BEAUTIFUL THINGS

What Reviewers Say About Emma L. McGeown's Work

Sugar Girl

"I loved this so much! It was exciting and fun, a little bit daring, and deeply heartfelt and emotional. There was so much packed into the story that I was hooked from the very first chapter and couldn't wait to join Ciara on this emotional adventure."—*LESBIreviewed*

Aurora

"I don't now what it is about the amnesia trope, but I can always get into it no matter how cheesy it is. Only this one wasn't silly at all. It was very realistic and completely convincing. ...Overall, this was a very emotional story worthy of your time. Read this when you are feeling like you need something that that will make your heart ache."—*Bookvark*

"McGeown debuts with an emotional, character-driven take on the soapy romance trope of amnesia. ...McGeown's off to a strong start."—*Publishers Weekly*

"A very good debut by a promising author. I'm looking forward to reading her next book."—*LezReviewBooks*

By the Author

Back to Belfast

Before She Was Mine

Sugar Girl

Aurora

Beautiful Things

BEAUTIFUL THINGS

by

Emma L. McGeown

2025

ISBN 13: 978-1-63679-934-6

This Trade Paperback Original Is Published By
Bold Strokes Books, Inc.
P.O. Box 249
Valley Falls, NY 12185

First Edition: December 2025

CREDITS
EDITOR: BARBARA ANN WRIGHT
PRODUCTION DESIGN: SUSAN RAMUNDO
COVER DESIGN BY INKSPIRAL DESIGN

Acknowledgments

Thank you to my parents and siblings for their continued support. I hope they know how much that means to me. They read everything I write. Every single page of every book. Even the pages I beg them to skip.

To my wife, Laura. Where do I even begin? You are my rock, my partner in crime, tag-team for wrestling the kids, therapist after a hard day at work, and whiskey buddy when the kids are finally in bed. Thank you for it all. To Avery, having Mama's picture on the back of the book is a little boring but you're only three so Mama is pretty boring in general. We're very proud of the kid you are becoming. Rua continues to be the best golden retriever on the planet. And then there's the newest edition. You're only a few months old, Rory, and while we were a little unsure of how a boy would fit into our household, I can confirm you were always meant to be part of the gang.

My family is my world.

PART ONE
2010

CHAPTER ONE

NIAMH DONNELLY

Six long weeks of sunshine. I'd never experienced anything like it in my life. Granted, I was only eighteen. But still, not one day of rain. I was actually starting to have withdrawals. It felt like most of the time, it rained in Northern Ireland, or on the precious, rainless days, it was just cloudy and grey. But on the Greek isle of Crete, it was summer every day.

It was an adjustment. Coming from cold, boring, old home where I had school every day to this, beaches and warmth. I got burnt a lot at the beginning, and very drunk, and of course, the sunstroke. I had to stop living off McDonalds and vodka and Coke. I'd learned that water was my friend and shade. I could never sunbathe anyway, thanks to my milk bottle complexion, but even walking the short distance to town was proving difficult in the heat. And the hills were exhausting. I ended up renting a quad for my duration, which was a surprisingly affordable method of transport. Sure, it was the literal number one cause of accidents in Crete, but that statistic was down to drunken tourists. I was a worker. We were exempt from the rules.

"Do you want to play cards?" Jenny asked from the balcony.

"My parents are calling in a bit."

"One game?"

I could hear the grin in her voice that made me shake my head.

"So you can add it to your long list of victories?" I said, making my way from my bed outside to her.

The late-afternoon heat engulfed me like a hug. It was mild, or perhaps I'd just climatised. Though, even I had struggled the last couple of days when it had been verging on forty degrees.

"Like it's hard." She quirked her brow. The sunglasses made her look like some kind of poker hustler. She was already confidently shuffling the deck, perhaps knowing that I'd agree to play. "Let's review the scoreboard."

"Let's not."

"Ninety-two to me, and thirteen to you."

She revealed the notepad for proof that, quite frankly, I didn't need. I sucked at Spit, a card game that Jenny had taught me when we'd first arrived. Honestly, I hated card games, but there was literally nothing else to do. We were renting a one-bedroom studio apartment on the outskirts of Stalis. It had two beds, a chest of drawers, and a very modest kitchen. It was basically two counter-cabinets, a sink, a camping stove, and a kettle. It was far from luxury, but considering how little time we spent in the apartment, it did the job.

Jenny shifted the large bag of crisps in my direction. It was probably our dinner. The seagulls swooped over our heads as we looked out onto the ocean. It was quiet. The swimming beaches didn't start for half a mile, so we got to enjoy this empty paradise of sand and sea just for us. We might see the odd person out walking, but most of them were locals.

Stalis was beautiful, quaint, and for the most part, pretty quiet. Especially where we lived. Thankfully, it was nothing like Malia. It was about four kilometres away or ten minutes on my quad bike. Malia was messy, loud, and full of drunk students. The Malia strip was also where Jenny and I worked. In the only Scottish pub in Malia, which was ironic because neither of us was Scottish. In fact, there wasn't a single employee who was Scottish. Even the owner was English.

"Is Mikey working tonight?" I asked Jenny as she dealt our cards.

"Yep,"

"Are you gonna talk to him?"

"Nope."

Mikey was a DJ who played a few nights a week at Salt Bar where we worked. He was an American guy in his mid-twenties who lived here. Full-time. There were a few like him. Those who couldn't just enjoy the summer, they had to uproot their whole life for the Crete experience. Some were nice, but they had a way of making me feel inferior. Because I was only here for the summer. Mikey was also a sleazeball, who had the emotional depth of a puddle. He was the kind of guy who exclusively hooked up with tourists because they would leave a couple of days later. Something about him really bothered me, but for some reason, Jenny liked him. Then, they'd finally slept together. She'd actually lost her virginity, which I'd really tried to talk her out of, but she had been adamant. They'd been sleeping together for a couple of weeks, and then she'd caught him in the toilets with a tourist a few days ago, and now, she was doing the mature thing. Pretending he didn't exist.

"So another awkward night at work?" I grimaced as we started playing the game.

"Thank God we're leaving in two weeks." She pulled her long dark hair back into a messy bun and shimmied her chair to the right a little to ensure she was still in the sun. At this time of the evening, there was only a sliver of the balcony still lit. I was happily in the shade, of course. There was little risk of being burnt this late in the day, but still, I didn't have the tanning abilities of Jenny.

"We can leave earlier if you want."

It was an empty offer. I actually wasn't ready to leave yet. Not to go back to boring Northern Ireland. Of course, I missed my family and friends, but nothing ever happened at home. At least working here, I got to meet new and interesting people every day.

"No, I'm not gonna let that dickweed ruin my summer. In fact, I'm probably going to spend my time flirting with every hot guy who walks into the bar. Just to piss him off."

"Okay." I felt relieved that we weren't leaving early but also had a bad feeling. I doubted Mikey was going to get jealous, and that would only upset Jenny more.

I focused on the game as Jenny's hands started moving a little faster, matching her face-down cards to the face-up cards. It was a game built on speed, and I just didn't have that kind of stamina. Or perhaps, my brain didn't work that fast.

"Besides, you'll need to get that undercut fixed when we get home." She sniggered.

"I like it."

"You can't see the back."

I'd really wanted an undercut for ages, just a little at the back, and that way, when my hair was down, no one could tell. I knew my mum would disapprove. I could hear her voice in my head: "You'll regret it when it takes years to grow back." We'd gotten drunk last week, and Jenny had cut it. It was a little crooked and not the most perfect length all the way round, but I loved it. And best of all, it made me look gayer.

I didn't feel like I looked "stereotypically" lesbian. This way, I felt like I could stand out a little. Signal my gayness a bit, especially when I tied up my hair, which I did at work because it got very sweaty. I'd definitely been getting more attention from girls lately, even though I hadn't asked anyone out yet. It was so hard to know who was just being friendly and who was flirting. Maybe my gaydar was broken, or it was just nonexistent. I'd hoped that maybe I would get to kiss a girl while in Crete. Sex seemed like a hugely ambitious concept at this stage.

Besides, I wasn't even sure I was ready to have sex, especially not some one-night stand with a tourist. I'd half hoped the first person I slept with would mean something. It didn't have to be love or my soulmate, but someone who meant something to me.

"Spit," Jenny shouted in delight. She added another victory to her side of the score sheet. "Another game?"

"I think I can hear Mum calling."

I lied, and I was sure Jenny knew. But we'd been best friends all our lives, so we were well-versed in knowing when the other needed space. Living in such confined spaces also helped us pick up on each other's need to be alone. She stayed outside while I moved into the apartment again. I dialled Mum's number on my phone, knowing it was going to cost a fortune but also knowing that, if I didn't check in every Friday, she would worry.

"Hey, Mum."

"Hello, honey." Mum's voice had a way of making me smile in contentment. I guessed everyone's mum's voice was just programmed to do that. "Has it been a week already?" She sounded tired. I could hear loud noises in the background. Screeching and beeping, it sounded like she was at the hospital.

"Are you still in work? I can call back if it's a bad time."

"No, it's okay. I'm due a break. I skipped my lunch."

"Mum," I whined in disapproval. It was dinner time at home. "You have to eat. And you shouldn't be working yourself—"

"Hey, who's the mum here?" I had to smile. "Huh?"

"You are."

"That's right. How's Malia?"

"Still standing."

"Good. And you're wearing suncream?"

"Yes."

"And eating, not just drinking beer?"

"Yes and yes."

"And what about Jenny? Not still pining over the DJ?"

"Not since he cheated on her." I said that part hushed, just in case Jenny was eavesdropping.

"We knew that was coming." I could hear she was talking while eating. That was common for Mum when at work. Being a nurse meant she didn't get a lot of time for a sit-down meal. "Poor Jenny. Take her out for dinner on me, will you, honey?"

"Sure." At times, it felt like Jenny was like another daughter to Mum. She always asked about her. I loved that because Jenny felt like a sister. She spent so much time at our house, it made me happy that Mum would care about her too. When I came out, Mum had asked if Jenny was my girlfriend. That was comical. Even the thought of it was completely preposterous.

"And what about you? Any girls?"

"As if."

"Niamh, you're going to have to try to put yourself out there a little more." I sighed, really not wanting to have this conversation. "You don't want to go to uni having never kissed anyone besides your teddy bears."

"Ha ha." I played along, knowing she was only teasing. I'd kissed guys before, and one girl at a party, but that had never amounted to anything. Mum didn't know all the details, but she knew enough.

"I'll still love you. And your teddy bears."

"Don't worry about my love life, it's weird. Speaking of things that are weird…how's Dad?"

"Touché." Mum seemed to really like that one. "He's good. He got moved from daytime shifts to nighttime shifts, which isn't great." Her voice dropped, and I could hear her disappointment. I was feeling down about it too. "But we're making it work. We always do." I wanted to ask more. Money was tight. Mum had said it in passing earlier in the year. I worried about it often, even though she'd never mentioned it again. Dad hated his job. He worked at a warehouse for a supermarket, and I could only imagine that nighttime shifts would be even worse. "He will be sorry he missed you tonight. Send him a text, will you?"

"I will. Hey, Mum, did Dad fill out my student finance forms?"

"Shoot." I knew she'd forgotten, and I tried my best not to sound mad. I'd asked her so many times in the last two weeks. The deadline was in a couple of days.

"Mum, if I miss the deadline, I don't qualify for the lower income grant." The frustration was coming out against my will. I really needed the extra money. I knew I couldn't ask them for money if things got tight during my first year at university.

"I know, I will speak to him tonight. After my shift. Don't stress. I will get it posted first thing in the morning before work, okay?" I couldn't even bring myself to say anything, still annoyed that she'd forgotten. I had to remind myself that she was busy, studying to become a doctor while also working a full-time job. "Honey, I love you, but I just got paged. But let's talk next week, okay? Unless, is anything wrong? Do you need money?" Money they didn't have.

"No, I'm good. Speak soon, Mum. Love you."

"Love you more."

She was gone. I texted my dad and resisted the urge to remind him about my university forms. They need his national insurance details and other tax information to determine if I qualified for the additional financial help. Otherwise, I'd never be able to afford university. I'd tried to save what little I could out here, but the wages were terrible. Twenty-five euros per night, which could be eight to ten hours. It was slave labour. A breach of human rights. But that was the going rate for unregistered workers. The only benefit they dangled at us workers was that the drinks were free.

"We better get ready soon," I shouted out to Jenny.

"Okay, I need to look hot tonight."

We got ready like we did every night before our shift. I applied light makeup, whereas Jenny went all out. She curled her hair, painted her nails, and was wearing her apparent "slutty" dress. She was definitely out for blood. We polished off dinner—cheese sandwiches and coffee—before we hopped on our quads and headed down to the strip.

It was pumping. Fridays were typically like that, where more of the locals came out too. Salt Bar had a healthy buzz, even though it was early. It didn't take long for me to clock Mikey. He was setting up his decks. He gave a wave in our direction, one which I returned, and one which Jenny most definitely did not. It was going to be an awkward night, for sure.

"Give me something strong," she asked from the serving side of the bar.

She was gone, then, off to wait tables. I made her a drink, rum and pineapple juice. I would tell her that it was a double, even though it was barely a single. She would be heavy drinking tonight. I could tell. Even if she didn't want to listen, I knew it was too early to get carried away on doubles. She still had to work, and I couldn't afford for her to lose her job. Not with rent due.

After a while, I forgot about the tension between the two. Mikey stayed at the DJ booth, and Jenny did everything to get those tips. Her flirting was almost entertaining. I didn't mind, especially when she was throwing a few of her tips in my direction. We could sometimes be a good double act. I didn't mind flirting with men as long as they were tipping me.

It seemed like any other night...well, until *she* walked in.

I knew the second I saw her that this would be a night to remember.

Chapter Two

Harriet Whitaker

White linen tablecloths. Again. People were just asking for them to get ruined when the menu choices were moussaka or grilled octopus on a bed of squid ink. I hated fine dining. I hated it before we took this stupid trip, and I could safely say after five weeks of travelling with my parents, I hated it more. I'd asked to go somewhere normal for dinner, I'd half begged, and this was where they'd brought us. After three weeks of travelling around Italy and now Greece for the past ten days, I was sick of it.

Some summer. My last summer holiday before university. Before Cambridge. Even thinking about Cambridge filled my insides with dread. I was supposed to be excited. I should have been excited. Cambridge was a privilege. It was the best education in England. Everyone knew it. Well, for some. Not for me. Not with who my father was, barrister Philip Whitaker.

It was a name that carried a punch in the world of law. And as his only child, I couldn't ignore the pressure to follow in those footsteps. Doors were already open for me. Doors that I so desperately wanted to slam shut. But how could I? I was his only child. How could I let him down by telling him I didn't want to go into his line of work? Not necessarily the lawyer part but corporate law specifically. It was just a shame that it was practically part of his personality.

However, if I wasn't going to have the powerful career, the alternative would be to marry someone powerful. Which seemed like an even worse fate. It was something I wouldn't say out loud, though. I wouldn't have wanted to offend Mama. Especially considering she had been practically grooming me to become a Lady of Surrey. Afternoon teas filled with dreary gossip about people we barely knew. It was as boring as it was tragic. But not impossible. I could easily do it. It wouldn't be hard to become a lady. I'd probably have an easier time of it. I'd still have to go to Cambridge, of course, because no respectful man would settle for a stupid wife without an education. But after that, I would be free to find a man to take care of me and eventually pump me full of children. The plot twist in all of this was that I didn't want to marry a *man*. Not if free will still existed. I doubted marrying a rich woman was even a possibility, not in the circles I'd grown up in.

"Darling, is everything all right?" Dad asked. I figured he was speaking to Mama. I continued to shift linguine from one small pile on my plate to another heap. I picked over some of it, and the seafood was good, but I just wasn't in the mood. Stuck between excited for this trip to be over and yet, dreading having to pack up my life for university. I needed a break. "Harriet, was something wrong with your food?"

"Oh no. It was lovely."

"You've barely touched it," Mama interjected. Their expressions showed concern.

"I'm just not that hungry."

"I'm sorry, dear. I thought this place did pizza. I know that was what you wanted tonight." Dad looked a little regretful. It had been my only request.

"Pizza is full of calories, Harriet," Mama remarked.

I could feel my fist clenching under the table, but I made sure to not show my frustration on my face. She wouldn't like that.

"We can go search for some," Dad tried.

"Must we?" Mama wasn't on board. Neither was I, honestly. The sooner I could go back to my room and be alone, the better. I'd order room service if I was hungry.

"I'm sure there's somewhere nearby that does food that you want," Dad said. "What about that Malia place? They might do some pizza."

I smirked. Malia would certainly have pizza; the quality would be questionable. I was certain that my parents would never approve of such a place full of debauchery and chaos. It would be too much fun for them to wrap their conservative heads around.

"Excuse me?" Dad ushered a waiter over, and I panicked.

"Dad, don't. It's fine. I'm okay."

"Is Malia nearby?" he asked the server. He was young, with long dark hair that was gelled back. He could have even been handsome if I gave a shit about boys.

"Yes, it is the next town across. Five minutes away," he said. His eyes shifted between all of us a little cautiously. "But it may not be the sort of place you'd want to visit. It's very…lively."

"Thank you." Dad let him go back to work. I appreciated his "watered-down" warning. It was definitely not the kind of place I wanted to visit with my parents, at least.

"I didn't realise it was so close," I said offhandedly. "Claudia is there right now."

"Elaine's daughter?" Mama asked. She was friends with Elaine. I nodded.

"Well, why don't you go see her?" Dad said.

"Really?"

I couldn't believe what I was hearing. My cousin Marco and I had asked for a night out when we were staying at his villa in Italy. Like me, Marco was trapped for the summer too. Spending time with him in Cinque Terre had actually been the highlight of the entire trip. Despite my parents refusing to let me out of their sight, even when I was with him, and now, they were allowing me to party in Malia. Had they no idea what happened there? Claudia's Facebook page was full of half-naked people, alcohol, drugs, and God knew what else. And then, it hit me. They had no idea what Malia was like. This was my chance. My opportunity for some space. Potentially my last night of freedom.

"Well…" Mama looked more hesitant. Typically. "Are Claudia's parents there?"

"No, but her older sister is," I lied.

I had no idea who Claudia was with. The truth was that Claudia and I were not that great of friends anymore. We used to be when we were children because our mothers hosted so many bridge club events together. I was never really a fan of her or her family, for that matter. But I didn't need to like her. I just needed her as an excuse.

"I'm not sure." Mama glanced to Dad.

"Claudia's sister goes to Cambridge too." That seemed to begin to sway them. "It could be a good opportunity to make friends. Network and such. And Malia isn't far from Stalis. Five minutes."

"Well, okay," Mama said, somewhat reluctantly. "I guess if it would be a good social experience."

I couldn't contain my excitement. I could feel myself already gathering my things when Dad spoke up again, "Don't forget, we have the tour of the Cathedral de Gustloff first thing tomorrow. Followed by tea on Sir Thomas's yacht."

"Who?"

"My old mentor, you remember," Dad said as if it were common knowledge. "So don't stay out too late."

Another cathedral? It felt like I had seen a hundred. Surely, there couldn't be any more left in Greece. And another lunch with some acquaintance of my parents. I couldn't bear it. Surely, I'd already sacrificed enough sanity to these monotonous activities in the last two weeks. It was almost ten anyway. I'd get out to Malia for maybe an hour. That was almost worse. A glimmer of fun only to be snatched away before I turned into a pumpkin at midnight. I had one option. I readied myself for the performance of a lifetime.

"Do you think that, perhaps, I could skip tomorrow's activities?"

Dad looked disappointed. Mama seemed to smile knowingly. Finally, she could see what this meant to me.

"You don't want to see the Cathedral de—"

"Darling." Mama placed her hand on my dad's. "Harriet is eighteen. She's young. And young people deserve to let the hair down every now and again." Finally, someone was speaking sense. Mama nudged Dad, who still seemed unsure.

"Please, Dad?" I said innocently.

"Oh, all right." I breathed a sigh of relief. "Just be careful, darling."

"I will."

They arranged a taxi to take me to Malia. I was to text as soon as I arrived and not stay out too late. All very manageable conditions for a night of freedom.

I only truly rejoiced when I stepped out of the taxi onto the Malia strip. I'd made it. It was carnage. Hundreds, maybe even thousands, of students walking around. It was late, but it looked like the party was only beginning. It was intimidating to say the least. My first point of call was to find Claudia. She wasn't exactly someone I wanted to spend all my time with, but I didn't really have any other option. I called her phone and was relieved when she answered.

"Harriet? Now's not a great time. I'm in Malia."

"Me too."

"Shut up. Oh my gosh, you must come meet us."

"Okay." She sounded drunk, her words slurred. I was already regretting this. Claudia was tiring to be around on a typical day, but adding in alcohol, especially when I was sober, was going to be draining.

"We're at, where are we?" she asked someone else. "Club Malibu, near the bottom of the strip." I had no idea where the strip started and ended, but I was definitely somewhere on it. At least, I thought so. "The VIP section. Say my name, and they'll let you in."

She was gone. Thankfully, Club Malibu wasn't hard to find. The queues snaked around the building; however, there was a separate line for VIPs, and to my delight, it was empty. Claudia's name did, in fact, carry as much weight as it did in London, and I was allowed in.

The music was pounding. So much so that I felt like it penetrated my skin. VIP was upstairs, overlooking the crowded dance floors below. It was moist, though blasts of air-con were thrust from above intermittently. Waitresses in illuminous bikinis walked around with trays of champagne. It was hard to not get distracted.

"Harriet?" I heard from up ahead. Claudia screamed my name again and rushed toward me. "Oh my God, what are you doing here?" She pecked my cheek and stumbled into a hug. "I cannot believe we're both here. In Malia. What are the odds? Who are you here with?"

"My parents."

"Ew, what are your parents doing here? I wouldn't have thought Philip and Pipa would be into raving." She poked fun, annoying me. Why would I bring my parents to a club?

"They're in Stalis. The next town across. But I convinced them to let me come alone."

"Cheeky girl." She ushered me to follow her. "I knew under that goody-two-shoes facade that you were actually cool." I couldn't resist the urge to roll my eyes. Claudia was already grating me. Everything that came out of her mouth was an insult dressed up as a compliment. "This way. We need to get you nice and liquored up." She was also dramatic as hell. "Everyone, this is Harriet. My mate from school. This is everyone."

Claudia handed me a glass of champagne as I received a couple of nods. Others went back to their own conversations, except two men from across the table. They watched me with curiosity, putting me a little on edge. They were older than the rest of the table. I tried to edge in on the conversation Claudia was having with another girl beside her as a distraction.

I couldn't put my finger on it, but the second I sat at their table, I felt uncomfortable. Like this wasn't where I belonged. It wasn't just because I didn't know anyone. Claudia ran in a lot of circles. She had a lot of friends in Cannes as well, which was where her family lived for half the year. Those people had money. A lot of it. That wasn't what put me off, though. It was the way they talked about money. As if wealth was their entire personality. I'd known people like this throughout my life; I just chose not to spend too much time with them. Surely, there were more interesting topics of conversation.

"Where do you go to school then, Harry?" one of the men asked from across the table. I knew he was talking to me, though I ignored him for a minute, hoping he'd lose interest.

Claudia nudged me.

"Sorry, were you talking to me?" I knew he was. It bothered me that he called me Harry, but I didn't have time to dwell because suddenly, everyone was awaiting my response. "I start Cambridge in a couple of weeks."

"Oh." That seemed to impress him. It did most. "A fresher, then. What are you studying? Art?" He smirked as if he had me all figured out. His pretentious friend sniggered.

"Law, actually. But it's another three-letter word, so you should have no problem spelling it out." I was glad to have gotten a laugh from the table, one that he wasn't pleased with.

"Harriet." Claudia threw me a wide-eyed expression. "Don't you know this is Oscar's table?" Her expression told me to watch what I said, and I did exactly that. I knew he was powerful. Just another reason to feel uncomfortable.

"It's five grand for this table. Just for the night. Spare change for me, really."

I hated him. I hated being here, and I wanted to go back to the hotel. I didn't want to stroke this asshole's ego all night, that was for sure. I stared at the glass of champagne but couldn't bring myself to even enjoy it. Something in it was lacking, or more likely, the environment was souring the taste. It felt fake. The people felt fake. More pretentious than even Claudia. I also didn't feel entirely safe, either.

When the cocaine arrived, I knew instantly I didn't want to be here. Each to their own, but it wasn't really my kind of thing. I made up an excuse to use the ladies room and left. I didn't even say good-bye to Claudia. I'd text her later if I remembered.

I felt instantly better the second I stepped foot outside. The strip had calmed a little. Perhaps everyone was in their club of choice. I took in a deep breath, relieved to be getting some fresh air, and when I looked up again, I saw Salt Bar. The Scottish flag hung proudly, touting its heritage. I liked Edinburgh. The people were always lovely. The music didn't sound too bad, either.

I walked inside. It wasn't overly big, a few tables scattered about with a DJ in the back and some people dancing. It was busy but not crowded. And best of all, the dark lighting meant that no one seemed to pay me any attention. Like it didn't matter who was there and what status they held. It was just a random bar. I already felt at home.

I spotted a free barstool.

"Hi." The bartender stopped me in my tracks. I'd already put my hands on the stool when I caught a glimpse of her. She was attractive. My age perhaps and her smile…it was inviting or maybe it was her blue eyes. Her long curly hair was fair, not quite blond, though, perhaps that was down to the dim lighting. I especially liked her piercings in her left ear, and the undercut was very hot.

"Is this seat free?" I asked, and that seemed to stump her.

"Yeah," she squeaked nervously. "I mean, sure. Go for it." I took a seat, noting the sexy accent. "You're not meeting someone here?" It seemed a harmless question, but I hesitated regardless. I wasn't about to tell a stranger that I was here all alone.

"I am, my friends are on their way."

She nodded, accepting my answer.

"Isn't this a Scottish bar?"

A coy smile appeared on her face. "Yes."

"You don't sound Scottish." It came out more accusatory than I intended.

"Neither do you." She cracked a smile daringly and raised her eyebrow.

"Suppose you're right."

"Most of us in here aren't Scottish. I'm from Northern Ireland."

"I'm from Sussex."

"England?" She squinted in confusion.

"Yes, England. How many Sussex do you know?"

"None, obviously. Hence, why I asked."

"Well, hence," I teased, and she played along, "I'm fairly sure there's only one."

"You want something to drink during your geography lesson or…"

"Sure, I'll take…" I thought carefully, but I wasn't really sure what I liked. "A beer?"

"What kind?"

"The beer kind."

She watched me suspiciously for a moment, and I squirmed a little under her gaze. I felt shy, like I didn't know how to react when a pretty girl like her was looking at me. It was unlike anything I'd ever felt. "I'm gonna need to see ID."

That was definitely not what I thought she was going to say. "Really?" I sighed in annoyance, pulling out my ID. It knocked my confidence that she thought I could be underage. She studied it for a moment and seemed satisfied, before handing it back. "You're not very good at promoting the local beverages. I'm new to Malia."

"You're not very good at being eighteen. Almost nineteen." Her brow quirked. She'd obviously read my birthday was in a couple of weeks. "You're acting an eejit." I had no idea what that was, but it didn't sound flattering. "How do you not know any beers?"

"I don't get out much." Plus, my parents always said beer was for "the poor man." Which I recognised was highly insulting and one of the reasons I wanted to order it. Just to see for myself. I was more familiar with wine or gin, but I couldn't see a single bottle of wine nearby to ask what they had to offer.

"Okay, can I make something, then? Because honestly, if you're not a beer drinker, this is not the place to explore. Trust me." She leant forward and whispered, "The pumps aren't cleaned very often."

As grossed out as I was, and trust me, I was, I also wasn't complaining about our closeness. Being in her personal space for just a few seconds left the smell of her perfume. It made my head a little dizzy. I nodded, not really prepared for the effect she was having on my breathing.

She got to work placing two highball glasses in front of me and squeezing lime into both. Her arms were pale and toned. Watching her work was deeply satisfying, if not a little entrancing. She mixed two measures of different clear alcohols before placing them in a cocktail shaker. The way she shook the shaker was oddly arousing, which made me want to look away. I couldn't be sure what my face was revealing. She poured the shaken drink into the glasses and topped them up with what looked like cranberry juice and fresh mint.

"Woo Woo."

"Excuse me?"

She laughed at my response, and I felt silly. If I wasn't blushing already…"That's the drink. A Woo Woo."

"Weird name."

"Try it and see."

I sucked the straw and took a moment to savour the taste. I could taste the cranberry, but an undertone of sweet peach emerged, blending a perfect balance of dry and sweet. "That's good." I took another healthy gulp, much to her surprise.

"It's a little strong, so don't be fooled. I wouldn't want to get in trouble with your mates for getting you wasted." She also took a sip of the drink before placing it behind the bar again.

A crowd of men arrived at the bar, and she was pulled away from me to serve them. I felt relaxed, even sitting by myself. No one seemed to bother me, and I found myself looking forward to a gap in her new customers in the hope she would come back to talk to me.

Chapter Three

Niamh Donnelly

Who's that?" Jenny whispered before sliding an order across the bar to me. I took the list of drinks and started making them.

"Who's who?"

"That girl." Jenny nodded to the other end of the bar.

"I don't know." I shrugged, not wanting to make a big deal out of the supermodel who'd just plunked herself down in front of me. "She's waiting on her friends, I think."

"She seemed into you."

"Please, I said, like, two words to her." I knew I'd felt some chemistry. There was something about her that made me want to be around her, and that wasn't really common for me. However, I wasn't about to let Jenny or myself get carried away. Besides, I'd been wrong in the past thinking a girl was flirting with me.

"Can you add a double rum and pineapple to that order too?"

"For you?" I asked, sceptical.

"Yeah, but they're buying. Give me it for free and put the price of the drink into my tips." She grinned in delight, although her eyes were a little unfocused, and I had to admit I was worried that she was getting a little carried away with the open bar.

"Jen, go easy, okay? I know you're pissed off at Mikey but..." I trailed off, throwing her a look that I hoped she would take as a warning.

"I'm good. Okay?"

I nodded, not fully convinced, before going back to serving the remaining drinks.

When I glanced up, Jenny was staring at the English girl curiously. I found myself watching her as well. Her free-flowing dark hair had a slight wave to it, but it was her green eyes that seemed to have left a lasting impression. She was beautiful. Really good-looking. Like, the kind of attractiveness that usually meant they didn't have a personality, or at least, not one anyone liked. But she was funny. I liked talking to her, and something even weirder was going on because when I looked in that direction of the bar, I found that she was watching me. I definitely wasn't used to that. Perhaps she was just being friendly. She couldn't actually be into me, could she? I was beginning to think I was the only lesbian in Malia.

"So," Jenny asked as I poured a couple of pints. "Have you talked to…anyone?" I could tell by her phoney nonchalant body language that she was fishing for information. Very specific information.

"Mikey?" She glanced at me, revealing her desire for his attention, and I felt bad for her. "Jen."

"What?" she snapped.

"He's not worth it. Jen, you could do so much better and—"

"Shut up, he's coming over."

She readied herself, almost bracing herself for some kind of argument. I just shook my head, wanting the pair of them to disappear so that I could go back to thinking about the English girl. Mikey moved toward us at the bar. It didn't look like he'd registered we had just been talking about him.

"It's dead tonight, huh?" he said, standing beside Jen.

I was forced to answer him when Jen practically turned her back on him. "Yeah, pretty dead."

"Can I get a pint when you get a chance?" Mikey asked me while surveying the bar, barely even noticing Jenny's annoyance beside him. I nodded, feeling the awkwardness of it all.

"I'm going to bring these drinks over to that table," Jenny said, "and I will come back for the rest, Niamh."

"Sure," I said, once again feeling so uncomfortable being around them.

The worst part was that I truly didn't think Mikey had registered that Jenny wasn't talking to him. He was such a dick.

I finished making up the drinks. It was a couple of doubles and Red Bull, nothing too difficult. I rang them into the till and placed them on the tray, only to find that Mikey was gone. Well, not totally gone. He was talking to *her*. I felt a pit of disappointment in my stomach. Especially when she laughed at something he said. Her smile was wide, and she looked happy in his company. I must have been imagining our chemistry after all.

It didn't take Jenny long to arrive back at the bar. "Is he fucking serious?"

"Apparently so," I said, still feeling a little dejected. And if I was being true to myself, jealous. As if he didn't already manage to get every girl in Malia. Not that she was mine or anything. I'd only called imaginary "dibs" in my head.

Jenny's expression looked hurt. Borderline heartbroken. Distraction was the best thing. Probably for both of us, actually. "Your order is all done." I shifted the tray a little closer to her on the other side of the bar in an attempt to refocus her attention. "And your drink is there." I gestured to it on the tray.

"Thanks," she muttered and begrudgingly left to go back to the group of guys waiting for their drinks.

I started to pour Mikey a pint of beer and stopped. Something a little unhinged settled over me. I switched mid-flow to another really cheap, shit beer. Yes, it was out of badness. Not my finest moment, but still. Not only had Mikey hurt my best friend, he had the audacity to chat up someone I liked. I placed his pint in front of him and couldn't help but smile a little to myself. Was this what revenge felt like?

They were deep in conversation, leaving me feeling a little awkward. I was about to leave them to it when she spoke up. "And what about you?"

I had to do a double take to make sure she was even talking to me.

"Nah," Mikey answered for me annoyingly, "she's just a worker. Only here for the summer."

"When do you go back?" she asked, giving me her full attention and making me want to stay put.

"A couple of weeks. I've been here since June. Besides, I start uni in September."

"Pfft." Mikey grimaced, which could have been because of his drink, but I didn't let on. "Who needs a degree these days? University is such a waste of time. What do you even learn? Anything you need to know, you can read on the internet anyway, and it's free."

I rolled my eyes, not wanting to get into it with him again. His opinions about university were far from my belief. As a rule, I tried not to take in too much of Mikey's nonsense.

"You just need to enrol in the university of life, like I did. Go travelling, see the world, get in touch with nature."

I was really happy to see that it looked like she didn't share that view, either. In fact, if the coy look she'd just thrown me was anything to go by, I'd say she looked just as unimpressed by him.

"Mikey, you know there's a difference between not going to university and not getting in."

She laughed at that, while Mikey looked a little affronted. "I can get into any university, okay, but it's a waste of money. You sit all day and listen to someone tell you how to think. Use your own mind, man." I rolled my eyes, eliciting another giggle from her. "I could do better things with my time."

"Like get drunk and pick up a different girl every night." I glanced in her direction. It was a warning to her, but he didn't miss my attempt to sabotage him.

"At least I get girls, kiddo," he snapped back, making me feel about an inch tall. He appeared to be joking, as always. I could see through him. He took another drink and rose from his seat. "Those pipes need cleaning again. Bring me a bottle of Bud instead." He slammed the drink in front of me. As if. I brought drinks to customers, not douchebag DJs.

He turned away from me but whispered just loud enough for me to overhear, "I got to get back, but come find me later, okay?" She didn't bother to respond to him, which made me feel a little less embarrassed.

"Wow." Her face scrunched up into annoyance once he was gone. "What a prick. You'll have to just hold me back from going to find him later."

I smirked at that. "Yeah, he's…" I shook my head, unable to find the words to describe how much I didn't like him. "I just wanted to warn you. He chats up a lot of pretty girls in here."

"Good to know." She smiled, holding my gaze in a way that felt a little intimate. "That you think I'm pretty."

I was speechless, and it felt like my brain was racing a million miles a minute. "Well, yeah." I couldn't think of anything cool to say. I felt like I was breathless and blushing and maybe even on fire. I'd never been flirted with, not by someone like her. "Obviously."

"Well, the feeling's mutual." She sipped her drink coyly. "Obviously."

The feeling was mutual. I allowed myself to gay panic for about two seconds before a strange yet exhilarating confidence came over me. "You know"—I leaned forward onto the bar—"you're actually very distracting."

"Really?" She played along, leaning on her elbow, coming a little closer. "I'm sorry I've been keeping you back from serving all your many, many customers." She glanced around the pub, pointing out that there wasn't a single person waiting for a drink. "There's also a customer waiting right here for a drink." She drunk the remainder of hers. "Oh, and I believe someone ordered a bottle of Bud too."

"Yeah, right," I muttered before starting to make her another Woo Woo. "He can wait all night on that."

"How do people fall for guys like that? Greasy hair, sleazy pickup lines, and the speech about the university of life." She shivered in what looked like disgust. "I mean, if I wasn't into girls before…"

"He's got charisma, that's for sure. More than me, anyway."

"I disagree," she said defiantly. "You're really nice to me."

"That's only because you're pretty." She laughed in outrage, and I really enjoyed receiving that kind of reaction from her. "I thought we established this."

"Hm, I don't know." She watched me suspiciously. Like she had some kind of a deeper read on me. Maybe she did. "I think there's more to you."

"You don't even know my name." I averted my eyes, finding it too hard to remain aloof when she was flirting like this. Deep down, I was a mess.

"Sure, I do," she said confidently, causing me to stop mid-shake of her cocktail. "Your name is…" She thought carefully before studying me from head to toe and then back up again. Her concentration made me laugh. "Levi."

"Levi?" I didn't see that coming. "That's not even a girl's name."

"And? Maybe your parents are super hippy and gave you this really cool, bohemian name. It would explain the piercings and undercut."

I played along. "Okay, and what's your name, then?"

"You tell me." She sat back and waited patiently.

I went back to shaking her cocktail again as I thought. Then, I made the mistake of looking at her again…she was *watching* me. The dip in her playful expression to something more. The air turned sexual; at least, that was how it felt. Something about the way she watched me made me think she *wanted* me. In a way I'd never felt wanted. It made me feel amazing.

"Jaq," I said once I'd served up her drink. "Short for Jaqueline."

She hummed in approval and reached out her hand to me. "It's nice to meet you, Levi." Her hand in mine sent a jolt all the way up my arm. It actually made my breathing falter for a moment. I couldn't be sure if she felt it too, but something shifted around us. Something felt right, even though I couldn't comprehend what.

I had to excuse myself to serve a stupid group of customers. I could feel myself rushing to make some of the cocktails. She was nowhere near me, and yet, she made me feel clumsy. Just her eyes on me. I also really wanted to be finished with the drinks so that I could get back to her. I just hoped her friends would never show. That way, I could keep her all to myself for a little longer.

"So tell me about yourself?" I asked, feeling out of breath by the time I made it back to her. "Do you come from a big family?"

"No, just me, Dad, and Mama."

"Weird that you call your mum that." I'd never heard anyone call someone Mama. It seemed really posh. Maybe Jaq was posh. Her accent seemed posh, to be fair.

"I have heard that it's unusual before," she admitted. "But then again, my parents are pretty…unusual."

"Wait, you've no brothers or sisters? What's that like being an only child?"

She seemed to close off, and I realised my mistake. It looked like something she didn't like being asked. "I don't know any different." She shrugged, leaning back on her stool, and it felt like she was literally pulling away from the conversation.

I immediately wanted to backtrack. "Sorry, stupid question." There was a brief silence that she didn't seem interested in filling. "I could tell you what it's like to be one of four kids."

Her expression lifted. "Okay."

"I've only had a spring roll twice in my life."

"What?" She laughed out of what seemed like confusion. "What does that have to do with coming from a big family?"

"When we order Chinese takeaway, you only get four spring rolls per portion. I rarely get to them first. My brother usually shoves two in his mouth as soon as the box is opened. It's like the Hunger Games in my house."

"I don't understand. Why not just get two portions?"

"We're not made of money," I teased, making her laugh again. "And don't even get me started on the bathroom situation. I've missed the bus so many times because someone wouldn't get out of the bathroom. And I used to have to get up at six in the morning just to play the PlayStation by myself. And then, the hand-me-downs."

I sighed, thinking back on school uniforms handed down by my sister. They never quite fit right and rarely felt like my own. It sucked sometimes.

"So you're the baby?"

"No way. I share the middle-child spot. I'm the third child down the pecking order. I'm not even sure my parents know I moved here six weeks ago."

She laughed at that. "Wait, really?"

"I'm joking, my parents are actually really great. I was just talking to my mum today." I could feel myself smiling just thinking about it.

"You must be close with her."

"Well, yeah, she's my mum." I shrugged as if that was obvious. But Jaq looked sad. I knew then that her homelife was likely very different from mine.

"What I'm hearing is that coming from a big family is like having no privacy and not having anything for just yourself?"

I thought carefully for a moment and couldn't help but think she was completely spot on. "Basically."

"That's exactly what it's like having no brothers or sisters." She sighed, leaving me to believe there was tension there. "I'm the only focus for my parents. They control...well, everything. My after-school activities, where I go, who I see, my friends."

"That sounds shit."

"It really is." I wanted to know more, especially because of how empty she looked. "You've another customer." She waved me off as if not having the strength to continue the conversation.

I reluctantly left to do my job but felt bad for the turn of conversation. I wanted to avoid talking about her family ever again if that was how she felt about them.

I had to change a keg and restock the bar, which provided a little breathing space from her. When I returned from the store room, Jenny was seated next to Jaq. It made me nervous seeing them talking together. I made it my mission to restock the fridges close to them. That way, I could eavesdrop.

"I'm just on holiday with my parents."

"And they let you out by yourself?" Jenny asked, but I had my back to them.

"Yeah, kind of." Jaq seemed a little shyer. Perhaps she was ashamed for lying about her friends coming, especially when she knew that I could overhear. Or maybe she was lying to Jenny now. I couldn't be sure. "They're in Stalis."

"That's where we live too." I knew Jenny was gesturing to me. I turned around to join the conversation.

"Oh, you guys *know* each other." There was a suggestion there. Jaq looked slightly surprised or perhaps disappointed.

"Yeah, we came over together," Jenny said and threw me a smile. "I couldn't have done this summer with anyone else."

"I didn't realise you two were together."

"No!" Jenny and I practically yelled in unison.

"We're not together," I said firmly, and Jaq looked relieved.

"Okay, you don't need to sound so…" Jenny said a little defensively. "Grossed out."

"No offence, but no."

"Excuse me, I am a catch."

"I live with you, Jen."

"How dare you? And I was just over here telling her all about how great you are."

I side-eyed Jaq, and she nodded in agreement.

"Jenny was actually really bigging you up. Not that she needed to," Jaq added, and I didn't miss the edge of flirting. Jenny threw me a miffed looked.

"I'm sorry, you are a catch…for any well-respecting gentleman."

"Thank you," she said before turning back to Jaq again. "We are just best friends," Jenny clarified, taking a long drink from the straw. The loud slurping at the end alerted me that she needed a refill. I was reluctant to serve her any more. "Can I grab a bottle of water?"

"Sure." I was happy to see she was being responsible. Thankfully, she'd been nowhere near Mikey, either, and that made me relax.

"Yeah, me too?" Jaq asked. I grabbed three water bottles.

"How old are you?" Jenny asked Jaq.

"I'm eighteen, but I'll be nineteen next month."

"We're eighteen too. Did you just finish your A-levels?"

"Yeah, you?"

"Just about," Jenny teased, throwing me a nod.

But I hated when she did that. She dumbed herself down often, even though I continued to tell her that being smart was nothing to be ashamed of. Especially in Malia. When we got here, she'd made me promise not to tell anyone that she was going to study medicine next year. I didn't even think she'd told Mikey, which made sense because he was so anti-education, but still. Perhaps Jenny liked to create an outgoing, carefree persona. Maybe she felt that being smart or wanting to be a doctor would make people think she wasn't fun.

"Are you into girls too?" Jenny asked boldly, and Jaq looked a little taken aback.

"Jen, maybe you should get back to work, huh?" I wide-eyed her, causing Jaq to giggle.

"It's just a question."

"It's a nosy question."

"I don't mind," Jaq interjected. "I'm not really into dudes... let's put it that way."

"Then, you're in good company with this one," Jenny said. I rolled my eyes. "Better get back to work."

"Thanks, Jen."

"Hey, I'm a good wingwoman."

"Oh yeah, you're the best," I said sarcastically as Jenny hopped off the barstool and returned to serving a couple of the remaining tables, leaving me and Jaq alone again. "So that's my roommate."

"She's lovely."

"She's a good person." I smiled, and a silence surrounded us.

I could tell the energy shifted a little. I wasn't sure why. Maybe because we both were attracted to each other. I felt like I didn't know how to bring it back to flirting again.

She looked a little regretful. "Hey, I just wanted to say, I'm sorry about earlier." I tried to bat it off, but she wouldn't let me. "How I reacted talking about my family was just—"

"You don't have to explain."

"Thanks, I appreciate that. I just, I'm not really myself sometimes, and I think my parents play a part in that."

"You can be yourself around me." A sudden vulnerability came over me. What I'd said was so heartfelt, and it just came out on its own.

"I feel like I can." Her eyes held mine for a moment, and it was nice. I felt like I could be myself with her as well.

CHAPTER FOUR

HARRIET WHITAKER

I was immensely relieved that I didn't just go back to my hotel room after seeing Claudia. It felt as though Salt Bar was exactly where I was supposed to be. Meeting Levi.

She was charming, sweet, and *really* attractive. That attraction was only being amplified the longer I was in her company. I'd lost count of the number of times she'd made me blush. Surely, there was a quota for the number of times one person could blush in an evening. She served customers while I watched subtly. At least, I hoped it was subtle. Watching her make cocktails or talking to customers, she was just so effortlessly charming. She had a way of talking to people. I admired it. It was her job at the end of the day, but something about her made me feel like it wasn't an act.

At times, I found myself envious of other customers who were stealing her attention, which was crazy. I was always pleased to see her keep returning to me. I got the feeling that she was just as into me. However, in the last couple of hours, I'd had quite a few Woo Woos. Maybe I was imagining things. I didn't really care at this point.

It was late, really late. I must have been one of the last people in the pub. And I could see other clubs starting to shut up for the night. It wasn't really all that shocking, considering it was after two a.m. I should have felt tired. We'd had a full day of sightseeing, I'd been awake since six this morning, and yet, I was wide awake. For the first time, it felt like.

"I hate to break it to you, Jaq." Levi came back toward me with this cocky expression. "But I think your mates have ditched you." I could feel my smile faltering. "I'm not complaining. Your friends standing you up just means I got you all to myself." A cute little dimple appeared in her left cheek, which I'd seen a handful of times. It felt like the dimple only appeared when she was flirting, which I really enjoyed.

I thought carefully but felt like I could trust her. We'd been talking all night. I felt like I was safe. "I don't really have mates coming."

A knowing smile appeared. "I kind of figured that. When you said to Jenny you were here with your parents. And also, you've been here for, like, three hours." I felt guilty for having lied; that must have shown on my face. "But I get why you said what you said."

"It's not really all that cool, is it? On holiday with my parents."

"At least they let you out for a night," I said. She quirked a brow. "That's pretty cool of them."

"Well, the only reason they let me out was to meet someone from home. I had this friend, you see, who isn't really that good of a friend. She's here right now." I struggled to hide my irritation. "I met her in the club across the street, but her friends were…" I breathed out speechlessly, feeling as though I was divulging a lot. "Not my kind of people." A bunch of straight posers only interested in what their selfies showed the world.

"I get it. The kind of people where you have to pretend to be someone you're not, right?"

"Exactly."

"It's draining."

"Yeah, I hated it. I left and literally had no idea where to go." Her eyes held mine in a trance. "Then, I just kinda ended up here. With you." She smiled, and I found myself wanting to lean onto the bar. Just to be closer to her.

"Lucky me," she said genuinely. "How are you getting back to Stalis?"

"I figured a taxi."

She seemed apprehensive. "By yourself?"

"I'm sure I will be all right. My hotel really isn't far."

"Won't your parents be mad that you woke them up coming home so late?"

"I have my own room."

"Really?" There was an edge of suggestion in her voice that made me excited.

"Yeah," I said, finding a confidence I didn't know I had. I guess that was just the effect Levi had on me. "Do you want to see it?"

Her eyes widened, and she looked a little flabbergasted. "I, eh, well." Her stuttering was sweet at first, but it turned nervous. "You don't waste time." She gave me a curt smile that looked a little uncomfortable, making me feel like I'd completely overstepped. "I should check to see if Jenny needs help cleaning down the tables." She left, and I felt like I'd just put my foot in it.

I wasn't normally this forward. And I was far from some kind of sexpert. I hadn't even kissed a girl before. There was just something about Levi. Something about her confidence that made me want to impress her, though it felt like I'd done the exact opposite.

Levi's friend, Jenny, began putting chairs on top of tables. Levi appeared out of the back room with a jacket and bag slung over her shoulder. She moved toward me. I felt an overwhelming need to apologise.

"I'm sorry. About before."

"Come on." She waved me off. "I'll make sure you get back to your hotel." Standing next to her, I realised she was around the same height as me. Behind the bar, she'd looked much taller.

We left the bar and started walking down the strip toward the beach. It was much quieter and a little cold. I wrapped my arms around myself, and before I knew it, Levi had slung her jacket over my shoulders. I smiled at the gesture.

"I'll not go upstairs, though. To your room," Levi said, and it seemed as though she was still stuck in our previous conversation.

"That's okay."

"It's not that I don't want to."

"You don't need to explain yourself, really." I felt stupid for even saying it in the first place. I felt grossed out, as well, like I was being predatory.

A silence settled over us. Unfortunately, it was a little awkward. I almost felt like I wanted to apologise again, make things right, when she spoke up.

"Hey, do you want to go somewhere?" Something playful appeared on her expression that seemed whimsical. I wanted to say yes, though I couldn't help but feel a little apprehensive. "It's on the way to your hotel. There's this beach." She put her hands in her jean shorts pockets, making her look shy. "People go there a lot around this time. It's safe, I promise. And it's the best place on the island to see the sunrise." Something in the air made me want to take a chance. "I just…I'm not really ready to say good night yet."

I was surprised by how happy that sentence made me. It was late, and she had been working. It would have made sense if she was ready to call it a night. I was happy she wasn't. "Okay."

"Okay," Levi repeated before her face scrunched up adorably. "One thing I probably should have mentioned. To get to this beach, you have to get on…" She motioned to the quad parked up at the side of the road.

"A quad? This is yours."

"Yeah, is that okay?"

"It's more than okay," I said excitedly, watching her climb on it. That was hot.

She reached out her hand to me, and I hopped on the back, noting the excitement in the pit of my belly. There wasn't a lot of room, which was no doubt fuelling my excitement. My front was practically touching her back, and I felt an excited rumble as she started up the engine. The vibrations felt like they were pulling me closer to her.

"I don't have a helmet, so just hold on."

I put her jacket on properly so that it didn't disappear on the drive. I didn't hesitate in wrapping my arms around her waist, which felt very intimate. I felt the heat of her back pressing up against my chest.

She glanced over her shoulder, giving me another jolt of excitement in my stomach. Her face was so close, and I wanted to lean forward and kiss her cheek, but I resisted the urge and instead whispered, "Ready."

We were off. The speed could have knocked the air from my lungs, but I loved it. My hair felt like it was going to fly away from me as I let out a nervous giggle. Levi must have heard it as she reached back and fleetingly patted my thigh. Her hand was cold, but it made me feel hot. I didn't think she meant to touch my bare thigh, but the wind was making my dress go crazy. It made me shimmy even closer to her. It was arousing to be this close and travelling at this speed. I felt reckless and rebellious for once in my life.

I could hear Mama's voice in my head telling me to never get on the back of some boy's motorcycle. Though, she'd never said anything about the back of a girl's quad.

She slowed up as we approached streetlights. I recognised the quiet, sleepy town to be Stalis, and I could even see my hotel in the distance. She parked up a short walk away from it and turned off the engine.

"How was that?" she said as I got off the quad first, followed by her.

"Windy," I joked, trying to fix my hair.

"Don't worry, you still look good."

"Are you always this smooth?"

"Actually, no." She laughed. "It must be your influence." I'd never evoked this kind of attention from someone before, therefore, I struggled to believe her. Perhaps she was just this charming with everyone.

"The quad must help you get the girls," I said, following her lead as she walked toward the beach.

"Yeah, there's a queue lining up right now," she said sarcastically.

"Or is it the invitation to watch the sunrise that seals the deal?"

"You tell me," she flirted before turning more serious. "Honestly, though, I've actually never brought anyone here." That surprised me. "Well, except for Jenny. But she doesn't count."

"Why?"

"Because she's like my sister. And besides, I wouldn't waste it on Jenny. She'd just fall asleep, which is super annoying because the sunrise is really special."

"What time is sunrise?"

"A couple of hours. I don't expect you to still be here when the sun rises, but the buildup is pretty good too." Something about her wording turned me on, but I really tried to ignore it. "The sky gets lighter and pinker, and it's really pretty. See?" She pointed out across the sky, and already, it was beginning to lighten.

"I would have never guessed you were a sunrise watcher."

She laughed, a little carefree. "Living here kind of does that to you." She shrugged. "I'm usually not so outdoorsy. At home, I watch a lot of TV. Like, loads. Nothing better than a night with back-to-back movies." I liked hearing about who she was outside of Malia. As if she was a real person and not just this cool mysterious bartender I had a crush on. It made her more real. "But I don't have a TV here. I haven't watched a movie in two months. I go for walks, read, listen to music, and just watch the ocean." I liked seeing this side of her, and I was disappointed to see an embarrassment had come over her. "Which I know sounds weird, and you probably think that I'm boring—"

"I don't." I touched her arm as reassurance and felt this tingle move from my fingertips up my arm. An exhilarating feeling that could have been only in my imagination, but I felt it every time we touched. "I get it. We don't have oceans and weather like this to appreciate back home. Well, I don't know about Northern Ireland."

"No way. You'd be lucky if it doesn't rain every day."

It was a warm evening, especially with Levi's jacket over my shoulders. The sand felt cool for a change.

As we got farther onto the beach, I could see a couple of fires lit sparingly and some small groups of people. Some looked like they were still partying. Others looked to be winding down for the night.

It was an interesting mix of people. I was glad when she directed us to a quiet spot where there were a few lounge chairs abandoned. They most likely belonged to the nearby hotel. She pulled two together and gestured for me to sit.

She sat and pulled her satchel around to her front. "I don't know about you." She was rustling around in the bag for something. "But I'm starving." She pulled out a large bag of crisps and shook them.

"Sounds divine. I hardly ate dinner." I thought back to the meal I had with my parents. That felt like two weeks ago.

"Me too. Though, I typically have a big lunch, and that does me until after my shift."

"I feel like in this heat, it's hard to feel hungry."

"Right?" Levi stared at me like I'd just said the most profound thing ever. "When I get out of work and it's cool like tonight, I'm so hungry. It's when I want to eat everything." She opened the bag and politely passed it to me first.

"Do you like working here?"

"Yeah." She thought carefully, taking out two bottles of water and passing one to me. "It's really fun. I mean, it's long nights, and the pay sucks, but you meet lots of cool and interesting people. And I'm lucky because I'm here with my best friend."

"Will she mind?" I asked, a little worried, thinking back to Jenny locking up without her help.

"That you took her fifty-cent bottle of water? I think she will live."

"No, I mean you guys live together. Will she mind that you're with me or that she has to go home alone?"

"No, I travel home plenty of nights by myself. She does too. That's why we have separate quads."

"Do they let anyone have a quad around here?"

"Pretty much," she quipped. "You can drive it sometime. If you have your licence."

"That's going to be a problem. Failed three times." I laughed. She threw me a wry expression. "I'm a good driver, though."

"Tell that to your driving instructor. All three of them."

"Harsh. You're lucky you're good looking and have a sexy quad, or I'd be gone."

"You're drunk," Levi said with a blush. I loved evoking this shyness from her. It was endearing and made me like her even more. "It's dark, it's clouding your vision."

I sat up straighter in my seat, a little offended that she didn't believe me. "How many drinks did you have before I walked into the bar tonight?"

"A lot less than you, I bet." When I didn't budge from the topic of conversation, she thought for a moment. "Before you came in? Maybe two drinks."

"I had none." Levi looked a bit shocked and perhaps sceptical if I was telling the truth. "Nothing," I repeated seriously. "That Woo Woo was my first drink."

"Huh," she said, looking a little embarrassed.

"So, yeah. I think you're..." Suddenly, it was my turn to feel embarrassed. "I'm kinda into you."

"So much so you wanted me back to your hotel room." She shimmied onto the edge of her lounger, bringing her closer to me. The air intensified around us. I felt panicked, and then, she reached up and pushed a strand of hair behind my ear. It felt like a thousand dragonflies were dancing in my chest, making sitting still a chore. "I'm kind of into you too."

She surprised me by leaning forward and pressing her lips against mine. I felt lighter, as if I was being inflated with something lighter than air. It caused my breathing to pick up and my hands to tremble. She pulled back and watched me carefully.

"Was that okay?" she whispered adorably. Sometimes, she could be the most confident person in the world, and the next, she could be so unsure of how she was making me feel.

"Yes," I said, unable to hide my mild annoyance. I leant forward and kissed her again. It was slow, tentative. I felt her become more daring when her hand glided onto my thigh. I pulled her head closer, enjoying the roughness of the short hair from her undercut. My thumb caressed the short patch of her hair as we kissed.

"That feels weird." She chuckled as we pulled apart, gesturing to her undercut. "In a good way."

"It's oddly satisfying." I went back to the bag of crisps, taking a handful and throwing the bag back to her. "I didn't think I would get to feel a shaven hairstyle like that when I finally got to kiss a girl."

"Wait." Her hand stopped riffling in the bag of crisps. "Was that your first kiss with a girl?"

It was my turn to feel very unsure. I could have lied. It wouldn't have mattered to Levi, considering we would probably never see each other again after tonight, but I didn't want to. Not with her.

"Yeah." She didn't say anything. "Actually, my first kiss ever. Now who's the loser?"

"That doesn't make you a loser. I'm just surprised. I figured you were full of experience."

"Why did you think that?"

"Maybe because you asked me back to your room."

"Fair point." I face-palmed, causing Levi to giggle. She turned more serious soon after.

"I was scared," she said in a small voice I wasn't familiar with.

"Of what?"

"You know."

"Sex?"

Levi tensed, looking a little self-conscious, and it became clear.

"So you haven't done it either?" I asked. She shook her head, but this time, she didn't look as embarrassed. And I just hoped that she was feeling more comfortable around me to be herself.

"We are both in the same boat." A silence fell over us.

I was surprised that she hadn't been with anyone. I figured with her confidence and charm, she would have had plenty of action. Part of me was glad she hadn't, either. "Hey, do you think it would be better to lose it with someone who hasn't had sex or someone who has?"

"Huh." She thought carefully. "I don't know. Maybe with someone who hasn't, either."

"Yeah, because at least that way, if you suck at it…"

"They wouldn't know any better." We both laughed. "I kind of hoped that I would do it while working here. That way, I could just go home and start university and not be, like, this kid anymore, you know. Because I'd have finally done it."

"But would you not want to lose your virginity to someone who really mattered?"

"Northern Ireland is pretty small. I could be waiting a very long time." Levi lay back on the lounger, staring up at the sky as she thought. I mirrored her on my own lounger, enjoying the turn in conversation. I felt like I could talk to her about absolutely anything.

"But at university, surely, you'll meet someone who wants to do it?"

"I fucking hope so." She laughed. It was a hope I had too.

We watched the stars and talked. I found that we could talk about everything and nothing all at the same time. Sometimes, it felt like we had so much in common, and other times, it sounded like she was from another planet. But there was something really nice about sitting on the beach with a stranger, waiting for the sun to rise. Enjoying the night for what it was. A chance meeting with a mysterious girl who I probably would never see again.

Chapter Five

Niamh Donnelly

No way." I said, refusing to listen to a word Jaq was saying. "It's raw fish we're talking about here."

"It's not all raw fish. Sushi can be cooked too."

"I'll take your word for it." I turned to face her on the lounger, propping myself up on my elbow. "I bet you're going to tell me that caviar is good next."

"Well," she started delicately, and I lost it.

"Oh my God, how rich are you?" She laughed, looking a little guilty. "I know you're going to Oxford and all—"

"Cambridge."

"But, like, how rich are we talking? Do you have servants?"

"No," she shouted and then thought carefully, perhaps afraid to tell me the truth.

"Jaq?"

"They're not servants." She paused. "We have staff, though."

"I knew it."

"But we aren't, like, *rich* rich."

"The fact that you have to say '*rich* rich' tells me everything. Okay, answer me this, and if you say yes, you're upper class, and that's the end of the discussion." She waited. "Do you have someone who drives you to school?" She cracked a smile. "I knew it. You're rich." She face-palmed, and I loved the way she laughed. It made me want to keep making her laugh.

I wasn't sure how long we'd been sitting on the beach. But pink streaks had painted the sky, and it wasn't dark anymore. It had to be getting close to sunrise, and yet, Jaq showed no signs of wanting to call it a night. I was pleased for that because it was turning into the greatest night of my life. And all we were doing was talking.

"Hey, are you cold?" she asked, a crease forming on her forehead.

"Nah," I lied. I didn't want her to feel like she had to give me my jacket back.

But the truth was, I was cold. It had gotten a lot colder in the last hour. I was starting to shiver, but I didn't want Jaq to know that. In case she suggested that we call it a night. I was hugging my arms. I had been for some time, but she hadn't noticed. Probably because of how dark it was before. Though, with sunrise approaching, I couldn't really hide it anymore.

"Yes, you are." She shimmied to one side of her lounger. "Come here." I didn't make a move at first until I realised that she was inviting me to lie under the jacket with her. It wasn't an offer I wanted to refuse. I took a seat on the edge of the lounger, and she gestured again for me to lie beside her.

The warmth was amazing. "You're ice-cold." She pulled me close to her chest and wrapped her arms around me, placing the jacket over me.

It was nice, and I could almost instantly feel my body temperature rising. I pulled her close to me, and she planted a soft kiss to my forehead. It was intimate, and I enjoyed feeling her this close. It felt like we were the only ones on the beach. Most people had tapered off, and now, there were just a couple of people truly committed to waiting out the sunrise. And us, of course. Birds chirping and the waves crashing were all I could hear, creating a peaceful environment. I could hear her heart beating and feel the warmth of her chest on my face. I didn't want to move or be anywhere else.

"Levi, what's your star sign?"

"Taurus. Why? Are you into star signs?"

"Maybe."

"Okay, what's yours?"

"Libra."

"Are they compatible?"

"No fucking idea," she teased. "I don't give a shit about star signs. It was you I wanted to know more about." That made me smile.

"Well, in that case, I broke my leg playing netball two years ago. I've never been to America. I have my first aid training certificate. And…what else?" She giggled as I thought. "I hate asparagus…and sushi."

"You have to try sushi to know if you don't like it," she said, sounding flabbergasted. "Okay, my turn. I've never broken anything. I have been to America before but never Australia, which I have always wanted to see. I don't have first aid training, but I have a grade five in the cello. Oh, and I really can't stand cucumber."

"Is a grade five good?"

"My parents seem to think so. I'm sure they'd prefer I'd a grade six, though."

"Well, it's five grades better than me. But what's your problem with cucumber? It's, like, the most inoffensive vegetable."

"Try having cucumber sandwiches at least once a week for your entire life, and you will know what I'm talking about."

"You're so upper class." I pinched her arm, making her squirm.

We stayed like that for some time. I liked lying beside her. Feeling her beating heart and the heat from her body. I'd started drawing patterns on her forearm. It was hypnotic, and she seemed to like it, almost as much as I was enjoying her playing with my hair. I could feel myself starting to doze off, perhaps I had fallen asleep until I felt Jaq nudge me gently.

The first thing I saw was the sun breaking through the horizon. Somehow, I could feel the strength of the sun on my face, and I knew I wasn't alone as Jaq squeezed me a little. Orange overwhelmed the sky, chasing away the streaks of pink and lightening the navy hue of the ocean.

"I told you it was worth seeing," I said.

She kissed my forehead, telling me she agreed. We stayed like that, watching the sun reveal itself more and more. I loved watching the beach transform. The transition from night to day seemed more gradual from this view.

"I don't do this much," Jaq said, but it had come out croaky and like a whisper. It had been a while since we'd talked.

"What?"

"Just stop. To not have every inch of my day filled with activities and events. To just…" She breathed in and exhaled slowly. "Just be. It's nice."

"You must be very busy back in England."

"Well, I had to be. Cambridge demands a lot of extracurricular activities."

"What are you studying?"

"Law," she said, and I could pick up on the change in her tone. She sounded deflated, and I was curious.

"Why?"

"What do you mean why?" She sounded confused, but I wanted to press her.

"Well, are you passionate about the law?"

"What does that have to do with it?" There was a hint of frustration that surprised me, but it didn't deter me. I thought about my own degree choice and treaded carefully.

"If it's going to be the thing you do for the rest of your life, shouldn't you be passionate about it?"

She was quiet. I knew she was thinking, I could tell by the change in her breathing. "What do you want to be, Levi?"

"A paramedic."

"Really?" She seemed surprised or maybe impressed, but I couldn't see her expression.

"I know it'll never make me a bunch of money." I thought about Mum, and everything she had gone through being a nurse. She always praised first responders. She said that it was the person who got to the patient first who did the hard work. The one who got a patient to her so that she could do her job. The person in the ambulance. It always inspired me. "It'll be hard. Long days, terribly hard days, maybe. But I would be helping people. Every single day."

She was silent for a moment, and part of me worried that maybe she had fallen asleep. I listened to the ocean and enjoyed the warmth of having her wrapped up in my arms, even if it was only for a little while longer.

"I want to be a human rights lawyer," she said in a voice that sounded so unsure. "Use knowledge to fight for the rights of marginalised people. People forgotten about. Immigrants, maybe. Or disadvantaged children." Her voice was quiet and unrecognisable. "I don't know."

"That sounds great."

"Yeah, if it ever happens."

"Why wouldn't it?" I turned to look at her, rising up on my elbow so that I was looking down on her. That was when I saw the sadness in her expression.

"You don't know my parents," she whispered, her hand reaching up and touching my face. Instinctively, I leaned into her palm, enjoying having her close. She stared into my eyes as the sadness evaporated, and something else took its place. "You're so beautiful."

I didn't kiss her, and she didn't kiss me. It was as if something greater pulled us together. It just kind of happened. Her lips on mine were soft, and I couldn't tear myself away. Her kiss was somehow empowering and graceful all at once. I deepened our kiss, and she let out a moan. It was creating a hunger in me that I'd never felt before. A desire to touch her, particularly when her thigh hooked around my hip, allowing me to position myself more on top of her.

Her hands clawed at my back and neck, pulling me closer to her. I kissed her neck as she parted her legs. Her dress had shimmied up her thighs, and I couldn't control the hormones and wild thoughts running through my head.

"Is that offer to come upstairs still there?"

She watched me with hooded eyes. I pulled back a little more and could see her thinking for a moment. I didn't know where those words had come from until she nodded, telling me she wanted me just as much as I wanted her. And while I was scared, something made me to want to. Wanted my first time to be with Jaq. Maybe she was the person I cared about enough to be brave. Our conversation from earlier replayed in my head, and I felt safe that even if it wasn't perfect, that it would be okay. We could figure it out together.

I was on my feet, pulling her up with me. Her hotel was nearby, and while she held my hand until we were outside, she dropped it just as we went inside the lobby. Perhaps she was afraid who would see us. I didn't mind. I already felt out of place being in such a fancy space. We got a couple of looks, but there were very few guests around at this time.

It was barely six, after all.

We rode the elevator to the top floor before we practically ran to her room. She opened the door, revealing a large bedroom with a sofa and balcony, which I knew meant that it wasn't a bog-standard room, reinforcing again that she came from money. The fact that her room was on the top floor was also a giveaway. I didn't have a moment to take in any more of the room before Jaq pushed me up against the wall.

Her kiss was hard, and her hands gripped my hips. She pulled my top over my head and threw it away somewhere. I'd barely made it into the room, and by her quick movements, I had concerns that we would be doing it right there by the door. I wasn't really complaining, either. She unbuttoned my jean shorts and began to lower them.

She seemed to know exactly what she was doing, even though, until about two hours ago, she'd never even kissed a girl. I removed her dress and could feel my hands trembling. Thankfully, she was moving so fast that I don't think she noticed my nervousness.

Soon enough, we found the bed. It was large, soft, and warm after being outside on the cold beach. Her kiss was insatiable, and her hands were...full of surprises. Our bodies seemed to collide with each other, but not in the rough way I'd imagined. I'd seen enough movies to know what sex looked like, but that wasn't what it felt like with Jaq. Feeling her body on mine felt invigorating. It was sensory overload.

We spent a lot of time exploring each other's bodies. She knew exactly where to touch me, which was a surprise. A happy surprise, of course. She was definitely working me up, and if her moaning was anything to go by, she was enjoying my touch as well.

I was kissing down her stomach when I suddenly felt nervous. The air seemed to intensify. I'd felt like I had touched her everywhere already, but I wanted more.

"Can I...go down on you?" I asked, noting the quiver in my voice. Jaq bit her lip, clearly open to the idea. She nodded, though I could see she was nervous. "I don't have to."

"No." She sat up slightly and kissed me. "I want you to. I just, I've never..."

"I know. Me neither, remember?" She cracked a smile of relief, "I'll stop if you aren't comfortable."

"I know." She lay back down as I kissed down her chest and stomach, seeming to relax.

I started slow. It was new for me too. I wasn't sure what I was doing, but Jaq seemed to be enjoying it. I could tell by her breathing. It made me want to pick up the pace.

"Slow down," she said, and I followed her lead. It was hot her telling me what to do and how to please her. She gripped my shoulder and gently ushered my head to where she needed me. "Right there." She gasped, and I was relieved for her vital instructions. I knew I wanted to make her feel good, but I had no idea just how much I would enjoy getting her there.

Her hips were struggling to remain fixed to the bed, and her breathing was ragged. I'd masturbated enough to know that she was getting close. I was enjoying hearing her moaning. I picked up the pace until she let out a loud groan. Her legs clamped around me, and everything quickened for a couple of seconds. Her movements slowed, confirming that she had reached her end. I thought as much, but I wasn't certain.

I felt proud of myself. I'd done it, and it wasn't as scary as I'd thought it was going to be. In fact, I really enjoyed it. I came up beside her and lay next to her, and she wasted no time rolling over and draping her leg over my pelvis. Her eyes were fluttering closed, and she had the sexiest expression, albeit a little tired.

"You sure you've never done it before?" she said, pressing kisses to my lips.

"So it was good?"

"Yes, couldn't you tell?"

I guessed, but I just needed the reassurance. I couldn't help but feel a little smug.

"Was it okay, for you, I mean?" she asked, sounding a little self-conscious.

"It was…" I shook my head before meeting her eyes. "Really good."

"Really?" She looked intrigued.

"Like, so hot."

"Really?" She seemed surprised, making me laugh, but she had this look of intrigue on her face. She began to draw patterns on my stomach, and her eyes darkened in a way that really turned me on. "Can I?"

I nodded, feeling a build of excitement between my hips.

She pulled back her hair and flipped it over her shoulder as she moved down my body. I was nervous but excited, and it felt like my heart was going to burst out of my chest. She kissed the inside of my thigh, and I could already feel myself getting worked up. When I felt her tongue, I struggled to compose myself. It was like nothing I'd ever done to myself. Everything turned into a blur. Somehow, she needed no instruction from me. It was as if she knew exactly what she was doing. I could feel it building fast, and I wanted to prolong it, but it was impossible. Before I knew it, there was an explosion.

She came up alongside me and let out a snigger. "Well, that was faster than I was expecting."

I felt too amazing to be embarrassed. "Are you mad that I came too fast?" I asked in mild outrage. "That means you're good at it."

"Sue me, I was enjoying myself." She rolled over and kissed me.

"It's good, isn't it?"

"Yeah." She kissed me some more as her hands started to explore my body again.

"Give me a second to catch my breath," I said, swatting away her wandering hand.

Rising from bed, she seemed to glide across the room. I watched her naked frame move to the fridge and lift out two bottles of water. She took a drink from one, and it was one of the sexiest things I'd ever seen. I'd never wanted to be a bottle of water more. Her eye contact was doing things to me as well.

"Okay, it looks like I'm ready to go again." I sat up and pulled her back onto the bed with me. Her giggles surrounded us, and I was sure at that moment, I was in heaven.

Until there was a knock at the door.

We pulled back, and she looked to the other side of the bed. The knock didn't come from the front door we'd walked in but rather, from the adjoining door just beside the bed. Barely three feet from us. I hadn't even noticed it until now.

"Harriet?"

Before I could say anything, Jaq's hand slammed across my mouth, and I saw panic on her face. She still had me pinned to the bed. "Yes, Mama?" she said, and I threw her a look of surprise. I would have never guessed her name was Harriet. It sounded...too posh for someone who'd just done that to me. She shot me a look of warning to behave, which of course, just made me want to do the exact opposite.

I slid my hand between her thighs teasingly, evoking a moan of pleasure that I greatly enjoyed.

"Can I come in?" her mother said.

I ceased my hand movement, suddenly feeling very panicked.

"Um." She jumped up. "Yeah." My eyes widened. "Just a sec," she called out. "Hide in the bathroom."

"What?" I barely got out, climbing from the bed. Naked.

"Don't say a word."

I begrudgingly ran into the bathroom and closed the door behind me, praying her mama didn't come in. I wrapped a hotel towel around me so I wasn't completely vulnerable and stood behind the door. I was terrified she would catch me, but I tried my best to be as quiet as a mouse.

CHAPTER SIX

HARRIET WHITAKER

I grabbed the robe from the closet and made sure that Levi had closed the bathroom door before I unlocked the adjoining door to my parents' room. "Mama?"

"Darling, what time did you come home?"

"Eh." I scratched my head, feeling vulnerable that she had brushed past and was in my bedroom.

"I knocked on your door around midnight, and I didn't hear anything."

I felt instant panic and couldn't help my eyes darting to the bathroom door, praying that Levi was quiet. "I got home around one, I think."

"You think? Were you drunk?"

"No," I said, trying to keep my voice level. I was usually a terrible liar, and quite frankly, I tried never to lie to my parents. It wasn't worth the punishment for getting caught. "I had a couple of drinks."

"How is Claudia?"

"Claudia?" Her pointed expression jogged my memory. "Yes, Claudia. Well, you know, Mama, she's Claudia. Always fun." I struggled to lie any better. My priority was to get her out of my bedroom. "I thought you were going to the Cathedral...thingy."

"The Cathedral de Gustloff, Harriet," she reprimanded, reminding me who I was talking to. It was humiliating because I knew Levi could hear everything. "Yes, I just wanted to make sure you hadn't changed your mind. About coming along."

"No," I said, faking a yawn. "I got home late. I could do with some more sleep."

"I just dread leaving you behind. Because remember, we are going straight to Sir Thomas's yacht. I wouldn't want you to miss out."

"I'll be fine." I could feel my frustration rising, I had to remind myself not to talk through gritted teeth. She didn't like that.

"Your father spoke to Sir Thomas last night. His son, you know, the handsome one studying at Yale, Matthew—"

"No, I don't think I do."

"Don't frown, it'll give you wrinkles." She forced me to relax my expression. "You do. You met him at Christmas three years ago." I was even more lost, but God forbid I'd be allowed to show that on my face. "Well, anyway, Matthew is visiting, and it would be an excellent opportunity for you two to spend some time together." I could tell by her tone that it was a setup.

I was embarrassed because not only was my mother trying to set me up with some guy, but she was basically outing me to Levi that I wasn't out yet. I just needed rid of her before she revealed anything else to prying ears. It was already bad enough that Levi knew my real name. I kind of liked our secret, made-up names. It made everything more exciting. Though, when I really thought about it, I didn't mind all that much that she knew my real name. It was like I was letting her get to know me.

"Mama, I can't." I struggled to conjure a real excuse until it hit me. "Because I've promised to see Claudia." The lies had begun.

"Oh, where are you going? Somewhere nice?" She took a seat on my bed, making me a little uncomfortable, considering what I'd just been doing in that very spot.

"Yes, a tour of the island." She looked to be buying it, prompting me to really sell it. "And a boat trip. I was rather looking forward to it, especially when her sister's Cambridge friends are coming along."

"Well, okay. If you're sure," she said, and I hoped that would be the end of it. "Did you have a nice night, then? Did you meet any boys?"

"It was lovely, yes, Claudia has a lot of friends, so—"

"Harriet, what on earth is that?"

"What?" I began checking myself over.

Mama was on her feet coming toward me. "You were definitely kissing a boy. Look at your neck."

I raced to the mirror and saw the tiny bruise there. I could have throttled Levi in that moment. I tried to come up with an explanation, but the panic had infiltrated my voice, making it near-impossible.

"Darling, aren't you coming?" Dad appeared at the door, and I begged for them both to just piss off. I covered my neck with my hair. "It'll be a lovely lunch with Sir Thomas and his son, Matthew."

"Philip, let's let her have a little freedom." Mama seemed to come to my rescue, which I was grateful for. Although, also suspicious. "She has plans with Claudia and a few friends."

I'd have thought she would have grounded me for life, but by the subtle wink she threw me, it would appear that my "dirty neck" made her happy. Which was weird in itself.

"Okay, darling. If you're sure," Dad said. "Oh, sunscreen. I knew I was forgetting something." He retreated into their room again. "Pipa, we don't want to be late," He called out.

"Coming," Mama said before whispering for my benefit only, "I want to know everything later."

"There's nothing, Mama," I said, holding my hair in place to shield my neck. "I burnt myself on hair straighteners." She clearly didn't believe a word of it.

"As long as he doesn't have any piercings or ride a motorcycle, I'm sure he's fine." Nothing like Levi, then, I thought. "Besides, it's only a holiday romance." She pecked my cheek, looking proudly at me. "You're only young once. See you tonight."

I followed her to the adjoining door and made sure to watch them leave their room. I even waited a couple of seconds just in case they forgot anything. I slammed the door shut and locked it.

"They're gone," I shouted to Levi before crashing into my bed in embarrassment, hiding my head underneath the pillow.

The bathroom door clicked open, but I was too ashamed to look up.

"Harriet?" It sounded strange coming from her.

I groaned a response. I couldn't even muster the pride to show my face again. I felt Levi sit on the bed when the mattress dipped. She lifted up the pillow and gave me the cutest head tilt. Her expression revealed a mix of confusion and humour. She was wrapped in a bath towel, managing to still look good.

"Say something."

"I'm just adjusting to you no longer being Jaq," Levi teased. "But Harriet?" She said it in an English accent. "How could you possibly miss tea with Matthew?" I pushed her away, resulting in her giggling. I sat up to face her as she said, "He goes to Yale, you know."

"Okay, make jokes."

"I'm done. Though, I am sorry." She reached over, removing my hair and caressing my neck. "That looks sore." Her touch sent butterflies to my stomach.

"It looks worse than it is. I always wanted a hickey, actually. Ever since I saw it in those bad films growing up."

"Well, I'm glad I could make all your dreams come true," Levi teased before her smile faded a bit.

"How much did you hear?" I could feel my face scrunching up.

"You're not out." I heard an edge of pity.

I sighed, a little annoyed that she'd heard but also happy that she wasn't going to lie about overhearing the conversation. "No." I could feel myself closing up.

"You never said."

"Why would I?" I said, feeling an overwhelming sense of shame. I felt like I couldn't even look her in the eye. I was sure she wasn't ashamed of her sexuality. "My parents would never be okay with it. My sexuality doesn't fit into their life or the life they have planned out for me." For some reason, I could feel myself getting upset, even though I was trying not to. I'd known I was a lesbian for years. At first, I'd hoped that if I didn't think about it, it would go away. That didn't work. I'd never felt confident enough with any of my friends to come out. I was too afraid that it would somehow get back to my parents. Even with some of my closest friends, it felt like too much of a dirty little secret to tell anyone. I'd been living with it. Silently. Perhaps suffering under the weight of it. "You're the first person I've ever come out to," I said, feeling pathetic.

"Thank you." Her words stunned me momentarily. "Thank you for trusting me enough to be the real you," she said, pushing my emotions over the edge in a way I wasn't prepared for. The tears were welling in my eyes before Levi could wrap her arms around me. I refused to let them fall, even though I knew I could be vulnerable with her. She whispered words of comfort into my ear as she hugged me, and I didn't know if she would ever know just how much I needed it.

"I'm sorry." I broke away, feeling embarrassed. "I'm not normally like this. It must be sleep deprivation or hunger or I don't know, sunstroke."

Levi laughed before taking my hand. "You not being out doesn't change anything. Not for me, at least."

"You're still kinda into this." I gestured to myself in disbelief, feeling anything but attractive.

"Very much so." I couldn't understand it, but I knew it was the truth. "But I should probably go. It's late." She grimaced. "Early."

I didn't want her to leave, but I didn't know her well enough to ask her to stay. Actually, that probably wasn't true. I felt like I knew her well enough, but that was part of the problem. Regardless of the strong feelings I had for her, the reality was, I hadn't even known this person an entire day. She got dressed, and I couldn't swallow the feeling of disappointment. And perhaps sadness that she was leaving and that I might never see her again.

"What are you doing today?" I asked, following her to the door.

"I'll probably sleep for a bit," she said, opening up the door to my room. "You?"

"Sleep is a must," I said, still feeling a little awkward.

"And after that?" she asked, looking shy in the jacket I'd been wearing all night. It made me want to have a little fun at her expense.

"You know, if you want to see me again, you could just ask me out."

Levi grinned, a blush forming on her cheeks that made my entire body tingle. I liked being the cause of it. She took a step forward, looking a little braver, until she was just a few inches from my lips. "Can I see you later?"

"I'll have to think about it," I quipped.

"Well, I'll be down on the beach at noon." Her eyes were glued to my lips, making me want to lean in.

"Where are we going?" It came out a little breathless.

"Meet me there, and you'll find out."

"Can I get your number—"

She kissed me gently before pulling away. She didn't move just yet, though. "If you want to see me, meet me on the beach. At noon." Her spontaneity was refreshing, even if it felt unorthodox to me. How could I get in touch with her if I was running late, or something happened? I wasn't used to not being able to contact someone. But it was also exciting.

I went with it. For once in my life, I embraced the unknown.

"And if I don't see you?" She shrugged. "It was a pleasure to meet you, Harriet." It was my turn to lean forward and kiss her. When I pulled back, she watched me for a moment, as something vulnerable passed over her features. "Niamh," she whispered, and it left me confused for a moment. "My name is Niamh."

She walked away from me, and something deep in my chest tugged with every step she took away. I couldn't help but watch her all the way to the elevator.

"See you at noon, Niamh."

She smiled back at me before shooting me a final good-bye and disappearing inside the elevator.

CHAPTER SEVEN
NIAMH DONNELLY

I drove home with a smile on my face. There was no one about except a couple of hotel staff and delivery drivers, most likely dropping off kitchen orders for the day. I was never usually awake at this time. I should have been exhausted, but I'd never felt more awake. My body felt as though it was still on an intense high. A high I never wanted to come down from. Perhaps that was just the aftereffects of being around Harriet. That was a surprise. Harriet? The more I thought about her real name, the more I liked it. Even thinking about her sent my heart racing. I felt like I could still feel her touch on my skin, and I loved it.

My smile couldn't be erased as I parked up outside my apartment and made my way inside. Turning the key, I got a scent of Harriet's perfume from my jacket. I found myself standing in the empty hallway just smelling my jacket like some kind of psychopath. I knew how it looked. I knew that my intense feelings were absurd. Beyond normal attraction, I thought. I was completely wrapped up in her.

The door opened, and Jenny looked furious. "What are you doing?"

"What?" I glanced around.

"You unlocked the door and didn't come in." She stepped back, letting me inside. "I thought you were a burglar or something. What time is it?" She groaned, climbing back into bed again.

"Like, seven thirty," I said, removing my jacket and Converse.

"Someone had a good night."

I couldn't resist the smile on my face. I was just glad Jenny was in bed and likely about to fall asleep; therefore, there would be no questions. I climbed into bed, still thinking about Harriet. I could have giggled. I felt happy to the point of being unable to remember what it felt like to be sad. It was crazy. Like there were no other feelings except this. It felt like elation, or maybe I was actually high.

"You had sex." Jenny's voice penetrated my thoughts, making me aware that she was awake. Her calculating stare was hard to read from the bed next to mine.

"What? No." I didn't know why I lied. I never hid anything from Jenny. But she seemed a little hostile, making me close up, and I didn't know why she was annoyed. It felt like an overreaction for just waking her up. Then, she threw me a look. I knew that look. It was the look she would throw me if I was hiding something. Without meaning to, I could feel my face starting to break.

"Oh my God," she squealed, throwing the pillow at me and making me giggle. "You had sex. Hold on, you had sex with a girl, right?"

"Yes," I said, a little miffed she even needed to ask.

"Wait, with the hot girl from the bar?" Her surprise made me even more smug. "Hell yeah, Niamh." She leaned forward, raising her hand up for a high five. "You need to rub that in Mikey's face tonight in work. Oh my God, dude, tell me everything."

"No, perv."

"Hey, I told you everything after I had sex with Mikey."

"Yeah, and I don't remember asking." She rolled her eyes, refusing to let me off the hook. "I'm still traumatised."

"Shut up. Now, come on. What was it like? I mean, with a girl. Did you like it?"

"Yeah, it was…amazing." The flashbacks made my insides squirm a little. "So much better than I'd even imagined it would be."

"Damn." She looked intrigued. "Did it hurt?"

"No."

"It did for me," Jenny said, a little confused. "Maybe you did it wrong."

"No." I rejected even the suggestion of it. If the right way was supposed to hurt, then, why would I want that? "I think it's different for lesbians," I said, but the seed of doubt remained. Maybe I did do it wrong?

"You didn't use, like..." She hesitated before whispering, "A dildo?"

"Jenny." I could feel my face heating up. I didn't want to have this conversation in the first place, but I definitely didn't think that was where she was going with this. "No. What the fuck? I don't even have a..." I couldn't even say it.

"Did she not have one? I figured somebody had to have one." She looked confused, making me confused.

"I'm pretty sure there's more than one way to do it."

"Oh, okay. It all just seems complicated. Like, with a dude." She threw me an obvious face. "You know where it goes. And that's kind of it. How did you know what to do?"

"I don't know." I thought back and couldn't wipe the smile from my face again. "I just kind of did."

"Did you..." She raised her brows, figuring I would understand what she meant. When I didn't respond, she elaborated, "You know." She gave a crude hand gesture involving her tongue.

"Oh my God, Jenny. Why?"

"What?" She looked innocent. "I'm curious."

"Why? Why do you—I don't know why you need this level of detail." I had to laugh because otherwise, I would have probably slapped her.

"Because we are best friends, and we tell each other everything."

"Okay, yes. Are you happy?"

She stared back at me, stunned, as her brain no doubt worked overtime. "Really?" she said, seemingly impressed. "Fair play. Wouldn't be my cup of tea, I don't think, but well done, Donnelly. You're obviously not a selfish lover."

"Jesus." I rolled away from her, shaking my head at her gumption. "Are we done?"

"For now," she said. "I'm sure I will come up with more questions when I'm fully awake, though."

"Can't wait," I snarked before letting myself be consumed with thoughts of her again. I allowed the idea of Harriet to lull me to sleep.

My alarm sounded later, and I knocked it off quickly. I could barely open my eyes, but somehow, I snatched my phone quick enough, ensuring the buzzing didn't wake Jenny. It had been months since I'd set an alarm. I was a little dazed as to why it was going off. So dazed that I almost allowed myself to fall back to sleep when I remembered.

Harriet.

It wasn't a dream. It was real. Last night had happened. To me. It had happened to me. I'd met the most amazing girl and had the most amazing time with her. I bounced out of bed and into the shower. I wasn't tired, even though I was functioning on barely three hours sleep. It didn't matter. I didn't need sleep. I felt beyond energised.

I got dressed quietly to avoid another inquisition from Jenny. It would be a while until she surfaced. We didn't usually get out of bed until lunch most days.

I went through quite a few outfits in my head, not really too sure what I should wear. A nervousness had settled in my stomach. I wanted to impress Harriet. Maybe something casual? Or dressier? What was she going to wear? I was getting inside my head, and time was ticking by. I especially didn't want to be late. I threw on my favourite pair of shorts and a cute T-shirt. I couldn't expose my shoulders during the day. They would be burnt to a crisp. I wrote Jenny a note on the kitchen counter. I didn't want her to worry, and I grabbed my snapback hat on the way out the door.

I was going to take Harriet to Hersonissos, a large town next to Stalis and farther away from Malia. Last night, she had told me a couple of the towns she'd visited, but Hersonissos hadn't come up. I figured it was probably a safe bet. I'd done the drive before on my quad. It wasn't far. There was a cycle route I could take along the water that, thankfully, quads were also permitted on.

I drove over to the entrance of the beach and waited. My phone revealed it was five to twelve, and I reminded myself to breathe. I felt nervous, like before a big test, but somehow, this felt bigger. I kept smoothing out my clothes. I hoped that I wasn't too underdressed.

I felt like I was waiting an eternity, and when I checked, I realised it was ten past twelve, and the panic set in. What if she wasn't coming? I knew where she was staying; I could always go over there, but maybe she didn't want to see me again.

Disappointment settled in my chest. Maybe I did imagine last night...no, that kind of thinking was crazy. It happened, I told myself.

I waited another few minutes, hoping that maybe she'd just slept in.

But she didn't show.

I didn't really know what to do with myself. I just stood there wallowing in the disappointment. I should have gotten her number. Why was I such an idiot? I thought it would be romantic, like in the olden days before mobile phones, where you just had to have faith that the other person would show up. This was my lesson learned. My generation needed phones. If nothing else to avoid getting stood up. My first date, and I got stood up. How humiliating. It was already bad enough that at eighteen, I'd never been on a date before, but when I finally got one, she didn't show.

"Niamh," I heard my name being called, and my heart started racing. "Hey." She appeared from somewhere behind me, coming from the direction of the ocean. "What the hell? You said noon. Does noon mean quarter past in Northern Ireland?" She looked cute when she was mad. For once, she was a little dishevelled. Her face was flushed, and there was a little bit of sweat on her forehead. "I thought you weren't gonna show. Where were you?" I liked seeing her not look like a Greek goddess for a change.

"I've been here for, like, twenty minutes," I said. "How did you get past me?"

"I've been standing—in the blistering sun, might I add—for, like, half an hour." She couldn't be stopped from her rant, but I struggled to take her seriously because I was just beyond relieved that she was standing here. "Look down, do you see sand? That's the fucking beach." She pointed behind us, and I had to laugh. She was right, and I was the idiot standing at the entrance.

"Sorry," I said, and she seemed to simmer a bit.

"I was about to leave." She sighed, her annoyance seeming to disappear.

"Me too. Thought you'd changed your mind and wanted to go off on Prince William's yacht."

"Sir Thomas."

"Whatever." I tutted, and she pursed her lips to hide a grin.

"Where are we going, anyway? I kind of hope it involves food."

"One hundred percent," I said, glad that she hadn't eaten either. I led the way to a café down the street.

"Good because that bag of crisps was the last thing I ate. Well, actually…not exactly," she added teasingly, making my face flush.

"Don't remind me about last night." I bit my lip, feeling a wave of arousal in my core. Harriet seemed to enjoy my reaction. "This morning…you know what I mean."

"Sorry, it was just very *memorable* when I was in the shower."

"Let's circle back to you thinking about me in the shower later. First, food."

"Agreed."

"I know this place. It does really good omelettes. I wouldn't even be that into eggs, but these are just that good."

"Is it in Stalis?" I heard a hint of concern.

"Yeah, but we can go somewhere else. You know, if you're worried about being seen with me."

"Why would I be worried?" Her hand grazed mine in what could be considered a bold move, though it sent a shock up my arm nonetheless.

I could feel the gay panic returning. I guessed it was still hard for me to believe someone like her was actually into me. It gave me the ultimate confidence boost, considering I'd never had a girlfriend, not even close to one.

"Stalis is really pretty," she said, and I liked seeing her check out the little town I'd come to know as home.

"Yeah, I really like it."

"What made you come out here to work?"

"My sister worked a summer in Ibiza when she was around my age, and she always talks about how great it was. And then, I talked

Jenny into coming too. She nearly made us live in Malia, but the strip was just too overwhelming for me."

"It really is, and I was only there for a couple of hours."

"It's what makes me glad that Jenny and I live even farther out of town. It's really peaceful. All of my neighbours are, like, old people."

"That's nice, though. I'd say it would be a nice place to retire to."

I couldn't have agreed more. I'd met a few older people from the UK who had moved out in their later years. It was always summer here, and it was just a slower pace of life. That was probably very appealing.

"What's it like living here?"

"It's nice. I mean, you get some crazy tourists." I threw her a look. "But I don't really hang out with them. The workers are my friends."

"I supposed it would get old saying good-bye to people every few days."

"Yeah. Sometimes, you see the same group of friends every night for a week. You get to know them, even party with them after work, and then, you go in the next day, and they're gone. You never see them again."

She looked a little sad at that. But there was something unique about my summer experience. I'd gotten used to people never staying put for long. Even other workers had started to leave. I wouldn't have wanted it to be my life, but it was a break from reality that I'd grown to appreciate.

"Did you meet many gay girls while here?" she asked a little innocently, but I knew what she was really asking. I decided to have a little fun.

"Oh, yeah. A ton." She nodded, but I saw her carefree demeanour falter. "I'm joking."

"Oh." She sighed in what looked like relief. "I'm glad." She grabbed ahold of my hand, and while I felt butterflies, I felt a little self-conscious. "Is this okay?" She must have sensed something.

"Yeah," I lied.

I had never held a girl's hand in public. It was scary. What if someone said something bad to us? I didn't know if I could handle that. There hadn't been any hate crimes while I'd been there, but I couldn't help feeling a little insecure to be open with Harriet. Greece was still a pretty traditional country. I wished I didn't care what people thought. I wished I was braver.

"Aren't you not worried about your parents seeing?" I asked, finding her confidence surprising. "In case they saw us. They were a little, um, intimidating," I said, trying my best to be respectful.

The truth was, her parents seemed really intense. And that was through a bathroom wall. I could only imagine what her ma was like in person. If I thought Harriet was posh, her mama was another level. Even the accent touted they were rich. It was beyond intimidating and far from my family's lifestyle. It wasn't just about the money, though. It was her mum's tone. The way she talked to Harriet, criticising her for frowning and for forgetting some old church nobody even cared about. It was super weird. My mum would never. Maybe I'd caught them on a bad day. Perhaps they were nice people. I told myself they couldn't be that bad; after all, they'd made Harriet. And she was exceptional. To be honest, it was more the change in her mood when she talked about them. Her whole energy changed, and she became reserved in a way she wasn't with me. And, of course, there was the blatant intolerance of their daughter's sexuality.

I remembered coming out to my parents. I was scared they wouldn't approve. Terrified that I would be thrown out, even though, deep down, I knew they would be okay with it. Everything in their characters told me they would love me no matter what. But I couldn't help being afraid. You can only ever come out once, and once you're out, you can't go back in again. I was one of the lucky ones. My coming out was great. My parents had told me they loved me no matter what. It saddened me that Harriet didn't feel like she would be accepted.

"They're probably sipping champagne somewhere on a big shiny boat by now."

"Some lifestyle."

"If you say so." Her tone dropped, and her energy flatlined again. I wanted to know why. Family wasn't supposed to bring a person down, surely. They were supposed to be uplifting. That was my experience, at least.

"This is us." I grabbed the door, and a small part of me was glad she dropped my hand.

I would have been too ashamed to tell her it scared me to hold her hand in public. We walked inside the café and found a table in the back. It was a small place and pretty traditional. Metal chairs and plastic tablecloths. It was air-conned, and it had nice people. Besides, it was the food we were really here for. I also knew one of the servers. He was a regular in Salt Bar. He usually gave me a discount because I gave him free drinks sometimes. He served us pretty quickly.

As soon as I placed my phone on the table, it pinged. I checked it but didn't bother reading it when I spotted it was from my younger brother, Oisin.

"Do you need to get that?" Harriet asked.

"No, it's just my brother. He's not important." I was being sarcastic, but she didn't pick up on it.

"Is this the brother that eats all the spring rolls?"

"No." I chuckled. "That's my big brother, Patrick. This is from my little brother, Oisin."

"You're close with your siblings?" she asked, still fiddling with the menu that was left behind in case we wanted to order anything else. It was as if the topic made her uncomfortable.

"Yeah, well, I'm really close to Oisin. We're close in age. Whereas, my older siblings, they moved out of the house a while ago." I wanted to keep it short. Conversations surrounding family never seemed to go well with Harriet.

"Do you have a lot of cousins too?"

"Last time I counted, it was, like, fifty."

"Fifty cousins, what the heck?" She looked horrified. "Do people in Northern Ireland not have any self-control?"

"Is that a lot? I mean, it's on both sides of my family." That did nothing to detract from her shock. "Well, how many do you have?"

"Two on my dad's side and one on my mum's side who I've never met."

"See, that's weird to me."

"My family is pretty weird." It seemed to come out a little withdrawn as our drinks arrived.

An awkwardness settled over us, and it seemed like it was fuelled by the topic of conversation yet again. We both ordered a latte, and while I let mine cool, she sipped hers.

"You know, we don't have to talk about family…" I trailed off, not fully knowing what I was trying to say.

"I'm sorry, Niamh." She sighed, her demeanour seeming to thaw. As if she'd had a light bulb moment. "I really like hearing about your family." I wasn't sure I believed that, and I wanted to know why. "They sound perfect. And I know you said it was hard with so many siblings, but don't you get it? You were able to get lost in the mix sometimes. You're close with your family, but you don't have to carry the weight of all your parents' hopes and dreams. You get to just be yourself. You've probably even come out to them."

I nodded sheepishly, feeling really sad that Harriet didn't have the same upbringing I had.

"See, that's amazing for you. I'm not close to mine. My parents control pretty much everything I do."

"Really?"

She pouted, showing a frustration.

"I want to know why. To understand. But I also know that you don't like talking about them. And the last thing I'd want is to make you uncomfortable."

"That's because I know you won't get it."

"Try me." I reached across and touched her hand. I almost pulled away, thinking it was the wrong thing to do, but she laced our hands and smiled.

"They're very good at controlling things." A coldness remained in her voice that actually gave me a chill. "And because of who my parents are, I socialise with people they approve of. Matthew, for example. Someone my father views as a good kid. Or Claudia, the daughter of one of my mother's friends at her bridge club." I could hear the strain in her voice, and it made me feel sorry for her. "And these people, they're all the same. They talk about money, status, and gossip." She stared at something over my shoulder. "Even the school I went to. I was driven two hours there and back, every day, just to go to the best private school in England. Even Cambridge." She shook her head. "It wasn't my decision. I have never had a say in any of it."

It was the first time I'd ever saw someone vanish before my very eyes. She looked small. She became someone so different. I struggled to fully comprehend what she was going through. I felt like just telling her not to listen to her parents and do whatever she wanted. Easier said than done, I supposed. Besides, something about her dejectedness told me that wasn't an option. She would lose everything.

"And the worst part of all is that one day, I'll probably become just like them. Marry some asshole alumni from Cambridge that my dad plays golf with. Have some kids so that they can also go to the same demonic private school."

"Break the cycle, Harriet." It came out of my mouth without me meaning to. "For your own sake."

"They're my parents." She shrugged.

"You're eighteen. You don't have to be anyone else. Who you are is pretty great."

"Niamh, you don't even know me."

"I feel like I do."

Her eyes turned a little sad and transitioned to a thoughtfulness that made me feel warm inside. "Me too." She squeezed my hand. "Promise me something?" I nodded. "You'll not take your nice family who loves you unconditionally for granted."

"I won't, as long as you promise me something. Be true to yourself. Don't waste your happiness trying to impress your parents."

"Maybe it's genetic. I will end up like them even if I don't want to."

"No, you won't." I rejected even the thought of it. Harriet could never be stuck up or hypercritical like her mum. She was too sweet.

She tilted her head like she didn't believe me. "Your pinkie doesn't stick up when you drink your coffee." She cracked a smile. "You'll never fit in."

"Thank God for my pinkie."

"Oh, and also, you're a lesbian. Sorry to break it to you, but you're not marrying a dude."

"Shoot, you're right." Her mood lifted, and I was glad to have helped get her there.

"It's a standard rule, no homos in bridge club." She laughed. "Okay, well, while we're on the topic. What is bridge?" That just made her laugh even more. "I know I'm really showing my working-class stripes over here, but I've never heard of it."

Our food arrived soon after, and I was glad that our conversation remained light and effortless. She'd ordered a Greek omelette served with a feta salad, and I got the house special omelette which had bacon, tomatoes, and a side of tzatziki sauce. I got to sample some of Harriet's, and she tried some of my food, excluding the tzatziki sauce, considering her dislike for cucumbers.

It was nice. We talked about music, the bands we listened to, and the TV we watched back home. I was glad we were able to clear the air a bit on her family. It felt like she was no longer hesitant when it came up again in conversation. And when it was time to pay up, I made sure to foot the bill. It was only right, considering I'd asked her out. It made me feel a little chivalrous in a way I wasn't expecting. I wondered if this was why guys liked paying too.

"Thank you for brunch."

"You're welcome."

"So, now, will you tell me where we are going?"

"Well, you told your mum you were going on a tour of the island, right?" Her brow furrowed suspiciously. "I was going to take you over to Hersonissos." Her face lit up, telling me I was on to a winner. "And I know there was something about a boat tour, but sorry, I don't have a boat." She didn't seem all that bothered. "I thought maybe we could go to the aquarium. That way, you'll still see some fish."

"That sounds really fun." Her reaction made me happy that I'd actually come up with a good date. I was relieved to have impressed her. And I especially wasn't expecting the soft kiss she planted on my cheek as we were walking back to my quad. It left my cheek all tingly. I was surprised she had kissed me in public. Especially when she wasn't out. "You're really cute when you blush."

"Shut up." I bumped her shoulder with mine. Anything to detract attention.

"God, why couldn't I have met you at Cambridge?"

"Because I'm not smart enough to get in somewhere like that."

"You're very smart. Hello, you want to go to med school. Besides, people at Cambridge aren't smart. They just have connections."

"Well, I don't have any of those, either. But I know what you mean." A sadness settled over us. It was the first time I'd thought about how this was a holiday romance. She would go home soon, and eventually, so would I.

"Do you think you would have asked me out back home?"

"No," I said honestly, and she looked a little disgruntled. "You're way out of my league."

"What are you talking about?" she said in outrage. "You have a sexy undercut, piercings, and are really good-looking."

Her hand laced mine as we made it to my quad. She leaned up against it and pulled me a little closer to her. The air intensified around us as she kissed me. Her arms snaked up and around my neck as she deepened our kiss. My hands found her hips, enjoying how it felt to have her body flush on mine. Flashbacks from this morning came back to me. Reluctantly, I pulled away, resting my forehead against hers and enjoying the contented sigh she let out.

"You taste as good as you did last night."

"You mean, this morning."

"Come on, you can have your wicked way with me later." I hopped onto my quad, and she shimmied up behind me.

She leant around to catch my eye. "You promise." I got another chaste kiss on the lips before starting up the engine.

Chapter Eight
Harriet Whitaker

We emerged into the late-afternoon light into a much more manageable heat. It wasn't nearly as hot as it was before we went into the aquarium. Riding on Niamh's quad had given us a false sense of the temperature. The breeze from the ocean had kept us from overheating on the drive. Not that I would have complained with my arms wrapped around her. However, I could handle the heat a little better than Niamh. Which was ironic considering she'd been living here for, like, two months already. We'd pulled over halfway to Hersonissos so we could apply more sunscreen. Niamh also had to wear a hat to avoid getting sunstroke, which was just the most Irish thing I'd ever heard. She looked hot in a snapback, though.

In the aquarium, I had spotted that her arms were a little red. I was pretty sure she'd gotten burnt, which was why I'd suggested we stay longer. At least that way, we were indoors and in the air-con. It wasn't much of a chore because the aquarium was awesome. I'd loved watching the crabs while Niamh had liked the seals. I could have done laps in that place just to spend more time talking to her.

"How is it still so warm?" Niamh said as we walked down the footpath into the old town. "I could swear Hersonissos is hotter than Stalis."

"It's more inland, I guess," I said, before dodging to the other side of her and nudging her closer to the walls of the buildings. That way, she had a better chance of being in the shade.

"Thanks," she muttered shyly, and it made me smile.

"How about ice cream? That'll keep you nice and cool."

"I'm sure there's some somewhere around here."

It was nice to explore the town with Niamh. She had only been to Hersonissos once before with Jenny, so it was like we were exploring it for the first time together. Hersonissos was a very different town than Stalis. Sure, Stalis had more class than Malia, however, it was still very touristy. Hersonissos was more like some of the old towns I'd visited in Athens. I enjoyed them more, well, as long as I didn't have to tour the cathedrals. I thought about my parents, where they were and when they would be back at the hotel. I subtly checked my phone to make sure they hadn't tried to contact me.

"Do you have to go?" Niamh asked, and I heard the edge of disappointment, making me stuff my phone back into my bag.

"No, I was just checking if I had any missed calls. I don't, so that's a good sign."

She nodded and didn't say any more on it. I was glad. I hated talking about my parents with Niamh. She couldn't possibly understand my life. And honestly, I was happy that she didn't have that kind of family dynamic. She had siblings and loving parents who seemed to accept her for who she was. It was beautiful, yet hard for me to understand. The fact that her parents even let her live abroad for the summer would never happen in my house. Maybe it was because she had siblings that she was afforded any sort of freedom. Honestly, I couldn't be sure. Perhaps my parents were just this way.

I tried to imagine what they would think of Niamh. They would never accept her, and they would probably ground me for the rest of my life. Even though Niamh had a heart of gold, they would never be able to see past her status long enough to see that she was probably ten times better than any of us. That made me really sad.

"This place looks good." Niamh stopped outside a gelato shop. I pulled myself from my thoughts, and we went inside.

We emerged again and took a seat on the wall outside the shop, giving us a sliver of a view of the ocean from behind some of the taller buildings at the oceanfront. I was just glad to still be in the shade.

"How's yours?" she asked between licks.

"You can't really go wrong with strawberry." I reached out my cone so she could try some of mine.

"It's good. I would never go for strawberry, usually."

"Me neither, but when I visited my cousin Marco in Italy a couple of weeks ago, we practically lived off the stuff."

"See, I usually like chocolate chip back home. But I was told by one of locals to try the pistachio, and honestly, it's all I get now. Here." She held out her cone for me to try.

"Oh wow," I said, unable to come up with anything more descriptive. It was nutty but sweet and refreshing. "I don't think I've ever had pistachio before, but that's so good. You've converted me. Strawberry just can't compete," I said, feeling a little disappointed with my flavour choice.

"Here." She swapped our cones before I could stop her.

"You don't have to give me your ice cream," I said, feeling touched by the gesture alone.

"Eh." She shrugged me off, licking the strawberry cone. "Maybe every time you get pistachio, you'll think of me." She winked, which I could just about see behind her sunglasses.

"What reminds you of me?"

"Hmm, a floral dress."

"Really?" I laughed because it was absurd.

"Oh yeah, I'll never look at a floral dress the same way," she teased before turning more serious. "You don't need to worry about me forgetting you." I watched her, but she didn't say anything. Something deeper lingered between us, and I couldn't help but feel closer to her.

"I'll not forget you, either." I reached for her hand and didn't miss the excited flip in my stomach. I held her hand as we finished our ice cream.

"When do you leave?" Niamh's voice was small, even though she was right beside me.

"The day after tomorrow."

She nodded a little sadly. "That's soon."

"Yeah, I know." I was feeling pretty down about leaving her. Then, something more positive consumed me. I liked Niamh. I really liked her, and when I really thought about it, I didn't want to never see her again in a couple of days. And why should we? "But you know, just because I'm leaving doesn't mean we won't see each other again."

"You gonna come to Northern Ireland?" she joked, but I felt serious.

"I mean it. Why couldn't we?"

"Like, long distance?"

"I don't know." I shrugged. "All I know is that I like you."

"I like you too." She seemed to think carefully. "I mean, I'm sure I could fly to Cambridge."

"You mean London. There are no airports in Cambridge."

"Even better. Cambridge sounds boring, no offence."

"I should take offence," I teased, "but I don't." Niamh laughed, turning to face me. "And besides, I've always wanted to visit Belfast."

"Harriet, are you serious right now?"

"About how I feel about you?" The air stilled around us.

"Well, I meant about dating when we're both back home, but yeah, that too."

I thought about her question. I understood her hesitation. Of course I could. We'd known each other less than a day, and yet, we were talking about staying in touch. Dating long distance. It was crazy. I knew it sounded insane in my head, but as cheesy as it sounded, it didn't feel too soon. It felt right. I wasn't ready to just have Niamh be a holiday romance. Someone to look back on fondly but eventually forget about. I didn't want to ever forget her.

"Yeah," I said, feeling incredibly vulnerable. "Niamh, I've never felt this way about anyone." Maybe I loved her. Which sounded crazy, but I couldn't deny how I felt. And maybe, one day, I would look back and think that I was just being a silly teenager, but for right now, I felt so complete.

"Me neither," she said before leaning forward and kissing me. She rested her forehead against mine, leaving me a little breathless. "Can I see you tomorrow as well?" she asked, a little hesitant, as if she was afraid that I would say no. "There's a boat trip to Santorini I've been dying to do."

"Oh my God, yes. I would love that."

Santorini was definitely on my bucket list. I asked if we could go while we were visiting Crete, but Mama had said it was a tourist trap. She'd said something about hiring a boat to take us out to circle the island, but that going onto the island would be a waste of time. I couldn't have disagreed more.

"Won't your parents mind?"

"I'll make something up. I want to spend my last day here with you." I could use Claudia as an excuse again, or maybe, I'd just lie and say I felt sick. I would do anything and face the consequences if it meant more time together.

Niamh's phone started ringing out of nowhere. She looked down at it and seemed torn. "It's my dad."

"Oh, okay. Take it, I can go—" I was about to hop off the wall to give her some privacy when he appeared on the screen.

"Hey, Dad." I was in view of the camera, so I shimmied away.

"How's it going, love?"

"Good, I'm just having ice cream."

"It's flippin' raining here. And was that Jenny I just saw?"

"Oh, no, that was…Harriet." Niamh glanced at me and threw me a look that pulled me closer to her.

"Hi, Harriet, nice to meet you." I shimmied closer to her so that I was in frame again. "I'm Sean."

"It's lovely to meet you, Sean."

"She's English." It didn't seem like he was annoyed about that. More as if stating a fact.

"Yes, Dad."

"What part are you from?"

"Sussex."

"A lovely part of the world. I used to work in Horsham."

"My cousin Marco lives in Horsham." Sean looked pleased, and Niamh looked happy that we were getting along too.

"Have you ever been to Belfast?"

"Not yet," I side-eyed Niamh and didn't miss the adorable look she threw me. "But I've always wanted to."

"I'm sure Niamh can help with that." He winked, causing Niamh to frown.

"Dad—"

"I'll leave you to it, love. I'll call you in a couple of days when you're not so busy."

"Okay, bye now."

"Bye, Sean."

"Bye, Harriet." I barely caught a glimpse before he was gone.

"My dad is so embarrassing."

"He was sweet. Do you think he knows we are on a date?"

"Yes, and now he's probably going to tell my whole family." She hopped off the wall and held her hand out for me. "But I guess that's not the worst thing in the world. Especially when you come visit." Her cute, lopsided smile told me she really didn't mind. It made me kind of excited to meet them. One day.

We stumbled upon a market on our way back to the oceanfront where the quad was parked. The stalls had an eclectic array of what some might consider junk. When we first saw it, I joked about not seeing anything worthwhile in somewhere like that, but it was Niamh who thought differently. At first, I thought she was mad. The lot of it was tat. Old clothes taken from the wardrobe of someone who'd probably passed away long ago or old furniture from a foreclosed house. No one could possibly find anything worthwhile. Except Niamh.

"Look at all these beautiful…"

"Things."

"Don't say it like that." She gave me a playful nudge. I struggled to hide my judgement. "They're beautiful things. Like this," she said, holding the silver ring. It was unique and rustic. It wouldn't have normally been my cup of tea, but I had to admit, it caught my eye too.

"I actually like it," I said, not missing the edge of surprise as she tried it on her ring finger. It was too big, so I suggested she put it on her thumb instead. "That looks cool."

She looked pleased with herself. "How much?" She held it up to the woman behind the table. She looked ancient and barely broke contact with her magazine. Her eyes found us over the rim of her glasses.

"Spoon," she said. Initially, I'd thought it was her broken English. Niamh and I gave each other a double take. "Spoon. I have two." Thankfully, Niamh looked as bewildered as I felt. The woman sighed defeatedly before rounding the table to us. She picked up a silver spoon that was from a set, also for sale on the table. She tapped the ring on Niamh's thumb. "I make from spoon."

"Oh," it seemed to click for both of us, and the woman smiled. Most likely from relief. "The ring is made from a spoon."

"Yes," she said. "They very popular. They sell out. And good quality. No green finger."

That had Niamh sold. "How much?"

"Ten." I was already riffling in my bag, and I was able to pull a twenty note from my bag before Niamh knew what was happening.

"What are you doing?" she said as the woman accepted my money.

"It looks good on you, and you've given me the best first date ever. Why not?"

Niamh looked touched. It was the best twenty I'd ever spent.

"I don't have change." The woman grunted, and I felt like rolling my eyes. I figured that was a classic trick at markets. I didn't really care about the change, not after seeing how happy the ring had made Niamh. "Here, you have this for your friend." She handed over another spoon ring. Niamh's face lit up as I started trying it on. It was smaller than hers and could only fit on my little finger. But I liked the way it looked, and there was something nice about knowing that Niamh had one too.

"Thank you." We waved good-bye to the woman, who just flicked her wrist as if she'd had enough of us.

"Matching jewellery, huh?" Niamh said as we left the market. "That's pretty gay."

"I won't tell if you don't."

"Okay, deal." We shook on it. "Where do you want to go now?"

"I assumed we were heading back to your quad. Back to Stalis." I tried to be suggestive. The truth was, I was excited to get her back to my room again. I didn't stop my arm from grazing hers.

"We can. If you want." Niamh looked a little disappointed.

"Don't you have work anyway?"

"Not for a few hours. I figured we could hang out for a bit longer."

"We can," I flirted. "You know, back in Stalis."

"Is there something you want to do?" She was not following at all.

"Yeah, you."

Her eyes widened adorably. I felt embarrassed too. Like maybe I was pressuring her or coming across as this sex-crazed woman, but the truth was, I was dying to get Niamh back into bed since last night. This morning. I knew what I meant.

"Oh," she said coyly. Nothing else followed, making me panic.

"Unless you don't want to. It's cool if you don't."

"No, I do. I just…Jenny is home."

"You can come to my room. My parents won't be back for hours."

"Okay." She snatched my hand and gave it a yank.

It was hard to stop my hands from wandering on the ride back to my hotel. Niamh had to focus on the road, of course, so I kept my hands firmly wrapped around her waist, but the anticipation was killing me. I wasn't the only one. As soon as we reached the elevator, Niamh had me pinned against the wall. Her hand hooked my thigh around her hip, and I couldn't help but melt against her front. She tasted like strawberry, and I was weirdly into it. The lift stopped, and I was pleased that no one was waiting to enter because they would have gotten an eyeful.

Once inside my room, it didn't take long for us to pick up where we'd left things off earlier this morning. I could touch her forever. I loved the reaction I got from her body. Everywhere I touched seemed to ignite a flutter of movement or a soft moan. I could kiss every inch of her, and I think I probably did at some stage. I loved the way her touch made me feel. She was my gay awakening, for sure. I knew without a shred of doubt that I liked sex with women. Specifically, Niamh. It was never ending but in a good way. Every time I orgasmed, which just seemed to be getting stronger, it was her turn. And vice versa, it felt endless. Like we would never be done, and I wasn't exactly complaining about it either.

Time felt irrelevant. Endless. Until...

The adjoining door burst open.

CHAPTER NINE
NIAMH DONNELLY

There was no warning. At least, not the kind of warning I could do anything about. I heard a brief knock at the adjoining door to Harriet's parents' room. I barely pulled away from her when it swung open. I caught a glimpse of shock on her face. There was no denying what we were doing. I knew that for sure. It happened so fast, and I sprang into action. I quickly got off her and turned my back to her mum. I had ahold of the sheets and wrapped them around my naked chest. I couldn't see what was going on behind me, but I could feel the most uncomfortable tension. It made my shoulders creep up as if bracing myself for impact.

"Harriet." Her tone was venomous, and it made me want to turn and shield Harriet from it, but I knew that would only make matters worse. "A word," she said, eerily politely.

The door closed again, and a silence settled over us. My mind was racing so fast that it felt like minutes passed when it had only been a few seconds. I still couldn't see Harriet's expression, but I could hear her shallow breathing. I wanted to comfort her, but I had no idea how. I turned slowly on the bed and saw the most heartbreaking look on her face. Her panic, fear, embarrassment, and devastation. I moved to her side, but she could barely register my proximity. It was like I wasn't even in the room.

"Harriet," I tried, but she remained in a trance. "Hey, are you okay?"

"I can't believe that just happened," she whispered, pressing her fingertips to her forehead. She looked crushed.

"I'm so sorry."

"You have to go." No words had ever hurt my heart more. I knew she was right. I couldn't be here while she talked to her mum. Not about something this big. But I wanted to comfort her. Protect her from what was potentially about to come. I only saw a glimmer of her mum's reaction, and it wasn't pretty. I couldn't imagine what faced her.

"Are you going to be okay?"

"Now." She finally met my eyes and placed her hand on my thigh. "You need to go now." The determination in her eyes had me nodding, even though it went against everything in my body. I started getting dressed, and Harriet threw on some sweats and a slouchy top.

She was panicked, and a little jittery. She attempted to make the bed, as if that was going to help. I wasn't even fully dressed when she started ushering me toward the door.

"Harriet, I don't want to leave you like this."

"It'll be fine. I'll make something up." She was being delusional, and I couldn't let her walk in there with that frame of mind.

"She knows what we were doing. She's not stupid."

"I'll figure something out." I could hear the quiver in her voice. Her fear was deafening. "But you need to go before she comes in here again." She opened the door and practically pushed me out of it.

"When can I see you?"

"At the beach. Tomorrow at noon. I'll be there." She tried to close the door, but I stopped it with my hand.

She locked eyes with me for a moment, and I saw her devastation. This was not how she had wanted to come out. If she'd wanted to come out at all. Her eyes filled with tears, and I stepped forward, pulling her into an embrace. She squeezed me back, and I breathed in deeply, memorising everything that was Harriet. Because something in my soul told me that this was the last time I would see her. I poured all of my strength into my hug.

"I'm sorry," I whispered against her neck as I felt her chest heave. When I pulled back, she wiped her tears away and looked at me once more.

"I've got to go."

And that was it. She was gone. I walked down to the beach in a daze. I imagined all of the things being said in that hotel room. I worried about her. I would have texted or called, but of course, we hadn't exchanged numbers. What a monumentally stupid idea I'd had. I was regretting it now. I had to have faith that tomorrow, I would see Harriet again. For now, I had to go to work. I couldn't even bring myself to tell Jenny what had happened, not at work at least. I couldn't trust my emotions enough.

On my way home from work, I passed Harriet's hotel. I thought about going up to her room. I parked up and everything. And just sat outside thinking. It was two in the morning. I was sure she would be asleep. In the end, I decided not to. I went home instead. It would only make things worse. And I had to trust Harriet. I had to have faith that tomorrow, I would see her again. Waiting at noon on the beach.

But I didn't. I went by at eleven thirty just in case, and I stayed until close to one. She never showed. I had to see her. I couldn't leave it this way. I didn't care if her parents were in her room, either. I would face them just so that I could see that Harriet was okay, or as okay as someone could be in her situation.

I went into the hotel, and thankfully, no one questioned my presence. I rode the lift to her floor and walked cautiously to her room. I waited outside for a moment, listening intently in case I could hear her parents. But it was quiet. I knocked on the door and could feel my heartbeat in my throat. It was booming in my ears. I was terrified of what storm awaited on the other side of the door. I just prayed that she was alone.

The door opened, and an older man stood there. "Hi." He had a Scottish accent. "Can I help you?"

I was stunned for a moment. He didn't look anything like her, and then, the panic settled in. "I'm looking for Harriet."

He shook his head. "No Harriet's here, love," he said pleasantly, leaving me feeling empty inside. "Maybe you have the wrong room."

"Yeah." I just about got out through the crushing force in my chest. "Sorry."

The door closed again, and I knew she was gone. They'd flown back home early. Or maybe, they'd moved rooms or even hotels. All I knew was that she was gone, and I had no way to reach her. I didn't know her surname. I felt crushed in a way I'd never experienced before.

By the time I got home, Jenny was awake.

"Hey, what happened with Harriet?" She was on the edge of the bed. I'd shared what had happened when we'd gotten home last night. I couldn't sleep, and the tossing and turning had seemed to be keeping her awake. "Did her ma flip?"

"She's gone," I said, but I couldn't be sure Jenny heard any of it before I started crying. She rushed to me and pulled me into a hug. I cried, and she hugged me for what seemed like a really long time. I couldn't form words. I couldn't bring myself to explain how I was feeling. It was too overwhelming. I was far beyond sadness. My heart hurt. My head felt like it couldn't make sense of anything. Everything felt broken. Nothing felt like it could make me happy. I hated myself for not going to her room last night. Perhaps I could have gotten to her before they'd made her leave. The regret felt unbearable. I hated myself for not getting her number or her last name or where she lived or anything that could have led me to get in touch with her. But most of all, I hated her parents. For taking her away. We were supposed to have another day. We were supposed to have time to figure out how we could stay in touch. That was ripped away from us, and the rage pulsating through me felt unnatural. And yet, the pain was so much more overwhelming. I felt like I could drown in my own tears.

"I'm so sorry, Niamh," Jenny whispered for what felt like it wasn't the first time. I'd almost forgotten she was still holding me. I'd forgotten where I was.

I didn't want to be here anymore. "Can we go home?"

"Yeah," she whispered over my shoulder, squeezing me tightly.

PART TWO
2018

CHAPTER TEN
HARRIET WHITAKER

It was a beautiful spring day. A definite chill in the air, but blue skies stretched beyond the city limits. I could have taken the tube, but London felt alive. For the first time in months. It had been a long winter, cold and miserable. The brisk walk would help shake out some of the jitters as well, a usual occurrence when I was meeting Mama. That was why I restricted our meetings to a maximum of once a month. It gave me ample time to recuperate and prepare for the next occasion.

She'd made a reservation at the prestigious Galvin La Chapelle, which was an extravagant lunch spot for a Tuesday. I could swear she was choosing these restaurants to impress Beth alone. At least she would be there to shelter me from the full brunt of Mama. Sometimes, I thought my parents preferred my fiancée over me.

When I arrived, the host lead me to a table in the back. Mama was waiting with the remnants of a glass of wine in her hand. Chardonnay, most likely. I could see the chilled bottle in the bucket from here. She spotted me, and a hint of a smile made its way onto her expression.

"Darling," she said, refusing to stand. I leant down and kissed both cheeks. She looked over my shoulder to the host. "Another glass. You'll have a drink, won't you?"

"I'm working."

"But you will, won't you?" The host was already on their way back with another glass for me. "And Beth?"

"I don't know." I could feel myself playing with my engagement ring. "You'll need to ask her when she arrives."

"I know Beth." Mama smiled in delight. "Another," she said to the host, and he left us again. It felt like she was enjoying making him do laps.

"She can have mine," I said, but it was like talking to a wall.

"Nonsense."

When the host returned, looking slightly out of puff, Mama tapped her glass, and he filled it from the chilled bottle. I hated the way she treated servers. You'd think after all these years, it wouldn't still bother me.

"Where's Dad?"

"Dubai," Mama said, gesturing to my wineglass for the host to fill. I was disappointed. Dad always made Mama more tolerable, and now, I would have to face her myself. Hopefully, Beth wouldn't be too late. "One of your father's clients ran into a little trouble. He flew out last night."

I gestured for the server to stop pouring when it was only half-full. I didn't want any to begin with. "Thanks," I said. He placed the bottle back in the bucket and draped it with a linen napkin before finally leaving us. "Is he away for long?"

"No idea, you know your father. He took his golf clubs with him." I nodded, knowing he would likely be gone the week. There probably wasn't even a work emergency. He just wanted a break from Mama. "Darling, did you get in touch with Dr. Quinn yet?" She narrowed her eyes, criticising my complexion.

"No." I tried to brush off the topic. I hadn't actually taken her suggestion seriously when she'd brought it up at last month's luncheon.

"You must. His wait list can be six months, and you'll want to start treatment before the big day."

"We haven't even set a date, yet," I said, my mind being drawn back to our argument last night. But I refused to dwell on that now,

Mama would only end up siding with Beth. "Besides, Mama, I really don't like needles."

"It's only Botox. You're better starting it early." I was twenty-six. She was getting worse. "You have a stressful job, Harriet. I can see it on your face."

"Okay." I opted to appease her. A usual tactic to get through these meetings.

"And your hands," she said in horror, and I clenched them into fists to hide my unmanicured nails. "I don't know how you keep someone like Beth around when you don't take care of yourself."

"Beth doesn't care about my nails," I said, not having the strength to go into detail about why lesbians didn't have long nails. That would certainly be a step too far. After all, it was only acceptable to be a lesbian if I was with someone "perfect." That was how it felt. At least to my parents.

Coming out hadn't been easy. After they'd caught me in Greece, my parents were so outraged that they'd flown us home that day. I didn't even have a chance to say good-bye to Niamh. I hadn't thought about her in years. I used to. A lot. I'd even tried to find her on Facebook a few times, but I didn't know her last name. I didn't even know what university she went to. Life kind of forced me to move on.

I'd dated other girls in university, but I'd known my parents wouldn't approve. There was no point in even bringing them up in conversation. I knew how my parents worked. The stakes would be higher for a woman. She would have to be out of this world. That was Beth.

I first saw Beth when I was in second year of university. I was nineteen, she was twenty-four. She was the whole package: smart, brilliant, charismatic and gorgeous. Beth was doing her PhD and taught one of my classes each week. I was completely mesmerised. The way she spoke was hypnotic. She made legislation sexy, somehow. Her being that bit older made her all the more irresistible. I was so attracted to her back then, and now when people asked how we'd met, she couldn't help but tease that she'd had no idea who I was. Not until we met at a bar the following year. By that stage, she was already working in a law firm.

Beth was from a high society family as well, adding some brownie points in my parents' minds. In fact, her family was distantly related to the royal family in Belgium, and yet, I had still worried about introducing her to my parents. It turned out that status was more important than even gender. The royalty link had sealed the deal for Mama, whereas Dad had been roped in by her ambition. All they would do was talk shop. So much so, he offered her a job a few years back, and six months ago, he'd made her partner. The youngest partner in their firm's history. It was impressive. Beth was impressive. I was sure my parents thought that I should have considered myself lucky to have been chosen by someone like her. And I did. Mostly. I loved her, and she would take good care of me. For that reason, I knew she was a keeper. She was the first woman that my parents approved of, and she was the only woman I'd ever brought home to meet them. Unless I counted Niamh, which I was positive Mama did not.

"How's work?" Mama asked, though I knew she didn't really care.

"Good," I lied. I did that a lot. It seemed to be the only way to get her to like me.

The truth was that work hadn't been fulfilling me lately. I had been working as a paralegal up until last year, when I'd been promoted to a solicitor in my firm. It wasn't nearly as high-flying or glamourous as Beth and Dad's firm. They managed big, well-known, *Fortune 500* kind of companies, some of whom I couldn't even say out loud for legal reasons. My firm was also corporate law but on a much smaller scale. I remembered Dad trying to get me into his firm, claiming I would climb the ranks in no time. But I couldn't imagine anything worse than having my father's legacy placed on my shoulders. I wanted to prove to them and myself that I could stand on my own two feet and succeed on my own.

They had been so proud when I became a solicitor. It made me feel amazing to have their approval. And yet, ever since, I had been feeling more and more withdrawn from my job. When I was a paralegal, I'd enjoyed the flexibility of cases, the banter with the other paralegals, and generally, less pressure. Now, everything fell to me. I was responsible for avoiding lawsuits with my clients, some of whom were incredibly hard to work with. They expected a lot, making the work tiresome. I often questioned if corporate law was really the right fit for me.

I'd talked to Beth about it recently, but she didn't really get it. She tried to be supportive, told me that it was just the promotion that was making me feel more stressed. She loved being a solicitor, and because of that, I was a little afraid to tell her that I didn't think I liked the work anymore. I had this horrible feeling that she would disapprove of me wanting to change careers. I wouldn't even know what else I would do, and I'd been working years toward this, therefore, I couldn't understand why it wasn't making me happy anymore.

"How's bridge club?" I asked, wanting to get off topic.

"The usual." She took another healthy swig of wine until something exciting popped into her head. "I meant to tell you, I ran into Claudia at the club the other day."

I forced an excited expression, refusing to reveal that I didn't associate with Claudia anymore. Ever since Greece, we hadn't really met up again. There were no bad feelings. We'd just grown apart. She went to a different university. She'd met her husband and settled down out in Surrey.

"And guess what?" She took a beat. "She just had a baby."

"Oh, whoa," I said, feeling very little about the news. "That's lovely."

"That'll be you soon."

That left me floored. She'd dropped a hint like this before, but she'd been drinking. A lot more than today. I hadn't really taken it seriously at the time, but this was unavoidable. "We're not really there yet." Correction, I was nowhere near ready for children.

"You will once you're married," she said excitedly.

"Beth doesn't really want to have kids, Mama." I felt the need to burst her bubble. For once, maybe Beth could be the bad guy. I always thought that I would have liked to have children one day, but Beth had never showed any interest.

"Of course, she won't carry them." The mere suggestion seemed ridiculous to Mama, and it annoyed me. "She's partner. She can't afford to take a year off on maternity." I was offended instantly, and I struggled to hide it from my face. "Be serious, Harriet. It makes much more sense for you to be at home with the children."

"At home with the children?" I could hear the disbelief in my tone.

"Beth's salary can more than support a healthy lifestyle for you both," she said as if it was written in law. Matter of fact, according to her. It enraged me. Once again, she was writing every inch of life. And I didn't even get a say in it. "A paralegal's salary wouldn't support a family."

"I'm not a paralegal." A fire inside made me want to stand up for myself. "I was promoted last year, and what does that have to do—"

"Beth." Mama spotted her stepping into the restaurant. Mama stood to greet her, pulling her into a hug and kissing her cheeks.

"Hello, my lovey." Beth sat next to me and gave me a chaste kiss on the cheek. "I'm terribly sorry for running late." The fire in my chest was extinguished. I felt disappointed in myself for letting it go. For once, I'd felt as though I was speaking up for myself, but it would be inappropriate to steer the conversation back. "Traffic was insane."

"The tube would have taken you half the time," I said, trying to ignore the overwhelming withdrawn feeling taking over me.

Beth smiled in apology.

"But it's horrid," Mama pointed out. "Dirty underground train. I don't know why you bother," she said to me.

"It is, Pipa, however, Harriet is right." She patted my thigh but removed contact quickly. Beth knew how to play it. The right amount of PDA in front of my parents. It was why she didn't kiss me on the lips or hold my hand in their presence. "I could have gotten here faster on the tube, but the firm's town car is much more comfortable," she quipped, receiving a laugh from Mama. "Have we ordered, ladies?"

"Just the chardonnay." Mama raised her glass to her lips.

"Are you trying to get me boozed up during lunch again, Pipa?" Mama laughed wickedly. "You know me too well." Beth played into her hands. It was almost like flirting between the two, which made me uncomfortable. However, I couldn't deny that Mama was much more palatable in Beth's presence. It was a trade-off I had come to accept. "Allow me." Beth made a show of topping up Mama's glass before pouring some into hers. She offered some to me as well, but I said no. I hated drinking during work, even the half glass that I hadn't touched was pushing it. "And Philip is in Dubai. I heard this morning he had to fly out last night."

"Another client in trouble," Mama said tiredly.

"I'm sure it came as quite a shock to you. I thought you and Philip were off to France this week." That was news to me, and I was surprised that Beth hadn't told me, either.

"He assures me that he will meet me in Paris on Saturday," Mama said, a little unconvinced, before a bright idea struck. "You girls should come join us next week. It would be lovely, and I'm sure Philip would love to see his favourite daughter..." I was his only daughter, and I was sure he would barely register my presence with Beth in the room. "And daughter-in-law," she corrected.

"Not yet," Beth teased. "But soon, mother-in-law." They laughed together, and I forced myself to join in. Anything to avoid the topic of conversation returning to Botox or children.

"When is the wedding, anyway? I've been dying to hear the details."

Beth hesitated for a moment.

"You've been engaged for months now."

I felt uncomfortable, and it transported me back to our argument from last night:

Beth was working at the kitchen table. She worked often in the evenings, claiming that it was necessary. There just weren't enough hours in the workday, she said, making light of it. Since making partner, she was working more. She travelled for work a lot. I often felt lonely when she was away. I told her as much once, but she'd said it was unfair of me to make her feel guilty for her success.

She'd said she had to work twice as hard as her male counterparts. She had to blow them out of the water, and at times, I knew what she meant. Being the youngest partner in her firm and one of the few women meant a lot of pressure. I'd felt this a bit in my work as well. A double standard for women. Especially those female solicitors with children. They were penalised or overlooked for promotions because they had to leave every day promptly to collect their kids from school. It was part of the reason I wasn't in a rush to have kids.

I tried to be more considerate of Beth's professional pressures. It was why I cooked dinner and tidied up, allowing her to be consumed in her work. Before she'd made partner, she'd been better at splitting her time between work and me.

"Are you still okay to have lunch tomorrow?" I asked after putting away leftovers into the fridge.

"Tomorrow?" she asked, barely tearing her concentration away from her laptop.

"Lunch with Mama."

"Oh, is that tomorrow?"

"Yes," I said awkwardly.

"All right, I'll be there." She went back to working.

"Thanks, you know what she's like." I felt like I was speaking into the void as her eyes were glued to the screen. "She's always easier to deal with when you're there."

"I think you're imagining that." She didn't look up from her screen, or else, she probably would have seen how much that hurt me. We'd fought about it before. She had this special relationship with my parents that was impossible for me. Beth could do no wrong, whereas it felt like I could do nothing right.

I thought about leaving it there, but we hadn't spoken at all today. I wanted some kind of interaction, especially because she had been in Scotland all last week on business. I had missed her. "I'm glad you're home." I felt stupid, like I was pestering her or something.

"Me too." She smiled briefly, but that was all I got.

We'd lived together for a couple of years. I'd experienced living with her before her promotion. We had been more spontaneous. Date nights during the week to the theatre or grabbing a drink after work. It had been fun and exciting, and as much as I didn't want to admit it, things had changed. The way we interacted had become more strained, unless it was with friends and family or at work events. I found Beth to be more attentive in company, compared to on our own. In public, we appeared flirty and finished each other's sentences. But at home, that seemed to fade.

"Was there something else?" she asked, putting me on the spot. I felt embarrassed for not just leaving her alone to work. That was clearly what she wanted.

"I was just going to put on a movie, if you wanted to join me."

"I can't, Harriet. I've this report due tomorrow."

"Okay." I tried to brush off my frustration.

I turned on the TV but watched nothing. I scrolled through my phone on Facebook or reading Reddit. When that didn't entertain me any longer, I decided to skim my email. One surprised me; it had ended up in the spam folder. It was just by chance that I'd spotted it. It was from a recruiter. I had no idea how they'd gotten my information, but they had a job opportunity. And for first time in a while, I was excited.

The job description was for a position within a human rights company I had heard of but had never worked with. They worked with undocumented immigrants arriving in the UK, particularly those arriving via the English Channel. I researched the company, and the more I delved into it, the more the opportunity sparked something in me. They worked with displaced refugees and helped with the legal side of seeking asylum. It sounded so much more fulfilling than anything I accomplished in my day-to-day. It was different, of course, but different sounded good. The opportunity was for a solicitor, but I was left feeling disappointment by the pay cut. If the job was right for me in other ways, I could make some lifestyle changes to accommodate the lower salary. However, I knew it wouldn't sit well with Beth. I could already hear her saying that it was a step backward.

I pulled out my laptop and applied for the position anyway. If nothing came of it, there would be no reason to have to talk to Beth about it.

"Hey." She appeared as I hit send on the application. "I'm going to go to bed soon."

I slammed shut the laptop and gave her my full attention.

"What were you doing?"

"Nothing. Just on Facebook." I got up and turned off the lights.

We got ready for bed and climbed under the sheets. She let out a sigh of relief. "It's so nice to be back in my bed again."

I curled into her side. "It's good to have you back." My fingers danced along her stomach, drawing lazy patterns.

"Not tonight." She removed my hand. "I'm exhausted." I felt rejected and a little upset. I wasn't angling for that. However, it was hard to deny that our sex life had turned into a bit of this.

Most nights, no one made a move, but when one of us did, it seemed like the other wasn't in the mood. We were not synced in that way. Which was partly understandable. We'd been dating for five years, and it was only natural to hit a bit of a lull. We used to have sex multiple times a week. However, this seemed more than a blip. Beth and I used to joke about lesbian bed death and how that would never happen to us. I'd never thought it would. We couldn't keep our hands off each other back then, but lately, we'd been going weeks without even properly kissing. It concerned me, and I had to admit I thought about it often. But I told myself it was temporary. That it was just a rough patch.

"I haven't seen you in, like, a week," I said in a small voice. "We don't have to sleep together, but could we at least talk?"

"About what?" Her voice revealed a frustration that I didn't like.

"About anything. Ideally, not work."

"What's that supposed to mean?" She was disgruntled, and it set me off. It felt like another rerun of a fight we seemed to be revisiting often.

"All we do is talk about work."

"Harriet, not this again, okay? You knew who I was when we met. I like my work—"

"Yeah, but I didn't know it was your whole personality. God, ever since you made partner—"

"There it is." She sat up in annoyance and turned, now looking down on me. "Every day you give me a hard time about being partner. Most fiancées encourage each other's career."

I sat up as well, feeling offended that she would accuse me of being unsupportive. "I support your career. But I didn't know it was the third person in our relationship. We never spend time together, go out for dinner, God forbid we have sex." I couldn't stop it from all coming out in one heated breath. "We compromise everything for your work commitments."

"You're always doing this, and it's getting old. If I'd known you were going to be such a nagging wife, I'd have never asked you to marry me."

I was shocked. She'd never talked to me like that before, but weirdly, it didn't feel like it had come out of nowhere. It didn't feel like it was a slipup said in the heat of the moment during an argument. She seemed tired, or rather, tired of me. That made me worried. It was as if she had thought about it before, but this was the first time she'd had the courage to say that she was unsure about us getting married. The hurt inside me made it difficult to form a response.

Beth didn't miss it, either. She let out a sigh, looking ashamed. "Look, I'm sorry, okay?" It seemed like she was trying to backpedal. "I'm tired. You know I love you—"

"Do I?"

That annoyed her. "Come on, Harriet. I'm trying to apologise here. Let's just forget about it. I shouldn't have said that. You're just nagging me so much."

"How? How am I nagging you?"

"I don't have time for this." She sprung out of bed. "I told you before. I have a meeting. I can't get into this imaginary argument again with you." She snatched her pillow. "I'm going to sleep in the guestroom."

I flopped back onto the bed, feeling flat. I hated arguing before bed, and I hated when she slept in the other room. It just felt like this was becoming more of a regular occurrence, and it was draining the life from me. Newly engaged relationships shouldn't be this hard.

I lay awake for what felt like hours until I started to regret fighting with her. She was tired. She'd said it enough times. I should have been more considerate instead of coming down hard on her.

I didn't want to break up.

We'd been together a long time to just throw in the towel after a few hard months. And we had a good life. We went on frequent holidays: ski breaks, city trips, and we had a lovely apartment in Nottingham, a very desirable location. If my eighteen-year-old-self could have seen me now, engaged to a beautiful and successful woman, she wouldn't have believed it. *Even my parents approved. Beth loved me and I loved her. Everything was right. So why wasn't I?*

A silence lingered as Mama looked expectantly between us. We hadn't talked since our fight. Beth had left for work before I'd woken up.

"Well, Pipa, we were just talking about the wedding last night, weren't we, Harriet?" Beth said, surprising me with just how good she was at deception. "We talked about maybe a summer wedding. Next year, perhaps." We had talked very loosely about that weeks ago, but had never been able to set it in stone. Somehow, Beth was doing that now. And infuriatingly, it was almost entirely without my input.

"Oh, you must do it in Italy. Philip's brother has the most luxurious villa."

"Definitely a possibility," Beth said, but I didn't believe a word of it. Beth never got on with my cousin Marco. Therefore, staying in his parents' villa would be a "favour" she would never accept. "We were actually thinking somewhere in Surrey."

"I love it. Close to home. I know the most perfect church. The minister may be open to marrying—"

"Two women?" I couldn't hide my scepticism. It felt like my life was getting written before my own eyes.

"With a little persuasion. Your father can help with that," Mama alluded, making me want to shut down, mentally check out of this conversation, but I was terrifyingly stuck in it. This wasn't how I wanted my big day to go. Paying off someone who didn't actually support our marriage. It sounded the opposite of what a wedding was supposed to be.

"Can I take your order?" a server asked. I was glad for the interruption. I felt like I was drowning.

"Yes." Beth took the lead as she did in most things in life. "We will have the Landes white asparagus and foie gras terrine. The truffle vinaigrette should be on the side. Pipa, would you like me to recommend something for you too?" I had lost my appetite anyway. It was safer for Beth to just order for me. She usually did.

"You know, I think I will have the same." Mama handed the server her menu, not bothering to say thank you. "It's sounds delicious."

"You won't regret it." They laughed together before Beth changed topic. "We still need to iron out the final details, don't we, lovey?" I glanced around at her, confused. "The wedding." She stared back at me, showing a hint of frustration.

I decided to play along. "Yes."

"It will be wonderful." Mama grinned at us, and I struggled to remain focused on this conversation at all. It seemed so far removed from how I was feeling.

Beth looked happy as they went on discussing potential reception venues. Once again, I was floored with just how convincing she was. Making herself look like the most perfect fiancée, when last night, she'd literally said that she didn't know why she'd asked me to marry her. I couldn't even muster involvement in the conversation, and instead, I took a swig of wine. The same wine I didn't want. Perhaps this would be my future, guzzling wine in order to get through the conversations around me. Discussions about me that didn't quite involve me.

"Well, I know an excellent wedding planner. Funny, she lives in Paris," Mama said, looking excited again. "Oh, you two must fly out next week. I could arrange an introduction."

"I wish we could, but, Harriet, don't you have that conference next week?" Beth addressed me, pulling me out of my thoughts.

"Yes." I was relieved to have been pencilled in to the tedious day event at Alton Hotel. I was once dreading it, though, now, it was saving me from another encounter with Mama.

I left lunch feeling that it was a particularly excruciating experience. Most of the time, Mama had a way of making me feel like I was a disappointment, but today, she'd really outdone herself. Perhaps it was the lingering unsettling feeling I had with Beth that was contributing to my low mood. Maybe—and it was a feeling I really couldn't shake—it was just my general dissatisfaction with my life.

CHAPTER ELEVEN
NIAMH DONNELLY

The wait seemed endless. My interview was supposed to start twenty minutes ago. I'd gotten there early and would take some responsibility for the fact that my butt was going dead. Hospital seats were like that, I guessed. I just wasn't normally the one sitting on them.

It was a quiet part of the building. It must have been because of its lack of chaos. And people. I hadn't seen a single person since I'd sat down. It did nothing to settle my nerves.

I could feel my knees bobbing uncontrollably. I hated interviews. I hated having to sell myself. I was far from a salesperson. That was why I was so good at being a paramedic. No one was ever cagey with me. There was instant trust. It was typically an emergency. They just wanted my help. I didn't need to be the best dressed in the room or have the best vocabulary. It was perfect for me.

Why was I interviewing for this job again?

The door to my left opened. "Thank you for coming down to see us. We will be in touch." The interviewee smiled, but I caught a glimpse of their panic and regret as they left the room. It made me even more anxious. I was the only one waiting when the interviewer set her sights on me. "Naimh Donnelly." I got up and put on a brave face. "Right this way." I didn't miss the way she surveyed me from head to toe.

The interviewer was older, late-fifties would have been my guess. She had short, curly, white hair and worse, glasses that were attached to beads around her neck. I'd had no idea they even still made those. I didn't miss the cross around her neck, making me just a tad intimidated. My suit felt a little hot, but I worried if I removed the jacket, she would see the sweaty armpits in my white shirt. Or worse, my full sleeve of tattoos.

I had been confident when I'd left home this morning. Mum had even complimented how good I looked, but now, I felt overly masculine. It was typically how I dressed anyway, though self-consciousness was settling over me. I wanted to impress this semi-conservative woman. What if I was too gay for her liking?

"It's lovely to meet you, Niamh." She sounded genuine, and that put me at ease. I took a seat in front of her desk. "I'm Cheryl Kelly, head of the General Practitioners Academy at the Royal Hospital. I oversee the training programme here and have done so for the past twelve years." She removed her glasses and sat back for a moment, seeming to relax. "I always warn the people I interview"—if I didn't already feel nervous—"acceptance into this programme is extremely competitive. We are interviewing around sixty applicants for a class of twenty-five, maximum. The dropout rate for this programme would shock you." She paused, perhaps gauging how intimidated I really was by what she was saying. I tried to keep my face neutral and my breathing steady. "I have to be sure on each candidate. It isn't called a fast track for no reason. This course will be the toughest eighteen months of your life. You could be working twelve-hour shifts in the ER, surviving on a couple of hours sleep, before a long day of classes the next day. Are you the kind of person who could handle that kind of lifestyle?"

"I think so," I said, more confident than I was feeling. "I feel I have worked in these kinds of stressful environments for years. I know how to prioritise my work and studies."

She smiled, seeming to approve of my answer. "I have to admit..." She scanned the page in front of her. "Your CV and application was one of the more, shall we put it, colourful ones in the stack."

I smiled a little. I'd had quite an adventurous couple of years, and I was glad to see it impressed Cheryl.

"Why don't you talk me through it?"

"Sure, where to start? Well, I graduated in the top ten percent of my class from Queens and came straight here. To the Royal. I worked in the first responders' unit for about nine months, and then, I packed it all in and packed up my life and moved to Australia. Which was the best thing I could have ever done." She tilted her head, perhaps a little sceptical. "Have you ever been?"

"My son moved out there last year. He loves it."

"But have *you* been?"

She shook her head, a little ashamed.

"Until you have, you can't understand."

"He tells me that every time I ask when he's coming home." We both laughed. And I felt like the scary tension in the room vanished. I felt more relaxed, like I was talking to an equal.

"I lived in Perth first, for about a year. I worked at the Royal Perth Hospital which was such an incredible experience. I got to learn from people who've been paramedics for forty years or more and respond to emergencies I'd never dealt with. Snake bites, for example."

Cheryl squirmed in her seat, but her smile didn't fade, telling me she wasn't bored of me yet. Working in Perth was like the trenches. I'd barely had any time to travel and explore. For that reason, the city didn't feel like home. It was why I'd decided to change locations.

"Then, I was in Melbourne for almost two years working at the Royal Melbourne hospital." I loved Melbourne. I couldn't help but smile, thinking back on the memories. "There, I moved up from a level one to level two and finally, a supervisor within the unit." I was proud of my achievements. I was hardworking. And in Australia, I'd found that was rewarded, which was why I was able to train and move up the ranks quickly. "In my application, I attached a letter of recommendation from my superior. I don't know if you got it?"

"I did, thank you. It was very impressive. It is all very impressive, Niamh."

I smiled, feeling a pressure ease. "When I left Australia, I went straight to Kenya to volunteer. I was responsible for providing vaccinations for everything from malaria to Ebola. It was a really enriching experience, though gruelling. Especially in the summer."

"I bet. Before we go on to talking about why you wanted to switch medical fields, there is a gap on your CV that I am curious about." Oh shit. I was a fool to have gotten cocky. How could I have thought she would have missed it? "Between Australia and Kenya, there was some time unaccounted for. Travelling, was it?"

It was because of Remy, but I couldn't exactly tell Cheryl that. My past relationship wasn't exactly easy to explain and not really appropriate for an interview, either. They were a free spirit. That was what had drawn me in first. Remy was nonbinary, and they were the first person I'd been with who didn't feel the need to label their gender. Meeting them had given me the confidence to explore my own gender and style. I identified as she-her but felt best when I leant into a more masculine presentation of myself.

Remy was a part-time tattoo artist and part-time poet. Which was a little unorthodox for someone like me, but Remy was just that good. They were unapologetically quirky, and I found it empowering and sexy. They used to walk around their house naked and stay up all night performing poetry in these alternative clubs. It was good when I was on night shifts but sucked when we had plans the next day because they couldn't get out of bed. We were so different, but I liked that. They got me into smoking weed, which I did...a lot. When I wasn't working, of course. Things were great, until our differences started to come between us.

After six months of dating, Remy invited me on a spiritual retreat on Tasmania. That was when things started to go downhill for us. It was supposed to be a weekend away, and I went along with it. Why not, right? What I wasn't prepared for was the volume of psychedelics I would be consuming without prior knowledge. It was fun and all but not worth losing my job over. Thankfully, it didn't come to that. We got frequent drug tests at work, and I cared too much about my reputation to take a chance. I handed in my notice and never went back. I could have spoken to my supervisor.

I was sure she would have understood. But I wasn't planning on staying in Australia permanently. I wanted to travel and volunteer before I travelled back to Northern Ireland again. It seemed to fit that timeline.

Remy wasn't interested in anything serious, and at the time, neither was I. We bought an old camper van, and she showed me around Australia. We drove all over from Killalea Beach to Sydney and up to Brisbane. It was an amazing time of my life. And going to travel Australia by myself was definitely a gamble, but I was so glad that I had done it. Because I felt like it had changed me. When I went out, I was fresh out of university and wanted nothing more than to earn money. I'd worked hard and partied hard in my spare time. I'd met some incredible people, got scammed a couple of times, and tried magic mushrooms. And while I could have stayed longer, I was glad that I'd moved to Kenya when I did.

"Yeah, I went travelling." I only half lied.

"Thought it was something as simple as that, but I like to check these things."

Thankfully, she didn't dig any deeper. I probably wouldn't have gotten a callback had I divulged the details of that spiritual retreat.

"So, Niamh, you have this wealth of experience in paramedics. We are crying out for first responders."

I felt myself grow sheepish. I knew there was huge demand for people with my skills. I felt ashamed to be abandoning it. But something stronger was pulling me in a different direction.

"Why do you want to be a GP?"

That was a tricky question. Cheryl wasn't the first to be surprised, especially in my life. Growing up, I had always wanted to be a paramedic. I'd told everyone as much, and after only being qualified for five years, I was switching fields. Of course it was suspicious. I had to be fully prepared to explain why.

"First responders have a crucial job. But in some cases, and you must know this, we're only really just holding people together until they get to a hospital." Cheryl mulled that statement over for a moment, seeming to disagree. "I mean, we obviously do a little more than that."

"I know what you mean." She smiled, letting me off the hook for almost diminishing the vital work of paramedics.

"I want to be the first person who can prevent illnesses from getting to an emergency. I used to always think it was a first responder, but I recently came to the realisation that it goes back further. From the first headache or fever or lump. To the person asking the questions. The doctor who supports patients when they're scared, and they don't know what is wrong with them." I could feel something working in my chest. An emotion rising that I tried desperately to push down. "GPs are the ones who investigate and use their knowledge to make the judgement call on where patients go next in discovering what's wrong. That's why I want to be a GP."

There was more, but I wasn't sure I wanted to share it. Not yet at least. I had only been in Kenya two months when I'd gotten the news about Dad. He'd just turned 60; he was fit and healthy. Gym a couple of times a week, an avid hiker, he didn't eat junk. He did everything you were supposed to do, and just like that... Cancer. My world had crumbled, and I'd wanted to leave and come straight home, but he'd encouraged me to stay. I always listened to what Dad told me to do. But I was terrified, and my whole family had come together in a way I'd never seen.

Dad was one of lucky ones, though; they'd caught it early, and he'd started treatment right away. He was doing great, just finished chemo last month. But that was what made me want to become a GP. From a child, I'd wanted to be a first responder, the one who got there first. Who prevented a patient from getting any worse until they could be treated in a hospital. But what I realised was that it was the GPs who actually did that. They were the ones to examine the patient at the first hint of something being wrong. To refer them on to the right physicians.

And if it wasn't for the GP in my local town, they would have never caught Dad's cancer until it was too late. I was from a pretty small village in Northern Ireland called Sherwood. It was pretty commonplace for one or two GPs to service the entire community. Dad went to see our family GP, Dr. Hyme, complaining about pains in his stomach and other symptoms that a doctor could have dismissed. It could have been chalked up to a stomach bug, stress, or maybe even pulling a muscle while hiking. A few days after Dad had visited Dr. Hyme, he'd called him back to check in. Out of the blue. Dr. Hyme had said he wasn't comfortable to wait and would refer him on to get a scan. Dad was worried at the time, but Dr. Hyme had assured him that it was probably nothing. And thank God he did. I felt like I would be forever indebted to Dr. Hyme.

I'd been hearing so many stories about the NHS being in trouble, especially GPs, and I wanted to do something about it. To be a cog in a flawed system, even though I knew it would frustrate me. Because it meant that I could really help people. I felt like I owed it to the place I grew up. The place that raised me. And I felt like I owed it to Dad.

"I have a couple of competency questions as well. Let's start with your ability to work under pressure."

The rest was a blur. I had prepped for questions like these. Jenny had completed this course three years ago and was now working as a GP in Derry. She had provided me with ample advice, and so I left the interview feeling that I had done my best.

I wanted to be on the programme so bad. It felt like my life depended on it. Any GP positions advertised online had this programme on the desirable criteria list. I knew I could do it, and I was at the stage in my life where I could dedicate myself to it. I was single, living at home, and ready to apply myself to a new challenge.

I walked through the front door of my parent's house. "Hey, loser." Oisin came bounding down the stairs toward me.

"You're still in your clothes from last night, so who's the real loser here?" I goaded as he gave me a playful shove. He looked rough, probably feeling pretty hungover. He was a student and had been out late last night.

"Nice suit, by the way." He patted the sleeves condescendingly. "Did you borrow it from Dad?"

"Ha ha. No, I borrowed it from your girlfriend."

"Dude." He threw me a wounded look. I instantly regretted it.

"I'm sorry, too far."

"We just broke up. Give me a week to grieve." He tried to play it down, but I knew he was still a little upset that things had ended with her.

"Sorry, my head is up my ass today."

"How'd the interview go?"

"I don't know." I shrugged, and he showed concern, which I was glad for.

Oisin was only twenty-two, but we were the closest. Perhaps because we still lived at home or maybe it was just Oisin's caring side. Besides, my other two siblings were in a different place in their lives. Sinead, my oldest sister, was in her mid-thirties with two kids, and my other brother, Patrick, was thirty, and his wife was expecting their first baby. As a whole, my family was still pretty close. There were arguments, sure, but Dad's cancer diagnosis had really pulled us all together. Most weekends, we met for family dinner, which, when everyone's partners and children were there, was utter chaos. But I wouldn't miss it. I'd already missed enough being away for four years. It was time to be at home.

"Well, you can tell me all about the interview while you're cooking dinner."

"Oh, is that right?" I followed him toward the kitchen, removing my suit jacket and already feeling ten pounds lighter. I went straight to the fridge. "Beer?" I asked Oisin.

"Yeah."

I handed him a bottle.

"I'll take one too," Dad said, clearly joking. He'd come out of the living room. He looked pale today.

He'd made the decision to stop drinking when he'd found out he was sick. Not that he was much of a drinker anyway. It was quite shocking seeing Dad when I got home from Kenya. I barely recognised him, he'd lost so much weight. Not only that, but his full head of fair hair was gone.

I gave him a hug, hating that there was barely anything to embrace. I pulled out the chair at the kitchen table for him. "Tea?"

"Go on then." He took the seat begrudgingly. I didn't miss the way he was out of breath.

"Oisin." I signalled for him to put on the kettle. He obliged as I pulled out the food for dinner.

"How'd the interview go...Dr. Donnelly?" He smiled proudly.

I rolled my eyes, but had to admit, I liked how it sounded. I knew Dad was proud of me already, but even he recognised why I was switching fields. He thought highly of the doctors who'd helped to treat him, and it wasn't exactly hard, considering Mum was an ER nurse.

"I don't know. There's sixty people interviewing, and there're only like twenty-five spots."

"Oh." Dad inhaled sharply, a nervousness settling in. "Not to worry, there's other programmes, right?"

"Yeah, and I have applied to them, but this one..."

"Is the best," Dad finished. "Well, as I always said, if it's meant for you, it won't go past you."

I nodded, starting to cut up the vegetables for dinner. "Spaghetti Bolognese okay for everyone?"

"Suits me," Oisin said, holding up his bottle of beer in cheers. "I've a good feeling about the job, Niamh." I knocked my bottle against his and went to take a drink.

"What am I, invisible?" Dad barked half-heartedly. We came to him to save him having to get up and did a cheers. We drank the beer, and he took a sip of his hot tea. "Save some dinner for Mum," Dad said as I went back to preparing dinner. "She's doing a split shift."

"Again?" I said, unable to hide my disapproving tone.

"Yeah, Dad, that must be, like, the fifth day in a row," Oisin chimed in. Dad shook his head but didn't say anything. I'd seen that look before. He was ashamed that Mum was working so much and that he couldn't provide for her like he used to.

A tension settled in the kitchen, and I knew Oisin could feel it too. We'd talked about it before. Oisin was giving half of his student loan to Mum and Dad to pay for his keep. He was probably giving them more than he would in rented accommodation, but they needed it. They also needed his help. Dad wouldn't let Mum shower him when he was too weak during chemo. I wasn't here, not that

I think Dad would have let me help. Oisin had stepped up, and I was eternally proud of my little brother. It was why I felt a little guilty about switching fields too. I would certainly earn more if I'd just got a paramedic job, especially a unit head role, but at least I had my parents encouragement to change roles. They'd always said all they cared about was our happiness. Even if I did get into the programme, at least I would be earning. Not much but it would be enough to contribute to the bills. That way, Mum didn't have to kill herself every day at work just to make ends meet.

We ate dinner, and I joined Dad in the living room to watch TV. Dad had become obsessed with this weird hiking show. I don't know how he even discovered it. It was on one of the random Sports channels, but I was sure he was their only viewer. It was this American guy reviewing hiking trails all over the world. It was clear the production team tried to make it really exciting, like, once, the host got lost, and another time, there was a bear nearby, but most of the time, nothing ever happened. Dad loved it, though. And seeing as he hadn't been able to hike in months, I kept my mouth shut and watched it with him.

Oisin joined us after cleaning up the dishes. "Is this on again?" I didn't hate the hiking show as much as him.

"Yep, but don't worry, it's just started." Dad teased. He knew no one else was into it like him. "Still don't know where Matty is going today."

"Oh goody, the suspense is killing me." Oisin threw me an exasperated look. He knew as well as I did that Dad would spend most days alone watching TV. It was the least we could do to sit and watch it with him.

"The Amalfi coast," Dad said, pointing to the screen. Matty, the host, hadn't even announced his destination for this episode yet. It was something the show did to build suspense. I was impressed Dad could tell just by a couple of seconds of flashing images.

"You sure?" I asked.

"Am I sure?" He spun to face me. "I've been there. I walked it."

"When?" Oisin asked in surprise.

"You weren't born yet, and Niamh was only a little one. One of my favourite hikes of all time."

"What's so special about it?"

"Look at it." He pointed to the TV.

It looked magical. Aerial shots of quaint villages that hugged the mountains. It was a spectacular backdrop next to the Mediterranean. From the small fishing boats at the dock to the rocky incline, the show was doing a good job was making the trail look desirable.

"Beautiful part of the world." Dad stared whimsically at the TV. "Cinque Terre was where the trail ended. Well, for me, at least. It was wonderful. From the food to the people. I'd go back tomorrow."

I couldn't help but smile sadly at that. Dad didn't have the strength to get himself dressed, let alone fly overseas.

"Maybe you will," Oisin said hopeful. "When you're better."

"Maybe, I will," Dad lied, and I knew it. I knew because of the sad wink he threw me. I hoped more than anything that he was wrong.

My phone rang all of a sudden. I checked the caller ID and saw it was from the hospital. I assumed it was Mum when I answered. "Hey, Mum." There was a long pause.

"Niamh?" The voice startled me.

"Yes."

"It's Cheryl Kelly, we met each other earlier—"

"Oh my God." Panic erupted like a volcano of nervous energy inside me. "I'm so sorry, I thought you were my mum. She works at the Royal, you see, and I never thought I'd hear from you so quickly." Dad watched intently and muted the TV.

"That's okay, Niamh. I understand this is a little out of left field." Her voice was soft but urgent. "What I'm calling you about is…well, it's a little odd. We don't normally do things like this."

"Okay." I sat on the edge of the sofa, nervous and feeling unprepared. It felt like Dad and Oisin had also stopped breathing in anticipation.

"Firstly, I would love to offer you a place on our programme."

"Really," I said, unable to believe my luck. I couldn't wipe the smile from my face. "That's great. Thank you. I'm so excited to get started, Cheryl."

"Be careful what you wish for," she said with trepidation that put me on the back foot. "Our term one class is set to go to London to complete training. Tomorrow. It's expensive training, and unfortunately, I have just had one person in the class pull out. Would you be able to fill the spot? It would be three days."

"Well." I hesitated as my eyes collided with Dad. My heart sank. I knew this programme was what I wanted to do, but I had a commitment to Dad these next few weeks. Mum had taken on extra shifts knowing that I would be home to take care of him.

"Say yes," Dad whispered.

"One sec, Cheryl. Dad…" I glanced at Oisin. He looked unsure. "I can't."

"This is the opportunity of a lifetime. You want this, right?" Dad asked.

"But what about you? Somebody has to be here."

"I'll be fine." I was torn. "Hey, you're not throwing your life away for me, kid." It didn't feel that way exactly, but he was swaying my decision. I struggled to argue with him. "You have to do this. I just know it." The level of conviction in his voice was hard to ignore.

I put the phone back to my ear. "Okay."

"I understand it is extremely short notice, but thank you, Niamh. I will have you back on a flight on Friday evening again."

"No, it's fine," I said, even though my head was spinning. I was still worried about Dad, but even Oisin looked to be supportive of the decision.

"You will be paid for your time away."

I hadn't figured it all out, but realistically, I wasn't working. I had nothing to lose, and it was a paid trip. I had to take it, especially with Dad practically putting me on the plane.

"I can send you through your itinerary and accommodation details this evening."

"Okay. I'll be there."

Dad looked elated, which helped to ease the guilt.

"I'm delighted to hear, thank you, Niamh. I will be in touch. Get some rest. You fly out at six a.m."

Lucky me.

"You got it!" Oisin shouted, and he jumped up from the sofa in celebration. "Congratulations."

"Thanks." I felt proud, and I was glad that I could celebrate it with them. Dad tried to get up from his seat, but I was over in a shot to make sure he didn't.

"Well done." He hugged me, and I found myself breathing him in. I did this for him. "I'm very proud of you, Niamh," he whispered holding me tight, and suddenly, I felt fragile. It felt like there was a surge of emotion rushing up my throat. I could feel my eyes blurring, but I tried to stop them by squeezing my eyes shut.

"I love you," I said, surprising even myself.

"I love you," he said before releasing his slight grip.

"When do you start?" Oisin asked from the sofa next to us.

"Yeah, about that. Can I get a ride to the airport tomorrow morning?"

Chapter Twelve
Harriet Whitaker

Running late was not in my nature. Growing up, it was unacceptable and seen as the height of rudeness. Mama despised it, and well, Dad was too OCD to ever fall behind. I'd stupidly slept in after having a rough night. I'd tossed and turned a lot, thinking about my job offer. I'd met with FD Solicitors on Monday morning. The interview had gone well, better than I'd expected. It felt right, and honestly, I had a good feeling after the meeting. Last night, they'd called and offered me the position. I was beyond thrilled. It was a role I was excited about. A change of pace. A new challenge.

But I wasn't convinced that everyone in my life would be as encouraging. I could understand why. A massive pay drop. Switching to the less lucrative civil law route. It was hardly a good look. But that wasn't how it felt. Not to me, at least. It was a career change but one that felt right. I wanted to make a difference. To help someone in need. It was something I'd always wanted to do but had forgotten about it along the way. I just had to bite the bullet and talk to Beth.

I had missed her last night. She'd stayed out late, business dinner on the other side of town, and therefore, she'd opted for the spare bedroom so as she wouldn't wake me. I didn't tell her that I was awake anyway. By the time I did fall asleep, I was so exhausted that I somehow managed to sleep through my alarm. Or perhaps, in a sleepy daze, I'd knocked it off.

Regardless, I was now running through the streets of London like a lunatic to reach the Alton Hotel. It was a conference on the change of legislation impacting the importation of goods from Commonwealth countries. It was boring. I was already bored, but I'd signed up to go long before I was offered this new job, and sadly, I'd made a commitment. I kind of had to see it through, and well, it was a break away from my depressing corporate job.

I finally reached the hotel, and there was a queue at reception, leaving me to scan the area for any signs of where this conference was. I spotted a large board on an easel up ahead and followed my gut instinct. The signage started with NHS training, and I blanked the rest. It had an arrow pointing downstairs anyway. To my relief, I spotted another whiteboard farther down the hall, leading me to my conference.

The door was closed, and I could hear a speaker inside had already started. I'd hoped they would have waited ten minutes to start. I was wrong. The lights were dim when I entered, and the door creaked closed, drawing the attention of a few in the last rows. I was mortified and wished more than anything I had been better prepared this morning. The only way I could describe my entrance was that I scurried to the closest seat I could find. It was on the last row, and thankfully, no one was beside me. I could pant in peace. Once I'd caught my breath, I pulled out my notepad to take notes. There were at least sixty people in the conference, most likely other lawyers and perhaps some students too.

I heard the door creak open again. Thank God, I wasn't the only latecomer. I spotted that they were moving in my direction, and I scooted over to the next seat.

"Thank you," she whispered once she had taken a seat.

"No problem."

"Did I miss much?" she asked, and something not unlike déjà vu overcame me. I tried to ignore it.

"Wouldn't know, I'm in about thirty seconds ahead of you," I teased and glanced over at her. She had short dark hair, but that was about all I could make out in the dark room.

"I'm not the only eejit late then." Instantly, I knew I recognised the voice. Even if it had been years.

I looked a little closer this time, and her eyes collided with mine. I knew her like it had been yesterday. Like I was back in Greece. She'd changed, older. Her long curly hair was gone, but her eyes, they were the same. She watched me for a moment, curious, but she clearly didn't recognise me. I hadn't changed that much. At least, I didn't think so.

"Niamh?" I whispered.

Her features contorted, and I was relieved that she remembered me. A wide smile appeared on her face, one which I couldn't help but mirror. "Jaq?" Hearing her made-up name for me sent chills throughout my body. I hadn't expected to feel such a reaction to a name that wasn't even mine. "I mean, Harriet."

"Hi, Levi," I teased.

"Hi," she said back in equal shock. I couldn't believe I had run into her like this. After all this time and at a regulation conference, of all places.

"What are you doing here?"

"I got a new job, well, yesterday, and they sent me to this conference." Someone hushed us from the row ahead, and we both shut our mouths. She threw me a mischievous look, and I found myself struggling not to laugh. Some things never changed.

"What are you doing here?" Niamh leaned closer and whispered.

"One of my clients is in Canada, so this regulation is affecting them."

She paused, and I could feel her energy tense. "Sorry, what?" I glanced at her, seeing the panic on her face. "This is medical training. Right?"

"No." I gestured up ahead. She started reading the presentation up front, and the realisation hitting her was so funny to me.

"Where the hell am I meant to be?" Niamh started looking around, as if that would help. My giggling made someone else hush us again.

"I'm pretty sure there's NHS training downstairs. I saw a sign on my way in."

"Okay, I got to go." She grabbed her bag, and I felt overwhelmingly disappointed. It was as if time started moving slower as she turned to get up and leave. But I couldn't just let her leave. Not again.

"Wait." I grabbed her forearm, preventing her from getting up.

The strangest sensation ran up my arm, and the air seemed to intensify around us. Like it was some kind of electronic magnetic zone. She stared at my hand, and I wondered if she felt it too. I couldn't let go for some reason. When her eyes met mine, they softened, and the hint of a smile appeared.

"Meet me in the foyer. After your conference."

"Okay," I didn't hesitate to reply. "Can I at least get your number this time?"

Niamh grinned, revealing a dimple that I'd somehow forgotten existed, and it was hard not to smile back. "Meet me at six." I nodded, and she was gone.

I watched her go and couldn't help but feel everything. I felt as if I'd somehow been transported to another planet. The high was hard to come back down from. I struggled for a while to start listening properly to the presentation. My mind was elsewhere. I didn't have the heart to tell Niamh that my conference was only on until lunchtime.

When it was over, I went to the office and did very little. I basically watched the clock until it turned 5:30.

After work, I went back to the Alton Hotel feeling excited and nervous. So much time had passed. Too much time. I was a completely different person. At eighteen, I had been a kid. A stupid teenager. Part of me wondered if I should even go and see Niamh now. Perhaps seeing her again would destroy the image I'd held on to of her for so long. It had taken me a long time to get over her. I just had to hear a Northern Irish accent to think of her. The curiosity would surely haunt me for the rest of my life if I didn't go.

When I arrived at the hotel, she was right there. Seated on one of sofas, scrolling through her phone. It didn't take long for her to find me.

"Hey." She stood and closed the gap. She had changed clothes. Before, she was casual, wearing a hoodie, but now she was in a button-up, black denim shirt, with a pair of skinny jeans and converse. The sleeves of her shirt were rolled up, revealing tattoos. She looked cool, a little more alternative than I remembered when we were young, but the new look suited her. I didn't miss the way she looked me up and down a little as well. It made me feel a little excited.

"You changed." I felt a little stiff still in my work clothes.

"Yeah, my training ended at half four. I got checked in and went upstairs and had a shower. I was all gross from the six a.m. flight."

"Brutal. What time did you get up at?"

"Like, 3:30. If I fall asleep, just leave me in the bar." She started leading us to the hotel bar.

"I don't know how you have the energy."

"Are you kidding? I'm dying to know what you've been doing the last eight years." She tilted her head, reminding me of the old way she used to look at me, and I felt my heart skip a beat. "Unless you want dinner?"

I hesitated. I didn't really know why. Beth came into my mind, and for some reason, I couldn't shake it. I hadn't told her that I was meeting Niamh. Not that she even knew who Niamh was. At least, not her name. Beth knew my coming-out story but not for the right reasons. It was more the butt of a joke. That I'd gotten caught by Mama. Beth didn't care about the woman in the story.

Niamh didn't miss my hesitation.

"Maybe just a drink for now?" I said, feeling a little awkward.

"Sure." Niamh didn't let the awkwardness linger, which I was thankful for. "Although, do you know the area? Because I'm here for three days, so I could do with some decent spots to eat."

"Yeah." We took a seat at a small round table near the window. The bar was pretty quiet, and they had these comfy armchairs that were perfect for people watching. She took one armchair while I sat at the one opposite. I crossed my legs, smoothing out my skirt. "There's a really good Italian next door." I pointed behind Niamh, and her eyes followed my directions. "Or there's a great sushi spot nearby…wait, I forgot, you don't like sushi."

Niamh looked sheepish. "I do actually eat sushi now."

"Really?" I couldn't help but goad her. "You gave me such a hard time about being posh for liking sushi."

"You are posh," she teased. "For many reasons but not just because you like sushi. I only really tried it when I moved to Australia."

"What?" I couldn't hide my surprise. "I've always wanted to go."

"I remember," she said in a way that somehow made me emotional. She moved on quickly. "Yeah, I lived all over Aussie for almost four years. And then, I lived in Kenya for, like, three months."

"That's incredible." I couldn't help but feel a little bit inadequate. "I've only lived in London." Even my voice dipped, as if I was ashamed. Was I ashamed? Perhaps a little. I had led a pretty sheltered life in comparison. "And, well, Cambridge."

"Ah, the infamous Cambridge." Niamh laughed, a glint appearing in her eye, and I already knew she was going to poke fun. "I wondered when it was going to come up. I had a bet on, figured you'd name-drop it within the first five minutes."

"Shut up," I said, but we were interrupted by our server. She was in her early twenties, pretty, and seemed to have an extra wide smile for Niamh.

"Sorry to interrupt, what can I get you both started with?"

"Hi," Niamh said. "Can I get a pint of Guinness, please?"

"We only have cans of Guinness, is that okay?"

"Oh no. Sorry," Niamh smiled adorably. "Cans are a disgrace to the Guinness name."

The server smirked and seemed to be enjoying Niamh's attention. It didn't really bother me all that much, mainly because I knew Niamh was only being her usual charming self.

"If you've ever drunk one, you'd know what I'm talking about."

"I'm more of a whiskey girl." She appeared to be flirting back. "I make a mean dark and stormy, if I can interest you."

"I do love a dark and stormy, but I'm a little jet lagged. Could I just get a pint of lager, whatever you have on tap. I trust your judgement."

"No pressure, then."

"None at all." Niamh nodded in my direction. "Harriet?"

"A glass of shiraz, please."

"Oh, and you can just give her the bill." Niamh smirked in my direction. "She lost a bet, you see."

I couldn't help but roll my eyes as the server left. "Niamh, you have not changed a bit." That resulted in her laughing uncontrollably, and I found myself joining in. "You're still as charming as ever. Chatting up everyone." I waved in the direction of where the server left.

"Please." She shook her head bashfully. "It's just the gift of the gab. All Irish people have it." She leaned back and watched me carefully. "Besides, you used to be sort of flirty back in the day too." Niamh was flirting, and it caused me to panic. I felt guilty. Beth came to the forefront of my mind. Niamh seemed to pick up on my discomfort.

"That was a long time ago." I didn't miss the odd tiredness that made its way into my voice. I kind of hated it. I didn't think Niamh missed it, either. Though she had the ability to avoid things getting awkward.

"Judging by the type of conferences you go to, can I make a wild assumption and say you became a solicitor after all?"

"Yes," I said, and I was pleased that she had remembered. "And you became a paramedic?"

"I did." She seemed a little unsure of that answer. "Well, I was." I waited for more. "I'm kind of changing fields. I literally got told I got the job yesterday."

"Really?" I couldn't believe what I was hearing. I was also considering changing my area of expertise. What were the odds that she would also get a new job offer yesterday too? "What are you changing to?"

"A GP. I kind of have to go backward, though, back to education."

"Wow, that is a bit of step back," I said, feeling it more than anything. It was odd. Niamh didn't seem like it was a big deal at all.

"Yeah, but it's the right move, I think, in the long term. And I'm only twenty-six, so changing careers is kinda expected in your twenties, right?"

I agreed, but it didn't feel like anyone else in my circle of friends and family would feel the same way. Well, except my cousin Marco. He was the only one I'd told about interviewing for the new job. He couldn't have been more supportive.

Our drinks arrived at that moment. The server placed my glass in front of me. "Here you go." She handed the pint directly to Niamh. "I just want to make sure you're satisfied," she said as she waited.

Niamh looked a little embarrassed at first, but she played along and took a sip. "That is an excellent beverage. Thank you," Niamh said, throwing me a look of awkwardness.

"My pleasure." She practically batted her eyes. "If you two need anything else, just give me a shout. I'm Tara."

"Thanks, Tara," Niamh said, and she left us alone again.

"Oh, thanks, Tara," I mocked, and Niamh's face turned beetroot.

"Maybe she is flirting." She sounded a little unsure when it was very blatant. I found it all quite hilarious. "That never happens to me."

"Yeah, right," I said, not believing a word of it.

"I'm serious. Maybe you have women hitting you up all the time but not me."

"No, I don't. I think people just sense I'm in a relationship, so they don't bother." I took a big drink of wine, feeling like I'd dropped a bomb into the conversation, but it wasn't something I was going to hide.

"That's nice. How long have you been with your partner?" Niamh asked and showed no signs of being awkward, which I was relieved at.

"Technically, she's my fiancée. We've—"

"Holy shit, you're engaged?" She looked surprised but also delighted for me. "Look at you, grown-up."

"I know, I'm super boring."

"Not at all," Niamh cut me off. "You found the person you want to be with for the rest of your life. That's magic." Her words were pure and genuine, and for some reason, having her seal of approval made me happy. "Some people spend their whole life searching for it. What's she like?"

"Her name is Beth. We've been together five years overall and six months engaged." Niamh nodded along. "We live together too and are saving up to buy a house."

"Good luck. London prices are crazy right now."

"I know, but Surrey is even worse, well, in the areas that Beth wants to buy. It's near my folks too, which…" I found myself trailing off. "I guess has its benefits."

"Wow, you want to live close to your folks? Things have definitely changed." Niamh seemed to struggle to hide her surprise, which made sense.

When I was eighteen, I couldn't wait to be free of them. Even now, I struggled to be around them for long periods of time. Why did I want to live near them again?

"So your parents are cool with you?"

"Yeah, it took them forever. I mean, especially after how they… found out."

Niamh's features hardened a little as if she were remembering it.

"It was really bad."

"They didn't…hurt you—"

"No, nothing like that. They just…" I trailed off, finding it too difficult to bring up those memories. "They said some really horrible things. They didn't understand it." I didn't even want to bring up their exact words. Our relationship had come so far that I feared if I thought too much about that time, I would resent my parents again. And of course, they'd said terrible things about Niamh as well. That she'd manipulated me, even accused her of drugging me. All kinds of accusations to avoid accepting the reality: I was a lesbian. "But when they met Beth, they knew they had to accept it or risk losing me."

"Good for you." Niamh gave a brief smile. "Beth must be some woman."

"She is."

"I'm really happy for you, Harriet," she said, and I believed it. Her smile faltered a little, and a shy energy came over her. Like she wasn't sure she wanted to divulge something, but after a sip of her drink, she seemed to have a little more courage. "You know, it's silly now, but back then…" She bit her lip, looking whimsical. "God, I used to think about you all the time. After Malia. I was so worried."

For some reason, a clamping started in my chest. It felt like validation or something. I'd thought about her so much, I didn't think I'd ever stop wondering about her and her life. It had taken me a long time to move on.

"I even tried to look you up, but I could never find you on Facebook or anything. Weirdly, there're a lot of Harriet's that go to Cambridge."

"Yeah, there's about a million Niamh's in Northern Ireland too."

That made her laugh. "You looked for me too?" I nodded enthusiastically, and her features washed over with relief. "Okay, good. I don't feel like that much of a loser anymore."

"I even called Salt Bar trying to find you."

"What?" That stunned her, and I felt like I'd overshared.

"Yeah." It was my turn to feel a little embarrassed.

"When?"

"When my parents, you know, caught us. They made me go straight to the airport, and we flew home." I found myself being pulled back into the memory. "They were…well, I'm sure you can imagine. I was grounded, and they took away my phone. I guess they were worried I'd call you, which, of course, I couldn't because we never bloody exchanged numbers." I couldn't hold back my frustration at that. Niamh mirrored my regret. "A few days after I was back home, I snuck in and logged on to my dad's computer and got the number for Salt Bar to try to call you. But they'd told me you left."

Niamh looked thoughtful for a moment. Perhaps she never thought I'd tried to find her after what happened. "Yeah." She cleared her throat, and her voice dropped. "After what happened, I…" She looked sad and couldn't seem to pull herself out of it. It touched me. After all these years, I had never gotten closure on it. "When you never showed at the beach the next day…"

I thought back and remembered that we were supposed to meet. I felt disappointment that she would have been waiting for me.

"I even went up to your room, just to make sure you were okay, but you were gone. It's sad, like…" She tried to joke but it fell flat. "I was just so heartbroken, I couldn't stay any longer in Stalis."

"Niamh." I sighed, feeling that heartbreak all over again. "I'm really sorry."

"Hey, come on, it wasn't me who got into trouble. I'm sorry it happened," she said, then seemed to check herself. "Well, I'm not sorry about that." I couldn't help but smile. "Honestly, I thought I'd never see you again." She watched me thoughtfully, and I felt lighter just being in her presence. "But here I am, sitting opposite you at a completely freak chance meeting."

"I know." I breathed out, still amazed that we'd ran into each other. "I mean, you weren't even meant to be in the same conference."

"Right." She nodded as if just realising that as well. "I guess the universe just has a way of pushing people together, doesn't it?" She took another gulp of her beer. "And it's nice because I get to see you again, and we're older and more secure in ourselves, and we're both…happy."

I felt disappointed and couldn't understand why. "Cheers." I raised my glass and ignored the confusing and conflicting feelings inside. "To Levi," I said, and Niamh's grin got a little bigger.

"To Jaq." We clinked glasses, and I was glad that the conversation didn't end there.

There was an endless stream of things to catch up on. From university stories to her time in Australia. It seemed like some adventure, one I couldn't help but feel a little envious of. I'd travelled, of course, and done my fair share of holidays, but I'd never backpacked. That wasn't Beth's thing at all. But I'd always thought I might have liked it. We ordered some bar snacks and shared them. I was glad for it because the second glass of wine had started to go to my head on an empty stomach.

Niamh talked about Jenny and her family. Her dad's cancer battle was heartbreaking. I knew how close Niamh was to her family, and I was relieved to hear he was on the mend, at least. Another round of drinks arrived, and I was starting to get conscious of time. It was close to ten. But something made me reluctant to leave. I wasn't ready to say good-bye to Niamh again. Not after all this time.

I sipped on my wine as Niamh talked about her new internship.

"Is it like going back to uni and being a fresher again?"

"I wish." She grimaced. "It's gruelling. Jenny did it a few years back, and honestly, she was so stressed out that she started to lose her hair."

"Wait, what? Is this really a programme you want to join willingly? It sounds like torture."

"Well, she was also on weird diet pills. Jenny is crazy." We laughed. "Besides, I'm ready to settle down back home. It feels like the right move after being gone so long." Her eyes looked a little glassy. I could tell the alcohol was starting to hit her as well. "You know when it just feels right, and even if it's scary and you know it's a step backward, it's like…" She trailed off, and I found myself completely moved by what she was saying. It was probably the alcohol. "Everything in your body is telling you that this is where you need to be. It was like me saying yes last night to flying to London to do this training. I just knew I had to do it."

I couldn't tear my eyes away from her. It was like she was helping me with my own internal dilemma. I knew the job with FD Solicitors was a step down in terms of salary, but it didn't feel that way. It felt right. Like exactly where I needed to be. And maybe that would mess with things elsewhere in my life, but I had to do it.

"And then, I run into you. Of all the people in London."

"I think us seeing each other was meant to be." I thought carefully and decided to let her in on what had been weighing me down this week. "You're not the only one who was offered a new job this week."

"You kept that quiet. Congratulations."

"Well, I don't know if it's a good thing. Well, to some people."

Niamh's brow furrowed. "What do you mean? Are you going to defend criminals and murderers or something?"

"No." That seemed preposterous. "It's for a position in FD Solicitors. It's total opposite to what I do now." Thankfully, I thought to myself. "They advocate for undocumented migrants coming through the English channel. They assist in getting them asylum and documentation to stay in the UK."

"Shit." Niamh looked taken aback. "That's awesome, Harriet." I couldn't contain my smile. Of course someone as completely selfless as her would understand. "You'd be helping so many people. What an amazing opportunity." I felt myself doubt that. "What?" she asked, seeming to pick up on my lack of enthusiasm.

"It's not in my field. There's so much opportunity in corporate law. You can make a lot of money." Niamh seemed unfazed by that. "FD solicitors is not-for-profit. The pay is…well…" I trailed off, taking another drink.

"Who cares about that? Money isn't everything."

"It is to my parents." I could hear their voices in my head. Money was everything to them. But it was Beth's voice I could hear as well. Disapproving. And I hated that.

"Harriet, you're twenty-six years old." Niamh's suggestion was loud and clear. "I have told you this before," she said, reminding me of what she'd said on our date when we were eighteen, "you don't have to do everything your parents say anymore."

"I know." I sighed, but I still felt so heavy. The pressure to be the best was weighing my shoulders down. The idea of disappointing them was like torture. I'd already shamed them enough by just being who I was.

"Well, what does Beth think?"

I could feel my eyes welling up, and I tried desperately to stop them.

"Hey." Niamh leaned forward in her chair, showing nothing but concern.

"I'm fine."

Niamh seemed unconvinced, but I was glad she didn't come over to my side of the table, or worse, try to hug me. I would have been a mess.

"I, uh." I cleared my throat and put every ounce of energy I had into pulling myself together. "I haven't told her. I will. Well, if I take the job."

She looked like there was a lot she wanted to say. Her features showed a mix of emotions, and I wished I could read her mind. It looked as though she was trying to tread carefully so as not to make my situation any worse. "It seems like you're in a tough situation." She kept it diplomatic. "Personally, I think you'd be crazy not to take the job. But that's just me."

I nodded, feeling as though she was right. I wanted the job. I knew I would be good at it.

"To hell with what your parents think. I mean…" She shook her head, a little flabbergasted. "The fact that you even talk to those people is incredibly big of you. I'd have cut them out. But not you. You're a much better person."

"I doubt that."

"I don't." Her eyes held me in a trance. So much so that I felt like I'd been transported back to sitting beside her on a wall in Hersonissos, enjoying ice cream. Feeling safe in her presence all over again. "Talk to Beth. If she's as incredible as you say, I think she will support you. Sure, it's maybe not a move she would make. But she loves you. All she wants is for you to be happy at the end of the day."

I felt a little calmer about the thought of telling Beth. Niamh was right. Beth would never take a career move like this, but she was open enough that I thought she would support me in it, especially if she thought it would make me happy.

My phone started ringing from my bag. Niamh gestured for me to take it. It was Beth. I answered and got up to take it out in the foyer. "Hey," I said.

"Hello, lovey. I'm about to turn in. Are you staying out much later?"

"No, I'm just finishing up."

"Where are you?"

I hesitated, for reasons I didn't fully understand, and decided to be honest. "I ran into an old friend at this conference. We had dinner and drinks. Catching up, you know."

"Oh, how lovely," Beth said with a yawn. "Who?"

"Niamh." Her silence prompted me. "I told you about her before."

"I can't think."

I sighed, a little miffed that she hadn't remembered the name of my first but not really surprised at the same time. "She's from Northern Ireland. I met her in Greece that summer I travelled with my parents."

"Wait, is she the girl Pipa caught you with?" I felt embarrassed that Niamh was known by something so humiliating.

"Yeah."

"Oh boy, that's…awkward."

I felt annoyed all of a sudden. Niamh was so much more than just some girl I hooked up with. I couldn't quite pinpoint why I was feeling so protective.

"Is she in town for long?"

"I think a couple of days."

"I'd love to meet her. She's famous in your house." Beth laughed again, and I chewed on my lip. "Set up dinner for tomorrow night."

I didn't respond for a moment. I didn't really want Beth to meet Niamh, but I wasn't really sure why. It wasn't an unfair request. I'd met plenty of Beth's exes over the years. She'd remained amicable with most of them. Whereas for me, there was no one as significant in my past as Niamh. Even though we had only known each other a couple of days.

"Harriet?"

"Uh, yeah. Sure," I said, resisting the urge to grind my teeth.

"Lovely. I'll see you when you get home."

"Good night," I said before hanging up and making my way back into the bar.

Niamh was talking to Tara again as she cleared away our empty glasses. They were laughing, and I could practically feel the sexual chemistry from here. It made me a little uncomfortable because I didn't think that Tara would be Niamh's type. The buttons on her shirt kept getting lower every time she came to take our drink order, and her laugh got a little more exaggerated as well. She was really throwing herself at Niamh. It was a little desperate.

"Hey," Niamh said, looking relieved at my return, which made me feel happy. I took my seat again.

"Can I get you a drink?" Tara asked.

"No, thanks. I actually should be getting home soon."

Tara looked thrilled at that. "Just one dark and stormy, then."

"Ah." Niamh looked a little awkward. "I probably should turn in too. I have training all day tomorrow."

"Come on, it's just one drink," I said, enjoying seeing Niamh squirm. "And you're only staying upstairs."

"Even better," Tara boldly said, and I witnessed her undress Niamh with her eyes. It would have been awkward if it didn't look like Niamh was into it. I felt like I should leave them to it.

"Sure, why not," Niamh said, and Tara left us again. "You're a bad influence."

"Why are you blaming me?" I laughed. "You're about to get lucky tonight. You're welcome."

"She is very attractive, I'll give you that." Niamh finished her drink. "Everything all right?"

"Yeah, it was just Beth. She's turning in and just wanted to make sure I was coming home."

"That's nice. Beth seems great. I'd love to meet her."

What was up with these two? I could feel my whole body stiffen in annoyance. "Funny, she said the same thing," I said, feeling that frustration again. "How about we all have dinner tomorrow night?"

Niamh looked a little uncomfortable. "Sure," she said but watched me carefully, as if she didn't know what to say. I felt agitated in my suit and a little hot. I couldn't really pinpoint why I was feeling uncomfortable at the thought of Beth and Niamh being face-to-face. Perhaps it was because they both knew very different versions of me. "I mean, only if that's what you want," Niamh said softly. "I won't meet her if you don't want me to."

"Why wouldn't I want you to meet my fiancée?" I could hear the change in my voice. I tried my best to hide the bitter edge. I didn't know why I was being short with her. I just wanted to leave. Tara was eying Niamh, and the thought of Niamh and Beth meeting was causing me anxiety in a way I'd never felt, like I'd been cornered into something I didn't want.

"Harriet." Niamh looked a little unsure. She leaned forward in her seat, and her voice lowered. "Are you okay?"

"Yes." I shook myself out of whatever weird funk had passed over me. "I'd love for you two to meet," I lied as best I could. "Tomorrow night, the Italian next door?"

"Okay," Niamh said, looking as though she didn't want to push the topic. Which I was thankful for.

"We will see you there at six," I said, collecting my things and standing. "I should go before I miss my last train." I wasn't going to miss the train, but I felt like I had to go, especially when out of the corner of my eye, I could see Tara making her way over with not one but two drinks.

Niamh was on her feet. "Get home safe."

I felt like she was going to hug me, but I deliberately took a step backward. The idea of being that close to her made me feel weird. As if it would be a disservice to Beth. And I didn't like that feeling. She didn't seem too annoyed, at least.

"See you tomorrow," I said and passed Tara on my way to the bar to pay up.

I settled the bill and glanced over at the table. Tara looked content in my seat. They looked to be getting very well acquainted. I couldn't help but feel a strange twinge inside my chest. I couldn't really fully understand what it was. I shouldn't have been jealous. Surely not. I was over Niamh. She had never really belonged to me in the first place. And I was engaged. It all seemed quite juvenile to even be feeling this way. I did the only thing that I thought would work. I ignored it and went home to my soon-to-be wife.

CHAPTER THIRTEEN
NIAMH DONNELLY

The ringing woke me up. It felt like it was sounding inside my head. I groaned, rolled over, and somehow found my phone to knock off the alarm. Tara let out a groan from beside me, clearly annoyed by the rude awakening as well.

"Morning." I rolled over and kissed her shoulder.

"I know you said you'd an early start," Tara grumbled before rolling back to return a kiss to my lips, "but this is ridiculous."

"I'm sorry," I said, enjoying feeling her soft skin against mine. "I really wish I could stay here all day—"

"Oh, but you can." She wrapped her legs around me, and I could feel the heat rising again between us. We'd barely slept last night. She seemed to have an insatiable sex drive. I wasn't exactly complaining, even if I was struggling to keep up.

"I have training. Downstairs, might I add." I reluctantly got up and left her in the sea of sheets.

It was a nice view. Tara was sexy, a little more dominant than what I typically went for. But she was sexually fluid, young, energetic, and she definitely knew how to please. We hadn't spent much time getting to know each other last night, but that hardly seemed like it mattered. I was leaving tomorrow night, anyway. We both knew what this was.

The hot water in the shower successfully dusted off the cobwebs I was feeling. It especially helped my sore head from all the drinks last night. I wrapped myself in the hotel robe and brushed my teeth. When I came out of the bathroom, she was dressed in her uniform from last night.

"Are you worried about going downstairs?" I asked, drying my hair with a towel. "I think we were a little obvious." After two cocktails, we were definitely making out at the bar. It would have been hard for her coworkers to have missed it.

"No." She laughed as if it was absurd. "You're not the first guest I have hooked up with." Her confidence was attractive. "What about tonight?" She moved toward me seductively. Her hands began untying my robe slowly, causing heat to grow in my core. "Can we do this all over again?"

"I'd like that. I just don't know when I will be back. I'm meeting my friend again tonight for dinner."

"The woman from the bar?" I nodded. "I have to say, I thought you two were a thing..." She trailed off as her nails lightly scraped my stomach.

"No." I didn't feel the need to go into detail. "We're just friends."

"You sure about that?"

I felt my heart skip a beat, and it wasn't because of Tara's teasing hand. I'd have been lying if I'd said I wasn't disappointed hearing that Harriet had a girlfriend and a little crushed that she was engaged. It was only for a split second. Of course the universe would present Harriet to me again when she was unavailable. Seeing her again in that conference, I had been overwhelmed. A flood of different emotions had hit me all at once. I'd struggled to focus on my training yesterday after we'd parted ways. I'd felt like a teenager again waiting for her to arrive for drinks last night. I had been nervous, sweaty palms, and had butterflies. I couldn't remember the last time that had happened.

I'd wanted to make a good impression. I'd made sure I looked the part. I'd changed my look since we were young, and I had to admit, I'd hoped she still liked what she saw. Harriet had only grown more beautiful. She wasn't as tan as I remembered, which made sense, considering she'd spent all summer in Italy and Greece. Her hair was more brunette. I'd always remembered it being practically black. But her smile was the same. Enough to leave me breathless. *And don't even get me started on her body.* She had known how to dress before, but corporate Harriet, especially in that pencil skirt, was distracting to say the least.

That had all tempered as soon as she'd told me about Beth. Her fiancée seemed incredible. And while initially, I was a little disappointed, it didn't stick with me. If I couldn't be the one for Harriet, she deserved only the best. Someone as wonderful as Harriet deserved everything, and I was just relieved to see that she'd found that person.

"I'm sure," I said as Tara's hand travelled south. I inhaled sharply.

"I couldn't tempt you to get back in bed?" she said, and I found it difficult to think straight. She was doing a great job at working me up again. But I had other plans, and I halted her hand.

"What time tonight?" I said, causing her to giggle in delight.

"I'll meet you in the bar. Come find me after your date." I watched her leave, already looking forward to later. She was definitely a good distraction.

My phone started ringing, and I was going to ignore it at first. I didn't want to be late to the training, especially considering how unprofessional my tardiness was yesterday. It started ringing again, telling me it was probably important. After checking the caller ID, I spotted it was Jenny.

"Hey, bitch," I said, flopping down on the bed. "What's up?"

"Okay, don't freak out," she said, and I could hear it in her voice. She was on edge. I was instantly worried.

"Jen, are you okay?"

"I just said, don't freak out. Why are you freaking out?" I could hear her panic loud on the other end of the phone. She was making strange panting and exhales, but I couldn't understand why.

"Okay, what happened? I love you no matter what. You can tell me."

"You can't freak out."

"Is this, like, a work thing? Damn, I hope it's not medical malpractice level because I was really counting on you to help me through this stupid training programme."

"Niamh, shut up."

"Do we need a lawyer? Because I actually might know someone…" I thought of Harriet, weirdly.

"I'm pregnant."

For once in my life, I was speechless. My breathing stopped for a moment, and my mind started racing. Jenny was pregnant. With a baby. Jenny didn't even know how to boil an egg, and now, she was going to be a mum. Someone, someday, would be calling Jenny Mum.

"You're freaking out."

"I'm not freaking out." I could hear my voice go high, and I willed myself to calm down. "I'm not, it's just…was this? How are you…what does Tom…how…what?"

"Oh my God—" Her panic had returned.

"Okay, wait." I focused my brain. "How do you feel? Are we happy, or are we booking flights to Liverpool to…you know, fix the problem? Because either, I am good with."

Jenny was quiet on the phone. "I don't know."

"Is it Tom's?" Her new boyfriend. They'd barely been dating three months.

"Yes."

"Okay, does he know?"

"No."

"Okay, well, let's figure this out."

"Niamh, I'm scared."

"Hey." I sat up. "We will figure this out, okay? And you know, you have so many options here. You're not alone."

"I feel alone." I heard her sniffle.

"I will be home tomorrow and come straight to your house."

"In Derry?"

"If I really have to," I teased. Jenny had moved up to Derry for work. It was an hour and a half away from our hometown. We still tried to meet up regularly, but it was hard. Well, not as hard as when I'd lived in Australia.

"I don't know if it's the hormones or what, but I don't think I want to get rid of them. Is that bad?"

"No," I said reassuringly, "nothing right now is bad. That's okay if you want to keep the baby."

"Yeah, but I'll be a single mum. You know my ma and dad will flip out."

"You have me. And give Tom a bit of credit, you know."

"He has Marvel bedsheets, Niamh."

"We can work on that," I said but didn't fully believe it.

"I'm such an idiot." She sighed. "I can't believe I got knocked up. I'm too young to be a mum."

"People have kids at our age all the time. Sometimes intentionally. And you're not an idiot. You're a doctor, remember?"

"That doesn't make me smart...hence, why I'm preggers." She groaned loudly. "Enough about me and my drama, how's London?"

"Weird," I said, not really wanting to tell her about Harriet. She had enough on her plate. "I'll have to tell you all about it when I'm home. Are you sure you're okay?"

"No, but I'll not be okay until my head stops spinning. But tell me why London is weird. So I don't obsess over the foetus inside me." Jenny gasped. "Did you sleep with someone?"

"Yeah, but that's not the weird part."

"Okay, whore." She laughed. "What's so weird?"

"Do you remember the girl I met in Stalis?"

"You mean the girl you were totally hung up on throughout uni?"

"I was not." I couldn't help but feel defensive.

"Yeah, you were. Wait, did you see Harriet?"

I was surprised Jenny remembered her name. Maybe I was a little hung up on her back then. "Yeah."

"Oh my God, and you guys hooked up?" Jenny was over the moon. *I wish.*

"No, we just had drinks."

"I'm confused."

"Well, she's engaged—"

"Oh, shit. Niamh." Her voice dropped, and I could feel her disappointment for me. It was kind. "She's engaged. I'm so sorry."

"I'm fine."

"Really?" Jen was sceptical. I guessed it made sense. Harriet was my first love. And I hadn't even gotten a chance to tell her that I loved her. The fact that Harriet and I hadn't necessarily broken up was probably playing a factor here too. We were kind of torn apart. Thinking about it now filled me with disappointment. "You're fine? I was there, remember. I know what she meant to you."

Jenny words stirred something inside me, and I didn't want to think too much about it. I tried to squash it down. "That was a long time ago." She remained silent. "Anyway, I kind of got roped into meeting her fiancée tonight for dinner."

"At least you said no." My silence prompted her to say more. "You did say no, right, Niamh?"

"Well—"

"What is wrong with lesbians? You don't have to be friends with your exes. Be like the straights, cut them out of your life, and block them on social media. Pretend they never existed."

"It's easier said than done sometimes."

"Niamh, listen to me carefully." Jenny had her serious voice, and I knew she meant business. "This is a bad idea. Ghost them."

"I can't do that, Jenny."

"Dude, nothing good can come of this. Cut your losses and pray that they break up."

"I'm not going to wish for that. What's the matter with you?"

"Maybe it's baby brain or some shit. Don't wish for them to break up, then. Whatever. Niamh, don't go tonight. I'm telling you, you're only going to torture yourself." She was making sense, but I didn't want to stand them up, either. That would be rude. It wasn't me. "Fuck."

"What?"

"My next patient is here."

"You're at work?" Classic, professional Jenny.

"Yeah, my boobs felt really sore, and I was being a total bitch to the receptionist, so I took a pregnancy test. For the craic, really. I wasn't expecting it to go this way." She sighed in frustration. "Okay, let's make a plan. Don't see Harriet—"

"Jenny—"

"Fine, do what you like. And then, come home, and come up this weekend to see me? I could do with a drink." My silence prompted her realisation. "Fucking hell, being pregnant sucks."

"We can have tea. I'll bring chocolate too."

"Deal. Good luck on your date." I wanted to argue that it wasn't a date, but she interjected. "And whatever you do, Niamh, don't get pulled in again. Maybe you're over her, which somehow, I doubt. Maybe she's not over you too." That thought alone caused my heartbeat to pick up, hopeful. "You guys meant something to each other. Seeing people from the past has a way of bringing up old shit. But honestly, and I feel it in my swollen breasts, I don't think you'll get the answers you want. Don't go chasing the past. She's engaged." My heart sank again because she was right. "Let her go."

I hung up the phone and continued to get dressed, all while thinking about tonight.

Chapter Fourteen

Harriet Whittaker

"D id you pick up almond milk?" Beth asked from behind me. She was rifling through the fridge.

"Yeah." I went in search and found it hiding under a bag of lettuce.

"Figures. I wouldn't have checked under the salad," she joked. I finished making our breakfasts: granola, fruit, and protein yogurt. The same as every day. "Have you a busy day?" she asked, making our coffee.

"I have a couple of meetings in the morning. And I'm seeing Marco for lunch."

"Oh." I heard the distain. Beth and Marco had never gotten along. Which was a real shame. Marco was my cousin, but he was also one of my best friends. It made it difficult for me. From the onset, they'd just seemed to find ways to bash each other. It was incredibly annoying. "Give my best."

"I always do." I didn't stay on the topic for long, knowing it would only start an argument. "Have you much on today?"

"Yes, I'm working with Philip on that merger," she said, taking a seat opposite me at the breakfast bar. It still felt weird when she talked about my dad in a professional environment. She talked to him much more than I did these days. Sometimes, it would have been nice to hear things first from my own dad. "They're not getting along very well."

"Always the way," I said, passing her a bowl.

"I fear we will have to go over to California to meet with them." She got stuck in to her breakfast.

"When?" I asked, already dreading her answer.

"Deadline for the merger is end of the month. I'd say we will be over next week if this call today doesn't go well."

I didn't say anything. I was upset. Another trip away. For God knew how long. I felt frustrated because I wasn't even asked. I understood that it was just a part of her job, but I hadn't signed up for this. I didn't want the marriage my mother had. My father was never home. But at the same time, I didn't want to be a nag. And we were doing better. Fewer disagreements. I shut my mouth, not wanting to start anything. Especially not when we were going to see Niamh later. I felt nervous again at the thought of seeing her. It stunted my appetite.

"I'm looking forward to dinner. What's her name again? Eve?"

"Niamh," I corrected. "It should be fun," I lied.

Niamh and Beth were just so different. Beth had a big personality, and she was chatty, way better than me in group settings. I sometimes had a habit of closing up. It was easier to let Beth do the talking for both of us. The only problem was that sometimes, people found her a little intense. That was Marco's biggest gripe with Beth. She showed interest in people to the extent that it could be perceived as intrusive. I knew it was all from a good place, but I worried about what Niamh would think. Niamh was kind and laid-back. I worried one was chalk and the other cheese.

"So what's she like? Your ex."

I didn't like her tone. It seemed a little condescending. But she was keeping it light, so I did the same. "Why are you saying it like *that*?"

"I'm just intrigued." She chuckled. "I've never met one of your exes before. What does she do?"

"She's studying to be a doctor."

"Still in education. How old is she?" I could hear her critical tone appearing, and I wasn't a fan. I felt this overwhelming need to protect Niamh.

"She's the same age as me. She's retraining to be a doctor."

Beth made a series of hums while she ate. I knew what she was thinking. Probably wondering why she didn't just stick to the field she'd studied for. The idea of restarting one's career would be unimaginable to someone like Beth. It was why I was still so reluctant to take the new job at FD Solicitors. That way, I wouldn't have to be judged in the same way.

"Is she hot?" Beth nudged her shoulder into mine playfully. I rolled my eyes, refusing to answer. "Is she prettier than me?" She double downed on the teasing.

"As if." I kissed her. I knew she wasn't insecure like that. You just had to look at Beth to know she'd never had a confidence issue.

"Good answer." She took a sip of coffee. "I was going to wear my Armani skirt with the stripes."

"Sounds good."

"You should wear that Chanel dress. It makes your boobs look good."

"Is that right?" I laughed.

"Yes. And I want your ex to know what she missed out on," Beth said competitively.

"Niamh's not like that. Besides, she always dressed very casually. T-shirts and Converse. I wouldn't want us to be too dressy."

"Nonsense. We shouldn't dress like slobs just to fit in."

"Niamh doesn't dress like a slob," I said, that protective nature coming back to the surface. "I think it's part of her look."

"Wait, is she a tomboy?" Beth found this very interesting. I hadn't realised that I was biting the inside of my cheek. "I didn't know that was your type back in the day."

"She wasn't as masculine presenting when I knew her," I said and kind of hated myself for justifying my attraction for Niamh. "Besides, I don't have a type." I didn't need to explain myself. I liked Niamh for the person she was, not how she looked. Although, honestly, I thought she was more attractive now.

"This is going to be fun." Beth sprang from her seat and put her bowl into the dishwasher. "I'm really excited to meet her." She poured her cup of coffee into a travel mug and pecked me on the cheek. "I'll see you back here later, and we can go to the restaurant together."

"Okay, love you."

"Love you too." Beth left, and I finished cleaning up before heading off into work.

❖

I was relieved when lunch finally came around. If I didn't already hate my job, today was pushing me over the edge. I had just been summoned to court with one of my clients. It was a couple of weeks away, but I was furious. I had specifically warned them not to dump waste unethically, and of course, they'd gone ahead anyway. I could hear their argument already: "It's cheaper to just go to court and take the fine." Never mind the countless fish and ecosystems their waste had destroyed, and it was probably polluting our drinking water. I really hated my choice of career sometimes.

"Why do people feel the need to break the law?" I slumped onto the chair opposite Marco. He laughed, and a giddy glint appeared in his eye. Clearly ready for some gossip. "Seriously, they make enough money already. Why do they have to be greedy and break the law?" I groaned, allowing my head to fall into my hands.

"Honey, being a solicitor is really not working out for you, is it?" he said, patting my hand. "What ever happened to that new job you applied for?"

"Well," I started and couldn't resist the smile pulling at my lips. "I was offered the job."

"Yay." He leaned across and pulled me into a hug. "I'm so proud of you," he said as his flat white coffee arrived.

We placed our orders for two salads, a usual order for us. I ordered a tea as well. The café was halfway between his work and mine. He was an investment broker, which made his dad, my uncle, eternally proud. Until he'd come out of the closet. Marco had come out the summer after I did. He'd teased that he was waiting to see if I was going to be ostracized before he made the plunge. Like me, there was a period of adjustment within the family. The wider family were beginning to fear it was in the water when we both turned out gay.

It just made Marco and I grow closer. He knew what it was like coming from a toxic family dynamic like ours. "Well, how'd Beth take it? This was the not-for-profit position, right?"

"Well, you see…" I could feel myself drawing a blank, the shame taking over. "I haven't exactly told her yet."

"Hm, I wonder why?" He sipped his coffee, looking pretty high and mighty. He already knew why, but he made me say it anyway.

"Because I don't even know if I'm going to take the job."

"But I thought you said the job was super exciting and fulfilling." He was right.

"It is, but…"

"Why are you even hesitating? You hate your current job."

"Hate's a strong word,"

"And yet, it's perfect for describing how you feel about your job." I didn't like that he was making sense. "You're afraid."

"I'll tell her," I told myself more than anything else.

"You think she won't approve," he said, hitting the nail on the head. I didn't say anything, and his voice dropped a little. "Beth is putting too much pressure on you. You don't have to climb the ranks like she did. She's so high-maintenance—"

"Stop it."

"Okay, no bad-mouthing." He sighed in defeat. "I just think you should have a partner who is less like your parents because let's face it, we all know your folks won't approve of you taking this job. Your mama is always going off about migrants coming into the Queen's good country," he pointed out, and I could see the frustration on his expression. "That's why I can't bring home Bobby." Marco's new man. They'd been dating a few months, and things seemed to be going in the right direction.

"You can be gay, Marco, but only with white guys. I thought that was clear," I joked, even though it was really heartbreaking.

Marco played along. "We know this already. Our family is full of bigots and racists. But think about the long game, Harriet." I paused, not sure what he meant. "Our trust funds."

"So we are supposed to be miserable until that generation dies off?"

"Who's miserable?" he asked as my tea arrived. "If you're having relationship problems, that's a different matter."

"Speaking of," I said, and I could feel my face scrunching up, not really sure why Niamh had come into my head.

"Oh, now I'm interested." He leant forward in his seat. "What's the latest with Cruella?"

"Marco," I warned. I didn't like him disrespecting Beth in front of me.

"Sorry." He seemed genuine. "I will listen with no judgement. What's going on with Beth?"

"It's not Beth." I deliberated over whether or not to say anything. But I told Marco everything. To hide this would almost be an admission that there was something to be ashamed of. Or something I was hiding. "I kind of ran into someone yesterday."

"Who?"

"Niamh."

"Niamh?" He looked a little clueless, and then it sunk in. "As in, Greece Niamh?"

I nodded. Seeing his reaction stirred something in me.

He looked taken aback, speechless. I could understand why. In our first year at university, I'd opened up about everything that had happened. I remembered him saying it was like a fairy tale. A modern-day Romeo and Juliet story, and we were tragically pulled apart. Though, obviously, not as tragic as the real story.

"Where?"

"We were at a conference, well, not the same one. But we met up afterward. We had dinner and drinks." I felt myself getting excited just thinking of it. "We caught up and it was…" I thought carefully. "Nice." He raised a brow, and I couldn't tell what he was thinking. "So much time has passed. And there she was. The same person I remember." I couldn't help but smile.

"Careful, girl."

"What?" I felt very self-conscious.

"Do you still have feelings for her?" He landed the huge question on me, and I felt myself squirming in my seat.

I couldn't hold eye contact; the question alone felt like a headache and an even bigger heartache. I wasn't sure how to feel. "I don't know." Given how Marco reacted with such a wry expression, I felt the need to elaborate. "I don't think so. How could I? I mean, it was a little summer romance…from years ago. Surely not, right?"

"Are you sure that's all it was?"

"I knew her for two days, Marco, what would you call it?"

He sighed. "I saw you afterward. And honestly, Harriet, you were different. Niamh just unlocked something in you."

"She was my first." I brushed it off. "That's just what happens."

"You said you loved her." I felt a crushing sensation in my chest. I'd forgotten I had told him that, and it was a reminder I didn't need.

"I was young."

"So you didn't love her?"

I refused to answer because it would unlock something within me that I needed to keep in the past. For the sake of my relationship.

"Okay," he said, unconvinced, as if he didn't believe me, but he didn't want to argue, either. I wasn't sure I believed me. "What are the chances you two would run into each other again?"

I had been thinking the same thing. Especially at a time when things were a little difficult for me. Not just in my career but in my relationship too.

"Maybe it's meant to be. Maybe she's supposed to be in your life."

"I can't do that. I'm with Beth. Besides, Niamh probably doesn't even feel the same way. I'm probably just getting swept up in the past."

"Have you asked her?" Marco asked carefully.

"Of course not."

"If Beth wasn't in the picture, would you be interested?"

"I can't." His question was irrelevant because Beth very much was in the picture, and I would never throw that away. Not for anyone. It would be dishonest and go against everything I believed in. I was not a cheater.

"I understand, I get it. But maybe there's another way you can find out."

"Find out what, exactly?"

"If Niamh is interested."

"I don't think I want to know." That worried me. I didn't want to know because if she was, that could stir something in me that I wasn't prepared for. And if she wasn't, I feared I might feel disappointed.

Our salads arrived, and we moved on from the topic. I was glad for it. Marco was asking the hard questions I didn't really want to think about.

I got home from work first and got dressed. I went straight to the Chanel dress, not because of what Beth had said about my full cleavage, but because it was my favourite dress. I felt confident in it, and I loved the floral pattern. It reminded me of summer.

Beth got home and was getting ready in the bedroom. I was in the walk-in closet, looking for some earrings in my jewellery box. I could only find one, prompting me to check in the tiny drawers.

And there it was: the ring I'd bought in Hersonissos. I lifted it out and couldn't help but feel thoughtful. I hadn't worn the ring in years. And yet, for some reason, I'd found it today. Of all days. It felt like too much of a coincidence to put it back. I tried it on the only finger it fit, my pinkie. But I knew Beth would be curious. She preferred I only wore my engagement ring. This new ring would definitely raise alarm bells. Instead, I placed it on a plain chain necklace, and I wore it around my neck.

I wondered if Niamh would even remember it. Perhaps she would, and it would bring her a little joy as well. Or worse, maybe she wouldn't remember it. I felt that would be more painful.

"All ready?" Beth asked from the closet doorway.

"Yeah, just grabbing my shoes."

"You look pretty, lovey."

"You too," I said, scanning her outfit. She was dressed to impress. She obviously wanted to make an impression. I just hoped she wouldn't go over-the-top with her questions for Niamh.

CHAPTER FIFTEEN
NIAMH DONNELLY

I felt a little drained after being stuck in the conference all day. Some of the training I had touched on in Melbourne, but the processes were different. They always were. It was educational, though, and I got to meet some of the trainees who had travelled from Belfast as well. They were in the term ahead of me and gave me some good tips on first term.

Then, the nerves kicked in. I felt nervous about seeing Harriet again. Perhaps it was because I would be meeting her fiancée, but when I really thought about it, I felt like we'd left things a little awkward last night. As soon as Harriet had taken the call from Beth, it felt like a light switch had gone off. When she'd returned, she'd seemed like a different person. I worried I'd said something. Perhaps she was embarrassed. I couldn't be sure.

Jenny's warning was also swirling in my head, and I wanted more than anything to support her new relationship. Nothing worse than coming across as some kind of needy ex.

I was annoyed for not packing better. I had two clean T-shirts left. I would have brought nicer clothes if I'd known I was going to be going out to a nice place, and I didn't have enough time to run into town to go shopping. I settled on the white T-shirt over the blue one. I still managed to feel incredibly underdressed when I arrived at the Italian restaurant. Not because the restaurant was overly fancy; it was when I came face-to-face with Beth.

She stood to greet me.

"You must be Niamh." She was gorgeous. Older, I would have guessed maybe in her early thirties, but she was dressed immaculately. She wore a stripey skirt that looked as though it was made to fit her. Her teeth were perfect, and her blond hair was long and glossy.

"It's lovely to meet you," I said. "Harriet has told me all about you."

When Beth stood back to take her seat again, Harriet was there. She looked breathtaking. She wore a purple floral dress that reminded me so much of when we were young. Part of me wondered if she had done it on purpose. I'd told her once how floral dresses would always remind me of her. But that wasn't the only thing that had my heart racing. It was her necklace, or rather, the ring on the chain. It was the one we'd bought together at the market in Hersonissos. I felt like seeing it put a trance over me and summoned these intense feelings I wasn't expecting. I tried desperately to resist because to indulge them would only taint my ability to be amicable to her fiancée.

When I met her eyes again, it was clear that she knew I'd recognised the necklace. She gave a small smile, as if telling me she'd worn the ring intentionally. We hugged, though it was brief and very awkward. Suited me. I didn't really trust myself to be too close. Not after the effect that ring had on me. It was sacred. I'd held on to the ring myself for sentimental reasons, but it felt like she was trying to get a reaction from me by wearing it. That annoyed me a little. Was she trying to torture me? Maybe Jenny had been right.

I took a seat opposite them at the rectangular table. Empty wineglasses were present, telling me they hadn't been waiting long on my arrival. I removed my jacket and didn't miss the brief shock on Beth's face.

"Nice tattoos."

I found the compliment a little fake. "Oh, yeah, thanks," I said, but the arched brow from her made me think she didn't actually like them all that much. I forced myself to keep my left arm on the table regardless.

They were pretty new, and I wasn't really used to people commenting. If I'd known I was going to a nice restaurant, I might have brought a shirt with long sleeves. I'd gotten my lower sleeve tattoos in Australia and had wanted them to reflect my travels, and the rest of my arm was finished when I'd arrived home a couple of months ago. Some of the tattoos had special meaning, while other ones, I just liked the look of them. I understood that tattoos weren't everyone's cup of tea, and while I didn't know Beth all that well, she didn't seem like the type. What was interesting was that Harriet hadn't seemed to have a problem with them yesterday or this evening. In fact, she seemed to be finding it difficult to tear her eyes away.

Beth took the lead. "How are you enjoying London?"

"I'm not really seeing much, to be honest," I said. Glancing in Harriet's direction was a mistake. She was touching the necklace in some kind of daze. Like she was somewhere else. Her eyes snapped to mine, and she seemed to check herself back into the conversation. "I'm stuck in boring lectures most of the day."

"Harriet tells me you're a doctor?"

"Not quite."

Beth frowned. "Well, studying to be one, right?" Harriet added, a little unsure. Her voice lacked any sort of confidence.

"Right," I said and went back to talking to Beth. For some reason, looking at Harriet was making me uncomfortable. It was stirring something from within that I didn't want to feel. Not right now. "I'm currently a paramedic, but I'm changing fields."

"A paramedic." Beth looked interested. "Frontline worker. That's very admirable. What makes you want to change fields?"

Harriet twisted in Beth's direction, looking a little annoyed. Perhaps she thought it was too intrusive. I didn't think it was, but regardless, Beth didn't notice Harriet's annoyance. I'd told Harriet about Dad's cancer diagnosis being a driving force behind wanting to become a GP, but I didn't really feel the need to offer that up to Beth.

"I'm just ready for a new challenge."

"There's a lot of pressure on GPs these days."

"Oh, I know. They're not exactly getting an easy time of it, either."

"Exactly, especially with the NHS in complete disarray," Beth said, a little disgruntled, and I could see Harriet tensing. She was surprisingly quiet and fidgeting. Perhaps she wasn't comfortable with the topic. "The sooner it's privatised, the better."

I could feel my face scrunching up in disagreement. The NHS being privatised would be a disaster. I would have said as much as well if the server hadn't arrived. "Good evening, ladies." I panicked, having not looked at the menu. I started quickly scanning it. "Are you ready to order?"

"We'll take a bottle of sauvignon blanc, number 83," Beth ordered from the wine list. "Is it good?"

"It's one of our finest bottles." The server started writing on a notepad.

"You drink white, right?" Beth asked me, but Harriet jumped in.

"You can order beer if you'd like."

I thought the sentiment behind her saying that was in the right place, but it made me feel a little embarrassed. Like, perhaps I wasn't posh enough to drink wine. I tried not to think too much into it. "Sauvignon blanc is great." I smiled through the awkwardness.

Harriet looked embarrassed and became reserved again, and it made me a little confused. I felt like she was a stranger sitting opposite me. The only reason I'd agreed to be here was to be around her, but this version of her was so standoffish. I was beginning to regret coming. Jenny had been right.

"Great. And is still water, okay?" Beth asked me, and I nodded. "A bottle of still water, as well. And for the entrees, we will have the veal."

I was surprised that Beth had ordered for Harriet. Perhaps they'd discussed it before I'd arrived. I wouldn't have thought Harriet was the kind of person who liked that. Maybe I didn't know her all that well. From first impressions, Beth had an air of confidence that could be intimidating, and Harriet seemed to completely withdraw, which was a little disappointing.

"And what does that come with?"

"Steamed seasonal vegetables and truffle potatoes."

"Good." Beth handed her menu to the server, and Harriet followed suit as if just going along with whatever Beth did.

"I'll have the chicken," I said, having no idea what I'd even ordered. It sounded simple, at least. I passed the menu back to the server. "Thank you."

"So, Beth," I said. "What do you do for a living?"

"I'm a partner at Shetland," she said confidently. "I'm not sure if you're familiar with it?" I shook my head. "It's one of the leading defence solicitors in London. Beth's father is one of the senior partners as well. One day, it'll be Shetland Whitaker on the business cards. Mark my words," she joked, but I didn't get it.

"Why?"

Beth frowned, and it was Harriet who looked a little embarrassed. "That's my surname."

"Oh." I thought on it. Harriet Whitaker. I'd never known.

"You don't know her last name?" Beth asked, a little perplexed.

"No." I glanced in Harriet's direction and spotted a change in her expression. More carefree and it made me settle a little. For half the time we'd known each other, I'd called her Jaq, but I wasn't about to reveal that to Beth. "It never really mattered."

Beth looked confused, whereas Harriet just smiled, and I could swear we were back on that beach in Stalis. For just a second.

"I don't know your last name, either."

"Donnelly."

She smiled pleasantly, as if approving.

"I thought you said she was your first love." Beth laughed, perhaps out of awkwardness.

My heart pulsated in a way that made me breathless. She'd loved me. Harriet's eyes collided with mine, confirming the truth. Her expression transitioned to regret, like perhaps she was embarrassed by Beth's oversharing. I wished that wasn't how I'd learned how Harriet had felt about me back then.

"How do you not even know each other's last name?"

"We went out, but it was only for, like, two days or something," I said, brushing off how much this conversation was affecting me on the inside. My emotions felt raw, and if I wasn't careful, they would make their way into my voice. "It was hardly anything serious."

I regretted my wording as soon as I said it because of the look on Harriet's face. Beth didn't see the hurt, but I did. I knew our time together had meant a lot more than that too, but I wasn't about to admit that to her fiancée. It was my turn to feel embarrassed, especially after witnessing just how uncomfortable Harriet was. She seemed to want off the topic just as badly as I did.

"We were so young." Harriet shrugged.

"Yeah." I brushed it off. Anything to change the topic. "That was a long time ago." To unpack that new information now would only torture me. I took the opportunity to move on. "So you work with Harriet's dad, huh? That must have been awkward when you guys started seeing each other."

"Not at all. Philip actually got me in as a paralegal. Harriet and I were already dating. I worked my way up to be the youngest partner they've ever had."

Beth seemed proud of the accomplishment but not in a boastful way, which I appreciated. She was ambitious, I could tell that a mile away. It made me also understand why Harriet was hesitant about taking the not-for-profit job. It seemed that Beth's career was very important to her. I felt bad for Harriet, and I just hoped that she would find the courage to do what was right for her.

"Philip is quite a mentor. We have a very good working relationship."

"That must come in handy with the in-laws."

"Pipa and Philip are like second parents. Isn't that right, lovey?" Beth said, taking hold of Harriet's hand.

Harriet smiled lovingly at her, but I couldn't help but feel it was put on. Maybe I was just hoping as much. Seeing them be affectionate affected me in a way I wasn't expecting. I didn't want to be feeling this way, but I made sure to hide any discomfort from my face. The last thing I wanted was to look jealous.

"That's great that you're so close with them. I've never met any of my ex's parents."

"Didn't you not meet Pipa? Briefly, at least," she teased, and I could see Harriet shudder. I laughed out of awkwardness alone. Getting caught in bed had been hugely humiliating. It bothered me slightly that Beth would poke fun, especially when it made Harriet look so uncomfortable. Thankfully, Beth moved on. "But really? You've never met any parents before?" I shook my head. "You mustn't have had many lasting relationships."

"Beth." Harriet's tone dropped argumentatively.

"No." Beth looked startled. "I don't mean in that way." She looked to me apologetically.

"It's okay." I tried to brush it off. I wasn't sure why Harriet felt the need to come to my aid. I could handle myself. "My ex lived in Melbourne, but their folks were from Sydney, so I never had the opportunity to meet them."

"That makes sense. How long were you and her together?"

"Remy is actually nonbinary, so they use the pronouns they-them. We were together for about two years."

"Oh, I'm sorry for using the wrong pronouns," Beth said genuinely, but I didn't take any offence. "We have a trans guy at work. I am familiar with the importance of calling him by the right pronouns. I have messed up once or twice, which I really hate."

"Honestly, I think nonbinary and trans people are more thankful if you make the effort. I don't think they mind when you mess up. Assuming it isn't intentional."

"Why did the relationship with Remy end, if you don't mind me asking?"

Again, Harriet looked annoyed at Beth for asking the question, but I was just glad to be talking to someone at the table. If it were up to Harriet, we would no doubt be sitting in silence.

"We wanted different things. I wanted to settle down, work on my career, get married, and maybe have kids." Harriet's eyes snapped up to mine. I wasn't sure why. The energy coming from her was so unpredictable. "Remy was more of a free spirit. They thought children would ruin their life," I joked, even though it had been a hard and difficult decision to break up. But I knew we couldn't be together. We wanted different things.

"I think we would be of the same opinion as Remy," Beth said, looking to Harriet. But weirdly, she didn't seem to agree. It left things a little awkward.

The wine arrived, and I couldn't help but notice how Harriet had absentmindedly started playing with her necklace again. She looked like she was on another planet, and I wished more than anything that I could figure out what was going through her head. She was so distant, and I was literally close enough to reach out and touch her. As soon as the wine was poured into her glass, she took a healthy gulp. Perhaps she was just nervous.

"Are you seeing anyone right now?" Beth asked. "I only ask because I have a friend in Belfast who would be perfect for you."

I could feel myself close up.

"I'm sure Niamh doesn't need help in that department," Harriet said, and it seemed like it was the first sentence she'd said all evening. "You seemed to be handling yourself all right last night."

I took a drink of wine to distract attention. It didn't help that my mind was replaying last night's activities with Tara.

"Only here one night and already found yourself a woman?" Beth teased. "Who is she?"

"The waitress from the bar last night," Harriet said between sips of wine. She revealed so little of how she was feeling. And I found I couldn't get a read on her at all, and trying to do so was draining my energy.

Thankfully, the conversation didn't stay on my romantic endeavours from last night. I was glad when we moved on and talked about all kinds of things, from current affairs to music.

Beth was incredible. Gorgeous, smart, and interesting. At times, I found her to be a little intense, but she was never nasty or anything like that. I enjoyed her company throughout dinner. The only downside of the night was actually Harriet. While I saw glimmers of her, she seemed to close herself away a lot too. It made me confused. However, it didn't seem to alarm Beth, which made me think that perhaps Harriet was just more reserved with Beth around. Which, frankly, was a crying shame. Reserved Harriet had nothing on the girl I used to know.

Dinner was finished, and we passed on dessert. Things were winding down for the night, and part of me was glad for it to be over. We were just finishing off our drinks when Beth excused herself from the table to use the ladies' room.

It was just me and Harriet. I felt a lot of different emotions. I wasn't sure how to be around her. She was so different from the woman I'd sat opposite just last night.

"Did you enjoy your meal?" Harriet leant on her elbows. Her posture seemed more relaxed. I would have said the wine did a lot of the hard work, but perhaps it was the absence of Beth.

"It was lovely. It's a nice place. I'll have to remember it for the next time I come back to London."

"You'll be back again? Like, for training?" Harriet looked optimistic for a moment, and it made me sad to have to break it to her.

"No, not really. I just meant, if I'm ever visiting again."

"Right." She looked disappointed. "You leave tomorrow?"

"Yeah."

An awkward silence lingered between us. I felt like there was so much I wanted to say to her. To maybe dig a little deeper as to why she was different with me than she was with Beth. But I realised the questions I had wouldn't help me. Jenny's advice was in my head as well. Digging around in the past was futile. Maybe I didn't know the real Harriet. And that was really difficult to comprehend. Beth surely knew Harriet far better than I could. They'd been together for, like, five years. Maybe this was who she was.

"Who knows, maybe we'll finally visit Northern Ireland. Beth and I." I couldn't help but feel a little dejected. "I'll have to get your number, and we can all do this again."

"Is that *really* what you want?"

Harriet looked taken aback. She looked a little upset as well, and I didn't like that I made her feel that way.

I tried another angle. "You just…were a little quiet tonight." She looked broken all of a sudden, and it made me sad. "You're different."

"It's not easy for me," she said, chewing her lip. I didn't know what she meant. "Seeing you again. Being reminded of the past."

I wanted so desperately to know what she meant by that. To hear her elaborate. But this wasn't the time. I couldn't help but feel that this conversation was going down a bad road. A road neither of us wanted.

"Beth's incredible," I said. She seemed to look indifferent. "She is. I can see why you're marrying her. You two look good together." Every word didn't sit well with me. And that was part of the problem.

Harriet watched me carefully. She reached up and held on to the ring on her necklace.

I couldn't tell what she was thinking, but I knew there was something she wanted to get off her chest. "You still have it." She nodded, never breaking eye contact. "Me too."

"Do you ever wonder..." Harriet whispered, as if she was afraid to say it out loud. "What might have happened if we'd stayed in touch?"

I could feel my chest tighten, and I hated that she was doing this. This wasn't me. And I hoped more than anything that it wasn't her, either. Because the truth was, sitting opposite Harriet's perfect fiancée was one of the hardest things I'd ever done. Beth was everything I wasn't. She was probably better in every single way. I was secure in myself to know that. And I was jealous. Because deep down, I still felt something for Harriet. I wished I didn't. But maybe I would always feel something for her. Because from time to time, I had wondered about what would have happened to us.

"I don't think we should exchange numbers." The words hurt to say out loud. Harriet looked devastated for a moment. It hurt because the idea of losing contact again seemed unforgivable. "We're in different places. You're here, and I have to go home." I had to be with Dad. I was just starting the programme. I couldn't dig around in the past when she wasn't available, regardless of what I felt. "That's where we're supposed to be, regardless of what... might have been." Her eyes stayed on mine. I felt that connection intensify, though I was glad that it was fleeting.

She nodded, as if accepting my proposal. "I think you're right. Besides, who knows?" she tried to say optimistically, but it fell flat. "Maybe we will run into each other again."

"Yeah." I chuckled. "Maybe when we're old and retired in Stalis."

"So just another forty years or so."

"Yeah," I said, despite the lump in my throat.

Beth arrived back in that moment. "Hey, lovey, ready to go? I just settled the bill."

"You didn't need to do that." I reached into my pocket for my wallet.

"Nonsense. It was a pleasure to meet you, Niamh. I do hope we can do it again sometime."

"Definitely," I lied.

We walked outside, and Beth hugged me good-bye first. I watched Harriet stare at the ground in a daze. She looked small. Then, it was Harriet's turn. She stepped forward and wrapped her arms around my shoulders. Her embrace was tight, as if she was holding on to something. I felt the surge rush through her chest and into mine. I felt at home in her embrace, and I breathed her in a little, knowing that I would probably never see her again.

It felt like a repeat. Our last hug outside her hotel room. And while part of me wished it wasn't good-bye, I knew it was the right thing to do. For both of us.

I pulled back and watched her carefully once more. "Take care," I said before whispering the last part, "Jaq."

"Bye," she said, before mouthing, *Levi.*

I went back to the hotel, and while I thought about going in search of Tara, I didn't want company tonight. I needed to be alone and process. Perhaps to grieve what could have been.

CHAPTER SIXTEEN
HARRIET WHITAKER

We arrived home to a dark apartment. Beth got the lights, and I kicked off my heels. I would have normally put them away in our bedroom, but that felt like too much work. I felt a bit woozy from dinner. I didn't think it was because I'd eaten too much. In fact, I'd struggled to relax enough to enjoy my meal. I wasn't a huge fan of veal, but it would have taken too much energy to go against what Beth wanted. I was on edge most of the evening from watching Niamh and Beth interact. The second bottle of wine had probably been a mistake. My head was a little unstable. I even stumbled when taking off my jacket.

"Steady there," Beth teased, making her way into the kitchen. "Would you like a nightcap?"

"Sure," I said, even though I knew I'd probably had enough.

I couldn't find the mental strength to fully engage with Beth on the taxi ride home. She'd only had good things to say about Niamh. And while that should have made me feel relieved or good in some way, there was an emptiness instead. I didn't know why.

I was overthinking my interactions with Niamh. Everything I'd said felt like it didn't come out the way I'd wanted. Beth's presence had made me feel insecure, as if I wasn't capable of holding my own. That wasn't exactly new for us. I let her talk for the both of us often. Marco had said before how he didn't like it, and now, in just one dinner, Niamh had commented on it too.

You're different.

Her words echoed in my mind, making my insides feel uncomfortable. A queasiness surged, and I felt like I could throw up.

I didn't want to be awkward. I wanted to be myself. The person sitting in Niamh's hotel bar. Not whoever that had been at dinner. Quiet, reversed, and second-guessing every word that left my mouth. I hated that Niamh had seen that side of me. But more than anything, I hated that I was becoming that person. It wasn't just in certain situations. I was becoming someone I didn't like. Secondary to Beth. This wasn't the first time I'd felt this way. Perhaps it took someone from my past to see it, for me to realise just how much of myself I was hiding, or rather, losing.

"Southern Comfort and ice?" Beth asked, reaching for two tumblers and placing them on the kitchen countertop. She made the drinks, and I took a seat on one of the stools at the breakfast bar. She placed it in front of me, and I stared at it for a moment.

"Cheers." She held up her glass and lowered her head to meet my eyes. "You okay?" She looked concerned. "Looks like something is on your mind."

"It is." I thought carefully. There was a lot on my mind. So much that I didn't know where to begin.

"Was it me?" Beth looked regretful. "I asked too many questions, didn't I?"

"No."

"I did, didn't I? Niamh is just such a fascinating person." I couldn't disagree. "I just wanted to do you proud."

"You did." I felt bad. Especially when I was questioning our relationship. "You were great."

"Then, what's up, lovey?"

I felt under scrutiny. She waited for me, though, which made me feel a little more comfortable. But I was terrified. I knew once I said what was bothering me, we would never be the same again. I was afraid the job offer would destroy the life I was building for myself. But then, the profound thought hit me, was this even the life I wanted? That gave me the courage to be brave. No one else could change the ways things were going except me.

"I was offered a job."

Beth's face showed surprise, and then transitioned into excitement. "That's fantastic, Harriet. What? Just out of the blue?"

"Well, no. I applied for it last week."

"Oh." She looked a little hurt, and I could tell it was because I hadn't told her about it. It made me feel guilty. "Well, where is the new firm? Is it a promotion, or…"

"It's with FD Solicitors," I said and could feel myself holding my breath.

Beth looked bewildered. "I can't think. I'm sure I have heard of them before but—"

I couldn't take it anymore. "They don't do corporate law." Her face faltered. "They help refugees and migrants coming into the UK." Her mind seemed to be racing and not in a good way. "It's not-for-profit."

"Excuse me?"

I heard the judgement loud and clear. Just like she'd heard exactly what I'd said. Which was why I didn't repeat myself. It looked as though she thought it was a mistake at first.

"Not-for-profit." It was as if she was mulling the idea in her head. I knew she disapproved by her body language. "And you applied for it knowing this?"

"Yes," I said, feeling my heart rate booming in my ears.

It felt good to get it out. For about a second, and then, it felt very hot. The queasiness returned, making the drink in front of me look repulsive. I got up and moved to the sink, filling up a glass of water. Beth said nothing. I sipped it, hoping it would settle the anxiety taking over my body. The tension just kept filling the room. I took my glass of water back to my seat and sat opposite her.

"Go on," she snapped, crossing her arms, leaning back against the fridge. It was like she couldn't wait to have a go, and that made me frustrated.

"And I am going to accept the offer." She let out a puff of air in shock. "I just thought you should know." My calmness was even a little eerie to me.

"Well, thank you," she said sarcastically. "Thank you ever so much for talking to me about this before you made any decision. You know, your fiancée."

"I am talking to you—"

"No, Harriet, you're telling me," she said, and I could understand where she was coming from. But weirdly, I was unfazed. I was sure of my decision, regardless of how she felt. Which made me struggle to be sympathetic.

"It's my decision."

She stared back at me, flabbergasted. She obviously didn't like what she was hearing. "Have you lost your mind?" She moved closer, placing her hands hard on the kitchen counter in front of me. "You have worked so hard to become a solicitor. You're making a name for yourself in this industry. You did the work, late nights sitting right there. You passed all your exams, and you've not even done a year before you're switching fields." The volume of her voice was causing me to sheepishly divert my eyes. "What has gotten into you, Harriet?"

"I'm not happy," I said, and it seemed like she didn't hear a word of it. It hurt just how much she was disregarding my feelings. It seemed to be all about her. As always. "I hate my job—"

"Then get another job. Don't commit career suicide."

"That's totally out of line, Beth." I completely rejected the notion, but I wasn't entirely surprised that she felt this way. "Career suicide is such a gross exaggeration."

"Not-for-profit, Harriet. Do you have any idea how bad that looks?"

"For who? You?"

"For yourself." She looked at me in disgust, as if I'd lost all self-respect. "Do pro bono if you need to ease your conscience or whatever. Don't jump from *our* level to the bottom of the barrel."

I couldn't believe the toxicity coming from her. It felt like a dark mist of negativity was seeping from her and clouding my view of her. I had expected some resistance but not to this degree. "Wow, refugees are the bottom of the barrel." I'd never seen her as an elitest. It made her unattractive and certainly not someone I wanted to spend the rest of my life with.

"That's not what I mean. Don't put words in my mouth."

"There's no need. Your morals are quite clear to me."

"You're being rash," she said, seeming to simmer. She was trying so hard to reason with me, but I wasn't sure I wanted to reason with her after those comments. "I'm just trying to explain that this isn't something to do on a whim. Not-for-profit solicitors are not on the same level as us." There it was again, and I felt annoyed. "They didn't have the kind of upbringing we did."

"And what, they didn't go to Cambridge?" I asked in disbelief.

"Exactly."

"You're unbelievable."

"Wake up, Harriet. It's a different class of law. Everyone knows that."

"This isn't about me at all. This is about you. And your ego."

"It's humiliating," she said, and I'd never felt more separated from her beliefs. Separate from her. "And what do you think this will do for your father's reputation?"

"I'm twenty-six old. I don't need my parents' approval." Niamh's words came to me in my moment of need and somehow managed to make me feel safe. Secure in my decision. "I don't need anyone's approval."

She looked taken aback. "I feel like I don't even know who you are right now. What has gotten into you?" Her eyes were shifting back and forth, scrutinising me in a way that felt intrusive. "Am I missing something here?" I shook my head, unsure what she meant. "Is this something to do with tonight?"

"What do you mean?"

"Well, we go to dinner with your ex, and you come home some kind of imposter."

"Okay." I waved her off, refusing to even entertain this.

"Is this to do with Niamh? She's changing fields so you want to do the same thing—"

"I got the job before I even saw Niamh."

"Well, I'm just trying to figure out where you got this idea from."

I was immediately offended. "Because I couldn't possibly come up with this idea by myself?"

"That's not what I mean. I just meant, we're a partnership, Harriet. We are supposed to figure this stuff out together. But that's not what's happening. You went behind my back—"

"Because I knew you wouldn't be happy, Beth. I knew you wouldn't approve of this, but I hate my job. I hate it." I felt relief at just vocalising that. "This is something fulfilling. I have wanted to do this kind of work since university. I talked to you about this before."

"Yeah, ages ago. I figured you'd grow up and forget about it," Beth said, and I couldn't be sure what my expression was revealing. I was devastated. The accusations and words she'd said could never be forgotten. I couldn't imagine ever forgiving her. "There's no money in this job. You'll be working for peanuts, Harriet. I just don't understand why you would want to take a step backward like this."

"Because I don't see it as a step backward." I felt uplifted. Like I could finally see clearly, and it filled me with joy. Perhaps it was a feeling of finally standing up for myself. "I see it as a step forward. A step toward something better."

Beth couldn't have looked more disgruntled. She looked fed up and as if she couldn't understand me at all. I felt the same way.

"This is what I want. I am taking the job. I want your support, but if you can't accept this then…" I let the implication remain unspoken.

A series of emotions passed across her expression. Anger to hurt and back around to disbelief. "I don't even know what to say to that." She slumped back against the fridge. "I think we both need some space."

There was nothing more to say. We both felt the way we felt. I wasn't even in the right headspace where I could have adjusted my thinking for her, and I didn't think she could do the same. We sat like that for another moment before she left. She packed a couple of things in a bag. I wasn't even sure where she was going, but it was clear she didn't want to be here. I didn't want her with me, either.

I got into bed feeling cold and low, and for some reason, my mind drifted to Niamh. I thought about what she was doing right now. Probably enjoying Tara's company, which made me squirm a little. An overwhelming disappointment settled in my chest. She was gone. Torn away once again. It wasn't Mama who was dragging me away from her, but oddly, it didn't feel any different than the first time. Life was pulling us apart. I only wanted the best for Niamh, and it seemed as though the path she was on would lead to that. It would have been nice to stay in touch, but I would have to settle for having gotten a glimpse into her life again. She was good. She was happy. I just had to work on getting to the same place as well.

CHAPTER SEVENTEEN
NIAMH DONNELLY

The drive to Derry was long and tiresome. It was dark, and I was never really a fan of driving at night. The Glen Shane Pass was a ropey road at the best of times, but the heavy rain and wind was putting me a little on edge. The headlights were giving me a bit of a headache too, though it wasn't fair to blame it all on the drive.

I hadn't gotten home from London until late last night, and I had to admit, I'd found it difficult to calm my thoughts. The training had been intense. I'd found it a lot more overwhelming, but I was pleased to know I was already one step ahead of the rest of my classmates. I started the programme in two weeks. It felt like the right move. I was excited for the new start. Until then, I could be close to home. Spending time with Dad and chipping in around the house some more to ease the pressure on Mum.

My mind kept returning to one place: Harriet. I must have thought about her dozens of times in the last two days. Even after I'd left the restaurant and gone back to my hotel, I couldn't shake the feeling that I'd made a mistake. Like, perhaps we should have exchanged numbers, even just to remain in each other's lives. It would have been nice.

Although, every time I started to feel regret like that, I had to remind myself that a friendship would have never been enough. Not for me. That had become very evident while sitting opposite her fiancée. I'd wanted to be the one holding her hand and the one to take her home. Even after all this time. Even though Harriet had changed, I still wanted to know her in *that* way. But we didn't always get to choose these things. She had her perfect fiancée, and they were probably going to have a pretty great life together. That was all I ever wanted for her. Even if it wasn't going to be with me.

I pulled up outside Jenny's apartment. Thankfully, the rain had eased. I lifted the bag of supplies from the back seat and made a break for her building. The bag of goodies consisted of Jenny's favourite chocolate, popcorn, and crisps, and I threw in a bottle of nonalcoholic wine. I'd never tried any, but maybe it would cheer her up a little. I usually brought a bottle of wine when visiting.

Jenny buzzed me up, and as soon as I got to her floor, her door swung open. She was wrapped up in a dressing gown, with furry slippers poking out at the bottom. Her black hair was scraped back into a messy bun, and she'd removed her makeup and fake tan. I'd rarely seen Jenny without fake tan on. It was her signature mark. It just told me how low she was. I pulled her into a hug, and we stood like that at her front door.

"What's in the bag?" she asked, still holding tight.

"Chocolate."

"You did good."

"And wine. Don't worry, it's nonalcoholic."

"Way to rub salt in the wound." She pulled back. "You can take that crap home with you."

"I thought it would be a nice gesture," I whined, following her into the apartment. She led me straight to the kitchen. "Maybe it's good." I pulled the bottle out of the bag and placed it on the counter.

"Why is it that shade? If that was pee, I would send it straight to the lab to be tested."

"Let's just not look too close at it," I said, pulling out two mugs and filling them with a serving each. At least the mugs would conceal the dodgy colour. "Cheers."

"To being knocked up." Jenny clinked my mug with hers. We both drank. She grimaced, and I was sure my face showed the same level of disgust.

"Okay, so that's terrible."

"Yeah." She chuckled. "How about tea instead?"

"Sounds good," I said and unpacked some of the snacks. "At least the snacks will be good." I put some crisps, popcorn, and chocolate into separate bowls while Jenny focused on making the tea.

We made our way back into the living room again. Jenny's apartment was a modest one-bedroom, but she lived alone, so it did the job. For now, at least. I took the seat beside her on the couch and turned to face her.

"How's work?"

"Shite."

"You're really selling being a GP, you know."

"I tried to talk you out of it, remember?"

I threw her a look that I hoped would relay that my mind was made up. I thought she got that.

"But honestly, if we had more good GPs out there who gave a shit, things would be a lot better."

"I'm hoping I will be one of the good ones."

"You will be. Caring is your superpower." She gave a small smile, but I could see the signs of wallowing returning. It brought my mind straight back to the bombshell she'd dropped on me in London.

"Did you talk to Tom?"

"Yeah." She sighed, taking a sip of her tea.

"How'd he take it?"

"I don't know. He hasn't texted me back yet."

"Jenny! You texted him?"

"What?" She looked startled.

"You didn't think something like this warranted a phone call, at least?"

"He doesn't like talking on the phone. His mum still makes his dentist appointments." I was speechless, and that seemed to speak volumes for Jenny. The look of realisation settled in. "Oh my God, I'm having that man's baby." I had to laugh, or I'd have freaked out with worry. "What am I going to do?" she said seriously as she pulled up her knees and rested her head on them.

"You're going to figure this out. And you have me. Always."

"Thank you." She grabbed a bowl of popcorn and took a handful before passing it to me. "So what happened in London?"

I let out a long, exasperated breath. I stared at the bowl in my hands while I thought carefully.

"I told you not to go," Jenny said, shaking her head.

"I probably should have listened to you." I felt the disappointment of leaving Harriet all over again.

"Hey, don't take advice from me. I got knocked up in the carpark of McDonald's."

I turned in horror, needing an explanation.

Jenny waved me off. "You don't want to know. What was her fiancée like?"

"Honestly," I said, popping a piece of popcorn in my mouth. "Perfect."

It was the truth. As much as I didn't want to admit it. As much as I wanted to poke holes in her personality or nitpick, the reality was that Beth would be able to give Harriet a life I could never. She came from royalty, for Christ's sake. I could never have competed, not that it was even a competition. She'd chosen Beth.

"Ouch." Jenny mirrored how I was feeling inside. "Would have been easier if she was a bitch. Or fat."

"She's gorgeous. Successful, the whole package."

"So she was all loved up?"

"Yeah." I sighed, but part of me didn't really believe it. I couldn't explain why I felt that. It was like a gut intuition.

"Hey, I've not seen that in a long time," Jenny said, reaching over and grabbing my hand. "You got that ring in Greece, right?"

She didn't know the story behind it, which I was glad for. It would have made me look really pathetic. I'd dug out the ring when I'd gotten home. I hadn't seen it in years. I hadn't meant to put it on, but once it was on my thumb again, I'd felt like I wanted it with me. Perhaps just for today.

"For the record, her fiancée has nothing on you, Niamh," Jenny said with conviction. I rolled my eyes, not agreeing. "I'm serious. It's Harriet's loss. One day, she will realise that."

"I don't know." I couldn't even come up with an argument. Mainly because I didn't believe her. Beth fitted perfectly into Harriet's life. Even her crazy parents seemed to love her. Maybe things had worked out the way they were supposed to.

A knock at the door caused Jenny to frown.

"Are you expecting—" I started but was interrupted with more urgent knocking.

"All right, all right." Jenny got up from the couch and made her way to the front door. I stood as well, feeling a little unsettled by the urgency.

A strange man stood there, and I was almost rushing to Jenny's side, but she seemed to recognise him. "Tom, what are you—"

"Are you actually pregnant?" he said, out of breath, barely registering my presence.

Jenny looked down as if feeling embarrassed. The room instantly plunged into tension. "Yeah."

He breathed out, releasing a breath he had probably been holding from the second he'd gotten that text message. He placed his hands on her shoulders. "Come here," he said and pulled her into a hug.

While I couldn't see Jenny's face. I saw his. I'd never met him. I'd heard so little about him because they were relatively new. But I could see something in his character. He was scared. There was no hiding that, but he was there for her. And weirdly, I got the feeling he would be there for her no matter what.

"I support whatever you want to do," he said. Jenny pulled back, and he stared down at her. "You want to raise this kid, then I'm here. You don't want to have it, and I will be there too. I know we've only been dating a couple of months, but I got you, Jenny."

My heart warmed a little bit. I didn't want to eavesdrop, but there wasn't really any escape from what was unfolding in front of me.

"Okay, take it easy." Jenny made light of the situation. I knew it was because his declaration had touched her. "Don't be getting down on one knee or anything." She turned back to me, and I didn't miss how she couldn't hide the small smile. "Oh, and meet Niamh." She gestured through to me, and I wished more than anything I wasn't still holding the bowl of popcorn. Like I was watching a movie.

"Hey," I said awkwardly and put the bowl on the coffee table.

"Hi," Tom said, probably feeling even more awkward. It was understandable. He'd just made a big declaration in front of a stranger. He moved farther into the living room and came toward me. "It's nice to meet you. Jenny talks about you a lot."

"Thanks, it's nice to meet you too. Dad," I joked, but it seemed to startle him. "Sorry." Jenny shot me an amused look. "Think I better leave you guys to it."

"You're not going home." Jenny put a stop to that. "You drove an hour and a half to get here. Besides, I need all the help I can get. And who better than my best friend and…" She looked over at a sheepish Tom. "My baby daddy."

"Okay, then. Welcome to the weird club, Tom."

"Thanks." He sat next to Jenny.

"Can I get you some wine?" I asked.

CHAPTER EIGHTEEN

HARRIET WHITAKER

I twirled the cup of coffee in my hands. It had gone cold. That was how long I'd been sat there. It was still early. I usually loved Saturday mornings. Nothing to do but plenty of options. Maybe go for a walk, grab a coffee, or some brunch in a nice café. Not today, though.

Beth hadn't come home yesterday. I would have known. I called in sick on Friday to make sure I was home. I had left a couple of missed calls, but she hadn't returned them. I worried that I had thrown my relationship away. All over a job. I felt like I was going out of my mind replaying our argument from Thursday.

I had felt so very alone. I wanted to talk to someone, but I couldn't. I wanted to call Marco. Though, he already disliked Beth, and I knew this would only give him more ammo. I wanted relationship advice, not someone telling me to break things off. That was the last thing I needed.

I thought of calling my other friends, however, a lot of them were also friends with Beth. I couldn't risk the rumour mill seeping out that there was trouble in paradise. It all felt hopeless. We had intertwined our lives to the point that I didn't even know how to untangle them. The thought of having to break up felt unimaginable. I could already hear my parents' disapproval and disappointment. I could feel myself shuddering just thinking about it. And when they discovered the reason for our breakup, they would surely disown me. Letting someone like Beth go for nothing more than some "charity" job.

I had so many regrets. I could have handled it all better. The things I'd said. I had to apologise for so much. I should have tried harder to see things from her perspective. I knew she would have concerns about the job at FD Solicitors, but I didn't expect her wholehearted rejection of my career change. It wasn't the company. It was the move from corporate law toward the not-for-profit industry. She couldn't seem to get past it, and it made me want to cut ties with FD Solicitors. Maybe I wasn't the right person for the role. Was it really worth throwing away everything I had built? My relationship? My parents' approval? I'd be risking it all.

But that didn't feel right, either. I wanted the job. Working with people who risked everything to get to the UK. Helping people who literally had nothing. Reuniting families and keeping people safe from extradition. Thinking about it now felt right, and imagining staying in my crumby job left me feeling empty. More than I wanted most things in life, I wanted this job.

Why did my career have to be tied to the relationships in my life? Surely, it shouldn't matter.

I heard the keys in the front door. It creaked open, and there she was. Beth looked a little startled to see me sitting at the breakfast bar. Perhaps she didn't think I would be home. It made me nervous that perhaps she was only here to collect more of her things. She didn't budge from behind the door, solidifying my theory.

I dropped my eyes to the coffee cup, filled with too much shame to make eye contact. Our argument was by far the worst we had ever had. Some of the things we'd said felt alien to me. We were never like that.

When she came into the kitchen, my head was down, and I couldn't stop the tears coming to my eyes. Part of me didn't want her to see it. Especially if she was here to end things. She stood somewhere in front of me.

"Harriet." Her voice sounded broken, making me look up. I saw a beautiful bouquet of flowers. It was enormous, filled with roses, lilies, and a dozen other kinds I didn't know the names of. She set them down to the side and came around to stand next to me. "I'm sorry." Her tired eyes were filled with tears. It broke my heart. I could feel my own eyes filling. "I'm so sorry, lovey."

I fell into her arms and sobbed. I could feel the pain in her embrace. She regretted our fight just as much as I did. I held on tight, cherishing our love. I thought I'd lost her. Thrown away our life together. I felt relief on a magnitude that was euphoric. I felt so relieved knowing that she wasn't walking away from our relationship. I didn't have to feel the shame of telling our friends and families. Just having her in my arms again filled me with gratitude.

"I'm sorry," I whispered, not missing the way my voice trembled. "I said some horrible things."

"You? What about me?" She sobbed. "I was awful. The way I spoke to you..." She trailed off, getting lost in another sob. "I will never treat you like that again." Her sincerity touched my heart. It felt good that she was taking accountability. I knew she would stand by her words too. That was just who she was.

I tried to take some of the responsibility. "I blindsided you. I shouldn't have—"

"I was shocked, yes." Beth pulled back and wiped her tears. Her mascara had run a bit, but I didn't want to stop her apology for something silly like that. "But that doesn't excuse those things I said. I should have never said this job was career suicide." She frowned, and I could see her guilt, and it made me feel seen. "I want to support you, always. I'm just so sorry we fought."

I took a breather, relishing having her here. Hearing her take accountability for the things she'd said filled me with hope. I felt that we were going to be okay. We had problems to work through, but the good thing was that Beth wanted to figure it out together.

"Beth," I started, and she listened openly, "some of the things you said..."

My mind brought me back to the argument, words burned into my mind. I needed to hear why she'd said, "don't jump from our level to the bottom of the barrel." There were other things that needed discussing. Perhaps it was in the heat of the moment, but still, I had to know, did she really view us as better-than just because of our line of work?

"Forget them, lovey," she said, clearly ashamed, but I felt a pang of reluctance. "They don't matter now. If you think this job is the right move, then you should do it." Something about the way she said it made me question if she really meant that. She sounded genuine, but her body language left me with concerns. "It will be an adjustment, you changing fields, but I'll get there." Her tone heighted, and it made me doubtful.

I felt my stomach drop, disappointed that she wasn't more supportive or willing to discuss what was said more. I felt like I needed closure or to air out some of the things she'd said, particularly about her views on not-for-profit. It seemed like these were issues that would be hard to overcome if we didn't talk about them.

"I love you, and that's all that matters." She took hold of my hands and kissed them. Her remorse was clearly written on her expression. I could tell by her dishevelled hair and the dark circles under her eyes. Beth would never leave the house looking anything less than perfect. It just demonstrated how much our fight had affected her. Her fingers played with my engagement ring. "I want to be better. You will be my wife soon, and I want to make sure I am the best I can be for you."

I believed her. Wholeheartedly, I believed she would do everything to make it up to me.

She kissed me. I allowed all of my unanswered questions and concerns to be washed away in her kiss. It felt like she was finally back, the Beth I fell in love with. Her kiss deepened, and I willed myself to move on from our fight. She had apologised, what more did I need, I told myself. Perhaps we didn't need to dissect the words we'd said when we were drunk. Maybe no good would come of it. She took charge, pulling me close, and I felt myself become breathless.

Her hands were hot on my body, and it felt incredible. Given the state of despair I'd been left in for the last two days, it felt like I was being resuscitated back to life by her. I was just so glad to have her back in my arms that I let her undress me in our kitchen.

We still had problems, but our love and commitment to a life together surely outweighed that. All of the energy built up from our explosive arguing was being redirected to a much better place. Her kiss was full of passion, and her hurried movements turned me on. Her hands on my skin made me feel desired in a way that had been lacking in our sex life in recent months. She kissed my neck, and once my clothes were gone, she ushered me to sit on the kitchen counter. Sitting on the cold surface was almost welcome, considering how hot and steamy things were getting between us. Her hand found its way between my legs, and after that, well, it was hard to hold on to any of the bad feelings anymore.

PART THREE
2026

CHAPTER NINETEEN

NIAMH DONNELLY

I didn't need to check the time to know that it was almost lunch. My stomach growling was a dead giveaway, but the heat was also making the hike a little more challenging. Hell, a lot more challenging. I was busted.

"Monterosso al Mare is just around the bend," our guide said. I was reluctant to believe Santino. He'd lied to me before.

"Thank God," James grunted from somewhere behind me. I didn't say anything, though it was a surprise seeing him at the back of the line.

I was sweaty and exhausted too, but I didn't want to appear to be any more of a wuss. I'd been back of the line most days. It would have been a little embarrassing if everyone wasn't really nice. Today, I was feeling it, though. It made me kind of relieved that this was the last day of our five-day hiking trip along the Amalfi Coast. We'd started in Florence and made our way to our final destination, Cinque Terre. This wasn't one of the more challenging trails, but still, my legs were aching.

The idea to hike across Italy hadn't come to me by accident. I had a couple of people to blame, or thank, whatever way I wanted to look at it.

Firstly, Mum was to blame. She'd said I was starting to look old. Grey hairs and wrinkles, she'd said the lot. It came from a place of love; therefore, I didn't hold any grudges. It had felt like a bit of an intervention. Especially after the year we'd had. She'd said I needed a break from work and well, life. I couldn't deny that the pandemic had left me in a state of burnout.

Jenny had also claimed it would be good for me, especially after a breakup. Granted, I'd booked the hiking trip almost six months ago. Therefore, I was over the end of my relationship with Julie. Sadly, it would have been our anniversary yesterday, had we still been together.

Jenny had to take extra blame, though, because she was supposed to be with me. It was her stupid idea anyway. "Let's relive our Greek summer abroad," she'd said. Then, she'd found out she was pregnant. Again. I was, of course, delighted for them. My godson, Leo, would make a good big brother, and she and Tom had been trying for a couple of years to have another. I'd shut my mouth and accepted my fate.

I had been excited about the challenge. I had even been hiking back home to build up resistance. I also found it to be a really great outlet from work pressures. To get out into nature and de-stress. The hiking bug had really gotten me after the breakdown in my relationship. Trails back home like the Slieve Donard, Ballintoy, and the Glenariff Forest Park had all helped to mend my broken heart a little and revealed an unknown passion I had for hiking. Hiking also made me feel closer to Dad. It felt like he'd been with me every step of the trip. He'd once said this hiking trail was one of the best he'd ever done.

Nothing could have prepared me for this level of intensity. The heat was turning out to be the most difficult part. And I'd been smart and planned to go in late September to avoid the blistering temperatures, but alas, there had been a late season heatwave. While it had been difficult, I couldn't deny loving every part of this experience. The views were spectacular. Especially today. I loved seeing the five villages that hugged the mountains in an incredibly unique way. Straight out of a travel magazine. Matty from that boring hiking show Dad loved so much wasn't lying. The vibrant colours of the townhouses were picturesque next to crisp blue ocean.

James let out a yelp from behind me. I turned and spotted him limping.

"Hey, you okay?" I went back. Everything in his expression told me he was in severe pain. "Here." I wrapped my arm around his waist and helped get him to a nearby rock to sit.

He was a big guy, probably a foot taller and three times the weight of me. He was made of pure muscle. I was sure it was a bit comical to witness me trying to help, but the group had went on ahead. He was stuck with me.

"Thanks." He panted, collapsing onto the rock. He rubbed his left knee. "It's the steps that are killing me."

"Just take a beat, there's no rush." I breathed out, enjoying the break myself.

"You don't have to stay with me. You shouldn't miss Santino's tour." I didn't have the heart to tell him that I'd missed most of what Santino had said about the surrounding areas. I was always at the back of the group, struggling to keep up.

"It's grand."

"What part of Ireland are you from?" he asked, and it made me realise just how little we had spoken on the trip. James was always up front, right beside Santino. Or he talked with the German couple who were close in second.

"Sherwood. It's just outside Belfast. What part of England?"

"Leeds," he said, reaching into his backpack and pulling out a bottle of water. He took a swig and poured some water onto his knee. He let out another grunt and rubbed the area where I could see a scar. "Fucking knee."

"I didn't realise you had an ACL tear." He smirked. "How bad?"

"Bad enough to end my career." He could have fooled me, especially considering his speed and resilience for the last four days. "I was fine until last night. That's why I missed dinner. I couldn't get out of an ice bath." It looked like the pain was easing, but he still looked worn out.

"Must have been a grade three tear, huh?"

"You had one too?" he asked, seemingly taken aback that I knew so much.

"No, I'm a doctor."

I was intrigued to know his story. On the outside, he looked like this big, hairy giant. A Jack the lad, perhaps. He'd been pretty loud during meals and even flirted with a few of the American women travelling with us. I'd thought he was just one of those guys who I would never get on with, but it was clear there was more beneath the surface.

"Were you a footballer?"

"Rugby." That would have been my second guess, considering his build.

"That'll do it. I see it all the time in the clinic." He nodded regretfully. "Professional?"

"Almost." The disappointment looked unbearable.

"I'm sorry, James."

"I had just been signed to Leicester Tigers when I got the injury." I was no rugby fan, but even I'd heard of them. They had to be one of the top teams in England. "I was twenty-three. Worst part was, it wasn't even on the pitch. I tore the bastard during training." He looked at his knee in disgust. "That was it. Overnight. Career gone. I'll be twenty-eight next week, and I really just wanted to prove that after five years, my knee wasn't holding me back anymore."

I felt sorry for him. It must have been difficult to give up on his passion at such a young age. "Hey, give yourself a little bit of credit. You haven't left top of the group in days. You're in a lot better shape than me."

He laughed. "I love it. I started hiking a couple of years back. It was good for building strength in my leg again. I feel good after a hike. Nothing else gives me quite the high."

I smiled, knowing exactly what he meant.

"When I got injured, I lost everything. My career. Friends. Even my girlfriend."

"It just keeps getting worse for you." I made light of the situation, and I thought he appreciated that. "What happened?"

"We were together for three years when I got injured. This was the woman I thought I was going to marry. Once my career was over, she didn't feel the need to stick around. Took her, like, two weeks after we broke up for her to hook up with one of my teammates." I could feel my face scrunching up, not quite believing someone would do that. He smirked at my expression. "She was a real keeper. But I've done enough of these hiking trips to know my story isn't as bad as others."

"Is that right?"

"In my experience, people seemed to get into hiking for one reason or another."

I could feel myself tensing.

"Sometimes for health and fitness, but for others, it's an escape. A way to deal with something difficult in their life." It felt like he was hitting a sore point. He watched me for a moment, and I struggled to make eye contact. I felt vulnerable. "I feel like you are part of the latter. But hey..." He dusted himself off and slowly stood. "You don't have to tell me your story. I always found, though, that talking to a stranger on a hike can be pretty therapeutic."

He had me there. "It's a long story."

"We've got time. Especially going at my snail's pace." He started hobbling in the direction of where the group had gone. He got into a better rhythm of walking, and I kept my pace slow so as to not rush him.

"Maybe I'm just really into hiking, ever think of that?"

"That part is true, I'm sure of it," he said. "You're too smiley to not love this. But if you were really a big-time hiker, you'd be up there with Santino."

"I'm a beginner."

"Interesting, you're only recently into hiking?" He posed it as a question.

"Okay." I could already tell where his mind was going. "You should really consider going into detective work." He laughed, and I allowed myself to be candid with a stranger. It was only fair after what he'd shared. "I started hiking about a year ago. After I broke up with my girlfriend." And to cope with losing Dad, but I left that part out. I didn't want a stranger's pity.

"Sorry."

"It happened a while ago." Fifteen months, to be exact. But he didn't need to know that. "I'm over it now. But it took a while." He had a way of making me feel comfortable, which was probably what made me unleash it all. "I thought I'd found the one too. We lived together, and things were good with us. At least, I thought so." It hurt to think back to that time with Julie.

I had been so blindsided:

I had arrived home from work after a very long day. Julie was in the kitchen, and I could smell dinner. I was surprised it was almost nine. She usually would have eaten long ago and been getting ready for bed. She was a personal trainer, so she started work at six a.m.

"Hey, babe," I called, making my way into the kitchen.

The table was set, and fresh flowers were in the centre. The candle was a nice touch, and I felt overwhelmed by the gesture. We hadn't made time for each other all week. Because she was in bed pretty early, it was easy to feel like passing ships in the night, especially when I stayed behind in the evenings to deal with paperwork at the clinic. Not only that, Julie had grown a bit of a following on social media too. I never really bothered with Instagram and stuff like that, but even I knew she was making it big when people came up to us in the street.

She never wanted to be called an influencer. That wasn't her style at all. She was kind and shy at times. But she could certainly motivate me if it was needed. She also ran boot camp training on Saturday and Sundays. That sometimes made it a little difficult to squeeze time in for each other. Especially because I worked all week so weekends were my only downtime. It was nice that she was making the effort this evening. And on a random school night too.

"Hey," she said as I kissed her cheek. "Take a seat. I made chicken parmesan."

"My favourite."

"I know."

I felt touched. "Do you want some wine?"

"Eh." She seemed unsure. "Okay. I'll fetch it."

"No, allow me." It was the least I could do after her making my favourite meal and waiting up for me to come home and enjoy it with her. "I have a pinot grigio or a rioja, or I'm sure we have a—"

"Either is fine."

I found that a little unusual. While Julie was very into fitness, she also appreciated good food. We'd been on several food and wine tours in France and Spain. It was a real passion of hers, and I enjoyed learning about new cuisines and wine pairings. She'd gone to the effort of cooking my favourite meal, and that would have usually warranted the optimal wine pairing. I tried not to think too much into it.

I opened a bottle of white and poured two glasses. Julie had plated up dinner and placed them on the table when I arrived back. I took a seat beside her.

"Cheers." I held up my glass, and I didn't miss Julie's reluctance to tap her wineglass to mine. She did eventually and smiled, though I could tell it was put on.

"How was your day?" she asked almost immediately after taking a sip of wine.

"It was good, busy as usual. Especially because we have a GP and nurse off sick." She started eating, and I followed suit. "Oh, this is so good." I groaned, and she smiled, clearly happy I was enjoying it. "Amazing, babe. You're the best." Her smile disappeared almost instantly, and I couldn't help but feel a little on edge. "How was your day?"

"It was fine." Her voice sounded empty.

She talked a little through dinner. About the traffic on her way home and the weather, but it was definitely strained. I was only halfway through my meal when I started to feel the need to be worried.

"Is everything all right?"

She seemed to tense, and I knew something was wrong. "Let's just enjoy dinner, okay?"

"If something is wrong"—I put down my knife and fork, feeling a little too concerned to eat—"tell me."

"Okay." She sighed and put down her utensils. She looked pale. Maybe tired too, but I couldn't be sure because she wasn't giving eye contact. "I don't think this is working."

I was confused. My heart rate jumped in panic, but I'd hoped I'd heard her wrong. "What?"

"I'm sorry," she said, confirming that I'd heard her correctly.

"I don't understand."

"I don't think I want this anymore. This."

She wasn't being clear. Our relationship? Our life together? I was panicking, and perhaps she was being evasive to save my feelings, but I felt more confused. "Where did this come from?"

"I've been feeling this way for a while."

"Why didn't you say?" I felt embarrassed and ashamed that I hadn't seen it coming.

"I just…" She showed me a heartbreaking look, and I realised why she hadn't told me until now. "You were already going through such a hard time. With work and then…"

"Dad," I said and was overcome with emotion.

"I didn't want to hurt you any more than you were already hurting."

"So you stayed with me out of pity?" I could feel myself getting worked up.

"No." She sighed, but her inability to look me in the eye told me it was the truth, making me angry. "You were going through a super difficult time, and I thought with time, you'd—"

"I'm sorry it's taking me a long time to get over losing my dad."

"Niamh," she breathed out in shock. I ground my teeth, still feeling that anger. "What you've been going through…" She couldn't seem to form a sentence, making me look at her, and her expression revealed her heartbreak.

I felt bad for saying it. "Sorry, I shouldn't have…I just, I'm trying to understand."

"I care so much about you." But not love? She reached across for my hand and squeezed it tight. "You are an amazingly kind person. I wanted to be there for you when you needed me."

I thought back on the last seven years. After a series of chemo treatments, Dad had gone into remission. He was okay for a few years. Until he went in for a routine scan and they'd found out his cancer had come back and spread to his brain and lungs. He'd seemed to deteriorate overnight. He'd died six weeks later. That was last year. It was sudden. Horribly sudden. It was the worst thing that had ever happened to me. To my family. I didn't think I could ever smile or really be happy again. Not after losing him.

Julie had helped put me back together again. We'd only been together a year or so before we'd found out he was dying. Dad had really liked her. It had made me happy that he'd liked the woman I was dating. The woman I'd thought I would spend the rest of my life with. I had no idea it would go this way.

"You will find a woman who makes you incredibly happy, Niamh. One day, I promise." She squeezed my hand again.

"I want to make you happy, Jules."

"I'm sorry. I don't think I can." She seemed like her mind was made up, and that devastated me all the more. That I couldn't even try to change her mind. "I've tried, Niamh. For months. I don't want to hurt you. But I can't help how I feel." Her tears were falling, and I could feel the tears on my own cheeks.

"I'm not in love with you anymore."

"What else was there to say after that?" I shrugged, thinking back on that heartbreaking time in my life.

I hadn't realised when I was in it, but losing Dad had changed me. Indefinitely. I guessed that was what happened when someone lost a parent. They were never the same again. Julie didn't want to be with the new me, and I couldn't blame her, either. It was why I struggled to want to date right now. I had to be by myself to really cope with losing him. I felt as though I had been hiding from it in work and with Julie. Deep down, I thought Julie had done me a favour. I hadn't been happy in our relationship, either. I just hadn't wanted to lose anyone else. It hurt to think about any potential future relationships. They would never meet Dad. Perhaps that was why I had been holding on to my relationship with Julie too. He was such a huge part of my life. Sometimes, I still picked up the phone to call him, forgetting he was no longer here. I wondered how long I would do that.

"I'm sorry about your dad," James said. I hadn't thought I was going to tell him that, but he was right. Offloading to a stranger was therapeutic. Especially on this trail. On the last day of the trip that my dad had such fond memories of. It would have been a disservice to not remember him with someone, walking in his footsteps. "And about your girlfriend. For what it's worth, you'd be surprised the kind of peace you can find hiking."

"My dad always said that."

"He hiked too, huh?" I nodded. "It makes sense now. Hiking isn't about the ex-girlfriend at all," James said, and I didn't need to disagree with him. I knew hiking helped me feel close to him. "It can even heal your spirit, you know."

"I think it already has." I believed my words. "Or at least, started to." We rounded the corner and spotted the group waiting for us.

"Are you both okay?" Santino called out with a wave. We waved back, and he started directing the group down another set of stairs.

James let out a groan, making me chuckle. Talking with him, and indeed, this trip altogether, had given me perspective on my life. I needed to do this, travel alone again. To gain clarity. It had helped me readjust my priorities. I had been working a lot before the trip. It was only natural that burnout was starting to affect my personality. After things with Julie ended, I was forced to really grieve Dad. And I'd tried to avoid it.

I'd thrown myself into my work. I'd wanted to prove myself as one of the more senior GPs in the clinic. Turnover of clinicians had been ridiculous in recent years, but I was determined to make things better for the new GPs we'd taken on. That had meant a few late nights managing the day-to-day running of the practise. I knew I was making a difference in my community, and that was what had kept me going. It made Mum proud, and I know it would have made Dad proud as well. The last year, I had been sleepwalking through life, not really fully sure of the direction I was going. I'd neglected myself. It was like I had lost sight of the work-life balance.

This trip had come at a time when I really needed it. It had been years since I'd travelled around Australia. I was overdue an adventure. The location was intentional too. I wanted to know why Dad loved this hike so much. I thought I might have felt a bit lonely, but the group turned out to be pretty friendly. I had gained something different from each of my interactions with them all.

There was a couple from Germany who had children a little younger than me. They were interesting and had travelled all over. And then, a father and son from India, who'd kept to themselves mostly, but we'd managed to talk an entire afternoon about Harry Potter. I think they thought I was English. The group of twenty-something friends from the US had turned out to be really fun, especially in the pub after a day of hiking. And then, there was James, who filled me in on the way he'd changed his life after his career and relationship ended. He was now an engineer, working for some aerospace company. He'd rediscovered new passions and found a way to make his peace with what happened in his early twenties.

It left me inspired to want to do the same.

To move on as this new version of me. I had to thank my dad, wherever he was now.

"Just a few more steps."

"Really, though, Santino? Because that's what you said last time." The group let out a collective laugh. I was glad one of the American women voiced what I was thinking. Her friends looked pretty exhausted as well.

The last step from the mountain trail led us into the village of Monterosso al Mare. It was the last stop for the day and the trip. We said our good-byes, and the group dispersed once we made it down to the village centre. Santino offered to walk the German couple to the train station, as they were travelling back to Milan tonight. The father and son said they were staying in a B&B in the next village across, while the group of Americans were off to a hostel for the night.

"It was nice meeting you, Niamh," James said when it was just us left.

"You too, James. Are you staying here?"

"No, I'm headed to Genoa. I'm flying to Rome in the morning. Would you kill me if I said I had another hiking tour?" He grimaced, and I shook my head in disbelief. "If you're ever in Leeds, look me up, okay?"

"I will. And good luck, don't overdo that knee," I said, more serious.

"I'll go easy this time," he said and walked off in the opposite direction.

It left me with a couple of days to enjoy the sights before I was set to head home as well.

It felt like the perfect place to relax if the live music pouring from a couple of the bars was anything to go by. I'd booked into a nice hotel in the town, somewhere to relax and unwind. I had been passing out in hostels with the group for the last few days. I figured I deserved a little bit of luxury. Hotel Antonio was located on the edge of the beach, with a pool that almost looked like it could blend into the ocean. And it was exactly where I wanted to spend my afternoon, and the next few days, relaxing and thinking about what I wanted my life to look like from here on out. Besides, it gave me an opportunity to discover why Dad loved Cinque Terre so much. Maybe I would fall in love too.

CHAPTER TWENTY

HARRIET WHITAKER

*B*uona sera," the server greeted me as I walked through the glass doors.

"*Grazie.*" I gladly took one of the glasses of champagne and could feel my smile growing a little bigger. The server's intense eye contact piqued my interest. She was gorgeously Italian, and just like that, I was happy to be back.

I was no stranger to Cinque Terre. My uncle's villa was a frequent holiday destination, especially when Marco was throwing one of his wild summer parties. I'd visited countless times since I was a child. However, I couldn't really class this trip as one of those. Although, Marco's wedding was likely to get pretty wild. One hundred and fifty guests were flying in from across the globe, including my entire demonic family.

The anxiety of being trapped for a weekend of back-to-back events felt a tad excruciating. I'd had months to prepare for it. I should have really been more accepting. Regardless of the dread I'd been feeling, I was Marco's best woman. I couldn't bail on him. And I was happy for them. Marco and Bobby were probably one of the only reasons I was still a believer in love.

I moved to the feature table that had montages of them. It was over-the-top and borderline obnoxious. They loved selfies, so there were about one thousand pictures. I made an appearance in a few.

It made me smile. There was a couple of pictures from early on in their relationship. I looked young. It was before I'd cut my hair to shoulder length. While other pictures were from the stag party, which was definitely one of the messiest nights of my life. I recalled the Elton John concert we were at from a few years ago and a festival in Barcelona. They lived a good life.

They were so in love. Had been for seven years. Marco was outspoken, bold, and hilarious, while Bobby was more introverted. He grounded Marco in a way that was endearing, while Marco brought out the carefree side of him. Together, they seemed to complement each other in almost every way.

Even tonight.

I found them in the patio area of the hotel's restaurant in matching crushed velvet suits. The emerald green was stunning against the ocean view. I wondered if it was their intention to stand out there all night. It was the perfect backdrop. The entire venue was stunning. Of course, my uncle, Richard, had booked the entirety of the five-star hotel. Most of the wedding guests had arrived this afternoon, while the remaining stragglers would arrive before tomorrow's buffet. The wedding was on Saturday, so I had to make it through the next two days.

I dodged some of my relatives en route to the couple. Mama hadn't spotted me yet, so I was already winning.

"Hello." Marco's smile took over his expression. It looked like relief. He kissed my cheeks. "Where have you been? You're the best woman." It came out like a hiss.

"My flight was delayed." I pulled back and saw gritted teeth. "I texted you."

"My mother is getting on my tits."

"We're a little stressed," Bobby said as he pulled me into a hug.

"Well, you don't look it. You two look gorgeous." I could see Marco's agitation simmering, while Bobby looked flattered. "You're setting the standards high, fellas. How are you supposed to top these suits?"

Marco looked excited. "Not a word," Bobby threatened when it looked like Marco was about to spill the tea. I knew what he was wearing on the wedding day, but Bobby's outfit was still a surprise. "They only get better, trust me. Speaking of..." Bobby reached for my hand and caught me off guard by pulling me into a twirl. "You look incredible, Harriet."

I was mortified because when I finally stopped spinning, I realised a few guests were staring in this direction.

"You really do," Marco said.

I felt flattered. I'd been meticulous when shopping for this weekend, so it felt good that they'd noticed. I felt like I had to look good. I didn't want another reason for my entire extended family to gossip about me. After all, I was supposed to be the one to get married first. I was sure that me calling off my wedding was still the talk of most family parties. I knew it was something my parents were probably still ashamed of, even if it had been five years ago.

"I'm just trying to keep up with you two," I said, giving nothing away.

Something caught Bobby's attention over my shoulder. "She's here," he whispered to Marco. "Harriet, your date has just arrived."

"What?" I felt uncomfortable, but Bobby had disappeared. "I thought that was a joke," I barked at Marco.

Raquel was one of Bobby's friends from LA. He had done her makeup at many fashion shows over the years. They'd tried to set me up with her before when she was over for London Fashion Week, but I'd had a work emergency.

"Raquel is a model, Harriet, you could do a lot fucking worse."

"I don't need a date to the wedding."

"She was already invited, so we figured we would do a little matchmaking." Marco fussed with my hair, giving it a volume. "You're overdue a weekend of filthy lesbian debauchery."

"Marco—"

"I heard she's a freak in the sack."

"What?" I felt panicked. "I didn't sign up for—"

"Hello, Marco," Raquel said, coming out of nowhere with Bobby struggling to catch up.

She was striking. There was no other way to describe her. She was easily a foot taller than me, and I was sure I would get a crick in my neck just staring up at her. Her blond hair was in a high ponytail, revealing her unique complexion. She looked like a model, which I guessed was fitting.

"Thank you for coming," he said once they'd pulled apart.

"Thank you for inviting me." Her green eyes were hypnotic. "And what a beautiful place. I've never had the pleasure of visiting Cinque Terre." Her French-Canadian accent was a major turn-on. I could listen to it all day. "Harriet?" The way she said my name was sexy. "I've heard so much about you, but I must admit"—she titled her head suggestively—"Bobby did you a disservice. He didn't tell me just how beautiful you are."

Marco and Bobby shared a look, but I was too distracted by her to really dissect it.

"Thank you," I managed to get out. "It's nice to meet you, Raquel." I hoped the nervousness wasn't seeping into my voice. Holding her gaze made me feel that way. Her confidence was a little intense. "At long last."

"We have to speak to the catering manager," Marco spoke up, throwing an obvious look in Bobby's direction. "Excuse us."

I rolled my eyes, knowing that it was nonsense. Marco gave me a thumbs-up when Raquel wasn't looking.

"It seems we have been set up," Raquel joked.

"Definitely," I said, enjoying her smile. "But I'm not complaining."

She seemed to like my flirting. Perhaps Marco's meddling wasn't the worst idea in the world. "Can I buy you a drink?" she asked.

I drank the remainder of my champagne in one gulp. She looked pleased, and I let her lead us toward the bar inside.

I could see Mama and Dad talking with my uncle, and I deliberately twisted my body as I walked to avoid them seeing me. I couldn't run from them all weekend, but I could at least have another drink or two to make them less insufferable.

We ordered more champagne and found a quiet table. It was out of sight from most of my family as well, which filled me with relief. It was practically in the foyer, but I didn't mind. I wanted to get to know Raquel a little better, especially if the grooms were going to be pushing us together all weekend.

"So, Harriet, tell me about yourself. Bobby says you are a lawyer, but I'm afraid I don't know anything else," she said, taking a sip. Her lips pursed in anticipation for what I had to say.

"I am a civil rights solicitor." I took a sip too, needing something to quench my thirst. The way Raquel's eyes drank me in was a little unnerving. "What do you do?" I knew she was a model already, but I wanted to hear it from her.

"I am a model, actor, influencer." She laughed, waving her hand as if it didn't matter. "I do many things in order to fund my real passions in life."

"Such as?"

"I love to travel. I love to dance. I love art. I love women." Her eyes fell to my lips, and I had to admit, her words were provocative. They made me feel a lot. I struggled to hide how her words put me on edge. "I like sex too."

"Oh," was about all I could get out through an awkward laugh. She was intense. I felt like she was trying to evoke this kind of reaction.

"What?" She shimmied a little closer in her chair in a power move that did nothing to simmer my panic. "You don't like sex?"

"I do," I said, feeling flustered. "I just..."

"Don't like to talk about sex?"

"That's not it."

"Do I make you uncomfortable?"

"Is that what you want?"

She smiled in delight, and I was glad I was finally able to find a way to deflect the unnerving attention. "I like to have fun." She leaned back, seeming to dial back the intensity, which I was thankful for. "You seem like someone I could do that with."

"Maybe we could get to know each other a little better. Then, who knows?"

She raised a glass in cheers. A server placed a couple of tapas plates on our table. He had been doing the laps for a while. Raquel picked over a couple of olives. "Ask me anything."

I couldn't think of anything. I liked her. She was gorgeous and sexy. And I got the feeling that she was attracted to me. Well, that much was obvious. I was attracted to her too, but I needed to get to know someone a little better to feel a sexual attraction. I was never good at one-night stands for that reason. In fact, the one and only time I'd slept with someone on the first night we'd met was with Niamh. And considering I was having to spend the rest of the weekend in Raquel's presence, I didn't want to just jump into something. The last thing I wanted to do was to make it awkward for her or Bobby. They were friends, after all. Not to mention, the idea of my entire family watching us like hawks was enough to turn me off the idea of pursuing anything.

"How long have you been a model?"

"Since I was a child."

"You must have a lot of stories," I said, reaching for the bread and ripping a piece off and dipping it into some tapenade.

"Yes, the industry can be brutal. That's why I am doing more acting as I get older. They won't want me to walk down the runway with a cane," she joked, nibbling on the bruschetta.

"You're a while off that, surely."

"I'm twenty-eight in a few months."

"And that's too old to walk the catwalk?" I asked in confusion.

"Of course," she said, as if that was common knowledge. "How old are you?"

I almost felt a little bit of shame for some reason. "I'm thirty-four." I could hear my voice go quiet. I didn't bring up that it was my thirty-fifth birthday tomorrow.

"That doesn't bother me. I've been with older women."

I was a little offended. I didn't consider myself in the category of older women. I was young. I mean, my back hurt more these days, and the hangovers were pretty rough, but I was sure I could still keep up.

"Do you like being a lawyer?"

"Yeah, I do. I find it really fulfilling." I would have gone into more detail on the topic, but she didn't seem overly interested.

"How long have you been doing it?"

"Twelve years, it must be." I reached for the baguette again. "I started in corporate law for a while, but I like this line of work better."

"That's a long time. I would have probably gotten bored by now." She'd been modelling since she was a child, so I found that a little hypocritical.

"Not me," I said, feeling a little defiant.

"It's just, and I don't mean to offend you…" It felt like that was exactly what she was about to do. "Being a lawyer just sounds so… heteronormative." That was definitely not what I thought she was going to say. Perhaps something got lost in translation.

"Well, queer people need lawyers too, you know."

"Eh." She dismissed me as if I was boring her. "It just wouldn't be very expressive, I'd imagine." I could feel myself hardening to her. For a couple of reasons but I still wanted to give her a chance. For Bobby's sake. "What do you like to do outside of work?"

"I don't know." I grappled to think of anything as I ripped off a huge chunk of bread. "I like yoga. It's relaxing." She seemed bored by that. "And running, I like to run sometimes—"

At that moment, a woman ran past the window. I took a glance and spotted her tattoos. I'd seen them before. I'd stared at them all through dinner once. Without warning, I found myself standing and watching her run past.

And before I could even think, I was running to the exit. My heels were loud on the marble floors, and I could see people watching me in confusion. Raquel called out, but I couldn't stop myself. It felt like a magnet was pulling me outside.

Once on the street, I knew for certain it was Niamh. It was impossible. How could she be here? But it *was* her. I didn't see her face, but that didn't matter. She was jogging away from me, and I felt fear in a way I'd never felt before. Like I didn't have a choice but to go after her.

I started running.

"Niamh," I called out, but she had oversized headphones on. My heels were making it incredibly difficult to pick up speed. "Niamh!" She was getting farther ahead, and I felt that desperation take over my limbs. "Niamh, wait," I called out again, and I panicked, looking down. I was still holding half a baguette and did the first thing that came to mind. I threw it.

It struck her on the back of the head, and finally, she stopped.

I breathed out a sigh of relief. It took her a moment to turn and recognise me. I knew the moment she did because the most infectious smile spread over her face. She removed her headphones and stared at me in shock.

"Harriet? I can't believe—" She cut herself off as her eyes scanned down my front. "You look," she breathed out, speechless. Niamh looked incredible as well. She was in workout shorts and a tank top, leaving very little to the imagination. "Did you just throw a loaf of bread at me?" She laughed, picking it up.

"Hi," I said, trying to think of an explanation through my heavy breathing. "Yeah." I suddenly remembered my manners. "Sorry." I tilted my head as she closed the gap between us. She handed me back the baguette. "Thanks." Her eyes were soft, and her smile was incredible. Just the way I remembered her. And just like that, a surge of emotion erupted from within. I couldn't be sure what I was feeling exactly, but it felt good. "What are you doing here?"

"I'm…" She seemed a little unsure. "On holiday, I guess." I had so many questions, especially because it seemed like there was a bigger story there. "What are you…"

"I'm at a wedding."

Niamh shook her head as if still in disbelief.

I felt the exact same way. "Oh my God, Niamh." I hugged her, feeling like I needed to make sure she was really there.

"You don't want to come near me. I'm all sweaty." She seemed uncomfortable, so I kept it brief. Though, she really didn't need to apologise. "I can't believe we're running into each other like this. Or rather, you're running after me." I laughed. Same old Niamh. "What are the chances?" she said, shaking her head, and then something came over her, and she seemed to pull herself together. "I'm sorry, I must be keeping you back." She looked a little disappointed, gesturing to my dress.

"You're not," I said, feeling this pull to her. It felt like a once in a million chance to run into Niamh in 2018, and now, here she was. We'd lost contact twice in the last sixteen years. I wasn't about to let that happen again. "Hey, do you want to get a drink or coffee?" She smiled adorably. "Or anything really."

"Yeah. I'd really like that."

We started walking back toward the hotel, and I remembered. "Oh bullocks." I stopped at the entrance.

"What?"

"I'm kind of on a date."

"Oh," she said, showing a range of expressions. She looked surprised at first—perhaps she thought I was married—then, she transitioned in an awkwardness, followed by disappointment again. "That's cool, some other time. Maybe."

"Well…" I trailed off, feeling a little disheartened as well. Until the thought popped into my head. "Will you come in?"

"On your date?"

"No." I laughed. "Besides, I don't think I'm really into her. She's a bit intense." Niamh seemed happy at that. "It's Marco's wedding, and I'm kind of the best woman. I was supposed to bring a plus one, but my friend couldn't make it. You'd actually be doing me a massive favour."

"I don't know." She seemed hesitant. "I don't want to crash your cousin's wedding. It would be weird, right?"

"Technically, his wedding isn't for two days. This is just a bunch of people drinking. It's an open bar, if that helps." She seemed to come around to the idea. "I don't want to put you on the spot, though."

"You're not." She bit her lip, and without meaning to, I felt myself stare at her lips. "I'll come in."

"Really? I couldn't contain my excitement, and she seemed to mirror it.

"Let me go shower and change, okay."

"Where are you staying?"

"Just down the street there." She pointed, and I recognised Hotel Antonio. It was a nice hotel.

"Great, that'll give me a minute to explain to my date. I kinda just ran away."

"Well, if it helps, I'm really glad you did."

Niamh flashed me one more of her all-encompassing smiles, the kind that made my heart skip a beat, before she jogged off. I couldn't help but watch her go, feeling a swell in my stomach. It felt like butterflies. A feeling I hadn't felt to this degree in what seemed like years. Perhaps sixteen years, to be exact.

CHAPTER TWENTY-ONE
NIAMH DONNELLY

I jogged away from Harriet in a daze. I couldn't believe that she was in Cinque Terre. I hadn't thought about her in so long. She looked amazing. Her hair was shorter; it made her look more mature, and I really liked it. Her body was the same, though, and in that dress, I struggled to remember my own name. She always did look good in a floral dress. Of course I would have to run into Harriet again looking like a scruffy, sweaty mess. I would have to rectify the situation. I'd spotted a clothing store on my run earlier, and I ran straight back to it.

Thankfully, it was still open. It had a few designer labels, and everything looked quite expensive. However, I was desperate. The nicest thing I had was a pair of cargo trousers, and they were filthy after hiking for the last five days. I needed something half-decent.

I found a black cotton shirt. It was in the men's aisle, but that'd never stopped me before. The shop assistant helped me find a pair of grey trousers that went along nicely with it. Her English wasn't great, but my Italian was even worse. We got there in the end. I bought a belt and necklace to go along with it.

I didn't care about the price of it all. There was no way I was walking into that hotel looking like a bum. Especially not if Harriet's well-to-do family were going to be inside. I had to impress them. I wanted to impress Harriet.

I resisted the urge to get ahead of myself, however, the fact that she was on a date implied that she was single. I had to admit, I was relieved to learn that she wasn't married. While in the shower, I couldn't help but wonder what had happened with her and Beth. Were they divorced, or did it not even come to that? I found myself unable to think of anything else. I wondered about Harriet's life in general. Where did she live, was she happy? To be honest, I just wanted to catch up with her at this point. Even if we were just friends. She was this person who always managed to fill me with good feelings. Even for just a moment. I hoped that hadn't changed. Even if I had.

I checked myself over again in the mirror. I applied a little bit of makeup and put some product in my hair. I'd wiped down my Converse and was pleased with my outfit. The expensive clothes were soft on my skin and gave me a confident spring in my step as I walked into the Marque Hotel.

It was probably the best hotel in the village, perhaps in the entire Amalfi Coast region. I'd have said the wedding guests had booked out the entire venue. At least, it seemed that way when I arrived in the function room. There were at least one hundred people, if not more. They were all well-dressed, and I was thankful again that I'd bought a new outfit. I would have felt like a sore thumb in my hiking wardrobe.

Harriet was at the bar. I made my way over to her slowly, allowing myself to take her in again. She looked better than ever. She always did know how to dress, but it really felt like she'd gone the extra mile tonight. Her dress was yellow, with a subtle green floral pattern to it. It looked summery and hugged every inch of her body. Though, she could have been wearing a ratty old T-shirt, and I would have probably still been into it.

She spotted me before I made it there, and her face transformed into excitement. I felt an excited thrill wash over me again. She came to meet me, and I didn't miss the way her eyes scanned my outfit. She seemed to approve.

"You look good."

"Well." I shrugged. "I'm just trying to keep up."

She looked bashful, sweeping some stray hairs behind her hair. I liked that I could have this effect on her. Her shorter hair really suited her face.

"Some party."

"My family doesn't do anything on a small scale."

"Speaking of, how is your dear mama?"

She didn't miss my teasing. "If you're not careful, she will be straight over."

"I'm sure I can handle her."

"I know you can." It felt like she was flirting, and that made me a little hopeful. "Do you want a drink?" I gestured for her to lead the way to the bar. "I have been on the bubbles, mostly, but I'm feeling a cocktail."

"Me too," I said.

She snatched the menu, and we shared it. Being close to Harriet again made me feel a little breathless. I could smell her perfume, and it stirred something from within. It didn't help that she was stealing glances at me that I pretended not to notice.

"Know what you want?"

"No idea." She laughed. "Ideally, something with alcohol."

"It's just a pity they don't do Woo Woos."

"Oh my God, I haven't had one of those since Malia."

"Honestly, I haven't either," I said as the bartender arrived.

"Hey, do you know what a Woo Woo is?" she asked out of the blue, making me laugh. He looked baffled. "It's vodka, cranberry…"

I helped her out. "And peach schnapps."

"I can make that," he said.

"We will have two, and can you put some fresh mint and lime in as well?" He left us to prepare our drinks, and when I turned back to Harriet, she was throwing me this look. "It just gives it that bit of…"

"That bit of…" She took the piss, successfully humbling me. "As if you're some kind of expert mixologist."

"Hey, I learned a lot that summer." I kept her going, enjoying the way our banter returned so easily.

"Such as?"

"How to make ten Jägerbombs in about a minute."

"So a summer full of life lessons and skills, huh?"

"Well, you tell me, you were there." I had her a little speechless, and I would never tire of making her flustered.

"Yeah, same old Niamh. Flirting with anyone with a pulse."

"Ouch," I said jokingly, though it left a little sore point. I didn't want her to think that I was just flirting with her for the sake of it.

"And who is this?"

I turned to the sound of an unfamiliar voice. I felt a little panicked. After all, I had reason to be. I'd crashed a party.

Harriet smiled, looking to be enjoying seeing me sweat. "This is my cousin, Marco." She started the introductions. "And, Marco, this is my old friend from way back. Niamh." I didn't miss the way her voice deepened when she said my name. As if it held deeper meaning. Marco gave a double take at her. The smile on his face disappeared, and it was like he'd just been introduced to some kind of celebrity. I knew then that he'd heard of me before. I hoped only good things.

"As in..." He reached out his hand to me, but his eyes fell on Harriet. I wished I could have read between the lines. "Greek Niamh?"

"I'm not actually Greek."

"Well, duh," he teased. "So you're *her*?" Now, I was panicking. "I love a girl with an accent, but Harriet, you said nothing about that bone structure. I feel like I'm looking at the gay Kiera Knightly."

I felt embarrassed by the attention, while Harriet just rolled her eyes. He must have been like this with everyone "Me?" I was a pro at deflection. "Look at that suit. Emerald?" He posed for the attention. "You look incredible. Your husband should watch out."

"He's not my husband yet." That made me laugh.

"Though, the jury is still out on who rocks it better," Harriet added playfully. She nodded to somewhere in the distance. "Bobby has the height advantage." I followed her gaze and spotted him a mile off. He looked amazing as well.

"He is very handsome, good work," I said, and Marco smiled proudly before a teasing glint appeared.

"I mean, he will do for my first marriage."

I liked him. He was funny, and he seemed to pull out the best side of Harriet. I knew a lot about him from her. She'd always talked so highly of her cousin.

Thankfully, Harriet's parents didn't come to our side of the bar. That filled me with relief. I wondered if Pipa would recognise me. However, she'd seen more of a naked ass than my face, so that was probably why. I knew her a mile off. She hadn't changed. It was actually a little frightening how little she appeared to have aged. Pipa was an attractive woman, there was no denying that, but I knew what lurked underneath. I knew just how hard she was on Harriet, and I would be sure to be on guard around her.

Bobby joined us with a few friends. They were fabulously dressed and clearly from the queer community, which made me relax a little. Especially, when the venue was bursting with stuffy, rich, old folks. The Woo Woos were going down nicely, so nice, in fact, that Marco ordered a pitcher of it for the entire table.

I liked their friends. They were fun and welcoming. Frank seemed to orchestrate most of the conversations. He was a photographer from London, and his much younger husband, Austin, was a makeup artist. There was Raquel, who was a model, I thought. But she hadn't said much. I loved hearing stories about photoshoots and diva behaviours of famous actors and models. It felt like I was getting insight into a world I'd never seen.

The only downside was that I hadn't really gotten a chance to catch up with Harriet. I wondered if she felt that disappointment too.

"I'll get the drinks in." I got up and took the empty pitcher to the bar.

While waiting for the pitcher to be refilled, Raquel appeared next to me.

"I'm not so into the Woo Woos, as you call it."

Her accent touted that she could have been French. She stood next to me, and it felt like she was towering over me a bit. She was gorgeous. Her long blond hair was sleeked back into a high ponytail. Her eyes gave nothing away, though she had this penetrating stare that I'd witnessed a couple of times at the table. It was clear she didn't miss much.

"I get it. It's an acquired taste, a bit like myself." I poked fun.

"You and Harriet?" She launched straight in with no warning. It threw me. Perhaps she'd been watching me closely as well. I wondered if I was being that obvious.

"Yeah, we're old friends." I batted it off. I hadn't even had a serious conversation with Harriet, let alone told this random stranger our history. I didn't even know how to properly define us.

"Is that all?" She pressed again, causing me to stumble on my words.

"I've known her for a long time."

"That much is clear," she said ominously. "I would just like to know if she's fair game is all." Fair game seemed degrading to me. "I don't like wasting my time."

I could feel myself standing a little straighter. Unexpectedly so. I felt protective. And then, I glanced back over at the table and caught a glimpse of Harriet. She was laughing with her friends. She looked happy and free.

It was nice to see her that way, especially after the last time we'd seen each other in London. A person who was so fretful, distant, and closed-up. She was a completely different person. While I didn't want to diminish the feelings I still had for her, I also wasn't willing to show all my cards to Raquel, either. I just wanted the chance to get to know Harriet again in whatever capacity that was.

"We're not together," I repeated again, this time with more conviction.

"Good." The bartender arrived with a pitcher of Woo Woos. Raquel placed her order, and it didn't seem like she was keen to continue the conversation.

I returned to the table. I didn't care for Raquel. She seemed forward and a little curt, but who knew, maybe Harriet was into that. That made me feel a little deflated. Part of me wished I'd put up a bit of a fight. However, Harriet didn't belong to me, and she certainly didn't need me to fight for her. She could do that on her own.

"Next thing I know, this one had pushed his way into my toilet cubicle," Bobby teased Marco, resulting in him rolling his eyes. They were telling us how they'd met. It seemed like a story that Harriet had heard before, but I was enjoying it.

"Pervert," Frank goaded. "What if he was taking a dump?"

"That's what I was hoping." The entire table erupted into various sounds of repulsion. "I'm joking," Marco teased before sharing a sweet smile. "We shared the hottest kiss." Bobby's eyes darkened. "I'd have had him there and then, but not this one." Bobby looked away sweetly. "He asked for my number and insisted we go for dinner." I couldn't help but smile just watching them. "That was it. I just knew."

"After only one night? And you didn't even hook up?" Austin asked sceptical. "How could anyone know after only one night?"

I was transported back to the beach in Stalis, curled up on a sun lounger with Harriet. Waiting for the sunrise. It left me a little breathless. I looked to my left and was surprised that at the precise moment, Harriet's eyes snapped to mine as well. It was a silent connection that I just couldn't put into words. I wondered if she thought of me in that moment too. The look on her face told me she did.

I was distracted when Raquel arrived back at the table with a glass of champagne. She gestured to sit next to Harriet, annoying me. Raquel had her own seat across the table, and Harriet was on a small loveseat. Once she sat, they were practically touching. I didn't like the way she looked at Harriet. I also knew myself enough to know that it was from a place of jealousy.

"I love you." Bobby smiled sweetly at Marco. They shared a nice kiss.

They seemed so different and yet, completely matched. My relationships never really seemed to get to that level of connection. The way they just knew what the other was thinking from one look or a smile. It was like a secret language. I thought of Harriet again. And willed myself to stop. I was just torturing myself now. Being in her presence was making it really hard for me to use my head.

"To Marco and Bobby," Raquel said, lifting her glass into the air. We clinked our glasses and took a drink.

"Ever been married, Niamh?" Frank asked, and I could feel all eyes on me.

"No, I guess I never found the right woman." For some reason, I could feel Harriet's eyes on me, and it made me feel a little nervous.

"The weekend is still young," Marco said, and I didn't miss the way he glanced at Harriet. I felt awkward, especially when I knew Raquel was moving in. "And she's a doctor. That'll make any mama proud." Harriet choked on her drink, causing her to cough.

"Are you all right?" Raquel was straight in, taking the words from my mouth. Unfortunately, I didn't miss the way her hand landed on Harriet's knee.

"I'm fine," Harriet said before wiping down the front of her dress. "Shit." She had spilled some of the drink onto her lap, leaving a red stain. The Woo Woos probably weren't the safest drink when wearing a dress like that. "I need to clean this up." She was on her feet.

"I can help," Raquel said, and I felt my jaw clench.

"Thanks, I'll be back in a minute," Harriet said to the group.

"Let's go to my room. I have something that'll take that out," Raquel said, and she placed her arm around Harriet's waist, leading her back to the foyer. And no doubt back to her room.

Conversations continued, and I felt a little uncomfortable. I enjoyed the craic, but I couldn't help feeling like I didn't have a reason to be there without Harriet. I found myself watching for her. Waiting for her to return. It felt like time was dragging on. Every person that came from the foyer caused my heart to skip a beat and be filled with disappointment when it wasn't Harriet. I finished the rest of my drink and couldn't shake the desire to want to go back to my hotel.

"Niamh?" Marco broke me from a trance I was in. He was standing behind me, placing a hand on my shoulder. "You must see the view from the patio. Come, I'll show you." I did as I was told.

"The venue is stunning," I said, following him through the thinning crowds. It looked like the party might have been winding down a little. It was past ten. "Is this where the wedding is? Tomorrow is the big day, right?"

"The wedding is on Saturday." Two days from now. "And while this hotel is beautiful, we're getting married at my father's villa. It's fifteen minutes from here. The views of the ocean will be breathtaking in the photos. Besides, the villa is special to us." Marco turned thoughtful as we emerged onto the patio. It was quiet out there. Almost everyone was inside, but I liked the crisp air. The sunset was a thing of the past, but there were still streaks of pink and orange across the dark sky. "It's where I introduced Bobby to my family, and it's where I asked him to marry me. On separate occasions, obviously."

"That's sweet." We stared out at the view. "I can see why you chose this place."

"I love Cinque Terre. Harriet and I have been coming for years."

"I remember," I said, and without meaning to, I could feel my mood plummeting. Just thinking about Harriet being in Raquel's room.

"Your reputation precedes you, Niamh." That surprised me.

"Yours does too, Marco." I kept it light, despite hearing the tone change.

"Yeah, but we're not talking about me here, are we?" he said, turning serious. "Don't think she hasn't talked about you." I felt vulnerable. I laughed to detract from the overwhelming way I was feeling. "Over the years."

"I hope all good."

"It's a real coincidence that you're here." He eyed me cautiously. "Or is it fate?"

"I don't think I believe in fate." I could feel my scepticism emerging, but I felt like I could be open with him. He had that energy about him. "It's weird, though. I came to Italy on a hiking trip…and I run into her." I couldn't help but think of Dad, like with some weird twist of ghostly powers, he'd meddled. But I knew that was ridiculous.

"But then again, everything about you two is a little unusual. You never had an easy time, did you?" I found myself getting caught up listening to what he was saying. He was right. Our time was cut short in Greece, and in London, the timing hadn't been right at all. "You know, I don't think she ever really got over you."

That stirred something within me. I met his eyes and saw him look just as regretful. I thought about London, and the curiosity was killing me. "Marco, what happened with Beth?"

"Oh." He smirked. "Yeah, you're to blame for that too."

"What?"

"It seems every time you come into her life, you leave a pretty big impression."

"I don't mean to," I said, a little self-conscious. I didn't want to upset Harriet's life. "And it's not like she's the only one left feeling…confused."

"I get that." He nodded a couple of times. "Ever think that maybe it's time you stop leaving each other?"

"Hey," Harriet said, causing us both to spin around. She was coming out onto the patio. "Am I interrupting something?" She made light, but I didn't miss her shooting a stern warning at Marco. We probably both looked pretty guilty. It must have been obvious we were talking about her. I just hoped she didn't hear anything.

"Niamh was just telling me about her hiking trip."

"Hiking?" Harriet looked surprised. "You hike?"

"I do, actually."

Harriet threw Marco a look. "Right. I should get back to the table," Marco said when it was obvious that Harriet wanted me alone. It gave me a little hope.

"Did you get the stain out okay?" I asked once he was gone.

Harriet took a couple of steps closer. "Yeah. And when I came back to the table, you were gone."

"Marco wanted to show me the view." I shrugged, thinking back on my interactions with her friends. "You have some nice friends."

"Yeah, they're pretty great." I liked seeing her expression soften. "They really took me in after Beth and I broke up. I lost loads of my mates who were friends with her as well."

"That's shit." I had been there over the years. That was pretty commonplace in lesbian relationships. After Jules and I broke up, a couple of friends distanced themselves from me, choosing her in the breakup. "I've been there too."

"I was a little worried, you know." I didn't miss the way her voice dropped. "That you'd left."

"You should know by now, I wouldn't leave without saying good-bye."

"And is this…good-bye? Again?" Her face revealed a disappointment that I'd felt time and time again when I'd said good-bye to her.

"I'm in Cinque Terre for another day." She looked relieved at my answer. "I'm sure you have a million wedding things to do, but could I see you tomorrow?"

"I'd liked that. I feel like…" She took a step closer. That way, we were both leaning against the railing of the balcony. "I barely got to talk to you."

"Well, you were a little busy." I left the suggestion there. She rolled her eyes. "How was Raquel's room?"

"I wouldn't know. We went to the toilets in foyer." I nodded, unable to hide how happy that made me. "She's a little intense."

"Tell me about it. She cornered me at the bar."

"I saw." I didn't miss the hardening of her expression, almost like she was jealous. "She is attractive, I can see why you'd be… interested."

"No!" I could feel my eyes widening in outrage. "She's not interested in me. It was you she was after." Harriet looked indifferent. "She wanted to know if you were, what she called, fair game."

"Ugh, gross."

"Yeah, my thoughts exactly."

"Well, I'm not interested. I thought I'd made that clear when I ran out on our blind date."

"Oh." It all made sense. "You were on a date with Raquel before you ran out on her?"

She nodded slowly as her eyes softened. I enjoyed being on the receiving end of that look. "So what did you say to Raquel? When she asked about me?" Her hand was gently running up and down the railing. Getting dangerously close to my hand.

"I said"—I was filled with regret—"that we were just friends."

She nodded, and her hand stopped its movements.

I deliberately inched my hand closer until my index finger had touched hers. She inhaled sharply but stared intently at our hands.

"You still have it."

It took me a moment to realise what she meant. Until her fingers danced over my thumb ring. The ring from Hersonissos. I hadn't taken it off in years. Perhaps it was in an effort to remember her. But somewhere over the years, it had just became part of my personality. Though I'd never forgotten the day I'd gotten it.

"You always did have a way with beautiful things," she whispered.

Our hands were barely touching, and yet, I couldn't ignore the roller coaster of feelings inside. Her touch was delicate, but it felt like my hand was on fire. Her eyes finally found mine. There was a yearning I hadn't seen in so many years. I wanted to kiss her, and I felt like if I did, she wouldn't object. She licked her lips, and I took a step closer. She did too as our hands intertwined. The air around us felt heightened but familiar. I wanted to reach up and touch her face, but I didn't make it that far.

"Harriet?" a woman called, and I took a step back, turning my back to the intruder. That was how I felt about whoever it was.

"Yes, Mama." Harriet's voice sounded strained. She seemed just as frustrated. Of course that was who it was.

"I've been looking everywhere for you," Pipa scolded, barely registering my presence. "I need your help taking in my dress. You promised."

"Right, I forgot." She sighed in annoyance. "You go on up. I'll be two minutes."

"Don't take all day." Her tone left an icy discharge behind. Her obnoxious heels clicking on the marble floors disappeared, and I felt like it was safe to turn around again.

"She's a peach," I said, and Harriet laughed.

"She's something all right."

"Your mama just loves to interrupt us."

"Some things never change," she flirted, and her eyes softened. I felt like I could stay there all day just looking into her eyes. Like we did when we were kids. "Tomorrow?" I nodded, letting out a contented sigh I didn't know I was holding. "I've a buffet in the afternoon, but what about in the morning?"

"Sure, I'll come by about ten. You can show me around the place."

"Sounds perfect," Harriet said, before taking a step closer and pecking me on the cheek. "Good night…Levi." I felt my heart flutter.

"Until tomorrow, Jaq."

It was sweet and brief, but I couldn't wipe the smile from my face. My cheek felt tingly as she walked me out of the hotel and waved me off into the night.

CHAPTER TWENTY-TWO
HARRIET WHITAKER

Where's Niamh?" Marco asked as I sat down. He had already finished his breakfast and was enjoying a cappuccino with Bobby. They both looked to me expectantly, making me self-conscious.

"I'm not seeing her until ten." I said, and then the thought occurred to me. "Hold on, how do you know I'm seeing Niamh again?"

I hadn't run into Marco last night to tell him. After Niamh left, I went straight to Mama's room and spent about two hours squeezing her into her wedding outfit. It was fine before we started, but Mama said she hadn't been on a keto diet for nothing. Embarrassingly, she insisted the dress was skintight.

"What do you mean again? Didn't you two sleep together last night?" Bobby asked, mirroring Marco's confusion.

"What?" The volume of my voice caused them both to jerk back in their seats. "No." I felt my face flush. The thought of Niamh being in my bed was enough to do that.

"When I left you two on the patio, things seemed to be going well. You never came back. I just assumed."

"No, nothing like that," I said but couldn't contain the smile creeping onto my face. "Well, except..."

"Did you guys kiss?"

"No. Almost. We, uh…" I felt nervous just thinking about. The excitement in the pit of my belly was making it difficult for me to sit still. "We…she touched my hand." They looked bewildered. "For like a second." I heard myself and grimaced. They looked at me like I'd lost my mind. I guessed I had. I'd never gotten giddy over holding hands. "What is wrong with me?" I palmed my forehead.

Marco patted my arm sympathetically. "For what it's worth, she's so nice," Bobby said, and it felt good to get their opinion. I cared what they thought. "And cute."

"Hot is a better word for it," Marco chimed in. "But Bobby is right. She's also a decent human being. She's hot enough that she could be a dick, and she really isn't." I loved hearing the nice things they had to say about her. "And the best part is, she's totally into you."

"Do you think?" I could feel myself growing doubtful.

"Yes," they said in unison.

The feeling was mutual. Niamh seemed so confident and comfortable in her own skin. She was gorgeous. I mean she always had been, but there was something about her now. I loved her style as well. I mean, that outfit was enough to make me want to invite her upstairs the second I saw her. But it wasn't all surface level, either. I loved the way she talked so kindly to people. She just had a warmth and charm that never faded. I'd found it attractive, but having my closest friends pick up on it too made me happy.

"You should have seen her face when you left with Raquel," Bobby teased.

"It was like a little lost golden retriever." Marco chuckled, but I felt terrible for making her think I was interested in Raquel.

"Raquel wouldn't leave me alone in the bathroom. I actually needed to pee, but I was afraid she'd gotten ideas from how you two met."

Marco let out a belly laugh. "You thought she would want to join you in the cubicle?"

"Basically."

"You'll have to let her down gently," Bobby explained. It must have been from experience.

"I thought I had."

After running into Niamh on the street, I had gone back into the bar and found Raquel. I'd explained that I had run into an old friend. She'd accepted it pretty well, which was why I'd felt brave enough to say I wasn't really looking for anything romantic. I would rather catch up with family. She'd seemed to accept it. But maybe Niamh's presence had made her competitive.

"She will get the message when you're making out with Niamh at the buffet."

"As if." I batted him off before realising there was an invitation there. "Wait, she's invited this evening?"

"Your plus-one cancelled." Marco made out like it was obvious. "Bringing her would actually clear up a headache for us rearranging the seating plan."

"She can come to the wedding as well?" The seed of doubt set in then. "That's a little weird, don't you think?"

"Not any weirder than you running into her in Italy." Marco had a point, and it made it difficult for me to argue. I was relieved that Niamh had been invited. It meant that I wouldn't have to spend my days dodging my mother and Raquel. I might actually enjoy myself with her by my side. That was, if she was even interested. "Besides, what kind of cousin would I be if I didn't invite your future wife to my wedding?"

"You're getting way ahead of yourself," I said, brushing them off, refusing to even think about that. "I'm getting something to eat. Do you want anything?" I got up and grabbed my plate to go over to the breakfast table.

I sat with them a little longer after breakfast. They had a revolving door of guests taking a seat at our table. They didn't seem to mind when I excused myself to meet Niamh.

She was waiting for me in the foyer. She was wearing a slouchy T-shirt and had her jean shorts rolled up a little. I was glad I'd kept my outfit casual as well. I was wearing a pair of sandals and a beach dress. I had my bikini on underneath, just in case.

"Hi." Niamh smiled, and I loved the way her eyes scanned me from head-to-toe.

"Hey."

"How do you always look so"—I quirked a brow teasingly—"good." It felt like she wanted to say something more suggestive, but perhaps she didn't know where we stood. Especially sober.

"It's a beach dress, Niamh. You'd look just as good."

"No, I would look like a dude in a dress."

"Shut up, you're too pretty to be mistaken for a guy." She seemed to get a little embarrassed. I would have doubled down, but her eyes flashed to something over my shoulder.

"Shit, your ma is coming this way."

I didn't even turn around and instead launched myself into Niamh, dragging her outside with me.

"Can we outrun her?" she asked seriously once we'd made it outside. Perhaps she was a little afraid of Mama. I guessed I hadn't really said anything about Mama to make her think differently.

"I don't know, she does Pilates." I didn't slow my pace, and neither did Niamh. We were on the streets. The morning sunshine was lovely on my skin, but the heat was a little uncomfortable to be running.

"Let's head down to the beach."

"Yeah, she won't look for me there." I was out of breath by the time we reached the bottom of the stairs. I caught Niamh's relief, and it caused us both to laugh.

"I don't normally run from people's parents, you know."

I was struggling to get a breath through laughing.

"Are you okay? Do you need to take a seat?"

"No, it's okay. I'm not in great shape clearly. Unlike you." I'd noticed her calves coming down the steps. They were toned and muscly. Though Niamh had always had a good figure, it was clear she'd gotten more into fitness in recent years. "What got you into hiking anyway?" I asked, feeling as though this was a passion of Niamh's that I'd never seen coming.

"That's a long story." I would have pressed more, but her energy shifted in a way that told me to leave it. I knew there was more there, even if she didn't feel comfortable sharing. "Besides, there's bound to be a couple of things you need to fill me in on since we last spoke." She threw me an intrigued look.

"Oh yes," I played along, "like how I changed careers?"

"That, but I think there was something else a little more... scandalous."

"When I sold my apartment? Or how I called off my marriage? Where should I start?"

"The fiancée, I would say." Her tone dropped, showing her deep interest. "What happened with Beth? I mean, only if you feel comfortable."

"I do. Feel comfortable with you." I glanced over and witnessed the most adorable smile. I took a beat, thinking back on that time in my life. "We broke up years ago. Things weren't great for a while. It was just a few things that kind of added up over time." Even now, I couldn't pinpoint the exact demise. "I'd say me joining FD Solicitors didn't help."

"That's the civil rights solicitors, right?"

"You have a good memory." I was impressed.

"Well, it is impressive. And I knew you were torn on it, but I was secretly hoping you would take it. Despite being afraid of what *people* would think." I couldn't be sure if she was referring to my parents or Beth, perhaps both.

"I'm still there, actually."

"I'm happy to hear that. Well, assuming you're happy there."

"I love it," I said. Niamh looked a little proud. "It was the right thing to do. I actually have you to thank."

"What'd I do?"

"It was after I saw you in London. You convinced me to take it."

"I did?" She looked guilty, and it caused me to giggle.

"Yeah, here you were changing fields in your mid-twenties, and you reminded me that I wasn't stuck in my boring corporate job."

Niamh said very little, but I could tell she was happy for me.

Once we made it closer to the shoreline, I took off my sandals. Niamh followed suit, removing her shoes. "Well, I'm glad I could help a little. Especially if it was the right move."

"I love the work. It's heartbreaking, and the system frustrates me. I have bad days, truly terrible, but I am able to do some good." The water was warm, and I couldn't help but feel content. The tide pulled the sand into the ocean, and my feet dipped farther. We kept walking and talking.

"Just last week, I was able to reunite a family. My client was stuck in Rwanda. She'd been deported months ago because her visa had been revoked. Illegally. It was awful. She was living on the streets." It was nice to see that the weight of my work wasn't lost on her. "And now she's home in Wales with her kids. I just feel like I'm doing something good in a world that's full of bad. It's the best feeling in the world."

"It sounds incredible, Harriet."

"Well, look who I'm talking to, you save people's lives every day. Did you become a GP?"

"Yeah, I did," she said but put the focus back on me. "But what you're doing is life-changing too. I'm really happy for you." She looked out at the ocean whimsically. "Really, I am. Because the last time we saw each other..." She sighed almost tiredly. "I have to admit, I left feeling as though I didn't know you anymore."

"You didn't," I said and pursed my lips, feeling a little triggered. "I was a shadow of myself. I look back and wonder who that was in my twenties."

"What happened that made you change so much?"

"I don't even know. It happened over years. I thought I was just maturing or something." I thought carefully. "I'd felt like I wasn't myself for some time. It got worse after Beth, and I got engaged. The pressure and expectations of what marriage would mean... changed us. Changed her."

When I reflected on it, I thought Beth was listening too much to my parents. They had signed us both up to be some sort of 1950's household with me becoming a housewife and Beth being the breadwinner. I had nothing against people who came out of work to be with their children, but that wasn't what I wanted. My parents had never seen a same-sex family. They assumed it would follow traditional values, just like when I was young, and they hoped I would marry a rich man. It was toxic and sexist.

My parents weren't picture-perfect, not even now, but they'd come a long way. I didn't feel the same pressures to live my life to their liking, or perhaps, I didn't listen to what they had to say anymore. It had taken many years of enforcing boundaries, and my parents had quickly realised that they weren't responsible for me anymore. They didn't have to worry about someone taking care of me. I could take care of myself.

"I was disappearing every day. And compromising things in my relationship that I would never do now. I was afraid of losing someone like Beth." It still hurt. Just how much of myself I'd hidden away to be the perfect fiancée. The perfect daughter. "And then, after we had dinner and you said…" I breathed out, feeling vulnerable. "You said I was different." I met her eyes, and she looked ashamed. "It was like a wake-up call."

"I hope what I said wasn't the reason you and Beth broke up."

"It wasn't." I touched her arm when she couldn't meet my eyes. "Marco had noticed too. And when you'd said it, I felt like I couldn't ignore it." We kept walking. The town across the coast proved to be a good distraction, and I found my eyes were fixated on it. "We had this huge fight." I shook my head, unable to tell her that it had happened right after dinner with her. Beth hadn't come home for two days. I'd thought we were over, but she'd come around. "And then, we made up again, which in hindsight was probably a mistake. It just dragged things on longer than they needed to be, especially because things were never the same. She didn't agree with my career move, and while she tried to be supportive, I knew she would never be on board, not fully, at least." Not in the way I needed. "Our work schedules started to clash more, and it all just fell apart."

It was a mess. Even interacting with Beth's solicitor friends once I'd made the career change became torturous. They looked down on me. I could tell in the way they asked about my work. Almost like they didn't see it as a real challenge. I hated it, but what was worse was that I never felt that Beth had my back. I found myself losing patience when she showed little interest in my work, and because I was out of corporate law, I found her work tedious and so very unimportant compared to my cases. It drove a wedge between us.

"Even wedding planning was a constant battle. We couldn't seem to agree on anything." She wanted a big, over-the-top traditional wedding, and I wanted nothing more than to run away and elope. "Until one day, I called off the wedding. It was mutual by that stage, thankfully."

I think she'd fallen out of love before I did. She had actually become really cruel and difficult to be with in the end, but I didn't want to share that with Niamh. Beth was just so unhappy, and years later, she'd apologised for her behaviour. I think she wanted me to be the one to end things, especially when she still had to work closely with Dad. She was just as trapped as I was, and all because she was afraid of disappointing my parents too. It had been hard breaking the news to them. They were devastated. More than we were.

"We sold the apartment six months later and had a clean break back in 2021. We email sometimes. Our schedules are too complicated to actually meet in person." Not that I thought either of us really wanted that. Beth had been in a long-term relationship for years, and we were both mature enough to accept that we didn't need to be in each other's lives anymore.

"So it's been over for a while." Niamh seemed happy to hear that. "I am sorry that you had to go through it. Well." She laughed. "Actually, I'm not." A teasing smirk appeared, and I bumped my shoulder into hers. She returned the gesture, a lot softer this time, and I couldn't help the way my breathing changed when she lingered, her bare arm still touching mine, and I could feel the heat. It felt nice. "It makes me a little mad that I didn't give you my number back then."

"But we've never had each other's numbers, why start now?"

"No, I *will* be getting your phone number before I go home tomorrow."

I felt disappointed that she was leaving so soon, and she didn't miss it. I felt myself create a little distance, but I missed the contact with her arm.

"Or not." She looked ahead, and it felt a little awkward. "You know, if you didn't want to stay in touch."

"No," I said, the idea of no contact feeling like a huge mistake. "That's not why…" I sighed, feeling like I wasn't able to properly articulate what I was feeling. "I'm just not ready to say good-bye." She was stealing glances at me, and I felt nervous. But I'd learned that nothing good came from hiding my feelings. "I wish you were staying another few days." I couldn't help but look, and our eyes connected.

"I could," she said, and I could tell she felt vulnerable. "Stay. For a few more days. If that's what you want."

"Is that what you want?"

She blushed and shrugged. "You're the one with a wedding. I don't want to be in the way of that."

"Oh, did I forget to mention that you're invited to the wedding?"

"What? I am?" She looked confused but also happy and then, doubtful. "Wouldn't that be a little weird?"

"That's what I said."

"Right? Like, it's weird, no?"

"Marco said we would actually be doing him a favour, seeing as my plus-one cancelled."

"You had a plus-one?" There was a hint of jealousy.

"A friend from work." I didn't miss the glimpse of relief on her expression. "Don't worry."

"I wasn't worried."

"Are you?" I suddenly felt dread.

"Seeing someone? No." That made my chest swell. "I *was* seeing someone, but we broke up last year." I already knew that, but I wasn't brave enough to admit it.

I had been travelling to Belfast for a concert. It was the last tickets Marco could get for Elton John. It was in 2024. I'd decided I wanted to reach out while I was there. I'd dated casually but no one serious. I hadn't tried looking for Niamh on social media for years, but I'd discovered her full name when at dinner with Beth, making it a lot easier to find her on Instagram. Her account was private, giving very little away. I'd nearly messaged her until I became suspicious of the girl in her profile picture. After a little digging, I'd found out they were together. I couldn't remember her name, but she was gorgeous. Her profile was public. She was a fitness influencer or something to that effect, from what I could tell from her posts. I was crushed. Part of me thought of messaging her anyway, just to keep in touch, but I worried what that relationship would look like. Did I even want to be friends? Furthermore, the last thing I wanted was to get in the way of her relationship. Her surprise appearance in London had caused me to question a lot of things with Beth, and they looked really happy. I didn't want history repeating itself.

"I'm sorry, breakups are hard," I said. Everything in her body language told me it was a difficult time in her life. "I would know. Was it amicable, at least?"

"Yeah, I mean, after the initial shock. She ended things with me." Her entire carefree demeanour seemed to fade away. "Kind of out of the blue. She said I'd changed." There was a long pause, and I wondered if maybe she didn't want to share. It made me think I should fill the silent void. "After my dad...he passed away."

"Niamh." Her eyes were cast down, and I felt the need to reach for her hand. The electric shock rippled up my arm. Perhaps she felt it too because she came to a stop. "I'm so sorry."

Her expression revealed a pain that made me emotional. She allowed me to wrap my arms around her, and she wrapped hers around my waist. Her face rested on my shoulder, and I could feel her breathe deeply. Feeling her in my arms again felt magical, even though it was weighed down by such heartache. I didn't let go until she did.

"He was such a nice man," I said when I could meet her eyes again. Her head snapped up in surprise. "I mean, I know we only talked for like five minutes, but he was really lovely—"

"You talked to him." It wasn't a question, more of a realisation. "I forgot about that day." She looked almost breathless. "You met my dad." I nodded, not really understanding what was going through her mind. Like I'd just given her a vital piece of information. "I'm glad he got to meet you."

"Me too. Do you mind me asking what happened? I know he was in remission so…"

Niamh started walking again, though I could see the beach was coming to an end. "The cancer came back more aggressive."

"I'm really sorry."

"After losing someone important like that, it's hard not to change, you know?"

"I can only imagine."

"Some time went by, and Jules, my ex, she sat me down and explained she wasn't happy anymore."

"And after losing your dad?" I couldn't help the judgemental edge to my tone. I kind of hated her for leaving when Niamh really needed someone.

"She had to put up with a lot. I was a mess after Dad. And I will be forever grateful to her for taking care of me. And though she never said, I'm sure she stayed a lot longer than she wanted to because of Dad." Niamh would forever amaze me. She wouldn't talk poorly of Jules, which oddly, made me a little jealous. I couldn't fully pinpoint why. However, it also made me like Niamh more. She was always thinking highly of others, even the people who hurt her. I was positive that her compassion was her superpower.

We kept walking until we got to rocks, signalling the end of the beach. There was a staircase that led back up to the village.

"Mind if we go inside, grab a coffee or something?" Niamh rubbed the back of neck, glancing up at the sky.

"Yes, of course. I forgot you burn easily."

"I'm wearing sunscreen, it's just…"

"There's a really nice café I know." I was a little out of puff by the time we got to the top, but Niamh gave me a little tug, helping me up. I liked the way her hand found my waist and helped to steady me. I could feel a heat there long after her hand was gone.

"What time is the buffet later?"

"Three."

"Shit." Niamh looked a bit annoyed.

"Have you somewhere else to be?"

"No, it's not that. I just…" She looked awkward. "I need to go shopping. I have a rucksack full of hiking gear."

"Well, I can help with that. I know a few places."

"Nice places? I don't want you walking in with some kind of street rat."

"I'll make sure you look good. Not that it's hard."

Flirting with Niamh was effortless. It felt like we'd been doing it for years. We hadn't even kissed yet, and I still managed to feel safe and secure with her. I felt like I could talk to her about anything, and she would happily listen without judgement. I wondered if that was just a Niamh trait, or perhaps she saved it especially for me.

CHAPTER TWENTY-THREE
NIAMH DONNELLY

I felt nervous putting on my shirt. The linen fabric felt soft on my slightly burnt skin. I guessed, considering how much it cost, that was to be expected. The blue and white stripes were sharp, and I liked that it was fitted too, making it easy to tuck into my navy trousers. I'd bought a new pair of white leather trainers, but they were posh, some kind of Italian designer. Not just bog-standard tennis shoes.

My phone rang. It was Mum.

"Hey, love."

"Hey, Mum." I waved at her through the screen.

"Hold on, I can't see you." She brought the phone down closer, and I couldn't help but laugh. It was an unflattering angle for her as she fumbled with the glasses on her head. She must have pressed mute because all of a sudden, she was speaking, but nothing was coming out.

"I can't hear you, you're on mute, Mum." She stared back confused and continued talking. "Mum, you're on mute. I can't hear you."

There was a lot of fumbling, and at one stage, the screen went back. I was sure I'd lost her all together when, "Bloody new iPhone you lot got me, fucking useless—"

"You're back."

"Can you hear me now?"

"Yes, how are you?"

"I feel like I need a drink after that."

I smiled.

"Well, let me see the view." I brought her over to the window so that she got to see the sights. "It's beautiful, love." Mum was quiet for a moment. "Daddy was right." I didn't miss the sadness in her voice.

"You should have come along."

"Not without him." The sadness was there again. I nodded along, but that was actually why I thought travelling a little would be good for her. She'd been staying close to home a lot in recent years, afraid to venture too far on her own. Though I wouldn't say it out loud, it worried me. She seemed to pull herself out of it, her tone lightening. "Sure, you know I can barely find my way out of the car park. Besides me and hiking don't go together."

"I know that. Dad told us enough stories about it."

Mum had been the one to convince me to go. After running into Harriet, I was a little glad I'd done this by myself. Maybe Mum and Dad were both meddling.

"What's the food like?" Mum asked.

"Incredible, you'd love it. The pizza is to die for."

"Sounds amazing. I can't wait to hear all about it. You're home tomorrow, what time do you need collecting?"

"Actually…" I could feel myself clamming up.

Changing my flight to Monday morning had turned out to easy enough. I didn't want to leave. Not when I had this chance to reconnect with Harriet. I'd been feeling like I wanted to meet someone new again lately. I was finally over Jules. Who would have thought someone new would be someone old?

"What's wrong?" Her tone dropped in concern.

"Nothing, I'm just going to stay another couple of days."

"Why?"

"Can't a girl have a little privacy?"

"What is going on? You're making me worried, and I don't like to be worried. I knew you shouldn't have went on this trip all by yourself." She was spinning out of control. "I told Jenny it was a bad idea and now—"

"Mum, I'm fine. I just..." I trailed off and realised that it might actually be nice to get a little advice on the topic. It was a little unorthodox, after all. "I met someone."

"A woman?"

"No, a man. Yes, a woman."

"Is she a hiker too?"

"No, definitely not." I laughed thinking about just how out of breath Harriet was during our walk on the beach today.

"Is she Italian?"

"No."

"Thank God, I thought we were losing you to Cinco de Pear."

"Cinque Terre?" She waved me off. "No, she's not Italian. She's actually English."

"What is it with you and English girls?"

"Excuse me?" I said in outrage. "There was only one English girl."

"Yeah, and she broke your heart. Let's just hope this one doesn't do the same."

I was speechless for a moment. I couldn't believe she'd remember Harriet all these years later. I'd told her what had happened when I'd come home from Greece and then about running into her again in London. But I didn't think she'd retained the information after all this time.

"Well, actually." I couldn't resist laughing at how ridiculous it all sounded. "It's her. That English girl." I shook my head, unsure why I couldn't just say her name. For some reason, it made me nervous. "It's Harriet."

"What? She's there? In Cinque Whatever?"

"Yes. Oddly enough."

"That's weird, Niamh."

"Yeah," I mused to myself, taking in Mum's wry expression.

"You just ran into her on the street?"

"That's exactly where I ran into her." I laughed, still in shock myself.

"But I thought she was married?"

"Well, she was engaged. But she didn't go through with it. It's been over for years."

"Oh my goodness, that is wild. Where is she now?"

"She's staying in another hotel. She invited me to her cousin's wedding."

"Well, what are you wearing?" I rolled my eyes. "You have to go, love."

"Don't worry I am." I walked to the floor-length mirror in the corner and turned the camera to get a full view of my outfit. "Lovely, you look great. Is that a new shirt?"

"Yes." I could feel myself turning shy.

"Niamh, this is huge." I nodded, feeling the weight of it too. "I mean, this is the girl. The girl you fell in love with when you were eighteen."

"I know." I plonked onto the bed with a sigh. "Mum, what if this is a mistake? It's been sixteen years. I mean, people change. I have." I felt my stomach drop. Mum's face softened. "What if reconnecting destroys the memories of what we were?"

"Well, nobody is telling you to get down on one knee for her." I had to laugh. Perhaps I was getting carried away with myself. "And, love, if you're still talking about how special things were between you when you were eighteen, then maybe you never got over her."

My heart squeezed, and I found myself unable to slow my breathing. I was glad I was seated because I felt a little shaky. Maybe she was right.

"You'll never know for sure unless you just go for it. Niamh, don't hold back because you're afraid of losing someone else."

I could feel a stinging in my eyes. I immediately thought of Dad. I hadn't realised that I was holding back. But I had been. Especially if Mum even noticed.

"I know you're afraid of being vulnerable and opening up again, but this is one of those times where you'll only live to regret it."

I sighed. "I don't know."

"How many more times are you gonna get the chance to run into this girl?"

"You've got a point there." I smiled before clocking the time. "Shit, Mum, I'm going to be late."

"Then, go. Go, love. I love you."

"I love you too. And thanks, Mum."

"Bye." She gave one last smile before the screen went back.

I looked myself over in the mirror one last time, feeling a little unsure of myself. I was glad I'd talked to Mum. She was always a romantic, and it was nice that I had her support. My outfit fit well, and I felt good in my clothes before I left my room. Harriet kept saying I didn't need to go out and buy a whole new wardrobe, but considering how flawless she had been dressed last night, I feared I didn't have a choice. Besides, I was supposed to be her plus-one, and the last thing I wanted was to embarrass her. Especially in front of her entire extended family.

She'd told me that they came from money. However, arriving back at the Marque Hotel, I couldn't help check out the expensive cars rolling up. Sparkly convertibles accompanied by bulky SUVs with blackout windows. It made me question if royalty was invited to this buffet. One thing for sure, it wouldn't be sausage rolls and egg mayo sandwiches kind of event.

I decided to wait in the foyer for Harriet. That way, I didn't have to go into the party alone. It meant I could also scout out a few of the fancy guests arriving.

I could feel myself fussing with my hair as I waited. I was nervous again to see Harriet. Being with her today, felt like we'd always stayed in touch. Which I recognised as ridiculous. Harriet had a way of making me feel alive. I also felt like there were no limits to what I could share. Perhaps she felt the same. She'd divulged what had happened with her and Beth. As someone external, the collapse of their relationship seemed inevitable, whether or not she knew that. I was just grateful that she saw how much of her wonderful self she was compromising to be with Beth. Harriet was confident and self-assured once again, restoring the version of her that I'd fallen in love with all those years ago. Thankfully, she'd overcome that self-consciousness I'd hated seeing in London, and if that was because of something I'd said to her, then so be it. I wasn't about to feel bad, especially because of where I was now. Reconnecting with her in yet another freaky chance meeting. Mum was right. I had to go for it, or I'd have to live with regret for the rest of my life.

The stakes felt high. Being around her again felt like breathing fresh air. Something felt right in a way I couldn't describe. She had a way of making me feel safe enough to be vulnerable. I'd opened up about Jules and Dad, which was so unlike me. It didn't feel like I was oversharing but rather, catching up with an old friend.

Were we just old friends? I hoped not. Our unforgettable chemistry was there. I didn't think it had ever really gone away. I'd been looking for that kind of chemistry ever since I was eighteen. Obviously, I had been looking in all the wrong places with the wrong people.

The elevator doors opened, and she emerged. I found myself unable to look anywhere, and thankfully, she hadn't spotted me yet. Her mid-length dress was simple and elegant. The camisole straps revealed her tanned, toned arms. It was the colour of the dress that had me smiling. It was almost an exact match of the blue in my shirt. She'd been insistent when we were shopping that I should wear this shirt tonight. She'd said the colour looked great on me, and even I had to admit that it did, but I couldn't have imagined just how good it looked on her as well.

I got up from where I was seated, and her eyes found mine. She scanned my outfit, and I didn't miss the arched brow and the way she supressed a sexy smile. I liked being the one to evoke that kind of reaction.

"Wow," I breathed out when I was close enough for her to hear. "Now I see why you liked the shirt so much."

"Yeah, because you look hot." Her voice was deep and raspy, and she took a step closer in a power move that made me a little breathless.

"I meant…" I lost the ability to speak or look her in the eyes. Harriet seemed like she was loving every second of my fumbling. "Blue. You wanted us to match." I gestured to her dress but got distracted by the way it hugged her waist.

"It's called coordinating, Niamh." Her smile was captivating, and the red lipstick made her lips irresistible.

"Harriet." Her name being called from someone approaching rudely interrupted my staring.

I took a step back, allowing Harriet to greet the older couple.

"Hi, Greta, you look lovely." She kissed her cheek. "Uncle Malcolm." She greeted him in a similar fashion as the two stood back.

"Harriet, you look wonderful," Greta said and eyed me suspiciously. Malcolm was sizing me up as well.

Harriet didn't miss the need for introductions. "This is…" she stuttered. Perhaps unsure of how to introduce me.

"Dr. Niamh Donnelly." I reached out with a strong handshake that left him a little gobsmacked.

"A doctor." Greta smiled approvingly in Harriet's direction.

"It's a pleasure to meet you," I said as Greta pecked me on the cheek. English people loved to kiss strangers, for some weird reason. "That is a beautiful dress, Greta."

"Thank you, Niamh. Well, you look like a woman who can show me where the bar is."

I liked her. I put out my arm for her to link. Harriet rolled her eyes, clearly unimpressed that she wasn't the one on my arm anymore. I could hear Malcolm asking Harriet about me, but I stayed on target and directed Greta to the bar. I got a glass of white wine and took a healthy gulp as Harriet talked to her uncle and Greta.

"The big day is tomorrow, huh?" Greta said excitedly. "Do you know what the boys are wearing?"

"Which one is wearing the dress?" Malcolm joked in bad taste, and I was glad that Harriet didn't humour him. When I threw him a hard look as well, he seemed embarrassed. Good.

"Malcolm." Greta smacked him on the chest.

"I've been sworn to secrecy, but they will look amazing," Harriet said. "They always do."

That was true. We hadn't been over to see them yet, however, I had spotted them at the other side of the bar. Bobby was wearing a shiny suit that looked like it was almost made of metal. It was a little sparkly as well, which I loved. Marco was in a pinstripe tuxedo, looking equally as fabulous.

"Do you have to do a speech?"

"Yeah," Harriet said nervously. "But that'll be tomorrow at the dinner, so I've plenty of time to perfect it."

"Have you heard it?" Greta asked me.

"Actually, no." Harriet side-eyed me. "But I know she will be great." I shared a sweet smile with her. That swell in my chest was back again.

"Will you excuse us?" Harriert said to them. "Bridal party stuff." She shrugged as if it couldn't be helped, but I got the feeling that she just wanted me alone.

We were moving farther into the party before she said, "Excuse my uncle, he's a prick."

"I figured as much."

"Mama's brother. It's a genetic disease." She halted at a secluded raised table. I placed my drink down and leaned against the table. She took a drink of wine before placing it down and giving me her full attention. "Nice power move back there."

"I'm sorry?"

"Dr. Niamh Donnelly," she teased, but I saw the glint in her eye. She liked it.

"Hey, I have to charm them with something. I don't got money."

"Money is overrated."

"What a rich person thing to say." Harriet laughed a little harder, and I was glad she still had her ability to poke fun of herself. I scanned the room. "So give me a debrief. Who are all these people?"

"I only know, like, half of them. Well, you met Malcolm and his third wife, Greta. And probably soon-to-be ex-wife, according to Mama,"

"Really? Well, it doesn't surprise with the whole dress comment."

Harriet rolled her eyes in annoyance. "Over there"—she gestured to the family beside us—"is my uncle Richard and Aunt Ethel. Marco's parents. My other cousin, Tilly, Marco's sister, is there with her husband. They're really fun...*big* into partying. They might offer you coke, but they're cool. And then, over there…" She gestured further away. "Are the other partners at my dad's firm."

"Okay." I nodded. "Boring old white dudes, check. And fun family we like, check."

"Speaking of people we like, there are some people we most definitely don't like." Harriet gestured over my shoulder. "Don't look but it's the ladies from my Mama's bridge club." I was dying to check over my shoulder. "The doctor title they will eat up but not the NHS part."

"Arseholes." I didn't bother to look back.

"My thoughts exactly." She laughed, placing her hand on my arm. It sent a tingly sensation up my forearm, and I found myself transfixed on her hand.

I glanced up at her eyes, and she was just as entranced. I twisted my wrist so that I could touch her hand instead. It felt like the noises in the room faded away to nothing. Her thumb caressed my hand, telling me that it wasn't a step too far. When I looked up again, I found her eyes were pulling me closer.

"This is crazy." Harriet bit her lip but didn't look away.

"What is?"

"That you're here." She shook her head, but the intensity of her eyes made me feel like I was anchored to the floor, keeping me in this moment. "This." She squeezed my hand. "I don't know about you, but…it's like no time has passed."

"I feel it too," I said and felt bold enough to say more. "I feel the same way every time I see you." It felt like I was revealing a secret. Telling her that I wasn't over her the last time we'd seen each other. She nodded, and I saw a glassiness appear in her eyes.

"You gave nothing away. Last time." Her tone was low.

"Watching you with her was one of the hardest things I've ever had to do."

"Letting you walk away was…" She sighed, and I really felt the weight of what she was saying. "I didn't think I would ever see you again." It came out in a desperate whisper. I could feel my fingers tightening on her hand. She touched my ring and smiled. "I love that you still wear this."

"I went looking for it after London, and I haven't taken it off since." The look on her face felt like it was shifting mountains inside me. "This is crazy." I couldn't help but laugh, feeling overwhelmed by the connection growing between us. If I hadn't laughed, I might have gotten teary. "The effect you have on me…"

"Like it's all my fault." She leaned forward seductively.

"God, I really want to kiss you."

That left her speechless. Without missing a beat, she leaned forward and captured my lips. I inhaled sharply as I felt her hand curve around my neck, holding me in place. My heart rate felt wild, and my brain was thinking a million things, but I silenced all of it.

"Harriet."

I pulled back only to find Pipa standing right next to us. I shifted back on my heel to give Harriet a little space. She turned to her mum and couldn't seem to hide her frustration.

Pipa eyed me next, and I felt cold. It was clear she didn't approve. "A word."

I was transported back to Harriet's hotel room again. The last time she'd caught us. *Harriet, a word.* It echoed in my mind and sent a cold shiver down my spine. Pipa motioned for Harriet to follow, and I could sense her reluctance. Everything in my body was telling me not to let go of her. Maybe it was just the eighteen-year-old version of me wanting to do what I should have done back then.

"Not this time," I said, surprising Harriet.

Pipa narrowed her eyes at me, clearly disgruntled. At least, that was the feeling I got, though her facial expressions hadn't really moved. I could feel myself shaking, but I took ahold of Harriet's hand anyway.

"Let's get a drink." We turned our backs on her and walked away.

Panic immediately set in, and I regretted pulling Harriet away from her mum. I felt like I had a target on my back. I could sense the hatred, but part of me didn't really care. I could practically feel a laser beam coming from the Robot Mama who lacked feelings… and was, well, scary as fuck.

"I can't believe you just did that."

"Should we go back?" I could feel my feet stumble.

"No, she'll see it as weakness." Harriet giggled as we made it to the bar. "Where did that come from?" She faced me, looking exhilarated.

"I don't know." I shrugged, but I knew exactly where it had come from: the resurgence of feelings for Harriet that had seemed to never go away and in fact, were amplified in her presence again. She dipped her head, and her eyes softened. It made me brave. "I wasn't about to let her take you away from me again." She looked touched, and it made me plant a soft kiss on her lips. We pulled apart, and I rested my forehead to hers.

"You are going to have to meet her eventually." She pulled back and threw me a cute look. "You know that."

"Yeah," I said, as my head fell into my hands.

"It was sweet of you to stand up for me, though."

"Yo, Mama Bear is pissed." Marco came out of nowhere. I raised my head again to see him looking elated.

"She is?" Harriet looked over her shoulder, but she didn't look upset. She seemed to find the whole encounter funny. I, on the other hand, was a little concerned.

"She was asking me all about who your date was. I said, just a friend." He popped his hip for dramatic effect. "Because I ain't no tout. And then, there you were, just snogging. Right in the middle of the party. It's like three thirty, Harriet, people haven't even finished their first Pimm's. Talk about X-rated."

"Calm down, we weren't even snogging." She struggled to downplay our kissing. "There was barely any tongue."

"There was a little tongue," I said, causing Harriet to bite her lip seductively.

"Steam came out of Aunt Pipa's ears." Marco giggled.

"She'll get over it," Harriet said soothingly as her hand cupped my face. I must have looked regretful. "Trust me, she's only annoyed at me that I didn't tell her about you. That I was bringing a new date." Her thumb stroked my face, and I begrudgingly met her eyes. "Dad will get a few vodka martinis, and she will simmer down, I promise." The contact was soothing and helped to erase my concerns.

"You guys are so cute. I want to die." Marco clapped his hands in delight. "Come with me, we have a table at the back far, far away from family. You can dry hump each other all you want."

"Marco," she reprimanded.

It didn't sound half-bad to me. Harriet grabbed my hand and proudly walked me to the back of the room. I could see a lot of people double glancing in our direction, but as long as Harriet wasn't worried, then I shouldn't be. Right?

CHAPTER TWENTY-FOUR
HARRIET WHITAKER

I woke up and groaned as my alarm sounded.

6:30 a.m.

I wanted to roll over to go back to sleep, especially with my mild hangover. It didn't take much these days to give me one. My second alarm sounded at 6:35, and I mentally thanked myself for setting two. The hair stylist and makeup artist would be here soon. I decided to shower and allow the thoughts of last night to return to me.

Having Niamh on my arm all night had felt incredible. She was so charming and funny with my friends and family that I found myself captivated by her. And the way she'd stood up to Mama had made me *want* her there and then. I'd struggled to keep my hands off her all night. Toward the end of the night, I definitely wanted her upstairs in my room, but it was late, and I had an early start. Niamh didn't seem annoyed, either. Thankfully, morning me was glad we'd cooled it last night. I was feeling nervous, and I still needed to rehearse my speech before I started getting ready.

Because I had a suite, it made sense that everyone got ready in my room. Tilly arrived at my door with some breakfast pastries and coffees. Hair and makeup arrived close to seven, and then Mama and Greta showed up. Marco's mother, Ethel, was last to show. The buzz in my room was lovely, with everyone excited about the wedding. Well, except for Mama. She was being frosty. It was only a matter of time before—

"Harriet, who was the woman with you last night?" Ethel asked. "I only got introduced to her in the washroom after a couple of brandies. She was fascinating."

My face felt flush. That could have been because the stylist was using hot curlers on my hair, but still. I didn't think Niamh had been speaking to Ethel. Not that I was annoyed. However, I hadn't even glanced in Mama's direction to know she wasn't happy. We'd avoided my parents most of the night. Which in hindsight had only made matters worse.

"Yeah, that's Niamh." I kept it short.

"I didn't know you were seeing someone?" Ethel said innocently, making me tense. I opened my mouth in an attempt to downplay last night, but Mama got there first.

"She keeps a lot to herself." It wasn't even eight. My head was already sore enough without having to coddle Mama's feelings of being "left out."

"I met her too. She's lovely. And a doctor." Greta said, unaware that she was only making Mama more annoyed. It was no use.

"I wouldn't know." Mama struck another chord in me. "Nobody tells me anything around here."

"Mama." I'd had enough. "Excuse me, can I have a moment to speak to my mother?" I said to the hairstylist. I didn't really give her a choice. Mama looked affronted, but I refused to spend Marco's entire wedding walking on eggshells around her. "My bedroom, please."

She followed me into my room and took a seat on the armchair in the corner. "Where is *she* anyway?"

"She?"

"Well, I don't know what to call her." Mama let it all out in an angry breath. "It's not like I was even introduced. You obviously think so little of me that—"

"Naimh," I said calmly, which seemed to simmer her. "Her name is Niamh. And she is staying at another hotel in town." Mama rolled her eyes, and I decided to take a beat myself before this escalated any further. "I'm sorry I didn't tell you about her."

"Do you have any idea how embarrassing it was to find out from…" She lowered her voice. "Greta." Mama had never gotten on with her brother's wives, and considering his marriage was on the rocks with Greta, it must have hurt. Appearances mattered a lot to Mama, especially being in the know. "And Ethel too."

"I didn't know Niamh had met Ethel, I swear. You heard her, it was in the washroom."

"Well, still. Why didn't you tell me you were dating someone?"

"We're not dating."

"Harriet." Mama looked borderline disgusted. "I'm not blind, I saw you two…canoodling."

"Ew, no one says canoodling anymore, Mama."

"Okay, well. You two were very affectionate. It was the talk of the night. And did you hear the way she spoke to me?"

"She's protective."

"You only just met."

"Not exactly," I said, feeling a little awkward.

"Who is she?"

"She's someone from my past. She's…Niamh is…" I sighed, giving up. "She's the girl I met in Stalis."

"Oh." Mama breathed out, and I could see a million things going through her head. I wished she could join up the dots faster and save me from all of the humiliation. "The girl that you were—"

"Yes."

"But she had long hair."

"Well, that was sixteen years ago," I said, flabbergasted. "She cut her hair and got tattoos and went to university and became a successful doctor—"

"Your first love."

I was speechless. "I…what?" I felt like she could see through me, and I kind of hated it. "How did you know I was in love with her?" I thought back on the difficult patch in my life, but I'd never revealed that to my parents. I wouldn't give that up to them.

"Young love like that burns, Harriet." I didn't really understand, but her voice was full of compassion. That surprised me. "Are you together?"

"I don't know." She threw me an unconvinced look. "Really, I don't know. We just ran into each other. Out of the blue."

"In Italy?" she asked, still deep in thought, making me worried. Mama thinking never led to anything good.

"And we just kind of…something just started again. I don't know how to explain it." I felt vulnerable.

"You should follow your heart. You owe it to yourself."

"Really?" I asked, sceptical of this compassionate imposter across the room from me.

"You haven't dated in so long." There was my mother, criticising me. "I was about to give up hope of you meeting someone new."

"Okay, it's not been that long." But her words made me think. "Niamh isn't new, anyway."

"Like I said, young love burns."

"What does that even mean?"

"You know I met your father when we were sixteen." I nodded, having heard this story before, but not sure of the importance of it now. "Did you know I was forbidden to see him?" She smirked mischievously. This was the part I'd never heard before, and I found myself so shocked that I needed to take a seat on the bed. "Your grandpa told me his family was no good. They weren't old money like we were. I was to stay away and meet someone my father approved of. But I never stopping loving him, and once I turned eighteen, I agreed to marry Philip. My father could do nothing."

It made sense why my mother would keep this vital piece of the story from me. After all, she'd always instilled a sense of loyalty to my parents. If I were to know that she disobeyed her own dad, it would undermine everything she wanted from me.

"I realised I had become my father the day I took you home from Greece." She revealed a pained expression I wasn't expecting. "You were heartbroken." My chest ached in a way that it hadn't done in years. I could feel the tears filling in my eyes. "I know you like to think the worst of me, Harriet, but I know when my daughter is heartbroken, and I hated that it was because of me." Her head dipped, ashamed. It was a side of her I'd rarely seen. "I couldn't get past my own hopes for your future so I took you away from someone who meant a great deal to you. Your first love. I was worse than my father."

"Mama." I moved closer and knelt in front of her.

"I am proud of you, Harriet, in case that was ever unclear." It had always been unclear. I couldn't understand where this was all coming from. Perhaps she just wanted to make up for past mistakes. "I'm proud of the woman you've become. You're so much braver than I ever was." I felt touched and confused about where this had all come from. "You've always suited yourself and done what's best for you. That takes courage. And if I'm honest, I think Niamh has a lot to answer for. She's the woman who changed you."

She did change me, but I never realised until now. She was my first sexual experience. The first woman to show me love. I thought back to London. How she'd helped me change the course of my life when it was going down such a dark path. Niamh was always there, helping to navigate my life. And in recent years, I learned that no one else was responsible for my happiness. Not my relationships, parents, or friends. I had done a lot of work to realise that it was me.

"You look happy."

"I am," I said. "But not entirely because of her."

Mama looked proud and pulled me into a hug. "Then I'm happy," she whispered and pulled back. I helped her up from her seat, and we made our way back into the living room. "I still want to meet her. A proper introduction, Harriet."

"You will, today."

"Good. She's Irish, then?"

"Yep."

"I guess not everyone is perfect." I scoffed. "She's a good-looking girl. That bone structure." It made me happy that I had Mama's approval, not that I needed it. "Think of the babies she'd make."

"Mama." I rolled my eyes, hoping that she was joking.

Chapter Twenty-five
Niamh Donnelly

The trail of mini buses pulled up outside a mansion on the bay. The gasps of the wedding guests made me feel like I wasn't the only one gobsmacked. It had been a long and windy road to get to the location. I was travelling alone, which didn't really bother me all that much. Harriet had texted this morning that she'd arrived earlier to get set up with Marco.

I got off the bus and was welcomed by the cool breeze rolling over the water. It was warm and pleasant. Turquoise waters glistened, clear enough to see the shadowy stones at the bottom. It looked like paradise. Stone statues lined the cobbled path to the entrance of the mansion. Large doors stretched over two stories, making them look as though they weighed a ton. I wondered how they closed them up at night.

Inside, it was cool and bright. The marble floors were shiny and stretched to the curved staircase. Upstairs looked out-of-bounds, and I followed the rest of the guests to the patio area. Servers greeted me with a tray of champagne. I gladly took one. I couldn't help but feel like some kind of celebrity. I could get used to this sort of treatment. I scanned the outside area that was filled with excitement. The staff were placing Chiavari chairs on the lawn while others were arranging the floral decorations. The ceremony would be held with the perfect backdrop. Beautiful mountains enclosing the water. I had to put on my sunglasses again to avoid the glare.

I spotted Frank and Austin and decided to join them outside. They must have been on one of the earlier buses. They were dressed in matching tuxedos, looking like the coolest couple in the place. Well, probably until the grooms arrived.

Austin was the first to see me. "You look gorgeous, Niamh." Frank seemed to approve as well.

I had to admit, I felt as though my outfit was a little revealing, I would never have chosen something like this for myself. But Harriet had been insistent. She'd helped me pick it out yesterday. I was wearing tapered, cream, tuxedo trousers with a matching waistcoat. The manikin in the shop had been wearing a white blouse underneath the waistcoat, but Harriet had opted to remove it. I'd enjoyed seeing her drink in my exposed skin when I'd tried it on. It had looked as though she'd wanted to reach out and touch, and I had been a little disappointed that she hadn't. Perhaps today would be different. Especially after how heated things had gotten between us last night. I would have gone back to her room last night, though I wouldn't have wanted to detract from her focus on today.

"Have you seen Harriet?" Frank asked.

"Not yet." I heard the nervous quiver in my voice.

"She looks *really* good," Austin said. I felt an odd disappointment settle over me. I hadn't expected him to have gotten to see her before me. "She's upstairs with Marco. If he's anything like Bobby, he will need all the help he can get."

"Have you seen Bobby?"

"I was helping him get ready all morning at the hotel," he explained, making me relax a little. I hadn't realised I was so nervous about seeing Harriet. I'd never seen her in formal wear, and I just hoped she liked how I looked too. "We arrived about an hour ago."

"They're both here? Hopefully, they don't run into each other," I said, causing Frank to laugh.

"This place is four thousand square feet. If you don't stay close to us, we will lose you too."

"He's in the east wing, and Marco is in the west wing," Austin explained.

I glanced at the building towering over us. I felt like I could finally grasp the level of wealth in Harriet's family. It was a little intimidating. I was just glad that she never exhibited any signs of being wealth obsessed. In fact, she was the opposite. Why else would she be so fulfilled working in a not-for-profit company? I admired her determination to not be defined by her family's power and wealth.

"He's a mess."

"Bobby is?" I asked, a little surprised, taking a sip of champagne.

"Hasn't stopped crying all morning," Frank added. "Wedding nerves. It's a big deal for Bobby, especially because his father arrived last night."

"There was an emotional reunion, that's for sure," Austin said. "Flew all the way from Nigeria. They didn't think he would come at all."

I asked what seemed obvious. "Bobby's dad isn't okay with him?"

"I think it was the wider family in Nigeria that wasn't okay," Frank said.

"I'm glad he came around," Austin said, and I knew from their interactions last night that Austin and Bobby would be close to each other. "For Bobby's sake."

A bell rung out, and a ceremony announcement was made. We were told to make our way to our seats, creating an excited buzz.

"That's my cue." Austin grinned excitedly. "Wish me good luck."

"Good luck," I said, and Frank gave Austin a kiss. I heard them whisper, "I love you," making me smile to myself.

People dashed to the toilets, others ordered another quick drink, and it was a little bit chaotic. It made me relieved that I had Frank to lead the way. Austin and he were good people, and it made me happy that Harriet had them in her life. We followed the string of guests to the lawn where the ceremony was about to take place.

Raquel and a couple of other friends had saved us seats at the end of the row. We were near the back, as family seemed to have nabbed the top few rows. That didn't bother me all that much. It meant I would have the perfect view of the grooms walking down the aisle. And Harriet, of course. I felt nervous and excited to see her. It wasn't something I ever thought I'd get to see.

The last wedding I had gone to was for my brother, Oisin, and because I was part of the groom's party, I'd had to stand at the altar. We'd waited ages for my sister-in-law to arrive; it wouldn't have been so bad if it wasn't in a drafty old church in January. This wedding was definitely more relaxed. I had a seat, with zero responsibilities, and hello, I was at a gorgeous mansion in Italy.

The string quartet started playing, and the crowd stood, as if knowing exactly what to do. The aisle stretched back, giving it a lengthy walkway all the way into the house. Sheer curtains had been trapped, hiding the wedding party from our view. After a moment, I saw Austin emerge first. He walked down the aisle confidently, even blowing a kiss to Frank as he passed. There was another groomsman who walked ahead, Bobby's brother, if the striking resemblance was anything to go by. Next, an older man appeared in a brightly coloured shirt and beige trousers. He would have looked a little underdressed if I didn't hear the buzz from some of the other guests. He must have been important. He stood back and welcomed Bobby into the light, resulting in a sea of gasps.

Bobby was styled in a white African dashiki suit with golden embroidery. He looked so handsome and happy standing next to the older man. That was when I realised who the gentleman was. His dad linked his arm and proudly walked him down the aisle. I could feel myself growing emotional watching them walk down the aisle together. I certainly wasn't the only one. Raquel and Frank were both crying next to me.

Marco's sister arrived next, Tilly. She dazzled in a black cocktail dress that flowed with each step. She was carrying a large floral bouquet that tied in with the accessories used in her updo. I didn't catch her entire walk to the top of the altar because Harriet stepped out next.

The air in my lungs seemed to evaporate. Her eyes were cast down as she started the long walk. I could tell she was nervous, but she really didn't need to be. She seemed to be moving in slow-motion, or perhaps that was just my brain unable to process how breathtaking she looked. Her hair was styled in simple waves, with a diamond broach clipping back a couple of strays. Her black V-neck gown seemed lightweight, allowing it to glide effortlessly with each step she took. It was different from Tilly's, but she looked radiant. She looked up and smiled welcomingly to the guests, but her eyes were searching. Almost frantically jumping between people. I couldn't contain what happened to my heartbeat when her eyes connected with mine. Her smile shifted from pleasant to something that seemed more content. I couldn't look away, and I didn't want to. I watched her all the way until she was at the top of the altar. Once there, she found me straightaway, and I didn't miss the glimmer in her eyes.

When Marco stepped out, people were struggling to compose themselves. Especially Bobby. I could hear him crying from the altar. People were incredibly emotional, which was endearing. Marco wore a simple black tuxedo that was bound to be designer. It might have been a little too simple for him if I'd not spotted the sparkly bow tie that also matched a pair of fabulous, golden glitter, pointed-toe laced shoes. Marco's father, Richard, walked him down the aisle, and I could look at nothing but the grin on Marco's face. He looked overjoyed. This was the best day of his life, that was obvious. The grooms held hands when Marco reached the top. I watched as they giggled and brushed away each other's tears.

The ceremony was beautiful and told the story of their lives. There was laughter and tender moments. I kept sneaking glances at Harriet, and occasionally, I caught her looking in my direction. I loved the way it made my heart dance. It didn't drag on long, though, which made me glad because church weddings were notoriously long-winded. The couple exchanged their vows and rings and sealed their love with a kiss.

The guests were on their feet again and cheering.

"What a ceremony," Frank said to me when it was our turn to join the queues of guests making their way back to the mansion.

"Bobby and Marco look amazing," Raquel added. "Everyone does," she said, and I didn't miss the way she threw me a flirtatious wink.

Given the way Harriet and I had struggled to keep our hands off each other last night, Raquel couldn't have missed it. She must have known we're together, and yet, it seemed like she was flirting with me. I felt like I needed to clear the air.

"They're off to get photos done, but they should be back in a little while," Frank explained hurriedly as we approached the bar. "I need the loo. Grab a table, will you? And a bottle of champagne," he said, disappearing.

I was a little disappointed I wouldn't get to see Harriet for a while yet, but at the same time, I understood. Being part of Oisin's groom's party had come with a lot of responsibilities. It had made it really tough to even enjoy the party.

It was just me and Raquel left.

"What are you drinking?" she asked in a seductive tone that I didn't miss.

"Champagne?"

"My kind of woman." She oozed charisma, and I felt even more awkward. Perhaps she hadn't caught on that Harriet and I were a thing. She requested a bottle of champagne from the bartender and then, her eyes were undressing me. "Some wedding, huh?"

"Yeah, it's a special day. How long have you known the guys?"

"I've worked on loads of projects with Frank and Austin. We kind of just stayed in touch."

The bartender passed us an ice bucket with champagne. It was an open bar, so no need to get out my card. Raquel grabbed several glasses, and we found a standing table to set down the drinks. It was loud and crowded, but the air-con was lovely.

"I'm surprised you came to the wedding. Didn't you just meet them?"

"Yeah." I laughed awkwardly. It was a blunt question. "Harriet's plus-one bailed, and she asked me to come along. I'm really enjoying myself."

"Me too, and what an excellent opportunity for us to get to know each other better." I choked on the champagne. "I hope I'm not making you nervous." More like uncomfortable.

"Not at all," I lied.

"I love your suit, Niamh, it's very sexy." She reached out and boldly stroked my shoulder. I could feel myself tensing afterward. "Who's it by?"

"I'm not sure. I bought it in town."

"I love Italian fashion, it is so…androgynous," she said, and I could tell she was flirting. "Anyone ever tell you, you wear a suit better than a man?"

"No," I said, feeling a little confused. Was that supposed to be a compliment?

"You do." Her eyes trailed down my front, making me even more uncomfortable. "Your body is masculine, but yet, your face is feminine. Ever thought of modelling?"

"No, modelling is definitely not my thing." I shut her down. I wanted to be clear that I wasn't interested. I didn't want to be rude since this was one of Harriet's friends. Maybe. "Sorry, Raquel. I think we've gotten off on the wrong foot." She stared at me blankly. "When we met the other night, you asked about me about Harriet." She nodded, as if recalling the conversation. "I should have been more honest with you. And probably myself." I laughed. "I'm very much interested in Harriet. We have a history and having reconnected, a lot of those old feelings have been stirred up again. I hope you understand."

"Well, that much was clear," she said. I laughed, feeling relieved that we were finally on the same page. "You two were very obvious last night." I laughed again, feeling myself blush. "You are both beautiful women. I guess I was just a little…jealous." That took a strange turn. "Perhaps we could all enjoy each other's company." She left the suggestion there.

"I don't think so."

"You can't blame me for trying." She held up her glass in cheers, and I felt relief. Frank arrived back at that precise moment.

I had done threesomes in the past, but for my first time reconnecting with Harriet, I certainly didn't want an intruder. The topic didn't come up again, and thankfully, with Frank in our company, she didn't circle back to it. I just found myself feeling impatient waiting on Harriet to return again.

Chapter Twenty-six
Harriet Whitaker

I had escaped the photographer on the strict instruction that I had to be back in eight minutes. Not ten, eight minutes. Enough time to see Niamh and maybe use the toilet really quick. The photographer was very strict, and I was afraid to piss him off. He had been regimented all morning.

The photoshoot of us getting ready had been tiresome. Marco had to pose with everyone while pretending to get dressed. There were multiple angles and different backdrops. My face was exhausted from smiling by the end of it, and it wasn't even noon yet.

The ceremony was beautiful, exactly how I would have imagined. Marco wanted it to be relaxed and full of love. Those were the instructions to the celebrant, and she'd delivered. I could barely keep it together half the time. Having Niamh there made it even more special. I wanted to share it with her. Marco was my family, my best friend, and watching him marry the man of his dreams made me eternally proud. This was the first day of the rest of their lives together. It was full of possibilities and excitement. It also made me realise just how much I wanted Niamh to be a part of my future. A scary thought but one I couldn't ignore.

We hadn't discussed what would happened between us after the wedding. I had no idea where she stood, but I knew in my heart that I didn't want to say good-bye to her again.

I ran from the waterfront all the way back to the villa. I was out of breath when I reached the lounge where the temporary bar had been set up. It was crowded and a little chaotic, but I wanted to see Niamh. I felt like I needed to see her. I'd invited her to Marco's wedding and left her alone. I hadn't even gotten to speak to her yet. I felt terrible for having been so caught up in wedding stuff. Hopefully, she understood.

The air-con in the bar was glorious, and I felt myself breathe what felt like fresh air. I was frantically searching for Niamh, but it was made really difficult by family members and guests trying to approach me. I tried my best to dodge everyone until I spotted her. Actually, I saw Raquel first. They were alone at a tall bench, though I could only see the back of Niamh. God, she looked so hot in that suit. I was closing in on them when I was overcome by a wary feeling. It caused me to slow in my tracks. I couldn't hear what was being said, but it was clear by Raquel's body language that she was flirting. Her hand reached over and stroked Niamh's bare shoulder, and I couldn't contain the crushing sensation in my chest. It made my feet feel heavy, making me unable to move any closer. Niamh leaned on her elbow and said something to Raquel that resulted in them both laughing. I felt the pulsating in my chest amplify; it made me feel sick.

I didn't want to see any more, and my time was almost up. I used the washroom, feeling as though I needed a moment to grasp what I had just witnessed. It looked like they were flirting. I didn't really have a right to be jealous. Niamh didn't belong to me, even though it felt like she did. We weren't together. However, at the same time, she was my date, so it was a little shitty of her to be flirting with someone else.

It was hard to sieve through my feelings, and therefore, I didn't. I went back outside again and found the rest of the wedding party. I smiled for the camera and swallowed the chopping feelings inside.

It was time for the couple of get their photos taken, and they were whisked off to the vineyard next door. The heat had become unbearable. Even Tilly's shoulders were starting to burn. Austin's nose had reddened as well, making him look a little ridiculous because he was usually so fair. We headed back inside to the bar where the air-con surrounded me again, and I felt a little less drained.

The idea of seeing Niamh left me with mixed emotions, especially after seeing her and Raquel together. It left a sour taste in my mouth. When I arrived at the table, Niamh wasn't there. Neither was Raquel. The churning in my stomach started again.

"Champagne, Harriet?" Frank said, somehow right next to me. He was already pouring me a glass.

"Sure, I am in desperate need of hydration," I said sarcastically. "Bubbles will just have to do."

"They're good bubbles. You look gorgeous."

"Almost as good as you." He clinked his glass to mine. "Identical suits?" I nodded in Austin's direction. He was talking to Tilly and her husband at the other side of the table.

"Of course, a fine man like that, I have to make sure everyone knows who he belongs to." I rolled my eyes, knowing that Frank wasn't insecure like that. "Speaking of, I believe you have some territory in need of claiming." He threw a coy look between sips of his flute. I frowned, not really following. "Raquel is hovering around Niamh."

"I know." I couldn't help the tension that crept into my voice.

"That girl." He sighed and shook his head. "She knows no boundaries."

"Well, maybe Niamh is into it." Frank's brow furrowed in confusion. "I mean, where is she right now? Both of them, in fact?" I knew I sounded jealous, and I hated it.

"I think it's time you go and look for her, don't you?" Frank said, and I found myself reluctant. I took another drink, but the champagne tasted off. Perhaps that was more to do with the insecurity and probably jealousy. I hadn't really eaten anything today. Maybe the excessive alcohol and coffee was clouding my perception. "Harriet." Frank touched my arm when I didn't move.

"What?" He looked a little taken aback by my snapping, and I knew I needed to cool myself. I was getting worked up over potentially nothing. "Sorry, I just…I didn't think I had anything to worry about. With Niamh."

"I'm sure you don't," Frank reassured before something over my shoulder caught his attention. "Look, she's coming this way."

I turned around, and there she was. She had two bottles of water in her hands and a smile that I hadn't realised I needed to see. Just seeing her seemed to relax the tension. I couldn't resist the way my heart raced seeing her scan my dress.

"Hi." she took a step closer, and Frank disappeared, allowing her to take his perch next to me at the table. "You look…" She breathed out speechlessly. "Incredible." Niamh's voice was velvety.

"It's all hair and makeup," I said, and she shook her head in defiance. "And what about you?" I bit my lip, taking her in. Niamh looked sexy and gorgeous. Her short hair was swept back, and the waistcoat revealed toned arms dotted with tattoos. It was a sight I thought I would always enjoy seeing. "I told you it was a good look."

"Well, you dressed me." Niamh blushed before placing the bottles of water on the table. "I figured you might be in need of this." She passed me the bottle, and I was a little touched by the gesture. I took a big drink of the icy water. I made me feel a little more normal again. "We could see you guys getting your pictures taken. It looks hot out there."

"Who's we?" I said, noting the accusation in my voice. Niamh didn't miss it.

"Me and Raquel." I could feel my jaw clench. "We were upstairs, and we saw you down by the water—"

"Why were you upstairs?"

She frowned, looking affronted, and shifted back on her heel. "I was using the bathroom." I still felt like I was on guard, and Niamh looked like she was grappling for some kind of explanation. "The queue was insane down here, so we went upstairs."

"Okay." I wanted to believe her.

"Are you okay?"

"I'm fine." I could feel myself hardening.

"No, you're not. What's going on?"

I didn't want confrontation, especially not here, but I felt like I didn't want to be around her. I had to get what was bothering me off my chest. "I saw you two."

"Saw who?"

"You and Raquel. Here." I felt hot, and I couldn't control the accusatory way it came out of my mouth. "Don't act like you don't know what I'm talking about—"

"Harriet, I don't know what you're talking about."

"If that's the way you're going to play it…" I shrugged, shocked that Niamh wouldn't just tell me that she was flirting. That way, I would know where I stood. I wouldn't be getting my hopes up for something more meaningful.

"Yeah, okay, Raquel came on to me, but I told her I'm not interested."

I nodded, my eyes were anywhere but on her. I could feel myself resistant to listening.

Niamh snapped, showing her frustration. "I'm at your family's party. Why would I start something with someone else?"

She was making sense, and I felt myself thawing. I knew I was being paranoid, but Raquel was beautiful and a model. The truth was, I really liked Niamh, and I didn't want competition. The fact that we hadn't discussed our future was also raising the stakes.

"Look, I don't play games." Niamh lowered her voice. "I figured you knew that about me by now." Her eyes revealed a hurt that stirred something in me. I knew on some level I was allowing my insecurity about our potential future, or lack thereof, to question her feelings for me. "I don't know what this weird jealousy thing is, but if you have doubts about how I feel about you, then—"

"How do you feel?" I felt vulnerable, but my question left her in a bit of a spiral. It didn't help my insecurity.

"Seriously? You want to talk about this right now?"

"You leave tomorrow. When are we gonna talk?" I couldn't hide the fear in my voice. I hated that I was being needy, but I needed to know.

"Harriet." She sighed, and everything in her demeanour seemed to soften. "I'm here, aren't I?"

But I needed more.

"Harriet," Tilly interrupted us and looked a little awkward, "Marco is asking for you. Everyone is about to be called for dinner. He wants us to stay behind."

"Okay." I sighed, feeling disappointed that we weren't able to finish our conversation. "I got to go. See you after," I said to Niamh, and she looked disappointed.

I walked away from her and followed Tilly. I felt bogged down, confused, and sad. My head felt full and sore. I was barely lucid to where Tilly was leading me. I was about to go upstairs when I felt a hand on my wrist. I was spun around and almost fell off the first step, but Niamh was there to catch me. I landed into her. She steadied me, but her hands stayed firm on my hips, creating an electricity between us.

"I want you," she said, and it was delivered with so much conviction that I couldn't have possibly been doubtful. "I want to be with you, Harriet. In whatever way that looks like. Whether that's long-distance until we figure stuff out, or you come to Belfast. I'll go to London. I actually don't care." I was overcome with her declaration and speechless in a good way. She wasn't afraid of rejection, and I think it made me fall for her a little bit more. "I don't want to say good-bye...not again." She rested her forehead against mine, and I could feel myself vibrating with joy.

"I don't either," I said. Niamh smiled with relief. "It's always been you." I wasn't expecting the crack in my voice. "I don't think I ever stopped wondering what could have happened..."

"I feel the same way, and that's scary."

"It's so scary." I couldn't help but giggle with her.

"I know we're not the same people we were back then. I've changed." Her voice cracked, and it broke my heart. I cupped her face, but she wasn't done. "But I want to know you. To be a part of your life. I know what I feel, and I feel like there's something amazing still between us. I feel it every time we run into each other. And if we walk away again," she said, exasperated, "then, I don't know if fate or God or whoever the hell is in charge up there will be arsed to put us back together again."

I laughed and couldn't hold back how happy she made me.

She leaned forward, kissing me softly.

A sea of cheers sounded from above us, and we both pulled back to find Marco and Bobby and my friends cheering from the top of the stairs.

"Well, that's not embarrassing."

"Having my friends hear you pour your heart out?" I asked. Niamh grinned, and I didn't miss the red shade of embarrassment on her cheeks. "Screw them." I kissed her again, loving the way it felt to have my arms wrapped around her.

"Can someone throw some ice on them?" Marco mocked from above.

"All right." She pulled back. "You better go." She kissed me once more and planted a soft kiss on my hand. "Promise me, you'll save me a dance."

"I promise." I reluctantly let go of her hand and went upstairs to be interrogated by my friends.

CHAPTER TWENTY-SEVEN
NIAMH DONNELLY

Bobby's brother was halfway through his speech. If he wasn't a public speaker professionally, then he was definitely in the wrong job. People were laughing and crying at the same time. Bobby looked embarrassed throughout most of it, but Marco seemed to be keeping him from crawling under the table. Which I probably would have if I'd gotten up to some of the things he had on his stag party.

I kept close watch on Harriet; she looked so cute and nervous. She was seated at the top table with the rest of the bridal party. I was seated next to Tilly's husband, a broker in London. His job was a little boring, but he was nice, and he had lived in Australia for a while in his twenties, so we managed to find something in common. The only problem was that Harriet's parents were also seated at my table. Thankfully at the far side. I couldn't help but feel a little bit on display. They both watched me cautiously throughout dinner. It was actually a little off-putting. I was going to have to talk to Pipa, or things were going to get mighty awkward.

His speech came to a close, and I could sense Harriet's nerves skyrocketing. She stood and took hold of the microphone.

"That's who I'm following." She shot daggers at Bobby, and the room let out a few laughs. "Thank you all for coming. What a wonderful day, huh? Can we have a cheers for the happy couple?"

People clinked their glasses together. Harriet took a long drink. It was clear she was nervous, but I was happy to see it wasn't too obvious. "I have known these two since day one. Literally, the night they met, I was there. Marco was in a right state. What's new there?"

I was glad that Harriet was able to keep the room entertained. She talked about Marco's stag party and how they'd all dressed up as the Spice Girls, with Marco being Posh Spice, and they went paragliding. I just hoped there was photographic evidence because that must have been hilarious. "I could tell a hundred stories worse than that about Marco—"

"You will not," Marco shouted, resulting in a sea of laughter.

"But I won't. I have seen them navigate the ups and downs, building their lives together. I am not confident about a lot of things in life, but it's clear to me that they were made for each other. It's a rarity to find your soulmate, and it's even harder to hold on to them." She locked eyes with me, and I felt like I was floating. I felt touched, and I knew her words weren't just for Marco and Bobby. "To happily ever after."

"To happily ever after," the room returned, followed by applause. Harriet was in her seat again, and I could feel her relief. I threw her a thumbs-up that I think she appreciated.

When the speeches were done, the room settled into comfortable chatter. I got up to stretch my legs. The food was delicious, though four courses was enough to make anyone a little sluggish. I went out to get some air, if that was even possible in twenty-eight degree heat. At half past six, the sun was still present in the sky, and the birds were chirping. I couldn't help but enjoy the view for a little while. It was quiet outside, and it gave me an opportunity to really process the last few days.

Reconnecting with Harriet had been one of the craziest things to ever happen. She was the same person I'd fallen in love with so hard at eighteen, but she was unbelievably different as well. It was hard to explain. She was more self-assured, perhaps, but so was I. We were in our thirties. There was a lot to consider before jumping into a serious relationship. Like my career. I'd worked so hard to get where I was, and I was positive that her career was a big part of her life as well. There were family dynamics, and of course, the logistical roadblock of where we both lived. Knowing myself as well as I did, those things isolated would have been enough to cause me to put on the brakes days ago, and yet, I was allowing myself to unapologetically get caught up in the fairy tale. The fairy tale of Levi and Jaq that still somehow existed.

I felt ready to settle down. Whether or not that was with Harriet still felt too premature to know. That was what my brain was telling me, at least. My heart seemed more confident. It was a battle between the rational thinking and the butterflies in my stomach, and it felt as though the butterflies were winning.

I decided to make my way back inside again when one of the party tables caught my eye. It had dozens, perhaps hundreds, of photographs of Marco and Bobby's life together. I found myself smiling seeing some of the goofy pictures. Harriet was in a lot of them too, which made me happy. One in particular stood out. I removed the thumbtack attaching the photo to the board. Marco, Bobby, and Harriet were standing in front of the Titanic museum in Belfast. It was an iconic building, and I knew there had been no mistaking that Harriet had visited Northern Ireland at some stage. It looked recent as well, and I felt disappointed. For reasons I wasn't entirely sure of. It kind of felt like a missed opportunity. I wished she'd reached out to tell me she was visiting.

"Hello." The voice made me jump a little. I turned and found none other than Pipa. "I didn't mean to frighten you." Something about her expression made her apology feel a little disingenuous. I set down the picture quickly to avoid any questions. "Niamh, is it?"

Words vanished from my vocabulary for a moment. I nodded and licked my lips, feeling very dry mouthed. "Yes." I faced her and stuck out my hand. She returned my gesture with a paper light handshake that made me feel uncomfortable. Limp handshakes always gave me the creeps. "It's nice to meet you, Pipa." Of course, it wasn't the first time we'd met, but I let that go.

I was a little taller than her, even in her heels. I hoped Harriet would realise that we were both missing and come looking. But until then, I was on my own. I could handle myself. I wasn't afraid of Pipa, but I didn't want her thinking her daughter was dating a disaster case either. I needed to be pleasant but firm.

"So you're *her*," she said. I wasn't quite sure what she meant. "The one from Greece." I was a little taken aback. I hadn't known that Harriet had shared that information with her mama. "I didn't recognise you."

"Well, you didn't see a lot of my face," I joked. After all, I had been naked on top of Harriet the last time she'd seen me in Stalis. I was glad she seemed to have a sense of humour.

"You should make better use of the in-room locking system. They're very effective."

I laughed. "Don't worry, I learned my lesson."

"I have too," she said ominously. I got the feeling she wasn't talking about locking the door, and it made me feel a little on guard. "So you're with my daughter?"

I found myself clamming up a little. She was such a small, yet extremely unpredictable, person. It made me realise that my best bet here was to put my cards on the table. I got the feeling that Pipa liked to be the one in control, though showing weakness would only go against me. "I hope so. We've only just reconnected again."

"Do you live in London?"

"No. I live in Belfast."

"How's that supposed to work?" she snapped.

"I don't know." I kept my cool. "We will have to figure it out."

"But you want to figure it out?"

"Very much so. I care deeply about Harriet. I always have."

"I am a good reader of people. I don't know if Harriet ever mentioned that?"

"She didn't." Though Harriet didn't talk much about her mama.

"Something about you, Niamh." She shook her head, unconvinced. I felt nervous. "I can't put my finger on it."

"Could be the accent."

She smirked. "Not that."

"It's probably because I'm working-class, then."

"Could be because you're a smart aleck." She was jesting, thankfully. "She likes you." Her features seemed to relax, and I felt like she was letting me see a softer side. "Well, I think we both know she more than likes you." I couldn't help the way my heart skipped a beat. "And my wonderful daughter is a much better reader of people than me, so I know you can't be all bad." Was that a compliment? I would never be sure. "She hasn't had it easy." Her voice dropped, and I wondered if she meant what had happened with Beth, or maybe, on some level, she was recognising the way she'd treated Harriet when she'd come out.

"No, she hasn't," I agreed and couldn't help the coldness in my tone.

She seemed to pick up on it too. "If anyone deserves to be happy…"

"I want to make her happy," I said, feeling every word. "Because she makes me happy."

Pipa smiled, and it looked genuine. "Right answer. There's a couple of things I'd like to know."

"Shoot."

"You're a doctor, correct?"

"Yes."

She seemed to approve. "Do you own any property?"

"I have an apartment in Belfast."

"Ever been married?" she asked. I shook my head. "Kids?" I shook my head, laughing. "Do you want them?"

"What is going on out here?" Harriet came up alongside me, placing her hand on my lower back. I felt myself exhale, and it felt glorious. I hadn't realised just how tightly I was wound talking to Pipa, and having Harriet next to me felt like I could be taken care of. "You don't have to answer that, obviously. Mama," she reprimanded Pipa.

"Yes," I said, surprising them both. "To answer your last question. But only with the right person."

Harriet looked pleased with my answer, though not as delighted as her mother. "Then you have my blessing. For now."

"Then we can be friends," I slung back at her, and she smirked once again. Perhaps not sure how she should take it. "For now."

I didn't need her blessing. Harriet was a grown woman, and it was for her to decide if I was worthy of her love. However, it would definitely make my life easier having Pipa on my side, so I didn't push it. Deep down, I didn't really care what she thought of me. I wasn't sure if I would ever really forgive her for the way she'd treated Harriet when she was younger.

"I'm sure Niamh will sleep easier tonight knowing she has your approval." Harriet teased, perhaps to defuse the tension.

"As long as you remember to lock the door." She winked at me. An unexpected joke that made me feel as though she didn't completely hate my guts. It was a start. "Your speech was wonderful, darling." She pecked Harriet on the cheek before leaving us alone.

"Lock the door, what's that all about?" Harriet asked me when Pipa was out of earshot.

"Your guess is as good as mine." I didn't let on as Harriet's hand found mine. "Hey, I have a question."

"Go for it." She turned sweetly to me.

I looked at the picture of her, Bobby, and Marco that I had been staring at before Pipa had begun her interrogation. "When was this taken?"

She looked guilty, and she grappled for an answer, which I found surprising. "You don't miss much, do you?" she joked, but I could tell I'd flustered her a little.

"You don't have to tell me about it—"

"No, that's not it." She seemed to shake herself before biting her lip nervously. "We were over for a gig a few years back. The tickets in London sold out, and I managed to find three Elton John tickets for resale in Belfast."

"No way," came out of my mouth, cutting her off.

"Yeah, I'm a huge fan—"

"No, Harriet," I stopped her. "I was there too. The farewell tour."

"Are you serious?" She gripped my hand, and I struggled to dismiss the feeling of unease. We could have run into each other at another freak chance meeting. How many times could this have happened over the years? Spontaneous run-ins that could have resulted in us reconnecting. It was hard to deny what was beginning to feel like fate.

Seeing Elton John was one of the best gigs I'd ever been to. Not because of how amazing he'd performed, but because it was the last family outings we had together before Dad died. It made me a little emotional, thinking about the fact that Harriet was even in the same arena as me and my whole family before we lost one.

"I went with my entire family. My dad was a huge fan."

Harriet smiled, and it felt like she understood the weight of what it meant to me. "Me too. See, I knew me and your dad would have gotten on like a house on fire." Her soft smile did indescribable things to me. My insides felt like they were dancing. Until her expression cracked, telling me there was more. "I have a confession, actually. Because when I was going over to Belfast, I actually tried to get in touch."

"You did?" That was a surprise.

"I knew your surname, and I actually managed to find you on Instagram."

"Why didn't you slip into my DMs?" I teased, but her hesitancy made me stop.

"I wanted to," she said in a small voice. "But I saw you had a girlfriend." The disappointment on her face was unbearable. The timeline meant it couldn't have been anyone but Julie. I felt disappointed as well. "And after what happened in London, when I was with Beth…" She trailed off, looking regretful. "I just didn't want to get in the way of that. You looked really happy with her." She looked sad, and it made me take a step closer to her. Her hands glided up the back of my forearms and stopped at the crease in my arm. Her fingers traced patterns on my tattoos. "And let's face it, Beth and I weren't the same again after I saw you. And if Julie was the one, then I would be silently happy for you from afar." The look on her face was heartbreaking.

"I think we both know she was never the one."

Harriet looked overcome by what I'd said. She cupped my face, pulling me toward her. It was so unexpected that it knocked the air from my lungs. She moaned into my kiss, her hand finding its way into my hair. I gripped her hips as she deepened our kiss. She tasted like wine, and feeling her front against mine sent a rush between my hips. It felt like electricity was powering my movements as I pulled her close.

CHAPTER TWENTY-EIGHT
HARRIET WHITAKER

Dancing with Niamh was something I hoped I never got used to. She was a good dancer, which I guessed surprised me. Dancing with her in front of my family felt empowering.

Sharing Marco and Bobby's big day with her also made me feel more connected to her than I was initially expecting. When I'd asked for her to stay longer in Cinque Terre, it was because I wasn't ready to say good-bye. I hadn't really thought about the intimacies of having her present for such an important event. But I was so glad that she'd agreed to be my date. My extended family loved her, and well, Mama would take some work. As she did with most things. I even caught Niamh at the bar talking to my dad. I knew he wouldn't be the problem.

As the evening ticked by, I could feel the energy between us amplify. The way Niamh looked at me made me feel alive and desired. It was difficult for me to keep my hands off her, in fact. Dancing with her felt like foreplay. It was clear that the anticipation of having her again was powering my movements on the dance floor. To the point that Marco had to pull me aside and bluntly told me to simmer down.

That was becoming increasingly difficult.

"Wanna get out of here?" I whispered to Niamh and enjoyed the way her eyes darkened. She nodded, and I latched on to her hand, removing her from the dance floor.

"Don't you want to say good-bye?" She chuckled as we made it outside to where some town cars were waiting to take guests back to town. It was around ten, but the party was still raging on. Well, for some.

"I'll see them tomorrow." I didn't even bother turning back to her and continued leading us to the first car waiting. "Tonight, I want you." I could feel her excitement passing through her body and into my hand.

Niamh didn't respond until we were in the car again, but she didn't say it in words. Her lips were on mine again. Her kiss was hungry, and her hands were a little wild. I had to remind myself not to straddle her in the back of the car. I was sure it would have given the driver a heart attack.

In no time at all, we were pulling up outside my hotel.

We clumsily made it into the elevator. I hadn't drunk that much this evening, but I felt intoxicated. Perhaps that was just the effect her kiss had on me. My knees were shaking as we made it into my room. I flicked on the lights and closed the door. Before I could move farther into the room, she twirled me around to face her and backed me into the wall. The second my back hit the cold surface, I let out a moan. Her lips started their assault on my neck as her thigh gently separated my legs. I relished the contact and might have even started a rhythmic grinding.

My breathing was erratic, and my thoughts were getting lost in her touch. She peppered kisses down my neck and chest before peeling back the fabric of my dress that cupped my breast. I'd never been gladder to have ditched the bra this morning, especially when her tongue teased my nipple, causing my head to rock back against the wall. My hand was pressed against the wall, helping to hold me up, while my other hand was held firm at the back of her neck. I could feel my knees becoming shaky, and I pulled her back up to my lips again. Her kiss was hurried, causing me to arch into her front. Feeling her body hot against me was such a turn-on. The slither of space between me and the wall gave her the opportunity to find my zipper. She was struggling, and it made me giggle.

She pulled back, finding the humour as well. "This is *not* a normal zipper, is it?"

"No." My lipstick was smeared on her lips, and I loved to see it.

"I knew I wasn't just rusty at this." She spun me around, causing me to laugh until I felt her plant a soft kiss to the base of my neck. It was soft and intimate, causing me to let out a slow exhale.

She unhooked the clasp and undid the couple of small buttons. It gave me a moment to calm myself. Though her delicate touch wasn't slowing my arousal. In fact, it was sensual in a way I'd never experienced with her. The zip glided slowly down my spine as I waited in anticipation. Her hands smoothed the length of my dress, surprising me when she knelt down. I let out another shaky breath and waited patiently as I felt her undoing the clasp of my left sandal.

"You won't need these anymore."

"Good." I was surprised by how raspy my voice sounded, clearly full of need.

She did the same on the other side, and I kicked my heels off, relieved when I felt the cold tile. It helped to soothe the aches in my feet from being in heels all day. I was still facing the wall, leaving me with no indication of what she would do next. I was never normally so submissive, but with Niamh, it excited me in a way I couldn't explain.

I felt her hands settle on my hips, and her breath was on my neck again. My eyes closed in anticipation. Her hands glided slowly up my waist, creating an exhilarating buildup. Her hands were warm and soft, travelling over my shoulder blades until she could get a handle on the fabric covering my shoulders. She removed my dress from my shoulders, and the entire thing pooled around my bare feet. I let out a shiver. It wasn't because I was cold but more because I felt exposed. She kissed my neck, and all of a sudden, I didn't feel vulnerable anymore. Especially when her hands started roaming my body from behind. My head rolled back on to her shoulder when she teased my breasts again.

Being submissive was fun and all, but I was running out of patience. I spun around and kissed her. It was her turn to be taken aback. I didn't miss the breathlessness that my kiss caused. I unbuttoned her waistcoat and removed it before my hands found the waistline of her trousers. I pulled back, resting my forehead against hers. Her breathing was wild as I unbuttoned the trousers. But instead of pulling them down, I took a firm hold of the fabric and pulled her with me as I led us to the bed. Her eyes never left mine as I walked backward to the bedroom. Her eyes were dark and entranced with mine, fuelling my steps. I felt so wanted by her, and it made me feel sexy. As soon as she spotted the bed over my shoulder, she was kissing me again. Once my legs felt the bed, I sat and kept her standing in front of me. My thighs were on either side of hers, as I gently removed her trousers. She helped me by kicking them off to the side.

I kissed her stomach, relishing the softness of her skin. I'd somehow forgotten how good she felt. I felt her hands get lost in my hair, enjoying my attention on her body. I pulled down her underwear next, receiving a loud exhale from her. I kissed her hipbone and left a trail down to her outer thigh. I couldn't explore any farther as she yanked me away.

I was lying back. I started to shimmy my way up the bed with her closely following. Once my head touched the pillow, she nestled between my legs, and her lips were hot on mine again. I could get lost in her kiss, particularly when she was grinding into my core. She travelled lower, stopping briefly at my chest. After she was satisfied to have tantalised my nipples, and left me panting uncontrollably as a result, she was on the move lower. I could feel her tongue teasing me through my underwear, resulting in my hips bucking. The teasing was becoming ridiculous, and without me actually losing it, she seemed to catch the hint, removing my underwear.

She always had known what she was doing down there, but it felt more incredible this time. I was struggling to stay quiet, especially when I felt her fingers get in on the action. I was a mess after that, riding the wave of arousal. One hand was gripping the pillow under my head while the other was aiding the back of her head. It didn't take long for me to tumble over the edge, causing my thighs to clamp down on her. It didn't stop her from finishing the job, though.

My lips should have been bruised and my body exhausted. It felt like we kissed for hours; perhaps we did, all while exploring each other's bodies. It felt like the perfect reintroduction. Some things had changed, while others seemed to stay the same. Being with her seemed to unlock a side of me that had felt hidden for a long time.

Chapter Twenty-nine
Niamh Donnelly

Coffee order?" We had somehow fallen into a lightning round of questions. I didn't know how we could go from having the most unbelievable roll in the sheets to talking about tea. Harriet looked sexy, and this room still smelled like debauchery but I didn't care. I could have stayed there forever.

"Oh, I'm basic." She giggled. "Latte all the way."

"I'm partial to a latte every now and then."

"I'm a seasonal sucker too: pumpkin spiced, cinnamon spiced," she rhymed off as we lay facing each other in bed. "Give me anything gingerbread, and I'm buying it." Her hair was ruffled and free.

"Now, you're losing me. I'm a flat white girl, through and through."

"Go-to treat with your coffee?"

"Can't beat a good muffin."

"Agreed, but I do love a croissant."

"Same. Oh, sandwich or salad?"

"Sandwich. Toasties, to be specific."

I should have known these things. I felt like I'd always known Harriet on a deep level, like, who she was as a person, but the problem was that we were always torn apart before we could learn the silly stuff. The normal, everyday, sometimes boring, and sometimes beautiful things about each other. I guessed now it was time to make up for it.

"Ham and cheese toasties are one of my primary foods at work. There's a café beside my clinic."

"You have your own practice?"

"No, but I'm one of the more senior doctors."

"That's so cool." Harriet looked impressed, and that made me feel a little proud until I remembered I had to go back to work.

I rolled onto my back and let out a sigh. "Now I'm thinking about work."

"Ever think about retirement?" she mused next to me.

"Does sleeping with me make you think about retirement?" I cocked my head, throwing her an exasperated look. "Because if so, then that was exactly what I was going for."

"Well, if I wasn't working, I could spend all my time in bed." She curled back into my side, and I felt myself relax. I raised my arm so that her head could rest on my chest. "But seriously."

"Seriously?" I thought for a moment. "I don't know if I will ever retire. I imagine it to be boring."

"You work too much."

"Look who I'm talking to? I saw you send a work email during the buffet yesterday. Or was it the day before?" I said before giving up, forgetting what day it was. The last few days had felt like a bit of a whirlwind.

"Okay, yes, I work a lot, but I can't wait until I don't have to."

"Well, you don't have to wait to retire for that. Don't you have a trust fund?"

"So just until my folks kick the bucket?"

I laughed. I was joking. Losing a parent wasn't something I'd wish on anyone.

"I just mean, I'd love to just get up and hang out. Do whatever you want. Maybe I'd bake or garden."

I smiled, imagining what Harriet in her sixties would look like and feeling this overwhelming desire to see it. One day.

"Maybe go swimming in the ocean."

"So you're not retiring in the UK, then?" I joked.

"I don't know. I guess, in my retirement fantasy, I'm in warmer climates."

"I'd say that would be nice. Live in Spain or something."

"Yeah." She breathed out, drawing lazy patterns on my stomach.

A silence settled over us again, and I enjoyed feeling her close to me. Being naked for hours was incredible with her, but I enjoyed the simple pleasures. Lying next to her and talking. It was nearly dawn. I could tell by the sky brightening. I felt too alive to be tired. Harriet had a suite that would have been impressive if I'd gotten the chance to look around, but we were too preoccupied. The balcony in her room was an extra special touch. We hadn't closed the curtains, and it provided something to stare out at: the Mediterranean water that stretched as far as the eye could see.

"This place is beautiful," I said.

"I know. I think it's my happy place. Especially after that."

"I'm glad I haven't lost my touch. You, on the other hand," I teased.

"Excuse me?" She was up on her elbow, looking offended.

"I mean that in the best way possible."

"I'm about thirty seconds away from locking you outside." She pinched my side, causing me to squirm.

"I'm joking," She lay back down on my chest as I started to stroke her hair. That seemed to wash away any of my teasing. "Hey, ever wondered what would have happened if we hadn't got...you know, caught by Pipa? Back then."

"Yeah, well, back then, I used to think about it a lot," she said thoughtfully. My chest tightened in disappointment at our missed opportunity. I used to spend a lot of nights wondering what if too. "I still do, the odd time." She seemed a little embarrassed. It made me smile because it had crossed my mind recently as well.

"And?"

"Well," she said, "I think we would have probably exchanged numbers and stayed in touch."

"Would you have become my long-distance girlfriend?"

"Would you have asked?"

I couldn't help the grin coming over my face. "I probably would have asked before letting you leave Stalis," I admitted, and Harriet's hesitancy prompted me to go deeper. "Harriet, I was crazy about you."

"I was too. I mean, I am." She let out a contented sigh, and I was glad I couldn't see her face because it gave me the confidence to share more.

"I imagine I would have tried to fly over to London. Maybe even as much as once a month. First year, the classes aren't too hard. I think I could have made it work."

"That much?"

"It would have been hard. I'd have lived off microwave noodles and frozen chips. I could have budgeted, and flights wouldn't have been that expensive if I planned it right."

She looked up at me, and I realised just how much she was enjoying my storytelling. "I would have probably come to Belfast once a month too."

"Really? Okay, so then, we took turns visiting each other."

"Yeah, and maybe I spent Christmas holidays at your family, and maybe you came to us for Easter." I could see it all in my mind, and it made me warm inside. Imagining Harriet sitting around our rickety old dining table. Mum getting out the good plates and Dad making sure the turkey wasn't overdone. It was a nice image, and I couldn't help but feel a little sad that it had never happened that way. "We could do summers here."

"With Marco and Tilly?"

"Exactly."

"That would have been unreal."

"And then, after university, maybe you would have come to London."

"Yeah, I'm sure I would have gotten a job no problem. So we would have lived together?"

"I think so."

It made me excited just to imagine what our lives would have looked like. But I realised that if I'd done that, I would have never gone to Australia. "Or maybe you would have come to Australia with me."

She gasped in delight. "I would have definitely come to Australia with you. That would have been awesome. Maybe we would still be there. We could have had a real life together."

I thought about what my life would have looked like. I really thought about how amazing it would have been to have Harriet in my life all these years. It made me happy inside until I felt as though her presence in those memories would have altered things. Would I have travelled in a beat-up old campervan into the wilderness with Harriet? It didn't seem like it was her kind of style. It wasn't even my style. The outback was dangerous, but Remy was adventurous in that way. They'd pushed me to do those things. Retreats into the outback filled with wild drug-induced trips. My experience would have been completely different because I wouldn't have travelled alone. Would I have gone to Kenya? Travelling alone was one of my greatest achievements. I always felt like it had shaped me in the best possible way.

And then, I thought of Dad. How his illness and passing had changed me. The hardships I'd gone through in recent years. My bouts of neglecting myself. Eating badly, drinking too much, poor mental health. I thought about how the pandemic had affected me as well, not just personally but professionally. I thought about the loss of my relationship with Jules. Would I have just pushed Harriet away instead of Julie?

And then, my mind went to the Harriet I'd met in London at twenty-six. She was so preoccupied with pleasing her parents and Beth that she was completely unrecognisable. She was miserable and trapped in a life she didn't even want. She'd grown to resent Beth because she'd felt she couldn't be her authentic self. What if that had happened to us? Would we have weathered the storm and made it out the other side?

I broke the silence. "Or maybe...things worked out the way they were supposed to." Perhaps timing was more important than any of us really realised.

"Maybe you're right." She yawned and curled into my side.

It was clear I was thinking more deeply on this than her. Perhaps we would talk about all of that again. "Are you tired?"

"A bit." She yawned.

"Mind if I stay?" I asked, feeling a nervous quiver. "I can go if—"

"Of course I want you to stay." She planted a soft kiss on my lips before resting her head on my chest again. I could feel myself starting to relax, enough to even doze off, until I heard her quiet voice. "Niamh?"

"Yeah?"

"What happens tomorrow?"

That roused me quickly. I felt dread in my stomach and then my chest. My body felt heavy, weak under the weight of her question. Her body had stiffened, perhaps a reaction to my senses becoming more charged.

I breathed out, not really sure of the answer. "What do you want to happen?"

"I don't know."

I waited a moment, but nothing followed. "Me neither."

She shifted back from where she was resting her head on my chest so that she was sharing the pillow again with me.

"I have to go back to Belfast."

She showed a glimpse of disappointment, but there was hope too.

"I have work, and honestly, Jenny is going to freak out when I tell her about this."

Harriet smiled. "Yeah, my therapist is going to have a field day too." Something softened in her eyes, and it made it difficult for me to look away. "Maybe I could come over."

"You better," I teased.

"I'm serious. I work remote, mostly."

I couldn't contain the excitement in my chest. "Really? You'd come to Belfast."

"Only if you want me to."

I kissed her, hoping that would relay my support.

"And it wouldn't have to be long-term."

I kissed her again, silencing whatever doubts were coming out.

"I could fly back for meetings, and—"

My lips on hers cut her off.

"Are you going to let me speak?" She pulled back, not showing any real annoyance.

"I am in complete agreement with all of this."

"Yeah?" She revealed the sweetest smile.

"I would be so happy if you came to Belfast. And we can take it slow, figure this all out, but I know I *want* to try to figure it out."

"I don't think it's going to be hard."

I decided to have a little fun with her. "You've never lived with me."

"You're asking me to move in? Talk about U-Haul lesbians."

"I figured, given our fourteen year history..." I rolled over, hooking her thigh over my hip. "I wasn't rushing things."

"If anything, this is overdue." She shimmied closer to me, and I enjoyed the way her body felt pressed against mine.

PART FOUR

2055

Chapter Thirty

Harriet Whitaker

"Niamh," I called from the kitchen. She didn't hear me. "Niamh," I yelled again, but silence floated through from the living room. I wiped off the flour dusting my hands and left the dough in the ceramic bowl. A little proving wouldn't do it any harm.

I made it into the living room and found her peacefully asleep in the armchair by the window. She'd been sat there since breakfast, and I couldn't help but smile. I walked over and removed the glasses that had slipped down to the tip of her nose. Her grey hair was a little wild as well, which told me she was in a pretty deep sleep. She hadn't slept well last night, too excited for the arrival of the kids.

I put her book to the side but kept her place with a bookmark. She was halfway through it. It would be her fourth book this week if she finished by Sunday, barely a challenge. Retirement suited her. She'd worked right the way up to the retirement age, and in the summer, she'd finally left the clinic. She was well due a rest; after all, she'd been in the same clinic since becoming a qualified doctor all those years ago. She didn't need to work all the way to sixty-five. We'd made sure to save up enough to enjoy healthy pension pots well into our eighties. That didn't even include my trust fund.

I'd retired three years ago from the civil service. While I'd enjoyed my work with FD Solicitors, the constant travel from Belfast to London had become tiresome. I'd found the idea of living in London less appealing after spending so much of my time in

Belfast. I was drawn to there in a way I hadn't imagined. Travelling to London for work became incredibly difficult when the twins came along. They anchored me to home. Then, I'd found a position in the NI civil service that had provided me the resources I'd needed to challenge the emigration system. To create a more equalised and transparent emigration policy. Over the years, I was able to lobby for real change within the system. It was one of the greatest honours of my life. Well, that, and my wife and children.

We'd downsized from our four-bedroom house in North Belfast a few years back. The extra cash had given us the freedom to buy a villa in Stalis like we'd always dreamed. That way, we could adequately split our time between Belfast with the kids in a more modest apartment, and the place we'd met and fallen in love. It was with a heavy heart that we'd left North Belfast, but then again, the upkeep was becoming too much for a pair of pensioners like us. Though, that house would always hold a special place in my mind. We'd raised Sian and Malachy in that house. They'd taken their first steps, gotten their first As at school, well, Sian had, at least. Malachy was never into school all that much. And that home was where I had some of my greatest memories.

There were hard times over the years, losing our parents and some friends along the way, but I could only seem to remember the good times now. It was strange, especially when I talked to Sian, and she complained about motherhood with her little baby, and yet, I could only recall the good years. When they had been little were some of our best years. Niamh and I talked about it all the time.

"Are they here yet?" Niamh asked, not bothering to open her eyes.

"No sign of them yet." I pecked her forehead and didn't miss the little smile.

"Was I snoring?"

"No," I lied, taking a seat on the armrest.

Her arm slung around my waist. "Mustn't have been asleep for long, then. I should have just driven and lifted them from the airport. Sian is terrible with directions." She sat up straighter, rubbing the tiredness from her face.

"We've been coming to Stalis for years, Sian knows where she's going. It's probably a hold up at the car rental place."

"Why did they need a car—"

"Don't start this again." I rolled my eyes. "They wanted to rent a car seat for the little one."

"I'd have bought a car seat."

"You know what Sian is like. When she gets something into her head, it's hard to shake it. I wonder where she gets that from?" I teased.

"You." Niamh pinched my ribcage, causing me to squirm and squeal.

"Get off!" I tried to get away, but she pulled me onto her lap again.

"Never." She kissed me just as we heard the sound of a car driving up the stoney path. We parted, and I could feel my eyes widening in excitement. "They're here."

We both bounced up from the armchair. Well, bounced was a stretch. Niamh had to pull me up. She threw me a teasing, borderline smug look. Her love for hiking had made her a little more limber than me these days. We walked through the living room and into the hallway. She got the front door, and sunshine heated up my face. It wasn't a warm time of year, but it was a hell of a lot warmer than in Belfast.

Sian emerged from the driver side of the car, and a huge grin appeared on her face. Her fair hair was tied back in a bun, and she looked a little tired. She hugged Niamh first. "Merry Christmas, Ma." And then, she found me. "Hey, Mum."

"It's good to see you." I hugged her back.

"All of you," Niamh said as Stephanie emerged from the car and moved to the back seat to get Archie.

"He was a nightmare on the flight," Sian said. "If he wasn't crying, he was chucking up all over me." She swiped at her shoulder, and I could see visible milk stains. "I can't wait to get a shower." She looked so like Niamh when she was fed up. They both hunched over with their hands on hips. It was actually a little comical.

"I'll get the bags," Niamh said, making her way past an exhausted Stephanie.

"You look wrecked," I said as Stephanie gave me an awkward hug with one arm, supporting Archie on her hip.

"He's still feeding through the night, I don't know what well-rested looks like anymore."

"Well, why don't you two go upstairs and get freshened up."

Sian glanced to Stephanie, who looked back at her in relief.

"Have a lie down. Granny and Nanny are on the job."

Stephanie passed him over to me, and all my attention was immediately derailed to my grandson. And only him.

"Yeah, don't worry about me," Niamh shouted from the car boot. "I'll sort the bags." I could hear her grumpiness, but I knew she was only jesting.

Sian took a hold of Stephanie's hand. "It's up this way." She led her upstairs, and the two shared a kiss and tired embrace as they slowly climbed the stairs. I forgot that Stephanie hadn't seen the place yet. We'd only had the place a year, but she'd had preeclampsia, so was advised against flying. I would have to give her a proper tour after she had a nap.

I could remember the exhaustion and endless sleepless nights with a new baby. They reminded me of us. However, we'd had two little ones at the same time. That was a real challenge. I would remind Sian of that later.

"Hey, where's Mal?" Niamh yelled upstairs.

"Didn't he call?" Sian shouted down. "He missed the flight."

"Figures." Niamh groaned from the hallway.

I had barely looked up after taking a seat on the armchair by the window. The same one Niamh had been stationed at most of the morning, awaiting their arrival. "Hey, little man," I cooed at him down on my lap.

He had red curls that bunched around his ears. His blue eyes and ginger hair were all Stephanie. He wrapped his fist around my index finger and brought it to his mouth. I distracted him just before he took a bite out of my finger. He was almost six months old.

"Can I get a squeeze?" Niamh asked, taking a seat next to me on the armchair.

I positioned him toward his nanny, and he let out a big gummy grin. It made both of us smile in delight, and for just a second, I was transported back to sitting with Sian or Mal on my lap. I felt twenty-six years younger again.

"Where is your silly old uncle, huh?" I asked Archie, who just dribbled a response. "I guess you'll be going to the airport anyway," I said to Niamh.

She rolled her eyes in response. "It wouldn't be like Malachy to add a little drama to Christmas."

"Remember the year we got the trampoline for the kids?"

"The same year we went to A&E with Mal's broken collarbone?" Niamh cut in, making me giggle. "What about when he asked for the quad bike?"

"We should have never told them how we met. Still my best parenting moment, swerving that one."

"Could you imagine? He would have driven it off a cliff. What about the Christmas Sian snuck in her first girlfriend for a sleepover?"

"At least we didn't crash them like Mama." I looked up at Niamh, feeling nostalgic.

Holding my grandson while remembering how it all began. How we'd gotten here in the first place. Niamh's eyes were warm and full of adoration. There were a few wrinkles, of course, but they were still the same as the ones I'd cherished for all those years.

"Don't get sentimental on me now, Jaq," she teased.

"Pop the kettle on, Levi. I'm sure this man is due a bottle, and I'd love a cuppa."

"For you, anything."

About the Author

Emma L. McGeown is an Irish writer who lives in Northern Ireland with her wife, two kids and dog. Previous work includes *Aurora*, *Sugar Girl*, *Back to Belfast*, and Golden Crown winner *Before She Was Mine*.

Books Available from Bold Strokes Books

Beautiful Things by Emma L McGeown. A warmhearted romance of missed chances, undeniable chemistry, and a stubborn love that maybe, just maybe, can find its way back. (978-1-63679-934-6)

Love Takes a Village by Karis Walsh. As Lena Preiss struggles to manage a busy restaurant in the Bavarian Christmas village of Leavenworth, Washington, chocolatier Devin Meyer brings an unexpected richness into her life, along with her delicious desserts. (978-1-63679-902-5)

Secrets of the Heart by Jenny Frame. When a beautiful stranger starts asking questions about Nikki Sharkey, head of an infamous crime syndicate, Nikki will stop at nothing to protect her daughter Isla. (978-1-63679-653-6)

Talon and the Songbird by Julia Underwood. In a world where survival depends on strategic alliances, Makayla and Talon must navigate not only complex politics but also the dangerous territory of their hearts. (978-1-63679-970-4)

The Great Popcorn Romance by Georgia Beers. Opposites attract, and Riley Shaw stands no chance of resisting Hannah Kramer's magnetic pull. But opposites know just how to drive each other crazy... (978-1-63679-910-0)

Three Blissful Days by Dena Blake. Kendall Jackson attempts to make her ex regret dumping her by announcing she's dating beautiful park ranger Ivy Patterson. But there's nothing fake about how attracted Ivy is to Kendall. (978-1-63679-707-6)

Chasing Her Scent by MJ Williamz. When Sheridan Rousseau walks into Lisette Mouton's charming little bookstore in Quebec City, she unknowingly holds the key to a mysterious box hidden in a secret room. (978-1-63679-900-1)

Heart's Run by D. Jackson Leigh. Hoping to recover an escaped racing mare, stock transporter Tobie Mason locks horns with local wild horse advocate Maggie Wilkes. (978-1-63679-825-7)

Scandalous by Kris Bryant. When a Hollywood actress trades places with her twin sister, everyone's in an uproar about getting duped, but Lindsay's more concerned about finding out which twin she made out with. (978-1-63679-874-5)

The Art of Love by Ali Vali. When Mimi and Bianca both set their sights on Jolly, sparks fly, loyalties are tested, and hearts collide as they navigate the unpredictable nature of their hearts (978-1-63679-719-9)

The Other Side of Forever by Kel McCord. Will Kenzie and Rachel be able to make love work when Rachel's cozy suburban dream feels like Kenzie's worst nightmare? (978-1-63679-812-7)

The Secrets of Rhydian Hill by Ronica Black. A doctor in need of a new start. A woman running from a killer. A love story that could end in tragedy. (978-1-63679-880-6)

Feeling Lucky by Krystina Rivers. What happens when, despite suddenly having enough money to buy almost anything, Lucy and Tanner start to discover that maybe all they need is each other? (978-1-63679-876-9)

Iceberg by Gun Brooke. When Lady Arabella hires Zandra, she never expects to find love, especially not as a disaster looms on the horizon. (978-1-63679-908-7)

It Happened One Semester by Aurora Rey. After a Pride night hookup, can eager new Assistant Professor Hudson Greene and Dean of Advising Callie Shaw overcome the odds and ace falling in love? (978-1-63679-814-1)

It's Kind of a Bad Idea by Sarah G. Levine. What happens when an emotionally unavailable serial dater meets the one woman she can't help but fall for—who happens to be the one woman who told her not to? (978-1-63679-920-9)

Thankful for You by Tagan Shepard. Everyone deserves to find their person, maybe Karen has finally found hers? (978-1-63679-884-4)

What Happens on Location by Nan Campbell. How can Helen produce a successful movie when its director is the woman responsible for the demise of her marriage? (978-1-63679-904-9)

When Love Comes Around by Radclyffe and Ronica Black. Can Maya Sanchez and Nolan Wright trust each other enough to build something real, or will the past tear them apart? (978-1-63679-930-8)

Anywhere with You by Margo Glynn. On a road trip through the Great American Southwest, two friends discover nature, hope, and each other. (978-1-63679-907-0)

Burning Bridges by Lesley Davis. Can Clancy and Jude crack the case of eight missing women—and the secrets of their own hearts? (978-1-63679-872-1)

Dreams Entangled by Sophia Kell Hagin. Amid self-doubt, secrets, a pandemic, fear of attack and attempted murder, Pirin and Gracie's attraction turns to love and their lives will never be the same. (978-1-63679-892-9)

Echoes of Love by Catherine Lane. As Hazel's and Jo's paths intertwine, they're swept up in a whirlwind of long-buried secrets, sizzling chemistry, and memories that won't be denied. (978-1-63679-835-6)

Moonlight Obsession by Sheri Lewis Wohl. All it takes to stop a clever killer is moonlight, love, and a silver bullet. (978-1-63679-831-8)

My Boyfriend's Wife by Joy Argento. Amid betrayal and heartbreak, can two women discover a love that could heal their pasts and rewrite their futures? (978-1-63679-866-0)

Tapout by Nicole Disney. A struggling MMA fighter finds her edge in an underground ring, but as she falls for the magnetic and ambitious promoter behind the matches, their dangerous world threatens to destroy everything they've fought to rebuild. (978-1-63679-924-7)

The Fame Game by Ronica Black. Wild child Hollywood actress Luna Kirkman begins dating Hollywood's leading man, only to fall for his straitlaced sister instead. (978-1-63679-858-5)

www.ingramcontent.com/pod-product-compliance
Lightning Source LLC
Chambersburg PA
CBHW021951010726
47494CB00003B/688